1967

1967

THE SEA GULL

Fernán Caballero

1314

TRANSLATED FROM THE SPANISH

AND WITH AN INTRODUCTION

BY

JOAN MACLEAN

BARRON'S EDUCATIONAL SERIES, INC.

WOODBURY, NEW YORK

FERNÁN CABALLERO
(1796-1877)

The Sea Gull, perhaps the most popular novel of its time in Spain, and still a milestone in Spanish literature, is here presented in a new English version.

Few novels in all Spanish literature have more successfully captured the essence of Andalusia than *The Sea Gull;* few more faithfully portray the manners and customs of a village and a great city alike.

The title, *The Sea Gull,* fails to convey in English all the meanings *La Gaviota* has in Spanish. This was the nickname given to the leading character, María Santaló, and carried with it the clue to María's character, for in Andalusia it has side meanings of a scold, an uncultivated and ill-mannered woman. The original title also contains a clue to the nature of María's story. Its author, Fernán Caballero, was a writer during the Romantic period of literature, yet she portrays María as the harsh, cold, and heartless savage she was. There is no trace in her of the romantic "noble savage" invented by Rousseau and further romanticized by Chateaubriand. Quite the contrary. The author was a realist, a forerunner of that school of literature, and a pioneer in that genre.

Fernán Caballero, whose masculine *nom de plume,* like George Eliot's, is a mask, was born Cecilia Böhl de Faber. *La Gaviota* was written originally in French and translated much later into Spanish. When the book was begun Fernán Cabal-

iii

lero was in private life the Marchioness de Arco-Hermoso, a young hostess with a brilliant salon near Seville; when it was published some fifteen years later, its author was poor, disillusioned, bereft of her family, and living in semi-retirement in a small village.

Cecilia Böhl de Faber was a remarkable woman, one of those "eminent Victorians" who rose above the inferior status then assigned women and who distinguished themselves in almost every country of Europe and in the United States. Some names come instantly to mind: George Sand, Elizabeth Barrett Browning, George Eliot, Harriet Beecher Stowe, Florence Nightingale, Lady Hester Stanhope, the Brontë sisters, and the lady who gave her name to an age, Queen Victoria. Yet though she was of this indomitable company, Cecilia Böhl de Faber, unlike many of the others, did her utmost to hide her light under a bushel, and denied to her dying day that she ever was or wanted to be a literary figure.

Much of this extreme modesty was the fruit of her father's training. Juan Nicolás Böhl de Faber gave his daughter an excellent education, but by some quirk of character, he heartily disliked "advanced women." The girl grew up in a household where English, German, French, and Spanish were spoken as a matter of course. Johann (or Juan) Böhl de Faber was a bibliophile by avocation, and by vocation a prosperous immigrant German business man in Cadiz.

His approach to his literary work was more that of a dilettante than a professional, yet he published two scholarly anthologies that won him renown throughout Europe: *Floresta de rimas antiguas castellanas* and *Teatro español anterior a Lope de Vega*. He was also interested in music, had a trained voice, and sang German *Lieder* most pleasingly.

His wife, Francisca (Frasquita) de Larrea, from Cadiz

(though her name would suggest a Basque origin) was as well known as her husband in Spain. She was one of the first women to gather about her a coterie who met at her house to converse on art, literature, music, and politics. This salon of hers resembled the more famous *salons romantiques* of Mme. de Staël and Mme. Récamier in Paris. In each case a brilliant woman, worthy of competing with the most learned and intellectual men of her time, led the cultural life of her city, if not of her country. In addition, Frasquita Böhl de Faber wrote under the pseudonym of Corina, chosen from the title of Mme. de Staël's most famous novel, *Corinne*.

Unfortunately, the marriage of Fernán Caballero's parents was not a happy one, owing in part to differences in temperament and in part to disagreements over religion. Böhl de Faber was a Protestant, Doña Frasquita an ardent Catholic. He disliked her literary bent and her independence of mind, and criticized her constantly for her intellectual pretensions. Indeed he said that "she did not constitute the ideal he had formed of a woman." A clue to his attitude toward his wife's and later his daughter's attainments lies in his vehement loathing for Mary Wollstonecraft because she wrote *Vindication of the Rights of Women*. The suspicion arises that Böhl de Faber's family life may have been marred by a trace of jealousy, as well as by his disapproval of intelligent women.

Inevitably the attitude of a father she adored exerted a strong influence on his favorite child. Cecilia never referred to her mother's literary accomplishments and seldom mentioned her at all, but she wrote and spoke of her father in terms akin to idolatry. She grew up with a horror of being considered a blue-stocking. Again and again she protested that she wrote her novels and stories mainly to practice the languages she knew; that they were written for herself alone. For many years she refused every offer to publish them. It seems evident, however, that Fernán Caballero wrote because she was a writer by nature and she had to write.

At about the time that she completed *La Familia de Alvareda* in German, she received one of her father's many hortatory letters which read in part: ". . . but believe me, my daughter, it is more important to teach (a girl) to be a good mother of a family than to stimulate her with imprudent flattery to be a ridiculous blue-stocking." Small wonder that the manuscript lay among her papers for twenty-five years!

The girl was intelligent and her tastes were intellectual. But as the dutiful daughter of socially prominent parents, she pursued the usual course of a debutante in her early life, both in Cadiz and in Germany. Her father's ties with Germany remained close as long as his parents still lived in Hamburg. Not long after his marriage, he took his wife and her Irish mother with him to visit the Böhl de Faber family. Their trip was interrupted by the birth of Cecilia at Morges, Switzerland on Christmas Day, 1796. The visit lasted two years and was terminated only by the illness of Doña Frasquita, who disliked Germany and longed so ardently to return to Cadiz that she became too ill to remain away from Spain. This pattern occurred several times during Cecilia's childhood. A good portion of her schooling was in Germany, and she completed her higher education at Hamburg University in 1812. While still a student, she made her debut at her grandparents' home, but like her mother, she returned to Spain full of joy at leaving behind the stiff formalism of German society.

The social life of Cadiz contrasted sharply with that of Hamburg. Although by today's standards, the manners of Cadiz were also somewhat formal, the city was not only a business and cultural metropolis at the time of the Napoleonic Wars, it was also the center of an international society composed of visitors from all over Europe and of titled Spanish refugees driven south by the campaigns. Fernán Caballero describes the quality of that society in the scenes laid in the salon of the Countess de Algar in *La Gaviota*.

The refugees from the north threw themselves into a round of feverish gaiety and brilliance while the French were moving steadily southward during the period between 1810 and 1812.

Cecilia Böhl de Faber was introduced to this dazzling scene at a famous ball given by the grandees of Madrid resident in Cadiz in honor of the Duke of Wellington. Until her death she preserved the pink satin slippers covered with lace in which she had danced with him. In the course of the evening, Wellington announced the beginning of Napoleon's retreat from Moscow.

While still very young, Cecilia also witnessed the liberal evolution in Spain begun under Charles III, who introduced the ideas of the French Enlightenment. This new thought brought about important changes. For the first time clandestine Masonic lodges sprang up in Spain. Among their early members were the type of grandee described as "proud of having spat in France." Charles IV continued this Francophile movement. Fernán Caballero portrayed this social upheaval with her characteristic effectiveness in *Elia: o La España Treinta Años Ha*. Also characteristically, she mourns there the decline of Old Spain. Nevertheless, Spain under Charles III had become more closely tied to the rest of Europe and moved once more with the stream of European thought. This new awakening was to be followed by a genuine renaissance in education, literature, and painting. European visitors were attracted there in numbers, partly by the climate, partly by the color and novelty of this hitherto little-known country with its strong national character and its integrity of customs and manners, but most of all by its romance and gaiety.

These developments are important to the scene of *La Gaviota*, colored by the author's reluctance to see change in her beloved Spain. They are contrasted with the old, unchanging Spain that, like Villamar, remained relatively untouched by civil war, foreign wars, new thought, or fashion.

When Cecilia was sixteen, she met a handsome young captain of grenadiers from the Balearic Islands. The young man, Antonio Planells y Bardaxi, was on the eve of departure for Puerto Rico with his regiment. It was love at first sight, and within a few days they were married. Cecilia sailed with him for Puerto Rico, where she remained for three years. The young people discovered they had little in common, and it was perhaps fortunate for the girl-wife that Planells y Bardaxi died very suddenly. How it happened that her parents consented to her marriage to a young man she hardly knew will always remain a mystery.

Much of this period in Fernán Caballero's life is related in *Clemencia*. After her bereavement, she returned to her parents' house, where she was courted almost immediately by a young Sevillian whom she had known before her marriage, the Marquis of Arco-Hermoso, Don Francisco Ruiz del Arco. But the girl could not yet think of remarrying and she went to Germany to spend two years with her grandparents. Shortly after her return to Cadiz, she and the marquis were married.

The estates of the Ruiz del Arco family were within a few miles of Seville; there the young couple took their place in Sevillian society. At that time the city was still "the grave matron with a rosary in hand." Social life was stiff and dull. But such was the social position and talent of the young marchioness that she was able to transform it. The fine old mansion at Arco-Hermoso became the meeting-ground of the Andalusian aristocracy and of the distinguished foreigners in Seville. Washington Irving, then Ambassador to Spain, met Fernán Caballero there in 1828.

After his first visit, he noted in his diary: "Call this morning . . . on the Marchioness of Arco-Hermoso; make a long visit; the Marchioness relates many village anecdotes of the village of Dos Hermanas. Return home and make a note of them."

This was the beginning of a long friendship. Washington Irving profited from Fernán Caballero's knowledge of the manners and customs of Spain and from her interest in folklore. Each encouraged the other to write. His developing interest in folklore bore fruit in *The Alhambra* and in his legends of the mid-Hudson valley. When their friendship was a few months old, the marchioness showed Irving some of her manuscripts on folklore, and received from him enthusiastic praise and encouragement.

But Arco-Hermoso was not alone a fashionable rendezvous for the aristocracy and the literati; it was also a refuge for the poor and unfortunate, and for political emigrés from the North.

This was the happiest period of Fernán Caballero's life. She was fully occupied with her salon, her good works, her writing, and the husband she loved. Her days were fruitful, though her literary work was confined largely to making notes and studies on Andalusian folklore. The materials for these came from her contacts with the villagers of Dos Hermanas, whom she encouraged to talk by her questions and by the warm informality of her manner. Frequently she journeyed to Paris, where she established close friendships with Mme. Récamier and Mme. Chateaubriand.

The death of the marquis abruptly closed Fernán Caballero's fourteen years of happiness. But this grievous loss was only the beginning of a series of tragedies and reverses that lasted until her death. Within three years both her parents died and she lost her fortune. The property of Arco-Hermoso had been deeply in debt. The widowed marchioness took on the responsibility of paying the creditors of the estate, a somewhat quixotic gesture that brought her no thanks and consumed almost all her inheritance. Moreover, the once wealthy Böhl de Faber shipping business had been ruined by the Napoleonic Wars and by piracy, and her legacy from her father's estate was small.

It was during that time while she was living with her sisters and her mother in Puerto de Santa María that she wrote *La Gaviota* in French; this was followed by *Clemencia, Relaciones populares,* a collection of folk tales, and *Una en otra.* In this same period she frequently met a young man from a prominent family in Ronda, keenly interested in literature and an excellent critic. While this Antonio Arrom de Ayala was courting her, he tried in vain to persuade her to permit the publication of her novels, in particular *La Gaviota,* which he considered her best.

After a time of indecision, Fernán Caballero married Arrom de Ayala. Through him she met the prominent man of letters, José Joaquín de Mara. Together Arrom and Mara had *La Gaviota* translated into Spanish and sold it to *El Heraldo* of Madrid as a serial. As its author she refused to let it appear under her name, they sought a pseudonym and chose "Fernán Caballero" as eminently Castilian, traditional, and masculine.

The novel appeared in 1849, when the author was fifty-two years old. It created a great stir and was widely and enthusiastically lauded by all the important literary figures of the day. Trying to guess the true name of the author became a sort of national pastime. Finally the secret came out and Cecilia Böhl de Faber was heaped with honors. Queen Isabel II sent her the Band of Lady-in-Waiting to María Luisa, the Infanta, and offered her a pension and the assumption of all publishing expenses of future books, as well as the grant of an apartment in the Alcázar as a home, and all the concomitant life of the court. The royal favors were gratefully declined.

Despite the honors and praise bestowed upon her work, the later years of this remarkable woman were increasingly unhappy. Personal misfortune struck again when her third husband, after losing what money she still had, blew his brains out in a London park.

Fernán Caballero felt so discredited by this episode that she retired to a convent about 1860. She had been living quietly in a small town near Seville, nearly penniless. She had long since ceased to write. All hope had left her, and she had fallen into a state of melancholy and indifference. Knowing her stringencies, the Infanta granted her an annuity. Once more she declined the royal bounty, and on the advice of a friend sold all the rights to her work to a Madrid publisher for a small sum that was sufficient to keep her until her death in 1877 at the age of eighty-one. Queen Isabel and her daughter, the Infanta, were at the author's bedside.

Some years before her death, she was the subject of a portrait showing an aging, but not aged woman—still handsome, and retaining traces of beauty. The forehead is broad and serene, the nose large. The eyes are big and beautifully shaped, their lids slightly heavy with an expression of sadness, and world-weariness. The corners of the small mouth are barely lifted in a Mona Lisa smile. The hands are extremely fine, white, and beautifully shaped. Like her mother, she was small and delicately made; like her father, blonde and blue-eyed. Her dress was somberly handsome and she wore the mantilla, her favorite headdress.

The artist revealed a woman who was an authentic *grande dame*. Yet beneath the pride, independence, and reserve of the great lady, there is a hint of the young girl who began life so richly endowed, but whose right to be a true intellectual, a professional writer, and a successful career woman was frustrated by her time, by the ambivalence of her adored father toward his wife and her, and by the inexorability of events. This frustration which, in the end, froze her in a state of immobility, was expressed in a letter she wrote several years before her death to her friend, Father Luis Coloma, author of *Recuerdos de Fernán Caballero:*

"My spirit is in a kind of inaction that might be called inertia. I neither enjoy nor suffer, and in this state of insensibility I await death in order to be purged at last of this lukewarmness . . ."

More than a century has passed since the publication of *La Gaviota,* but it has retained its place in Spanish literature —not for its great literary merit, but because it was a welltold story, gracefully written. Within the compass of this novel, Fernán Caballero managed to include all the significant social phenomena of Victorian Spain: the recovery from the Civil War with its enduring effects; the changing styles and ideas of the new Spain, as represened by the *habitués* of the countess's salon, contrasted with the enduring Spain of Villamar.

This photographic portrayal arises in part from the unique position or Fernán Caballero. She spans the period of the Romantic movement and the beginning of Realism in literature. Thus she was the first of a line of illustrious novelists—

Alarcón, Pereda, Palacio Valdés, Emilia Pardo Bazán—which culminates in the greatest of them all, Pérez Galdós. In part, her success as a novelist arose from the fresh viewpoint and enthusiasm of a foreigner who had adopted Spain *con amore,* though she was willing to admit its faults with sorrow and to strive vigorously to correct them by her moralizing. At times she displayed the sentimentality of the Romantic writer, but she offset that with a keen irony which would seem more natural to such an intelligent woman.

James Fitzmaurice-Kelly, author of *A History of Spanish Literature,* has said of Fernán Caballero: "It would be difficult to maintain that Fernán Caballero was a great literary artist, but it is certain that she was a born teller of stories . . . She came into Spain at a most happy moment, before the new order had perceptibly disturbed the old, and she brought to bear not alone a fine natural gift for observation, but a freshness of vision, undulled by long familiarity. She combined the advantages of being both a foreigner and a native. . . ."

Throughout *La Gaviota,* and all her other novels and stories, Fernán Caballero clung faithfully to her own experience. The portrayal of her characters is almost photographic. All the minor characters are briefly and successfully realized. The male characters, more fully developed, are less successful. Rafael, the Duke, and Stein are probably the weakest. Stein, in particular, is somewhat effeminate and always too good to be true. Rafael, partially successful as a young dandy, is a wit who lacks the brevity to sharpen his point.

In her treatment of the women, however, Fernán Caballero reveals their monolithic character. Their submission is more apparent than real. Aunt María and Marysal in particular are wrought of iron. Aunt María is the prototype of the matriarch, while Marysal is the Spanish woman of fire and ice. She has the complete integrity of her heartless amorality, first seen by Momo who kept prophesying that her admirers were "raising a crow to pick out their eyes." That the women characters are true to life is evidenced by the fact that Spain was ruled by several queens of remarkable character, the greatest of whom was Isabel I.

Fernán Caballero's work held a three-fold significance in Spain. She rescued the novel from the doldrums and gave it new vigor; she was a devout apologist for Spain and all things Spanish (hence she vindicated the inborn patriotism and pride of the Spaniard); and she transcribed the life of her time as she saw it, with a keen, loving, and faithful eye.

THE SEA GULL

In November of the year 1836 the passenger ship *Royal Sovereign* was drawing away from the foggy coast of Falmouth, breasting the seas with all her might, and spreading her sails, dark and wet from the fog that was even darker and damper than they were.

The interior of the ship presented the dreary spectacle of the commencement of a sea voyage. The passengers crowded aboard her were fighting off the ravages of seasickness. Half-fainting women could be seen, their hair dishevelled, the fronts of their dresses rumpled, their hats awry. The men, pale and out of sorts; the children neglected and wailing; the stewards crossing the staterooms with staggering step to bring the sufferers tea, coffee, or other supposed remedies, while the ship, lord and master of the waters, battled the seas, heedless of the ills it was causing, over-riding the seas when they fought back, and hotly pursuing them when they gave way.

Those men who, either through constitutional immunity or experience in sailing, had escaped the common scourge, were pacing the deck. Among them, accompanied by two aides, was the governor of an English colony, tall and aristocratic in appearance. Several of the others were bundled up in their mackintoshes, hands in pockets, faces flushed, bluish, or leaden, all wearing a general air of malaise. In short, that handsome vessel appeared to have become the seat of ill humor and queasiness.

Outstanding among the passengers was one young man who looked to be about twenty-four years old, his unassuming and well-bred air and calm, handsome face giving no indication of the slightest disturbance. He was tall and well-built, and in the carriage of his head there was grace as well as dignity. His black, curly hair crowned his high forehead; the look in his large, black eyes was both calm and keen. A soft smile, betokening competence and alertness, played about his lips, which were shadowed by a thin, black mustache, and his high class and character shone forth from his whole person, his manner of walking, and his gestures, without the slightest trace of the disdainful air unfairly attributed by some people to any kind of superiority.

He was travelling for pleasure, and being essentially a good-natured man, was not to be drawn into any assaults upon the vices and the foibles of society; that is, he felt no call to tilt with windmills, like Don Quijote. To him, it was much pleasanter to look for the good, and this he sought with the pure and uncomplicated satisfaction of a girl gathering violets. His face, his dress, the manner in which he wrapped himself in his cloak, his indifference to the cold and to the general misery, proclaimed him a Spaniard.

He was strolling along, observing the mosaic-like joining of the side timbers with a quick, appraising glance, estimating the number of those boards whose sum total is called a ship, or in smaller dimensions a coffin. But there was little to note about men who seemed drunk and women who looked like corpses.

Nevertheless, his interest was aroused by the family of an English official whose wife had come aboard so ill she had to be carried to her stateroom, as did the nurse whom the father followed with the suckling infant in his arms, first ordering

three other children of two, three, and four years to seat themselves on the deck, admonishing them to be good and not to
move from the spot. The poor children, doubtless very strictly
reared, stayed there as still and quiet as the angels painted
around the feet of the Virgin.

Little by little, the lovely rose color faded from their
cheeks; their big eyes, opened to the fullest, stared ahead as
though they were stunned or paralyzed. Their suffering was
evident in their pinched and frightened faces, but they made
no move nor murmur to proclaim their plight.

No one paid heed to this silent misery, this docile and
dolorous resignation.

The Spaniard was about to summon the steward when
he overheard him replying in a surly manner to a young man
who appeared to be asking help, in German and with expressive gestures, for those abandoned little children.

Inasmuch as this young man lacked outward elegance or
distinction, and as he spoke nothing but German, the steward
turned his back, saying he did not understand.

The young German then went down to his stateroom in
the bow and returned promptly carrying a pillow, a blanket,
and a coarse woolen coat. With these he made a kind of bed,
laid the children down on it, and covered them with the greatest care. But scarcely had they stretched out when seasickness,
until then checked by lack of movement, suddenly erupted;
and instantly the pillow, the blanket, and the coat were reeking
and stained.

The Spaniard stared at the German whose face betrayed
nothing but a smile of benevolent satisfaction which seemed
to say: "Thank God, they're relieved."

The Spaniard spoke to him in English, French, and Spanish, to all of which he received no reply beyond an awkward salute and the repeated phrase *Ich verstehe nicht* (I don't understand).

When the Spaniard went up on deck again, after dining, the cold had increased. He wrapped his cape around him and began to take his constitutional. He saw the German then, sitting on a bench and staring out at the sea which was coming up to the sides of the ship as if showing off, displaying its foamy pearls and phosphorescent diamonds.

The young watcher was coatless, his own having been rendered unwearable, and the cold must have bitten him deep.

The Spaniard took a few steps toward him, but, not knowing how to address him, came to a halt. Suddenly he smiled as though struck by a happy thought, and going straight to the other man, he said to him in Latin:

"You must be very cold."

This voice, this sentence, brought the keenest satisfaction to the stranger, and smiling back at the speaker, he answered in the same language:

"The night is indeed quite bitter; but I wasn't thinking about that."

"Well, what were you thinking about?" asked the Spaniard.

"I was thinking of my father, my mother, my brothers and sisters."

"If you miss them so much, then why are you travelling?"

"Ah, señor; necessity . . . That hard taskmaster."

"So you're not travelling for pleasure?"

"That sort of pleasure is for the rich, and I'm poor. For my own enjoyment! . . . If you could guess the object of my trip, you'd realize how far it is from pleasure."

"Where are you going then?"

"To war, to the civil war—the worst kind of war; to Navarre." [1]

"To war!" cried the Spaniard, thinking of the kind, gentle, almost humble and most unbellicose aspect of the German. "Then you're a soldier?"

"No, señor; that's not my calling. Neither my tastes nor my principles would lead me to take up arms except to defend the sacred cause of Germany's independence if she should again be invaded by foreigners. I'm going into the army of Navarre to try to get a job as a surgeon."

"And you don't know the language!"

"No, señor; but I shall learn it."

"Nor the country either?"

"Not that either. I've never been outside my village except to the university."

"But you have references."

"None whatever."

"You must have a patron to turn to."

"I don't know a soul in Spain."

"Well, what do you have then?"

"My skill, my good will, my youth, and my trust in God."

The Spaniard reflected før a moment or two on those words. As he studied that face portraying candor and gentleness; those blue eyes pure as a child's; that wistful and yet trusting smile, hc felt keenly interested and somewhat touched.

"Would you like to come below with me and have a hot

---

[1] This northern province of Spain was the scene of the first Carlist War (1833-1840), supported by the clergy and extreme conservatives, for the purpose of restoring the throne to Don Carlos, brother of Ferdinand VII, who had passed it to his daughter Isabella. The rebels wanted to preserve the male succession, but Don Carlos was a poor leader and they failed.

drink to keep out the cold?" he asked. "Meanwhile, we can talk."

The German bowed his gratitude and followed the Spaniard to the dining saloon where he ordered a drink.

At the head of the table sat the governor with his two aides; two Frenchmen were on one side. The Spaniard and the German seated themselves at the foot of the table.

"But how did you conceive the notion of coming to this unhappy land?" asked the former.

The German launched upon a faithful account of his life. He was the sixth son of a professor in a small village in Saxony. His father had spent all he had on the education of his children. Upon graduation, the young man we are coming to know found himself, like so many other poor boys in Germany, without a practice or a post after dedicating his youth to hard and meritorious study and internship under the best teachers. His support was becoming a burden to his family; undiscouraged, he resolved, with all his Germanic equanimity, to come to Spain, where the bloody war in the North had aroused the hope that his services might be put to good use.

"Beneath the lindens that cast their shade over the doorway of my house," he said at the conclusion of his story, "I gave a last embrace to my good father, my dear mother, my sister Lotte, and my little brothers who were clamoring to go with me on my journey. I stepped forth into life, deeply moved and in tears. For some people it is a bed of roses. But, after all, man was born to work; Heaven will bless my efforts. I love my profession because it is fine and worthy. Its object is the healing of one's neighbor, and though the task may be painful, the results are rewarding."

"And your name is . . . ?"

"Fritz Stein," replied the German, half-rising from his chair and making a little bow.

Shortly afterward, the two new friends left the saloon.

One of the Frenchmen, sitting near the door, saw that as they were going up the companionway, the Spaniard threw his handsome fur-lined cape across the German's shoulders; the German made as if to refuse; but the Spaniard eluded him and went into his stateroom.

"Did you understand what they were saying?" he asked his fellow-countryman.

"As a matter of fact," replied the latter, a commission agent, "Latin is not my strong point; but I'd guess that the pale blonde fellow is some sort of weepy Werther[2] and I gathered that there's some little Charlotte in his story, to say nothing of some kids, just like the German novel. Chances are that instead of picking up his pistol to console himself, he's taken to drink. While that's not so sentimental, it's certainly more philosophical and more German. As for the Spaniard, I take him for a Don Quijote, a champion of the downtrodden, with overtones of Saint Martin who shared his cloak with the poor. This fellow, with his tall figure, his straight and fiery glance, and his pale, colorless complexion like a landscape in the moonlight, makes a perfect picture of a Spaniard, for his part."

"You know," replied the other, "I'm going to Tarifa[3] as an historical painter. I aim to paint the scene of the siege at

---

[2] Werther was the hero of Goethe's romance, *The Sorrows of Young Werther* (1774), a sentimental account of a tender young German student, so overcome by love for his Lotte that he took his life.
[3] A seaport near Cádiz, reclaimed from the Moors by Sancho IV of Castile in 1292.

the moment when Guzmán's[4] son signals his father to sacrifice him rather than surrender the citadel. If this young man would like to sit for me as a model, I'm sure my painting would be a success. I've never seen Nature come closer to the ideal."

"That's the way with you artists; all poets!" answered the commission agent. "As for me, unless I'm mistaken in judging this man's grace, his foot like a woman's and the way he sets it down, and his elegant, slim waist, I'd class him right now as a bullfighter. Maybe he's Montes himself, for he looks more or less like him, and besides, he's rich and open-handed."

"A bullfighter!" exclaimed the artist. "A man of the people! Are you fooling?"

"No, honestly," said the other. "I'm not joking at all. You haven't lived in Spain as I have, and you don't know the aristocratic temperament of the people. You'll see. It's my opinion that thanks to the spread of equality and fraternity, well-marked aristocratic manners are declining; soon there won't be any except in Spain, among the common people themselves."

"Imagine a man like that being a bullfighter!" said the artist with a smile so scornful as to nettle the other man, who got up and cried:

"I'll soon find out who he is; come with me and we'll go hunt up his servant."

The two men went up on deck where they soon found the man they were looking for.

The commission agent, who spoke a little Spanish, started a conversation with him, and after a few commonplaces, said:

"Has your master gone to bed?"

---

[4] Alonso Pérez de Guzmán, "El Bueno" (the Stout-Hearted), was so called because he permitted his son to be killed rather than surrender Tarifa during the Moorish War. He was the founder of one of the richest and most illustrious dukedoms in Spain.

"Yes, sir," replied the servant, casting at the speaker a knowing glance full of suspicion.

"Is he very rich?"

"I'm his valet, not his business manager."

"Is he travelling on business?"

"I don't think he has a business."

"Is he travelling for his health?"

"He's in very good health."

"Is he travelling incognito?"

"No, sir; under his own given name and surname."

"And his name is . . . ?"

"Don Carlos de la Cerda."

"That's certainly an illustrious name!" cried the painter.

"Mine is Pedro de Guzmán, at your service," added the valet. With this, he bowed to them and retired.

"That Gil Blas[5] is right," said the Frenchman, "There's nothing commoner in Spain than illustrious names; but to be sure, my shoemaker in Paris is named Martel,[6] my tailor Roland,[7] my laundress Mme. Bayard.[8] In Scotland there are more Stuarts than stones. We've had our legs pulled! That rascal of a servant was making fun of us. But, on the whole, I suspect he's an agent of the Rebels, some underling of Don Carlos."

"What difference does it make?" exclaimed the artist. "He's

---

[5] Gil Blas was the picaresque hero of a novel with that title by Le Sage (1715), a French priest. The merry rogue earned the reputation of a scholar before serving as valet to one of his many masters.

[6] Charles Martel, drove the Moors out of France at the Battle of Tours, 732.

[7] Roland, hero of the French epic *Le Chanson de Roland,* which celebrated his stand against the Saracens at Roncesvalles in the Pyrenees in 778.

[8] The Chevalier de Bayard was the famous French knight "sans peur et sans reproche," hero of the Italian campaigns of Charles VIII, Louis XII, and François I.

still my Alonso Pérez de Guzmán, el Bueno; the hero of my dreams."

The other Frenchman shrugged.

When the ship landed at Cádiz, the Spaniard took leave of Stein.

"I have to stay a while in Andalusia," he said. "But my servant will go with you to Seville and book a seat for you on the stagecoach to Madrid. Here's a letter of recommendation to the Minister of War and another to the Commander in Chief of the Army. If you need me at any time, write to me in Madrid at this address."

Stein was so moved he could not speak. With one hand he took the letters and with the other rejected the card the Spaniard held out to him.

"Your name is engraved here," said the German, putting his hand to his heart. "Oh! I'll never forget it as long as I live. It stands for the noblest heart, the loftiest and most generous soul, the best of mortals."

"Your letters wouldn't reach me at that address," replied Don Carlos, smiling. "You'll need something plainer and shorter."

He handed Stein the card and took his leave.

Stein read: *The Duke of Almansa.*

And Pedro de Guzmán who was standing nearby, added:

"Marquis of Guadalmonte, of Val de Flores and of Roca Fiel; Count of Santa Clara, of Encinasola and of Lara; Knight of the Golden Fleece and of the Grand Cross of Charles III; gentleman in waiting to His Majesty; Grandee of Spain of the first class, etc. etc."

CHAPTER II

On a morning in October of 1838, a man was coming down on foot from one of the villages in the county of Niebla, heading toward the shore. So great was his impatience to arrive at a little seaport which had been pointed out to him that, thinking to take a short cut, he entered one of the huge ranches common to southern Spain which are used for raising cattle, completely uninhabited tracts whose herds never leave them.

This man looked old, though he was only twenty-six. He was dressed in a kind of military blouse, buttoned to the neck. His headgear was a worn, visored cap. On his shoulder he was carrying a stout pole which held suspended a small mahogany box covered with green baize; a stack of books tied together with strips of selvage, a kerchief containing some articles of white clothing, and a big, rolled cape.

Even this light luggage seemed too much for his strength. From time to time he would stop, press a hand to his laboring chest or wipe his burning forehead, or perhaps fix his eyes on a poor dog following him, which lay down at every stop, exhausted, beside his feet.

"Poor *Treu*," he said to it, "the only creature offering proof to me that affection and gratitude still exist in this world! No, I shall never forget the first day I saw you! You were with a poor shepherd who was shot for refusing to turn traitor. At the moment when death overtook him, he was kneeling and trying in vain to drive you from his side. He asked them to take you away but no one dared to do it. The volley rang out and you, the faithful friend of the poor wretch, fell seriously wounded

11

beside your master's dead body. I picked you up, I healed your wounds, and since then you've never abandoned me. When the jokers in the regiment used to make fun of me and call me a dog doctor, you'd come and lick the hand that saved you as if to say: 'Dogs are grateful.' Oh, God! I used to love my neighbor so much! . . . Two years ago I came to this country, full of life, hope, and good will; and I offered them my vigils, my care, my skill, and my heart. I've healed many a wound, and in exchange I've been deeply wounded in spirit. Dear God! Dear God! My heart is broken. Here I am, ignominiously thrown out of the army after two years of service, two years of working tirelessly, here I am accused and persecuted, only because I treated a man from the opposite side, an unfortunate fellow who came to die in my arms after being hunted down like a wild beast. How is it that the rules of war can make a crime of what morality has established as a virtue, and religion as a duty? And what am I to do now? Am I to go back and rest my poverty-stricken head and my heavy-laden heart under my father's roof tree? They wouldn't think there that it was a crime to take pity on a dying man."

After a few moments of rest, the unhappy man made an effort.

"Let's go, *Treu; vorwärts, vorwärts!*"

The traveller and his faithful animal went on their painful way.

But in a short while he lost the narrow path, worn by the feet of shepherds, which he had been following.

The terrain was becoming more and more thickly covered with brambles, with tall, dense, briar bushes; it was impossible to follow a straight line; he could not walk without veering to one side or the other.

The sun was completing its course and no slightest trace

of human habitation was visible anywhere on the horizon; nothing could be seen but endless open pastureland, a desert as green and featureless as the sea.

Fritz Stein, whom our readers will doubtless have recognized, realized too late that his impatience had led him to call upon more strength than he possessed. He could hardly keep himself on his sore and swollen feet; his pulse was fluttering violently; his head was splitting; a burning thirst was devouring him. Then, to add to the horror of his situation, a deep, long-drawn bellowing warned him of the nearness of some of the half-wild herds of bulls that are so dangerous in Spain.

"God has rescued me from many perils," said the wretched man, "He will protect me now; and if not, His will be done!"

Whereupon he hastened his steps as much as he was able; but what was his terror when, having rounded a thick clump of mastic[9] bushes, he found himself face to face with a bull only a few paces away!

Stein stood motionless as if turned to stone. The brute, surprised by the encounter and by such audacity, also stood still, fixing on Stein his big, fierce eyes, burning like two bonfires. The traveller knew he was a doomed man if he made the slightest movement. The bull, owing to the instinct of his kind, based on his strength and courage, must be provoked to attack. He tossed his head twice, impatiently pawing the earth and raising clouds of dust, as if issuing a challenge. Stein made no move. Then the animal took a step backward, lowered his head, and prepared to charge, when he felt his hocks nipped. At the same time, the furious barking of his loyal companion identified Stein's savior. The bull, enraged, turned to repel the unexpected attacker, a move that gave Stein the opportunity to run. The terrible situation from which he had barely escaped

---

[9] A shrub with a heavy sap, belonging to the sumac family.

lent him new strength to flee among the pin-oaks and the mastics whose density hid him from his formidable opponent.

He had already crossed a narrow glen, and, climbing a hill, he stopped at its crest, completely out of breath, to turn around and look back at the site of his critical moment of jeopardy. Thence he could see among the briars at a distance his poor companion being tossed repeatedly by the ferocious brute. Stein held out his arms to his faithful companion, and said, sobbing:

"Poor, poor *Treu!* My one friend! How well you earned your name! How dearly you've paid for the love you bore your masters!"

To escape the dreadful spectacle, Stein hurried onward, shedding copious tears. Thus he reached the crest of another rise whence a magnificent view unrolled before his eyes. The land sloped gently toward the sea which, calm and still, reflected the fire of the setting sun, looking like a field sown with diamonds, rubies, and sapphires. In the midst of this extravaganza of brilliance, the white spread of a ship's sails stood out like a pearl set in the waves. The irregular line of the coast displayed now a beach of golden sand splashed with silver spray by the gentle combers, now high, broken cliffs seeming content to face the formidable element and to stand firm against its assaults like steadfastness itself in the face of fury. On one of the cliffs at his left, he could make out in the distance the ruins of a fort, an artifact of man, hence able to withstand nothing, founded on the rock which is the work of God, hence able to withstand anything. Some clumps of pines lifted their dark, enduring heads above the brambles. To the right a huge structure could be seen on a hilltop, but it was impossible to determine whether it was a village, a castle with outbuildings, or a convent.

Enfeebled by his last flight and the emotion that had recently shaken him, he turned his steps toward that point.

By the time he arrived, night had fallen. The building was a convent like those built in centuries past when faith and zeal reigned: virtues so great, so fine, so lofty that by the same token they no longer fit into the narrow and paltry ideas of this century; for in those days gold was not hoarded nor spent knavishly but was turned to noble and worthy uses, as though the men of that time thought of grandeur and beauty before comfort and utility. It was a convent that, in other sumptuous, rich, hospitable days, used to give bread to the poor, help to the needy, and healing to the ills of soul and body; but now, abandoned, empty, poor, dilapidated, it was up for sale in exchange for some pieces of paper, yet no one had wanted to buy it even at that low price.

Though swollen to gigantic dimensions, though moving forward like a conqueror invading everything and undeterred by obstacles, speculation usually stops at the temples of God, as sand borne by the wind of the desert halts at the feet of the Pyramids.

The bell-tower, despoiled of its appropriate ornament, reared up like a lifeless giant from whose vacant eye-sockets the spark of life had departed. A white marble cross still stood before the entrance, its half-ruined pedestal causing it to tilt, as if in weakness and grief. The door, once opened wide to all, was now closed.

Stein's strength deserted him and he fell half-fainting to a stone bench made fast to the wall near the doorway. His delirious brain was in a turmoil; it seemed to him that the waves of the sea were approaching him like huge serpents, quickly drawing back and showering him with a white and venomous spittle; that the moon was shining down on him with

a pale and astonished face; that the stars were whirling about
him, looking down and mocking him. Then came the bellowing of bulls, one of which came out from behind the cross to
cast at the feet of the fever-ridden man the mangled body of
his poor dog. The cross itself wavered toward him as though
about to fall and pin him beneath its weight. Everything
moved and whirled around the unhappy man! But in the
midst of this chaos where his thoughts were becoming more
and more confused, he no longer heard muted and fantastic
murmurings like distant drums, as the rapid beating of his
pulses had sounded to him, but a clear, distinct cry, one that
could not be mistaken for any other—the crowing of a cock.

As though this rural and domestic sound had suddenly
given him back the power to think and to move, Stein got to his
feet, tottered to the door and knocked on it with a stone; he was
answered by barking. He made an effort to repeat his knock
and fell unconscious to the ground.

The door opened, and two people appeared.

One was a young woman with a lamp in her hand. Directing the light on the object she saw at her feet, she cried:

"Good heavens, it isn't Manuel; it's a stranger . . . And
he's dead! God help us!"

"Let's help him," exclaimed the other, a mature woman,
very neatly dressed. "Brother Gabriel, Brother Gabriel!" she
called, going into the patio. "Come quickly. Here's a poor man
who's dying."

Quick but heavy footsteps were heard. They were those of
an old man, not very tall, whose peaceful and candid face proclaimed a pure and simple soul. His grotesque attire, consisting
of a pair of trousers and a ragged waistcoat of dark sackcloth,
seemed at first glance to be cut from a monk's habit. He was

shod in sandals, and his shining tonsure was covered by a dark woolen cap.

"Brother Gabriel," said the old woman, "we must help this man."

"We must help this man," replied Brother Gabriel.

"Heavens, señora," exclaimed the girl with the lamp, "where are you intending to put a dying man?"

"Daughter," replied the old woman, "if there's no other place to put him, in my own bed."

"And you're going to let him into the house," said the other, "without knowing who he is?"

"What does it matter?" said the old woman. "Don't you know the proverb, 'Grant a boon, nor ask to whom'? Come, Dolores, help me, and let's get to work."

Dolores obeyed with a mixture of willingness and fear.

"I hope to goodness there's no fuss when Manuel comes," she said.

"What if there is?" answered the good old woman. "I'd like to see the day when a son can tell his mother what to do!"

Among them, the trio carried Stein to Brother Gabriel's room. A bed was quickly made up with clean straw and a large, fleecy sheepskin. Aunt María[10] took a pair of coarse but snow-white sheets from a chest, together with a woolen blanket.

Brother Gabriel wanted to give up his pillow, but Aunt María opposed that, saying she had two and could very well sleep with only one. It was not long before Stein was undressed and put to bed.

Meanwhile, a repeated knocking was heard at the door.

---

[10] Tía and tío, aunt and uncle, are respectful, lower-class titles given to people somewhat advanced in years in the Spanish villages and in the country.

"Here's Manuel," said his wife then. "Come with me, mother, for I don't care to be alone with him when he finds out that we've taken a man we don't know into the house."

The mother-in-law followed in her daughter-in-law's steps.

"Praise God! Good evening, mother; good evening, wife," said a tall, well-built man, some thirty-eight or forty years old. He was followed by a boy of about thirteen.

"Come, Momo," [11] he added. "Unload the burro and take her to the stable. Poor Golondrina is about worn out."

Momo brought a good supply of big white loaves, some panniers, and his father's cloak into the kitchen, which was the family living room. Immediately afterward, he led Golondrina away by the bridle.

Dolores went back to close the door and joined her husband and his mother in the kitchen.

"Did you bring me the soap and the starch?" she asked.

"Here they are."

"And my thread?" asked the mother.

"I didn't want to bring it," replied Manuel, smiling and handing his mother some skeins.

"Why, son?"

"It reminded me of the fellow going to the fair who was given a commission by all the neighbors. Bring me a hat; bring me a pair of leggings; one cousin wanted a comb; an aunt wanted chocolate; but no one gave him a cent for it all. When he was already on his mule a little boy went up to him and said: 'Here are two pennies for a whistle, would you like to bring me it?' Suiting the deed to the word, he put the money in the man's hand. The man bent down, took the money and said, 'You're going to whistle!' And when he came back from

---

[11] An Andalusian nickname for Gerónimo.

the fair, of all the orders he brought nothing but the whistle."

"Well, I like that!" said the mother. "Whom am I spinning for day and night? Isn't it for you and your children? Do you want me to be like the tailor of Campillo who sewed for nothing and supplied his own thread?"

Just then Momo appeared in the kitchen doorway. He was short and chubby; his shoulders were high, and he had a habit of holding them still higher in a gesture of "who cares" until they almost touched his huge ears, broad as fans. His head was large, his hair sparse, his lips thick. Moreover, he was snub-nosed and extremely cross-eyed.

"Father," he said with a malicious expression, "There's a man in bed in Brother Gabriel's room."

"A man in my house! Dolores, what does this mean?"

"Manuel, he's a poor sick man. Your mother wanted to take him in. I was against it, but the señora prevailed. What was I to do?"

"All very well! But even if she is my mother, that's no reason for letting the first man that comes along into the house."

"No, let him die like a dog instead," said the old woman. "Is that it?"

"But, mother," replied Manuel, "is my house some sort of hospital?"

"No, but it is the home of a Christian; and if you'd been here, you'd have done the same as I."

"No, sir!" replied Manuel, "I'd have set him on top of the donkey and taken him to town since there are no convents now."

"We had no donkey here to carry him, nor any living soul to take charge of this unfortunate man."

"What if he's a thief?"

"A dying man doesn't steal."

"Who's going to pay for him if he's sick a long time?"

"Somebody killed a chicken to make a stew," said Momo. "I saw the feathers in the yard."

"Mother, have you lost your mind?" cried Manuel angrily.

"That will do; that's enough," said the mother in a stern voice and with dignity. "You ought to be ashamed of yourself, getting angry with your mother for doing no more than God's law commands! If your father were alive, he'd never believe a son of his would close his door to a wretched man who came to it dying and with no roof over his head."

Manuel lowered his head and there came a silent pause.

"Come, mother," he said at last. "Forget I said anything. Do as you wish. Everyone knows women will have the last word."

"How good he is!" Dolores said cheerfully to her mother-in-law.

"You might doubt it," said the latter, smiling at her daughter-in-law of whom she was very fond, and getting up to take her place beside the sick man's bed. "I, who bore him, have never doubted it."

As she passed by Momo, the grandmother said to him:

"I always knew you had a bad disposition; but I never saw it more plainly than now. Go with God; I feel sorry for you. You're a bad boy, and anyone who is bad carries his own punishment with him."

"Old women are good for nothing but preaching," Momo grumbled, casting a sidelong look at his grandmother.

But scarcely had he pronounced the last word when his mother, who had overheard him, flew at him and gave him a slap.

"I'll teach you," she said, "to be insolent to your father's mother, who is twice your own mother."

Momo took refuge, snivelling, in the back of the corral, and vented his anger by beating the dog.

CHAPTER III

Aunt María and Brother Gabriel tried to outdo each other in taking care of the sick man; but they could not agree upon the method to be used in treating him. Aunt María, though she had never read Brown,[12] favored nourishing stews and stimulants, for she kept saying he was very weak and emaciated.

Brother Gabriel, though he had never heard the name of Broussais,[13] preferred cool drinks and compresses, for, in his opinion, there was cerebral fever, the blood was inflamed, and the skin burning.

Both were right; and under the combined system, consisting of María's stews and Brother Gabriel's lemonades, Stein recovered life and health on the very day that the good woman killed the last hen and the friar picked the last lemon on the lemon tree.

"Brother Gabriel," said Aunt María, "what manner of bird do you take our invalid to be? A soldier?"

"He might well be a soldier," answered Brother Gabriel, who, apart from the fine points of medicine and horticulture, customarily regarded Aunt María as an oracle, and eschewed any opinion different from hers, just as he had done with the

---

[12] John Brown (1735-1788), a Scottish physician who attacked all systems of medicine then existing, wrote *Elementa Medicina* expounding his Brunonian theory that all disease is due to excessive or deficient stimulation.

[13] François Joseph Victor Broussais (1772-1838), a Parisian physician who theorized that irritation, the cause of all disease, proceeds from inflammation of the gastroenteric tract, and that all treatments must be directed to curing the gastroenteritis.

prior of his monastery; hence he would repeat, almost mechanically, whatever the good old lady said.

"He can't be," went on Aunt María, shaking her head. "If he were a soldier he would carry arms, and he hasn't any. It's true that when I was folding his coat to put it away, I found in the pocket something more or less like a pistol; but when I examined it closely, just in case, I caught on that it wasn't a pistol, but a flute. So he can't be a soldier."

"He can't be a soldier," echoed Brother Gabriel.

"What if he's a smuggler?"

"He might be a smuggler!" said the good lay-brother.

"But no," the old woman answered, "because you have to have goods or money to work at smuggling, and he has neither."

"That's right. He can't be a smuggler!" affirmed Brother Gabriel.

"Brother Gabriel, let's see what the titles of those books say? Perhaps we can find out from them what his work is."

The monk got up, took out his horn-rimmed spectacles, set them on his nose, reached for the pile of books and, going to the window which opened on the main inner patio, he spent a long time examining them.

"Brother Gabriel," said Aunt María at last, "Have you forgotten how to read?"

"No, but I don't recognize these characters; it looks to me like Hebrew."

"Hebrew!" cried Aunt María. "Holy Mother! What if he's a Jew?"

At that moment, Stein who had been semiconscious for some time, opened his eyes and said in German:

"Gott, wo bin ich?" (My God, where am I?)

Aunt María was in the middle of the room in one bound.

Brother Gabriel let the books fall and stood as if turned to stone, opening his eyes as round as his spectacles.

"What did he say?" asked Aunt María.

"It must be in Hebrew like his books," answered Brother Gabriel. "Perhaps he is a Jew, as you said, Aunt María."

"God help us!" cried the old woman. "But no. If he were a Jew, wouldn't we have seen his tail when we undressed him?"

"Aunt María," replied the lay-brother. "The Father Prior said that business about Jews' tails is a hoax, a stupid notion, and that the Jews have no such thing."

"Brother Gabriel," said Aunt María, "there's been a lot of chopping and changing ever since that blessed Constitution came. That lot ruling us in place of the king don't want to hold on to anything that came before them, so they don't want the Jews to have tails, but they've had them all their lives, like the devil. If the Father Prior said anything different, they forced him to, just the way they make him say 'Constitutional King' in the Mass."

"It might well be so," said the monk.

"He can't be a Jew," went on the old woman, "but he could be a Moor or a Turk shipwrecked on these shores."

"A pirate from Morocco!" echoed the good lay-brother. "He could be."

"But then he'd wear a turban and yellow slippers like the Moor I saw thirty years ago when I went to Cádiz. His name was Selim the Moor. How handsome he was! But in my opinion all his good looks came to naught because he wasn't a Christian. Whatever he is, Jew or Moor, it's no matter; we've saved him."

"We saved him, even if he's a Jew or a Moor," echoed the monk.

And the two of them went back to the bed.

Stein had raised himself and was staring in bewilderment at all the objects around him.

"He won't understand what we say to him," said Aunt María, "but we must make the attempt."

"Let's try," repeated Brother Gabriel.

As a rule, the common people in Spain believe that the best way to make themselves understood is to speak at the top of their voices. Aunt María and Brother Gabriel, fully convinced of that, shouted in unison. She, "Do you want some stew?" and he, "Do you want lemonade?"

Stein, who was emerging little by little from the chaos in his mind, asked in Spanish:

"Where am I? Who are you?"

"The gentleman," replied the old woman, "is Brother Gabriel, and I am Aunt María, at your service."

"Ah," said Stein. "The Archangel and the Blessed Virgin, whose names you bear. She who is health to the sick, consolation to the afflicted, and succor to Christians, will repay you for the good you have done me."

"He speaks Spanish," exclaimed Aunt María, overjoyed. "And he's a Christian who knows the Litany."

Full of jubilation, she flung herself at Stein, pressed him in her arms, and kissed him on the forehead.

"And now who are you, after all?" said Aunt María, after giving him a cup of stew. "How did you happen to stop at this lonely spot, sick and dying?"

"My name is Stein and I'm a surgeon. I was in the war in Navarre and came back to Extremadura looking for a port where I could take ship to Cádiz and from there to my own country, which is Germany. I lost my way and wandered for a long time in circles until at last I came here, sick, worn out, and almost dead."

"Now you see," said Aunt María to Brother Gabriel, "his books aren't in Hebrew, they're in the language of the surgeons."

"That's it; they're written in the language of the surgeons," repeated Brother Gabriel.

"Which side were you on?" asked the old woman. "Don Carlos or the others'?"

"I was serving with the Queen's troops," answered Stein.

Aunt María turned to her companion and said to him in a low voice and with a wink:

"He isn't one of the good ones."

"He isn't one of the good ones!" echoed Brother Gabriel, hanging his head.

"But where am I?" asked Stein again.

"You are in a convent which is no longer a convent," replied the old woman, "it's a body without a soul. Nothing is left of it but the walls, the white cross, and Brother Gabriel. The other side carried off all the rest. When there was nothing left to be sacked, some gentlemen who call themselves Public Auditors were looking for a good man to be a watchman for the convent, that is, for its shell. They heard of my son and we came here and established ourselves. I live with that son, the only one left to me. When we moved into the convent, the fathers moved out. Some went to America, others to missions in China, others to stay with their families, and still others set out to make their living by labor or begging. We saw one of the lay brothers, old and heartbroken, sitting on the steps leading to the white cross, weeping partly for his brothers who were leaving and partly for the abandoned convent. 'Aren't you coming, sir?' asked a member of the choir. 'Where am I to go?' he answered. 'I've never been outside these walls since I was taken in by the fathers as an orphan child. I don't know anybody out in the world and I don't know anything except how to take care of the convent garden. Where am I to go? What am I to do? I can't live anywhere but here!' 'Then stay with us,' I said to him. 'Very well, Mother,' replied my son. 'Seven of us sit down at the table now; eight of us will sit down; more will eat less, as the saying goes.' "

"And thanks to this loving-kindness," added Brother Gabriel, "you see me here taking care of the garden; but ever since the chain pump was sold I haven't been able to irrigate one handsbreadth of earth; so the orange and lemon trees are drying up."

"Brother Gabriel," went on Aunt María, "has stayed right here inside these walls; he clings to them like ivy; but, as I was saying, there's nothing left but the walls. Imagine such knavery! Nothing at all. It's as they say: 'Let's destroy the nest so the birds won't come back.' "

"Nevertheless," said Stein, "I've heard that there were too many convents in Spain.

Aunt María fixed the German with her sharp, black, shocked eyes; then, turning to the lay-brother, she said to him in a low voice:

"Were our first suspicions right or not?"

"Maybe our first suspicions were right," replied the monk.

CHAPTER IV

Stein, whose convalescence was proceeding rapidly, could soon leave his room with Brother Gabriel's help, and examine at his leisure that noble structure, so sumptuous, so magnificent, so full of beauty and artistic riches, which, withdrawn from the sight of man, situated beneath the sky in open country, had been a fitting habitation for the many rich and famous men who once lived in the monastery, further embellishing its beauty and magnificence with whatever graces and good works God had endowed them, unseen by anyone but their Creator, and with no purpose other than to glorify Him, for those who believe that modesty and humility hide always beneath the cloak of poverty are vastly mistaken. No, patches and huts may sometimes cover a greater pride than palaces.

The great vaulted gateway, through which Stein had been admitted, opened on a large, square patio. From the gateway to the back of the patio stretched an alley of enormous cypresses. There stood an immense grilled gate of iron, dividing the main patio from another long, narrow one, where the alley of cypresses continued majestically, forming an honor guard to the magnificent doorway of the church, which stood at the end of this second, narrower patio.

When the outer gate and the grilled gate were both opened wide, the superb main altar, covered with gold-leaf from floor to ceiling, like the gilded walls at the upper end of the church, could be seen perfectly from the steps of the marble cross situated at some distance outside the building, for convent churches are not obstructed by choir stalls. When hundreds of lights were reflected from the glittering moldings and shone on the heads of the numberless angels which formed a part of the ornamentation; when the sound of the organ, in keeping with the grandeur of the place and the solemnity of the Catholic services, thundered in the vaulted roof of the church, too small to contain it, and soared to lose itself in the music of the spheres; when this grand spectacle unrolled with no one to see it but the open countryside, the sea, and the sky, it must have seemed that this edifice had been erected and the divine offices performed for the sole enjoyment of the natural elements.

On either side of the grillework, beyond the alley of cypresses, stood two huge doors. The one on the left, the seaward side, opened upon an inner patio of gigantic dimensions. A broad cloister encircled it, its roof supported by twenty white marble columns on either side. Its flagstones were of blue and white marble. In the center of the patio stood a fountain fed by a chain pump always in motion. It portrayed one of the acts of mercy, showing a woman giving water to a pilgrim who, prostrate at her feet, was receiving the water she offered him in a shell. The interior walls of the cloister were encrusted to a height of twelve feet with small tiles whose brilliant colors composed artistic mosaics. Across from the entryway rose a broad staircase of marble, an airy construction without any base or support other than the masterly proportioning of its enormous mass. These admirable masterworks of architecture were very common in our convents. The great artists, creators of such marvels, were motivated by a high religious zeal, and by the noble hope and belief that they were working for remote posterity. It is well known that the greatest and most popular of them[14] never would work on any religious subject without first taking communion.

The upper cloister was supported by twenty columns smaller than the lower ones. This, in its turn, was surmounted by a balustrade of pierced white marble of exquisite workmanship. The mahogany cell doors, small, but decorated with carvings, opened on these cloisters. Each cell consisted of a small anteroom, leading into a parlor, also small, with its corresponding alcove. Some pine chairs, a table and a bench furnished the main room; the bedroom contained a bed of four planks without a mattress, and two chairs.

Behind this patio was another in the same style. The novitiate, the infirmary, the kitchen, and the refectories were all there. The latter contained long marble tables and a kind of lectern for the man who read during meals.

The section at the right of the alley of cypresses contained a patio like that on the opposite side. Here was the hospice where travellers were lodged, whether they were laymen or clerics. The library, the sacristies, the wardrobes and other offices were also there. In the second patio, entered through an outside door, were storerooms for oil below, and granaries above. These four patios formed the main portion of that majestic group of buildings in the midst of which, preceded by the alley of cypresses, rose the church with its campanile like an enormous stone cypress. The roof was composed of a million tiles, each one made fast with a huge iron spike to keep it from being torn off by the strong winds common to that high ground and the nearby sea. At the cost of a nickel per nail, that part of the materials alone had cost fifty thousand dollars.

---

[14] Bartolomé Estéban Murillo (1617-1682), friend of Velázquez, and a great genre and religious painter whose works adorn many Andalusian churches and cathedrals.

The convent had at its front the main patio, which we have already mentioned, and within the patio, to left and right of the entrance, there were small one-storied rooms for lodging farm laborers during the days when the brotherhood had cultivated its lands. It was there that Manuel Alerza, the custodian, was living with his family at the time of our story. To the left, on the seaward side, a great orchard spread out, displaying beneath the cell windows its cool greenness, its trees, its blossoms, its murmuring irrigation canals, its birdsong, and the tinkle of the bell on the ox which turned the chain-pump. This all formed a small oasis in a dry and featureless wilderness, close to that sea which delights in havoc and destruction, and which comes to a stop along a fringe of sand. But what most abounded in this solitary, silent spot were the cypresses and the palms, typical convent trees, the former standing erect and austere, aspiring to heaven; the latter no less tall, but bending their fronds toward the earth as if drawing to themselves the delicate plants growing there.

The wells and the whole framework of the pumps, set up on artificial mounds to raise the water level, were sheltered under rampant pyramids of ivy so thick that if the door of the wellhouse were closed it was almost impossible, without artificial light, to distinguish objects within. The shaft holding the wheel was supported on two olive stumps which had put down roots and were covered with a crown of dark green foliage. The density of the ivy provided a shelter for numberless gay little birds, content to build their hidden nests there, while the ox went around and round with slow steps to the ringing of his neck bell, whose silence would tell the gardener that the beast was enjoying sweet idleness.

The cells of the lower level opened on a terrace with wooden benches, and when the friars sat there they were able to gaze upon that narrow, pleasant enclosure, enlivened by birdsong and perfumed by the breath of flowers, like a calm, contemplative life; or, if they wished, they might scan open space in the vast spread of the ocean, as splendid as it is treacherous, sometimes calm and meek as a lamb, at other times turbulent and violent as a fury, like those noisy, monstrous lives that get themselves embroiled in the world's affairs.

These men of profound learning, these scholars who lived an austere and inward life, used to cultivate potted flowers on their terraces and raise little birds with paternal solicitude, for if paganism equated the sublime with heroic action, Christianity has equated it with simplicity.

On the side facing the orchard a space of equal size, enclosed within the walls of the convent, contained the olive-presses whose mill-beams, fifty feet long and four wide, were of mahogany, and also the bakeries, the ovens, the stables, and the barns.

With good Brother Gabriel as his guide, Stein was able to admire that past grandeur, that condemned ruin, that abandonment which was devouring so many marvels like a cancer, that destruction which would eat away an empty edifice, however strong and solid, as the worms will possess the body of a young and robust man.

Brother Gabriel never used to interrupt the German surgeon's reflections. He belonged to the blessed group of the poor in spirit who are also sparing of words. He contained his drab sadness, his featureless memories, his monotonous thoughts, within himself. As Aunt María used to say to him:

"You're one of the blessed, Brother Gabriel; but it hardly seems as though your blood runs through your veins; it seems to stroll instead. If something exciting should happen to you some day (and that would be only if the fathers were to come back to the convent, the bells to the bell-tower, the pumps to the orchard), you'd die of shortness of breath."

In the stripped and vacant church there still remained some residue of magnificence by which to gauge the extent of the loss. That gilded high altar, as brilliant as when it used to reflect the tapers lighted in devotion by the faithful, was growing dim beneath the dust of neglect. Those beautiful cherubs' heads; those windows with broken panes that now let in owls and other birds whose nests befouled the fine carvings and gilded cornices and made the rich marble floor a noisome depositary for their droppings; those remains of altars, despoiled of all their adornment; those beautiful big angels seeming to soar from their pilasters holding ever-lighted silver lamps, and still stretching forth their arms, gazing sorrowfully at their empty hands. The beautiful frescoes on the vaulted arches, which could not be carried off, were washed by the weeping clouds in the sky, assaulted by storms; the empty sanctuary, once guarded by doors of solid silver decorated with bas-reliefs by Berruguete; the holy-water fonts, dry and dust-covered. . . . Dear God! What artist would not sigh to see them? What Christian be not downcast? What Catholic not prostrate himself and weep?

In the sacristy, its wall lined with chests of drawers, the upper section of which formed a long counter, the drawers stood open and vacant. Formerly they held the lace-trimmed, batiste robes, the sacred vestments of velvet and lamé—the velvet embroidered with silver, the silver with gold, and the gold with pearls. The ropes for the bells were still in a nearby corner; one of them, thinner than the others, rang the high, sweet bell which summoned the faithful to mass; another rang the melodious and resonant bronze bell, like a military band, sober, yet animated, which, with its companions, used to proclaim the great Christian feast days. The remaining bell used to strike very deep and solemn reverbations, like a cannon, to solicit the prayers of men and the mercy of heaven for a dead sinner.

Stein sat on the bottom step of the low stairway leading to the pulpit, supported by a black marble eagle. Brother Gabriel went down on his knees on the jasper steps to the main altar.

"Dear God!" cried Stein, burying his face in his hands. "Those cracks, that water seeping into the vaulted arches and dropping, wearing away the whole structure with its slow, steady work; those rotting timbers, those mouldering ornaments. What a sad and frightening spectacle! Added to the sorrow aroused by what is left here, there's the horror inspired by what is dying a violent death at the hands of man. This building, erected to the honor of God by devout men is condemned to oblivion by their descendants!"

"Dear God!" said Brother Gabriel, "I've never seen so many cobwebs in my life. Every little angel is wearing a skull cap of them. Saint Michael is carrying one on the point of his sword and it almost seems as if he's holding it out to me. If the Father Prior could see this!"

Stein fell into a deep melancholy. This holy place, he was thinking, respected in the world on the lips of men and by the light of day, where kings used to come to bow their heads and the poor to lift theirs; this place which offered stern lessons to the proud, and gentle happiness to the humble, is today fallen into decline and given over to chance, like a ship without a helmsman.

At this moment a bright ray of sunlight came through one of the windows and struck the finial of the main altar, making a group of embracing figures stand out from the darkness in splendor, as though in response to Stein's plaints: they were Faith, Hope, and Charity.[15]

---

[15] We had decided to cut short the perhaps over-long description of the convent, convinced on the one hand that it is of slight interest and no surprise to the present generation, which is acquainted with these marvelous works scattered throughout Spain; and, on the other hand, convinced that the prevailing opinion may class such sumptuousness as useless at best; a reflection, let us say in passing, that does not occur to the moulders of modern opinion when they dig up such marvels of art from the ruins of Greek temples, erected to false gods, nor when they search for and recover the riches stored in American and Indian temples. Let us say, then, that we had decided to cut short this description of the convents for the above reasons. But we have not done this, perhaps because we have a presentiment that this may be of interest to foreigners who do not know our magnificent and beautiful religious buildings. (FERNÁN CABALLERO'S NOTE.)

CHAPTER V

The end of October had been rainy, and November was dressed for winter in her green and sheltering cloak.

Stein was walking one day in front of the convent from which an immense and unbroken view lay open. To the right, the limitless sea; to the left, the endless pasture land. Along the line of the middle horizon, the dark profile of the ruins of Fort Saint Christopher stood forth, like the image of nothingness in the midst of that immensity. The sea, undisturbed by the lightest breath of wind, was rolling gently, effortlessly lifting its swells gilded by reflections from the sun, like a queen who permits her golden cloak to sway. The convent, with its grand, severe, and angular lines, was in harmony with the somber and monotonous countryside; its mass dominated the only spot that broke the horizon in all that uniform panorama.

At that spot stood the village of Villamar, situated beside a river as full and turbulent in winter as it was sparse and stagnant in summer. The well-cultivated environs looked from afar like a checkerboard, each square of which presented some variation of a thousand tones of green: here the yellowish green of grapevines still covered with new leaves; there the ashy green of an olive tree, or the emerald of wheat shooting up after the autumn rains; or the somber green of the fig-trees; and all this divided by the blue-green of the cactus fences. Some fishing boats were passing before the mouth of the river. On the side of the convent, a chapel stood on a hill; before it rose a huge cross on a pyramidal base of whitewashed stone; behind it was an enclosure covered with crosses painted black. This was the cemetery.

A lantern, always lighted, hung in front of the cross; and the cross, the symbol of salvation, served as a beacon to seamen, as if the Lord had wished to make His parables real to those simple country folk, as He daily makes Himself real to men of strong and humble faith who deserve such grace.

This dry and featureless landscape cannot be compared with the valleys of Switzerland, the banks of the Rhine, or the coast of the Isle of Wight. Yet there is a magic in the works of Nature so powerful that they never lack beauties and attractions; there is never a single object totally without interest, and if at times words fail to explain wherein that interest lies, the intelligence grasps it and the heart feels it.

While Stein was reflecting thus, he noticed that Momo, having left the estate, was coming toward him en route to the village. When the boy saw Stein, he suggested that they go together; Stein accepted, and they set off.

The day was so beautiful that it could be compared only to a diamond of the first water, of maximum brilliance, its value not impaired by even the slightest defect. The spirit and the ear relaxed gently amid the profound silence of Nature. Against the turquoise blue of the sky, a single little white cloud was visible, its indolent stillness suggesting an odalisque wrapped in veils of gauze and softly reclining on her blue ottoman.

In a short time they had come to the hill nearest the village where the cross and chapel stood.

The climb to the crest, though short and easy, had exhausted Stein's strength, not yet fully regained. He wanted to rest a moment, and began to look closely at the place.

He approached the cemetery. It was green and flowering, as though attempting to stand apart from death and the horror it inspires. The crosses were encircled with showy ramblers through whose branches small birds fluttered, singing, "Rest in peace!" No one would have believed it was an abode of the dead, were it not for this inscription: "I believe in the forgiveness of sins, the resurrection of the body, and life everlasting. Amen." The chapel was small, a square, simple building closed at the front with an iron grille; its modest, half-sphere dome crowned with a iron cross. The only entrance was through a little door next to the altar.

On the altar was a large oil painting which showed one of Christ's falls with His cross. Behind the Lord, the Virgin, Saint John, and the two Marys were grouped, and at His side the fierce Roman soldiers. This painting had taken on such a dark tone with age that it was difficult to discern the figures; but by the same token, time had heightened the effect of deep devotion the painting inspired, whether because meditation and spirituality accord badly with bright and showy colors, or because of the seal of veneration stamped by time on works of art, particularly when they represent religious subjects which then seem twice sanctified by the worship of so many generations. All things happen and all things change in the vicinity of religious monuments like that; they alone endure, and their treasures of consolation, offered with lavish hands, are never exhausted.

The devoutly faithful had adorned the painting with various objects of silver leaf, placed in such a way that they seemed to form a part of the composition. These were a crown of thorns on the head of the Lord, a rayed diadem on the Virgin's, and flowers at the foot of the cross. In the eyes of an artist, this pious custom appears strange and even ridiculous, to be sure; but after all, the chapel of Christ the Redeemer was not a museum; no artist had ever crossed its threshold; only devout, simple folk gathered there, and they went only to pray.

The two side walls were covered from ceiling to floor with votive offerings.

These offerings were public and authentic testimonials to benefits received, laid in gratitude at the foot of the altars, sometimes when the grace asked for had been granted, sometimes to fulfill a vow made during times of great trouble and anxiety. Long braids of hair were there, offered as her most priceless treasure by a loving daughter on the day when her mother was snatched from the talons of death; little silver children hanging by pink ribbons, which an afflicted mother had dedicated to the Lord of Succour for the recovery of her son, grievously stricken; arms, eyes, legs of silver or wax, according to the means of the person making the vow; pictures of shipwrecked men, or men in other great perils, during which they and theirs had prayed with what unbelievers would label simple-mindedness, but what was actually a simple faith that their pleas would be heard and answered through divine mercy; for it would appear that intellectuals, the enlightened, the people who call themselves somebodies and consider themselves the best, do not believe that prayer constitutes a bond between God and man.

These paintings were not masterpieces, but perhaps if they were they might have lost their best qualities, and particularly, their candor. And yet there are people today who, having the presumption to find in themselves gifts of superior merit, will close their minds to the sweet impressions made by candor, the very innocence and serenity of the spirit. Are they not aware that in proportion as enthusiasm wanes, candor perishes? Spaniards: conserve and respect the vestiges still remaining to you of things as holy as they are priceless. Do not model yourselves on the Dead Sea, which kills with its breath the birds flying over its waters; nor, like it, dry up the roots of the trees in the shadow of which so many lands and so many generations have lived contentedly!

Among the votive offerings there was one that made Stein wonder at its singularity. The altar did not run in a perfectly straight line from top to bottom but tapered in a curve toward the foot. Between its base and the brick paving there was a small space. There in the shadow Stein noticed an object propped against the wall; and by examining it closely, he finally made out that it was a wide-mouthed blunderbuss. So great was its size and its undoubted weight that he could not imagine how a man had been able to handle it; this happens to us when we look at the armor of the Middle Ages. Its mouth was so huge that an orange could easily have been dropped into it. It was broken, and its various parts were clumsily tied together with cords.

"Momo," said Stein, "what is the meaning of that? Is it a real blunderbuss?"

"It seems to me that it certainly looks like one," said Momo.

"But what is a deadly weapon doing in this peaceful and consecrated spot? Here you can rightly say that it sticks out like a sore thumb, like Christ with a pair of pistols."

"But don't you see that it isn't in the Lord's hands; it's an offering at his feet?" replied Momo. "The day this blunderbuss was brought here, many years ago, was the same day this Christ was given the name of the Lord of Succour."

"And what was the reason?" asked Stein.

"Don Federico!" cried Momo, staring at him wide-eyed, "Everyone knows that. Don't you know it?"

"Have you forgotten that I'm a foreigner?" asked Stein.

"That's right," answered Momo. "Well, I'll tell you about it. There was a highwayman hereabouts who, not content to

rob people, killed men like flies, either so they couldn't inform
on him, or because he enjoyed doing it.

"One day two brothers who lived here had to take a trip.
The whole village came to say good-bye to them and to wish
them the luck not to come upon that outlaw who refused to
spare a life and had everyone terrorized. But the brothers, like
good Christians, commended themselves to this Lord, and went
on their way, trusting in His protection. As they came abreast
of an olive tree, they met the robber face to face. He came out
to confront them with his blunderbuss in his hand. He threw
it up to his shoulder and aimed at them. At that crucial moment, the brothers fell on their knees, calling to Christ: 'Help
us, Lord.' The soulless creature fired the gun, but he himself
was the one dispatched to another world, for it was God's will
that the blunderbuss burst in his hands. By the grace of God,
the gun misfired. You're looking at it right now. They tied it
together with those cords and brought it here to commemorate that miraculous rescue, and ever since then the Lord
has been called the Lord of Succour.[16] So you didn't know
about it, Don Federico?"

"No, I didn't know about it, Momo," replied the latter,
and as if in answer to his own reflections, he added: "If you

---

[16] This legend of the Lord of Succour, or more properly, this true story
of the happening that became the subject of a painting, is verified by
the aforementioned blunderbuss which could be seen at the foot of the
altar of the chapel situated on Ganado Street in Puerto de Santa María.
Not long ago (1855) it was closed. The Vicar of the said chapel, according to what we have understood, is claiming the painting so that
it may be venerated in the Main Church. We are persuaded that if he
achieves his wish, he will not venture to place at the foot of the altar
the old and broken blunderbuss which, by bursting, saved the lives of
two devout men who begged help of the Lord. What would the proper
Protestant say, he who keeps innoculating our lives with a cold humor,
if he were to see a blunderbuss in a church? What would those who
cleave to "the letter," but not to "the spirit . . ."? AUTHOR'S NOTE.

only knew how ignorant those people who are said to know everything really are!"

"Let's go. Are you coming, Don Federico?" asked Momo after a moment of silence. "I can't tarry any longer."

"I'm tired," replied Stein. "You go ahead and I'll wait for you here."

"Well, so long," replied Momo, and he set off, singing:

"Stay with the Lord, and adiós,
That's how the saying goes,
The poorest man can gather pence
But even the rich man can't buy sense."

Stein remained staring at that tranquil little village, half fisherman, half sailor, carrying in one hand the plow and in the other the oar. Unlike the villages in Germany, it was not made up of a few scattered houses in no particular order, with their rustic thatched roofs and their gardens; nor did it rest, like those in England, in the shade of picturesque trees; nor yet, like those in Flanders, was it in the form of a double line of pretty houses along the sides of the road. It consisted of some wide but ill-laid streets. The one-story houses, of unequal height, were covered with old tiles; the windows were few, and fewer still the panes or any type of trimming. But there was a big square, now green as a meadow, and in it a very lovely church. The whole effect was bright, clean and gay.

Fourteen crosses like the one near Stein were placed at regular intervals until the last, rising in the middle of the square, stood in front of the church. This was the Way of the Cross.

Momo returned, but not alone. He was accompanied by an elderly gentleman—tall, dry, thin, and stiff as a candle. He was dressed in a jacket and trousers of dark homespun, a waist-

coat of piqué in funereal colors, adorned with some drawn-
work that was a masterpiece of its kind; a sash of red wool,
like those habitually worn by the country people, a broad-
brimmed Andalusian hat with a cockade that had once been
red, but which time, rain, and sun had turned carrot-colored.
On the shoulders of the jacket were two narrow galloon straps
of dubious gold, intended to hold epaulets, and an old sword,
hanging from a belt of the same, completed this half-military,
half-rustic costume. The years had taken their toll at the front
of this person's long, narrow head: in order to make up for
the lack of its natural adornment, he had combed up and
brought forward the few remnants of hair left to him. They
were tied in the middle with a black silk cord on the top of
his head, forming a Chinese topknot that was truly elegant.

"Momo, who is this gentleman?" asked Stein under his
breath.

"The Commander," replied the latter in his natural voice.

"The Commander! Of what?" persisted Stein.

"Of Fort Saint Christopher's!"

"Of Fort Saint Christopher's! . . ." exclaimed Stein, delighted.

"At your service," said the newcomer, saluting politely.
"My name is Modesto Guerrero, and I place my useless self
at your command."

That set form of courtesy was so appropriate to this man
that Stein could not help smiling as he returned the soldier's
salute.

"I know who you are," went on Don Modesto. "I feel
for you in your reverses, and congratulate you on your recovery
and on having fallen into the hands of the Alerzas who are,
in my opinion, very fine people; I and my house are at your
disposal for whatever you desire. I live on the church square,

I mean Constitution Square, as it's now called. If at any time you'd like to favor me with a visit, the sign will direct you to the square."

"As long as there's no other square, why all the directions?" said Momo.

"Does it have a sign?" asked Stein, who had not had occasion during his busy camp life to acquire the usual polite forms, and knew not how to reply to the punctilious Spaniard.

"Yes, sir," the latter replied. "The mayor was obliged to obey orders from above. You can see that in a little village it would not be easy to provide a marble slab with gold letters like the stone markers of Cádiz and Seville. The schoolmaster had to be ordered to make the sign. He writes a good hand, and he had to get up high enough on the wall of the Town Hall. The master mixed some black paint from lampblack and vinegar and started to work tracing letters a foot high whilst perched on a step-ladder. Unfortunately, as he was attempting to make a graceful flourish, he shook the ladder so hard that it came down with the poor master and the pot of ink, and he fell into the creek with the pot. Rosita, my landlady, who witnessed the catastrophe from her window and saw the poor man get up as black as coal, was so frightened that she suffered from indigestion for three days and I was really worried about her. The mayor, however, ordered the schoolmaster to finish the job in spite of his bruises, for the sign just said CONSTI; so the poor teacher had to push ahead with the job; but this time he wanted no part of a step-ladder, and they had to fetch a cart for him and set up a table on it, tied down with ropes. The poor fellow, perched up like that, was so upset thinking of his accident that he had only one thing on his mind, to get it done quickly. And so the last letters, instead of being a foot high like the first ones, were only an inch high;

and that wasn't the worst of it, for in his haste he left one letter still in the inkpot, so now the sign says: PLAZA DE LA CONSTITUCIN. The mayor was furious; but the master stuck to his guns and swore that he wouldn't do it over for God Himself and all His saints, and that he'd rather get on an eight-year-old bull than go through that act again. So the sign has stayed like that; but luckily no one in the place can read it. And it's a pity that the schoolmaster hasn't corrected it, for it was very fine and would have done honor to Villamar."

Momo, who was carrying some full saddlebags on his shoulders, was in a hurry, and he asked the Commander if he was going to Fort St. Christopher.

"Yes," he replied, "and on the way I'm going to see Pedro Santaló's daughter, who is ill."

"Who? The Sea Gull?" asked Momo. "Don't you believe it. Yesterday I saw her on top of a cliff, screaming like the rest of the gulls."

"Sea Gull!" exclaimed Stein.

"That's a bad name Momo has given this poor girl," said the Commander.

"Because she's got such long legs," Momo answered. "Because she's in the water as much as she's on land; because she sings and yells, and jumps from rock to rock like the rest of them."

"Well," observed Don Modesto, "your grandmother likes her very much, and she never calls her anything but Marysal[17] on account of her funny little tricks, and because she sings and dances so gracefully, and mimics the birds."

"That's not why," said Momo; "it's because her father is a fisherman and she brings us salt and fish."

---

[17] A nickname formed by a play on words, meaning Salty Mary, thus implying salt, i.e. a dry wit, grace, and a liking for the sea.

"And she lives near the fort?" asked Stein, whose curiosity had been aroused by those descriptive details.

"Very near," the Commander replied. "Pedro Santaló used to have a Catalonian boat which ran into a storm en route to Cádiz, and was wrecked on the coast. Everything was lost—both the ship and the men, except for Pedro, who had his daughter with him. His desire to save her lent him twice his ordinary strength. He made land, but he was ruined, and that so discouraged and saddened him that he didn't want to go back home. What he did was to knock together a hut among the rocks from the flotsam of his boat, and turn to fishing. It was he who used to supply the monastery with fish, and in return, the fathers gave him bread, olive oil, and vinegar. He's lived here twelve years now at peace with the world."

At this point they reached the spot where the path branched, and they separated.

"We shall see each other soon," said the veteran. "I'll come to call on you and to see your benefactors before long."

"Say hello to the Sea Gull for me," said Momo. "I'm not worried about her being sick; you can't kill weeds."

"Has the Commander been in Villamar very long?" Stein asked Momo.

"Long! . . . A hundred and one years; since long before my father's time."

"And who is this Rosita, his landlady?"

"Who? Miss Mystical Rose?" replied Momo with a scornful gesture. "She our schoolmistress. She's uglier than sin; one of her eyes looks east and the other west, and she's got smallpox scars big enough to hold an echo. But, the sky is clouding over, Don Federico; the clouds are running like greyhounds. Let's get a move on."

CHAPTER VI

Before going any further, it might not be a bad idea to make the acquaintance of this new character.

Don Modesto Guerrero was the son of an honest farmer who yet held letters patent of nobility, until the French burned them during the War of Independence, as they also burned his house, under the pretext that his sons were brigands, that is, criminals guilty of the grave offense of defending their country. The good man could rebuild his house, but the parchments lacked the luck of the phoenix.

Modesto was drafted, and as his father had not the means to buy him a substitute, he entered the ranks of an infantry regiment as a private first class.

As he was somewhat simple, and had a long, dry face besides, he soon became the butt of the offensive taunts and practical jokes of his mates. Spurred on by his meekness, they carried their jokes to an extreme, until Modesto put a sudden end to them in the following way. One day when there was a dress parade of troops in preparation for a review, Modesto took his place at the end of one rank. A long, narrow cart was standing nearby; his mates quickly and skilfully tied a rope with a running knot to one of his legs and fastened the other end to one of the cart wheels.

The colonel shouted the order to march. The drums beat, and the whole corps began to move, except for Modesto, who remained tied up, with one leg in the air like the sculptured figures of Zephyr.

When the review was over, Modesto went back to the

barracks as quietly as he had left, and with no change of pace, demanded satisfaction of his mates. As no one wished to take the responsibility for the trick, he announced with the same calm that he would challenge them all to a fight, one by one. Then the man who had thought of the joke and engineered it came forward; they fought, and the outcome was that his adversary lost an eye. Modesto told him, with his usual serenity that if he would like to lose the other, he would be glad to oblige at any time.

Meanwhile, lacking relatives or friends at court, Modesto, with no apparent ambition, and no temperament for intrigue, was moving ahead in his chosen career at a snail's pace, until the time of the siege of Gaeta,[18] in 1805, when his regiment was ordered to join Napoleon's troops as an auxiliary. There Modesto distinguished himself for his courage and coolness to a degree which won him a cross and the highest eulogies of his commanding officers.

His name blazed like a meteor in the *Gazette,* only to fall later into eternal obscurity. These laurels were the first and the last to be offered him in the course of his military career, for after receiving a deep wound in the arm, he was deemed unfit for active duty, and in recompense was named commander of the abandoned little Fort Saint Christopher. It was forty years now since he had taken under his command the skeleton of a castle and a garrison of lizards.

In the beginning our warrior could not adjust himself to that neglect. Never a year went by that he did not send a petition to the Government, asking for needed repairs and for the guns and troops required for that bastion of defense. All these pleas went unanswered despite the fact that, under the

---

[18] A fortified seaport near Rome, besieged by the French during the Napoleonic Wars. After an heroic defense, it was captured by Massena.

circumstances of the day, he had not omitted the warning of a
possibility of a landing by the English, the American insur-
gents, the French, or the Rebels and the Carlists. His constant
requests for pay met with the same reception. The Government
paid no heed whatsoever to the two ruins: the castle and its
commander. Don Modesto was long-suffering; and ultimately
he accepted his fate without bitterness or despair.

When he arrived in Villamar, he became a lodger in the
house of the sacristan's widow, a lady who had given over her
whole life, in company with her daughter, who was then
young, to religious devotion. They were excellent women;
somewhat prudish, withered, and intolerant; but good, charitable, frugal, and shiningly neat.

The villagers regarded the Commander, or the Commender, as they called him, with affection, and as they also
knew his stringencies, they did what they could to alleviate
them. There was never a slaughtering but that he was sent
his supply of bacon and blood pudding. At harvest-time one
farmer would send him wheat, another chickpeas; still others
would contribute with their share of honey or olive oil. Women
used to send him the products of the poultry-yard; so that his
pious landlady always had a well-filled larder, thanks to the
general benevolence inspired by Don Modesto; he, whose temperament matched his name, far from being puffed up by so
many kindnesses, was accustomed to say that Providence lay
all about, but its headquarters was Villamar. To be sure he
knew how to respond to so many gifts, for he was extremely
accommodating and polite to everyone. He got up with the
sun, and his first act of the day was to serve at mass for the
priest.

One village woman would have an errand for him, another
would ask him to write a letter for her to her soldier son;

another, to take care of the children while she went out on business. He would watch over the sick, he would pray with his landladies; in short, he tried to make himself useful to everyone, always provided that nothing he did would besmirch his honor or his decorum. This is not at all uncommon in Spain, thanks to the boundless charity of the Spanish people, plus their noble character which forbids them to lay up treasures, and bids them give what they have to him who is in need: the excloistered clergy, the nuns, the artisans, the soldiers' widows, the dismissed public employees can all attest to that.

The sacristan's widow died, leaving her daughter Rosa, with a full forty years on earth and an ugliness that could be seen from afar. What most contributed to that misfortune was the doleful result of smallpox. The scars were concentrated on one eye, particularly on the lid which she could lift only half-way; so that the half-covered pupil gave to her whole face a lifeless and unintelligent look, in notable contrast to the other, turned-in eye, which at the slightest hint of scandal would send forth sparks like those from a bonfire of twigs; and the truth is that she seemed to find such hints with remarkable frequency.

After the burial of her mother and the customary nine days of mourning, Miss Rosa said to Don Modesto one day:

"Don Modesto, I'm very sorry to have to tell you that we must part."

"We must part!" cried the good gentleman, opening his eyes wide and placing the cup of chocolate on the tablecloth instead of on its saucer. "Why, Rosita?"

Don Modesto had grown accustomed to using this nickname over a period of thirty years.

"It seems to me," she replied, raising her eyebrows, "that

it shouldn't be necessary for you to ask that. You surely know that it won't look right for two respectable people to live together alone. That would be honey to evil tongues."

"And what could evil tongues have to say about you?" said Don Modesto. "You, the most circumspect woman in the village?"

"Is there anything at all that's safe from them? What would you say if you knew that you, despite your years, your uniform, and your Cross, and I, a poor woman with no thought other than to serve God, are providing diversion for foul months?"

"What are you saying, Rosita?" cried Don Modesto, stunned.

"Just what you're hearing. We're now known only by the bad names those wicked acolytes have given us."

"I'm amazed, Rosita! I can't believe . . ."

"You'll be better off not to believe it," said the pious woman. "But I assure you that those wicked boys (may God forgive them) say to one another every morning when they see us coming to low mass: 'Ring the bell, for here come Mystical Rose and the Tower of David, together and in love as they are in the Litany.' They call you by that nickname because you're so tall and straight."

Don Modesto stood still with open mouth and eyes staring at the floor.

"Yes, sir," went on Mystical Rose, "my neighbor told me that. She was scandalized and advised me to complain to the priest. I told her I'd rather suffer in silence. Our Savior suffered much more without complaining."

"Well," said Don Modesto, "I won't stand for anyone making a mock of me, and still less of you."

"It would be better," went on Rosa, "to prove by our

patience that we're good Christians, and by our indifference
how little attention we pay to the world's judgments. On the
other hand, if those miscreants are punished, it will only make
matters worse."

"You're right as always, Rosita," said Don Modesto. "I
know what those 'funny' people are like; if you cut off their
tongues, they'd talk with their noses. But if any of my mess-
mates had dared to call me Tower of David when I was young,
he'd better have added: 'Pray for us.' [19] But you're such a
blessed saint, how can you be afraid of scandalmongers?"

"Don Modesto, you know the vulgar saying of those people
who think the worst of everyone: 'Between male and female
saint, a wall of rough stone and mortar.' "

"But between you and me," said the Commander, "there's
no need to put even a thin partition; I, with so many years
on my back; I, who have been in love only once in my whole
life, . . . and to prove my point, she was a good-looking girl
and I would have married her if I hadn't caught her flirting
with the drum major, who . . ."

"Don Modesto, Don Modesto," cried Rosa, drawing herself up, "honor your name and my modesty and spare me your
amorous memoirs."

"It was not my intention to scandalize you," said Don
Modesto in a contrite tone. "Suffice it for me to swear and you
to realize that no evil thought has entered or will enter my
head."

"Don Modesto," said Mystical Rose impatiently, fixing
him with the one burning eye while the other tried in vain
to imitate it, "do you think me so simple-minded as to believe

---

[19] This again refers to the Litany to the Virgin where the priest says,
"Mystical Rose," "Tower of David," etc., and the congregation answers
to each: "Pray for us."

that two people like you and me, sensible and God-fearing, would conduct ourselves like those barefaced fools without chastity and the fear of sin? But in this world it's not enough to behave well; it's also necessary to provide no food for talk by always keeping up appearances."

"That's another thing," replied the Commander. "What appearances can there be between us? Don't you know that he who excuses himself accuses himself?"

"I tell you," answered the pious lady, "that people are talking."

"But what would I do without you?" asked Don Modesto, downcast. "What would you do without me, alone in the world as you are?"

"He whose eye is on the sparrow," said Rosa solemnly, "will take care of those who trust in Him."

Disconcerted and knowing not whereon to lay his head, Don Modesto went to see his friend the priest, also Rosita's pastor, and recounted all that had taken place.

The priest made clear to Rosita that her scruples were exaggerated or that her fears were groundless, and that, on the contrary, the proposed separation would give rise to ridicule.

Accordingly they went on living together as before, in peace and the grace of God. The Commander, ever good and helpful; Rosa, ever careful, attentive, and disinterested; for Don Modesto was not in such means as to be able to pay her for her services in money, indeed had the guard on his dress sword not been made of silver, he might easily have forgotten what silver looked like.

CHAPTER VII

When Stein reached the convent, he found the whole family together, sunning themselves in the patio.

Dolores, seated on a low chair, was mending one of her husband's shirts. Her two little girls, Pepa and Paca, were playing near her. They were pretty children, six and eight years old. The infant boy, in his reed walker, was providing amusement to another five-year-old boy, his brother, who was showing him tricks very suitable for the development of the young mind, always precocious in that region. The five-year-old was good-looking, though under-sized; therefore Momo often made him furious by calling him Francis of Anise,[20] instead of Francis of Assisi, his real name. He was dressed in diminutive trousers of rough wool with a jacket to match, so shrunken in size that his shirt fell into a large pouch at his waist, as the trousers were held up by a single draw-string of selvage.

"Make an old woman, Manolillo," said Anise.

The boy made a funny face, half-closing his eyes, puckering his lips, and bowing his head.

"Manolito, kill a Moor."

The little boy opened his eyes very wide, knitted his brows, doubled his fist, and turned scarlet as a consequence of swelling up in a warlike pose. Then Anise took his hands and swung them back and forth, singing:

"See what pretty little hands I have;
How small, how white,
How cute they are!"

---

[20] A herbaceous plant with a small, pungent seed, like celery seed.

Aunt María was spinning. Brother Gabriel was making baskets from the dried leaves of the dwarf palm.

An enormous, woolly white dog, called Palomo, one of the fine breed of Extremaduran sheep dogs, lay stretched out full length asleep, taking up a great deal of space with his strong legs and bushy tail, while Morrongo, a fat yellow cat, denuded since kittenhood of ears and tail, was sleeping on the ground upon the border of Aunt María's petticoat.

Stein, Momo, and Manuel all arrived together from different directions. Manuel had just made the rounds of the property in the exercise of his function as custodian; he was carrying a gun in one hand and three partridges and two rabbits in the other.

The boys ran to Momo, who emptied the saddlebags in one motion. A great quantity of winter fruits poured forth as from a cornucopia, fruits that are served in Spain on Hallowe'en—walnuts, chestnuts, pomegranates, sweet potatoes, and so on.

"We'll have a feast," said the elder girl, "if Marysal brings us some fish tomorrow."

"Tomorrow," said the grandmother, "is All Saints' Day; surely Pedro won't go out to fish."

"All right," said the little girl, "the day after, then."

"There's no fishing on All Souls' Day either."

"Why not?" asked the child.

"Because that would profane a day that the Church has consecrated to the souls of the blest. And to prove it, I'm going to tell you a story. Once upon a time some fishermen went out to fish on a day like the day after tomorrow; and when they came to pull in their nets, they were happy because the nets were so heavy; but instead of fish there was nothing in the nets but skulls. Isn't that so, Brother Gabriel?"

"Of course! I didn't see it, but it's true," said the monk.

"Is that why you make us pray so much at the hour of the Rosary on All Souls' Day?" asked the little girl.

"That's just why," answered the grandmother. "It's a religious custom, and God does not wish us to neglect it. I'm going to give you an example as proof. Once upon a time there was a bishop who didn't put much stock in this pious practice, and he failed to tell the faithful to do it. One night he dreamed that he saw a frightful abyss, and on the edge of it an angel with a chain of white and red roses was pulling a beautiful woman, dishevelled and weeping, out of the abyss. When she saw she was outside that dark place, the woman began to fly up to Heaven, covered with glory. On the following day, the bishop wanted to have the dream explained, and he prayed to God to enlighten him. He went to the church and the first thing that met his eyes was a little boy on his knees saying the rosary beside the tomb of his mother."

"Didn't you know that, little one?" said Pepa to her sister. "Well, let me tell you about a little shepherd boy who was very pious and fond of praying; and also about a soul in Purgatory who wanted more than anyone to see God. And when he saw the little shepherd boy praying from his heart, he went to him and said: 'Will you give me what you're praying for?' 'Take it,' said the boy, and the soul appeared before God and entered into glory all of a sudden. So you can see whether or not God listens to prayer."

"Certainly," said Manuel. "There is nothing better than to pray to God for the dead. I remember a member of the brotherhood of souls who once was begging for them at the door of a chapel, shouting: 'Anyone who throws a peseta on this tray will release a soul from Purgatory.' A joker came along, and after throwing down a peseta, he asked: 'Tell me, brother, do you think the soul is out now?' 'No doubt about it,' replied the monk. 'Well, then,' said the other, 'I'll take back my peseta for she can't be so stupid that she'll go back in.' "

"You may be quite sure," said Aunt María, "that there's no subject on which my son doesn't have a story, Don Federico, funny or spicy, to the point or not."

At this moment Don Modesto came into the patio, as erect and as stern as when he was introduced to Stein in the village, the only difference being that he was carrying a large fish wrapped in cabbage leaves, which hung from his cane.

"The Commender! The Commender!" shouted everyone there.

"Are you coming from your castle of Saint Christopher?" Manuel asked Don Modesto after the first exchange of greetings and the invitation to have a seat on a stone bench against the wall where Stein was also sitting. "You might well enlist my mother, who's such a good Christian, to ask the Blessed Saint to set up the walls of the fort again, the reverse of what Joshua did to other walls."

"I have more important things to ask the Saint," replied the grandmother.

"Very true," said Brother Gabriel. "Aunt María has more important things to ask the Saint than to rebuild the castle walls. It would be better to ask him to re-establish the convent."

At these words, Don Modesto turned on the brother with a brusque gesture. The monk, seeing the movement, got behind Aunt María, drawing himself together in such a way that he almost disappeared from the sight of the gathering.

"From what I can see," said the veteran, "Brother Gabriel does not belong to the Church Militant. Don't you remember that before they built the Temple, the Jews had conquered the Promised Land by the sword? Would there be churches and

priests in the Holy Land if the Crusaders hadn't taken it with
their lances at the ready?"

"But why should Aunt María ask for impossible things?"
said Stein then, with the good intention of distracting the
Commander from the subject.

"It doesn't matter," answered Manuel. "Old ladies don't
pay any heed to that, except the one who asked God to let
her win the lottery, and who, when asked if she'd bought a
ticket, said: 'Where would the miracle be if I had a ticket?'"

"The truth is," opined Don Modesto, "that I would be
most obliged if the Saint were to undertake to inspire the
Government with the idea of rehabilitating the fort."

"Of rebuilding it, you should say," answered Manuel.
"But you'd have to be careful not to repent of it later, as once
happened to a devotee of the Saint who had such an ugly,
stupid, and worthless daughter that she could not find a man
desperate enough to want to take care of her. The poor worried
woman spent her days on her knees before the image of the
blessed Saint, begging him for a suitor for her daughter. Finally
one turned up, and the mother's joy was boundless; but it
didn't last long, for he turned out to be so wicked, and he
treated both his wife and his mother-in-law so badly, that the
mother went to the church and, standing before the Saint,
she said to him:

> 'Enormous Saint Christopher,
> Big feet, huge fists, hide like a rhino,
> You're a lout like that son-in-law of mine-o.'"

During this conversation, Morrongo, the cat, arched his
back like a camel, yawned widely, washed his whiskers, and,
sniffing in the air certain scents that pleased him, approached

Don Modesto little by little until he had taken a position behind the redolent package hanging from the cane.

Instantly he was struck on his velvet paws by a pebble thrown by Momo with that extraordinary manual dexterity displayed by boys of his age at throwing things. The cat promptly withdrew, but before long he was back and waiting as if he had nothing on his mind. Don Modesto caught on, and his peace of mind was disturbed.

While these maneuvers were taking place, Anise asked the little boy:

"Manolito, how many gods are there?"

The boy held up three fingers.

"No," said Aanise, raising one finger. "There's only one, one, one."

But the other kept his three fingers raised.

"Grandma," shouted Anise, confused. "This boy says there's three gods."

"Silly," she replied. "Aren't you afraid you'll be carried off by the Inquisition? Can't you see he's too young to understand what's said and to learn what he's taught?"

"Some people," said Manuel, "are no smarter for being older, like that goose who went to confession and when the father confessor asked him, 'How many gods are there?' he confidently said, 'Seven!' 'Seven!' exclaimed the astonished priest, 'How did you arrive at that figure?' 'How? Why, this way: the Father, the Son, and the Holy Ghost make three; three separate persons make another three, so that's six, and one true God, makes exactly seven.' 'You clown!' said the priest, 'Don't you know that there's only one God in Three Persons?' 'Only one!' said the penitent, 'Dear me! How the family has shrunk!' "

"Well," said Aunt María, "it's plain to see that my son learned a great many jokes while he was in the king's service. But, changing the subject, you haven't told us, Commander, how is little Marysal?"

"Ill, very ill, Aunt María, and getting worse every day. I feel so sorry for her poor father, who's almost beside himself with anxiety. This morning the girl had a high fever; she wouldn't eat a thing, and she was coughing constantly."

"Is that so, señor?" exclaimed Aunt María. "Don Federico! You've cured so many people; you removed a wen from Brother Gabriel and straightened Momo's eyes; couldn't you do something for that poor child?"

"Gladly," replied Stein, "I'll do all I can to relieve her."

"God will repay you. Let's go and see her tomorrow morning. You're tired from your walk today."

"I wouldn't care to be in your shoes," grumbled Momo. "She's the most stuck-up girl . . ."

"She isn't at all," replied the grandmother. "She's a little bit unruly, a little bit strange . . . And why not? She grew up alone on a lonely headland with a father who's gentler than a dove; though, like any good Catalonian seaman, he has rather a hard face. But Momo hasn't been able to stand Marysal since she called him a flat-nose one day, because he is one."

Just then a commotion arose; it was the Commander running full speed after the rascal Morrongo who had carried off the fish under its owner's very eyes.

"Oh, Commander!" shouted Manuel, laughing. "The sardine carried off by the cat arrives at the table late or never. But here's a partridge in exchange."

Don Modesto accepted the partridge, thanked them, said good-bye, and went off muttering curses on all cats.

Throughout this scene, Dolores had been nursing the baby

and trying to put him to sleep by rocking him in her arms
and singing to him:

> "High up on the hill of Calvary,
> Sweet with the olive thicket's breath,
> The nightingale and four little linnets
> Mourned in song our dear Lord's death."

It would be difficult for anyone to capture in flight, like
a boy chasing butterflies, these poetic emanations from the
people; difficult to give answer to anyone wishing to analyze
why the nightingales and the linnets should mourn the death
of the Redeemer; why the swallow pulled the thorns from His
crown; why rosemary is looked upon with a measure of veneration, owing to the belief that the Virgin used to dry the
diapers of the Infant Jesus on a bed of rosemary; why, or
rather how, it came about that the alder is a tree of ill omen
because Judas hanged himself from an alder; why no evil will
befall a house fumigated with rosemary on Christmas Night;
why all the instruments of the Passion should be seen in the
blossom that has earned the name of passion flower. Indeed
there is no answer to such questions. The people neither have
answers nor seek them; they have gathered together these fig-
ments like vague echoes of some distant music, without inquir-
ing into their origin or questioning their authenticity. Savants
and realists will greet the person composing these lines with
a smile of pity. But we shall be content to hope to arouse some
sympathy in the heart of a mother, or beneath the humble
roof-tree of a man who knows little and feels much, or in the
meditative inwardness of a cloister, when we say that for our
part we believe that there are now and always have been
mystical revelations granted to devout and ascetic persons,
revelations which the world labels the delirium of over-stimu-

lated imaginations but which people of a meek and fervent faith regard as special favors from God.

Henri Blaze says: "How many seeds of ideas tradition launches into the air for the poet to breathe life into!" These words seem to us to apply to things which no one is obliged to believe, nor entitled to condemn either. A mysterious source sent the seeds of these ideas into the air, and they take root in believing and devout hearts. However hard the apostles of rationalism may strive to fell the tree of faith, it will forever send forth vigorous and flowering branches aspiring to heaven if it is rooted in good soil, that is to say in a strong and fervent heart.

"But, Don Federico," said Aunt María as Stein was engaged in the preceding reflections, "up to now you haven't told us what you think of our village."

"I can't say," answered Stein, "for I haven't seen it; I stayed outside the village waiting for Momo."

"Is it possible you haven't seen the church, nor our Lady of Sorrows, nor Saint Christopher, so handsome and strapping, holding his huge palm tree and carrying the Infant Jesus on his shoulders, with a city at his feet that he could crush like a toadstool if he took a step? Nor the picture where Saint Anne is teaching the Virgin to read? Haven't you seen any of those?"

"I haven't seen anything but the chapel of the Lord of Succour," Stein replied.

"I never go out of the convent," said Brother Gabriel, "except to go to that chapel every Friday to pray the Lord for a good death."

"And didn't you notice the miracles, Don Federico?" Aunt María continued. "Ah, Don Federico! There's no Lord in the whole world more miraculous. The Way of the Cross begins at Calvary. From there to the last cross there's the same number of steps as from Pilate's house to Calvary. One of those crosses happens to come face to face with my house on Royal Street. Didn't you notice it? It's at that very eighth station that our Savior said to the women of Jerusalem: 'Weep not for me; weep for yourselves and your children!' Those children," added Aunt María, addressing Brother Gabriel, "are the benighted Jews."

"They're the Jews!" echoed Brother Gabriel.

"At this station," the old lady went on, "the faithful sing:

'If Christ teaches you to weep,
And the lesson you don't keep,
You don't have a heart, alas,
Or else it's made of stone or brass.' "

"Next to my mother's house," said Dolores, "is the ninth cross, where they sing:

'Think how cruel you must be
To our exhausted Christ,
Unless you offer your hand once
Ere he has fallen thrice.'

"They also sing this:

'Now He lies there once again;
Three times did Jesus fall.
I have sinned so frequently,
My sins upon me pall.
Moan and weep; yes, wail and cry,
For it is God who's going to die.' "

"Ah, Don Federico," the good old woman continued, "there's nothing that so moves my heart as the Passion of Him who came to redeem us. The Lord has revealed to the saints the three great sorrows he suffered: first, the scanty fruit borne by the land he watered with His blood; second, His pain when He was stretched out and nailed to the cross, dislocating all His bones, as David had prophesied. The third," she continued, turning loving eyes on her son, "when He beheld the anguish of His mother. The only reason," she resumed after a moment's silence, "I'm not so happy here as in the village is that I can't carry on my devotions. My husband—yes, Manuel, your father—who was never a soldier and a better Christian than you are, thought as I do. The poor man, may he dwell in glory, belonged to the Brotherhood of the Dawn Rosary which goes out just after midnight to pray for the souls of all the dead. He used to lie down to sleep, worn out from his day's work, and exactly at twelve, a brother would come to the door and sing as he rang a little bell:

> 'There's a little bell at your door;
> It does not call you, nor do I.
> It is your parents rousing you
> To pray God for their souls, for aye.'

"When your father heard this verse, he no longer felt weary nor in need of sleep. In a twinkling of an eye he would get up and go running after the brother. I think I can still hear him singing as he went:

> 'Mary handed Christ her crown,
> And to her Son was heard to say:
> No longer will I be a queen
> Unless Thou willst Thy just wrath stay.
> Then Jesus to his Mother said:
> Had thy pleas not softened me,
> I would have struck that sinner dead.' "

The children, who took so much delight in imitating whatever the grown-ups were doing, began to sing the charming lyrics from the song to the Dawn:

> "You should've been there so see
>   How Heaven's King entered Jerusalem!
>   No fancy coach and four had he;
>   Just a burro lent to Him."

"Don Federico," said Aunt María after a silence, "isn't it a fact that there are men of no faith in this world God made?"

Stein was silent.

"Well, you couldn't have done what you did for Momo's eyes if you had looked at things the way those people do," the good old lady answered sadly.

CHAPTER VIII

On the following day Aunt María set out for the sick girl's house accompanied by Stein and Momo, who walked beside his grandmother's donkey. She was mounted on the stately *Golondrina,* ever obliging, meek, and docile, moving steadily ahead with her head and ears drooping, without a single spontaneous movement unless she found within reach of her muzzle a thistle, her special dish.

When they had arrived, Stein was surprised to find a leafy, pleasant spot amid the naturally dry and stern terrain of that featureless district, like an oasis in the desert.

The sea had cleft an opening between two tall headlands, forming a small, circular cove shaped like a horseshoe. This was fringed with very fine sand and looked like a glass plate set on a gilded table. Some rocks protruded timidly through the sand, as though offering a place to sit and rest on that tranquil beach. The fisherman's boat was made fast to one of the stones, rocking with the swell of the sea like a mettlesome charger which has been gentled.

Dominating the foremost cliff rose the Fort Saint Christopher, crowned by crests of wild fig trees like an old Druid priest garlanded with oak leaves.

A few paces away Stein discovered to his surprise a kind of marshy kitchen garden, one of those called *navazos* in Andalusia. They are made by removing the top soil to a certain depth and diligently cultivating the bottom. A bed of reeds with dense, fresh foliage surrounded that sunken garden, firming up the perpendicular planes that encircled it and protecting the garden with its tall, lush stalks and network of fibrous roots against the encroachment of the sand. In that hollow, the land produces abundant, well-ripened vegetables without irrigation, despite the proximity of the sea; for the sea-water, filtered through thick layers of sand, is cleansed of its salt, and when it reaches the plants it is ready to nourish them. The watermelons from the *navazos* are particularly delicious, and some of them grow to such a size that two are a load for a beast of burden.

"Look how beautiful Pedro's garden is!" said Aunt María. "It looks exactly as though he waters it with holy water. The poor man is forever working at it, and it shows it. I'll bet he'll gather tomatoes as big as oranges this year, and watermelons like millstones."

"The ones we gather from the *cojumbral* on the banks of the river are bound to be better," said Momo.

A *cojumbral* is a garden planted to melons, corn, and vegetables, seeded on a damp patch of land which the owner of the pasture-land customarily sets aside for the free use of the poor country people, who cultivate it for their own use.

"I don't care much for *cojumbrales*," said the grandmother, shaking her head.

"Well, señora," answered Momo, "perhaps you haven't heard the old saying that goes: 'a *cojumbral* brings its owner two thousand *reales,* a cloak, a fat hog, and one more child."

"You left off the ending," replied Aunt María. "It goes: 'and a year of fever which swallows up all the other gains except for the son.'"

The fisherman had built his house from the flotsam of his boat which the sea had cast up on the beach. He had set the roof against a rock face so that it sheltered a kind of natural stairway formed by the stone, with the result that the house was three stories high. The first consisted of a tall room big enough to serve as parlor, kitchen, hen-house, and winter quarters for the donkey.

The second, reached by some open stairs cut into the stone, was subdivided into two small rooms. Pedro slept in the one on the left, which was dark and attached to the rock-face; the one on the right was his daughter's. She enjoyed exclusive use of a little window that had served as a port-hole on the boat and now offered a view of the cove. The third story, reached by the narrow corridor dividing the father's and the daughter's bedrooms, was a dark and airless attic. The roof, as we have said, was supported by the cliff; it was flat and covered with thatch, the first layer of which, watered by the rain, yielded a thicket of grass and little flowers, so that when Nature was awakened from the drought of summer by the autumn rains, the hut seemed to be crowned with a charming roof garden.

Upon entering the cabin, the arriving visitors found the fisherman downcast and sad. He was sitting in the firelight, facing his daughter. She was shrunken and shivering, her fleshless limbs wrapped in a dark flannel shawl, her dishevelled hair hanging loose about her pallid face. She seemed no more than thirteen years old. With an expression of ill will, the sick girl fixed her large, wild, black eyes on the people who entered, and then immediately turned around to huddle in the corner beside the hearth.

"Pedro," said Aunt María, "you're forgetting your friends, but they don't forget you. Can you tell me why the good Lord gave you a mouth? Couldn't you have come to tell me that the child was ill? The sooner I'd been told, the sooner I'd have been here with this gentleman who is a doctor that can't be beat, and who's going to make your daughter well in the twinkling of an eye."

Pedro Santaló got up abruptly and went to Stein, wishing to talk with him; but he was so upset he could not speak a word, and covered his face with his hands.

He was a man advanced in years, a rough-hewn Colossus. His face, tanned by the sun, was crowned with a thick, unruly head of white hair; his chest, red as an Indian from Ohio, was covered with hair.

"Come, Uncle Pedro," continued Aunt María, whose tears made a path down her cheeks when she saw the distress of the poor father. "A man like you, as big as a house, looking as if you'd eat little children raw, and now scared to death for no reason! Come! Anyone can see you're all front!"

"Aunt María," replied the fisherman in a broken voice, "if I bury her, she'll be the fifth of my children."

"Dear Lord! What is there for you to get so downhearted about? Remember your namesake, Saint Peter, who sank into the sea when he lost the faith that had been holding him up. I tell you that with the help of God, Don Federico will make this child well before you can say Jack Robinson."

Pedro shook his head sadly.

"How stubborn these Catalans are!" said Aunt María with spirit.

And passing in front of the fisherman she went up to the sick girl and said:

"Come, Marysal; come, get up, girl."

Marysal made no move.

"Come, child," repeated the good woman, "you'll see how he'll make you better like a charm."

With these words, she took the girl by the arm and tried to raise her.

"I don't want to!" said the sick child, trying to shake off the hand that held her.

"The daughter is as soft as the father; she comes by it naturally," murmured Momo from the doorway.

"She's cross because she's sick," said her father, trying to excuse her.

Marysal was shaken by a fit of coughing. The fisherman wrung his hands with anxiety.

"A cold," said Aunt María. "Come, this is nothing unusual. But all the same, my foolish Pedro, who is it that has allowed this girl to run around over the rocks barefooted and bare-legged in this cold weather and these freezing winds?"

"She wanted to!" answered Pedro.

"And why wasn't she given proper food—soups, milk, eggs? Not to mention that all she ever eats is mussels."

"She doesn't want to!" replied the downcast father.

"She'll die of being given a free rein," interjected Momo, who was leaning against the door jamb with his arms crossed.

"How would you like to put your tongue in your pocket?" said his grandmother impatiently; then turning to Stein: "Don Federico, try to examine her without having to move her, for she won't do it even if they kill her."

Stein began by questioning the father about some details of the daughter's illness; then, approaching the patient, who was growing drowsy, he observed that her lungs were cramped inside her narrow rib-cage, and had become irritated from the pressure. Her case was serious. She was very weak from lack of food; she had a deep, dry cough and a constant fever; in short, she was on the road to consumption.

"Does she still feel like singing?" asked the old lady during the examination.

"She'd sing crucified upside down like a bat," said Momo putting his head outside the door so the wind could carry away his low words before his grandmother could hear them.

"The first thing to be done," said Stein, "is to dress this girl against the bad weather."

"Do you hear that?" said the worried father to the girl. "She'll have to wear shoes and stockings and outdoor wraps."

"But she doesn't want to!" cried the fisherman, getting up suddenly and opening a cedar chest from which he took a number of garments. "She doesn't lack for a thing; everything I have and all I can save is for her. María, my daughter, won't you put on these clothes? Please do it, little Mary; you hear the doctor's orders."

The girl, aroused by the sound her father had made, shot a peevish glance at Stein, saying hoarsely:

"Who's my boss?"

"Give me an olive switch and I'll show her right now," muttered Momo.

"She must be properly fed and must take some nourishing broth," Stein went on.

Aunt María made a gesture of approval.

"She must be built up with milk, chicken, fresh eggs and all such things."

"What did I tell you!" interrupted the little grandmother, turning to Uncle Pedro. "The gentleman is the best doctor in the whole wide world."

"Be careful not to let her sing," warned Stein.

"I'm afraid I'll never hear her again!" cried poor Pedro dolefully.

"That's a fine thing to say!" answered Aunt María. "Let her get better, and then let her sing day and night like a cuckoo clock. But I'm thinking that the best thing to do would be for me to take her to my house, for there's no one here to take

care of her nor to make her a good pot of stew like the kind
I can make."

"I know that by experience," said Stein, smiling, "and
I can testify that the stew made by my good nurse's hands is
fit for a king."

Aunt María glowed with pleasure.

"So, Uncle Pedro, there's no more to be said; I'm taking
her."

"Leave me without her? No, no, you can't!"

"Uncle Pedro, Uncle Pedro, that's not the way to love
your children," replied Aunt María. "If you love your children,
you put what's best for them above anything."

"Well, all right then," answered the fisherman, getting up
suddenly. "Take her. I'm placing her in your hands; I'm turning her over to that gentleman's care, and I commend her to
the protection of God."

So saying, he rushed precipitately from the house, as if
he were afraid of changing his mind, and went to saddle the
donkey.

"Don Federico," asked Aunt María when they were alone
with the girl, who remained lethargic, "isn't it true that with
God's help you can heal her?"

"I hope so," replied Stein. "I can't tell you how interested
I am in that poor father!"

Aunt María made a bundle of the clothing the fisherman
had brought out, and he came back leading the donkey by the
halter. Among them, they put the sick girl on top of the
animal. She offered no resistance, being still drowsy with
fever. Before Aunt María could climb on *Golondrina,* who
seemed very pleased to be going home in company with Urca
(for that was the name of Pedro's burro), the father called
Aunt María aside, and handing her some gold coins he said:

"I've managed to save this from my shipwreck; take it and give it to the doctor, for I'll give all I have to the man who will save my daughter's life."

"Keep your money," said Aunt María. "I tell you the doctor came here first of all to please God, and second to please me . . ." Aunt María spoke the last words with a touch of vanity.

With this, they started on their way.

"Grandmother," said Momo, walking behind *Golondrina,* "you won't stop until you have the convent full of people, big as it is. Anyway, isn't the shack good enough for Princess Sea Gull?"

"Momo," replied the grandmother, "you're getting too big for your britches."

"Well, but what's she to you? What have you to do with that wild sea gull to make you take her under your wing like this?"

"Momo, remember the old saying: 'Who is your sister?: your next-door neighbor.' And another one adds, 'Wipe the nose of your neighbor's child and take him home,' and then there's the commandment, 'Love thy neighbor as thyself.' "

"And then there's still another that says: 'You'll always be at odds with your neighbor,' " replied Momo. "But what's the use? You're stubbornly determined to take the laurels away from Saint John of God."

"You'll never be the angel that helps me," said Aunt María sadly.

Dolores received the sick girl with open arms, applauding her mother-in-law's decision as very wise.

Pedro Santaló, who had carried his daughter in, called aside the charitable nurse, and putting the gold coins in her hand, he said:

"This is to pay for her stay here, and to see that she lacks nothing. As for your loving kindness, Aunt María, God will reward it."

The good old woman hesitated a moment, then took the money and said:

"All right. She'll lack nothing. You needn't worry, Pedro, for your daughter is in good hands."

The poor father hastened away and did not pause until he reached the beach. There he stopped, turned toward the convent, and began to weep bitterly.

Meanwhile, Aunt María said to Momo:

"Hurry up. Go to the village and bring me a ham from Serrano's; ask him to give you one that is well cured, seeing it's for a sick person; bring me a pound of sugar, and a quarter of a pound of almonds."

"Go on, don't get excited!" cried Momo. "Do you think they're going to give it to me on faith, or on account of my honest face?"

"Here's money to pay for it," replied the grandmother, putting in his hand a gold coin worth four dollars.

"Gold!" exclaimed Momo in stupefaction, for it was the first time in his life he had seen that metal minted. "Where in the world did you get this coin from?"

"What does it matter to you?" replied Aunt María. "Don't stick your nose in other people's affairs. Run, fly! Why are you coming back?"

"Well," replied Momo, "all I needed was to be a servant to that beachcomber, that damned sea gull! I'm not going, not for any Catalans!"

"Get on your way, boy, and right now."

"I'm not going if you beat me to smithereens."

"José," said Aunt María, seeing the shepherd about to leave, "are you going to the village?"

"Yes, señora. Is there anything you'd like?"

The good lady gave him the list, and added:

"That Momo, that bad boy doesn't want to go, and I don't want to tell his father on him; he'd send him off like a shot, and he'd give him such a whaling there wouldn't be a sound bone left in his body."

"Yes, yes, be sure and take good care of that crow so she can pick out your eyes," said Momo. "You'll see how she'll pay you back . . . you just wait!"

CHAPTER IX

A month after the scenes just related, Marysal felt noticeably better and was showing not the slightest desire to go back to her father.

Stein was completely recovered. His kindly disposition, his modest ambitions, his natural sympathies held him more closely each day within the peaceful circle of good, simple, and generous people among whom he was living. His bitter discouragement gradually waned, his spirits revived, and he was growing cordially reconciled with life and mankind.

One afternoon he was watching from a sheltered corner of the convent facing toward the sea the awesome spectacle of one of those storms which generally usher in the winter. A triple layer of clouds was scudding above him, shoved along by gale winds from the sea. The lowest layer, black and heavy, resembled the cupola of a ruined old cathedral on the point of collapse. When these clouds sank lower, breaking off in the water, the second layer, thinner and less black, rivalled the speed of the wind which tore it in places, disclosing through the openings still higher and whiter clouds, running before the wind still more rapidly as if fearing to soil their whiteness by contact with the others. The breaks in the clouds made a path for fugitive gleams of sunlight, falling now on the waves, now on the land, quickly vanishing, to be replaced by the shadows of the slower-moving clouds, with a play of light and shade that lent an extraordinary animation to the landscape. Every living creature had sought refuge from the fury of the elements, and nothing could be heard but the mournful duet of the roaring waves and the howling gale. The vegetation of the open land bowed its rough head before the violence of the wind that lashed it and passed on to lose itself in the distance with muted threats. The turbulent ocean was shaping up into enormous seas that gradually "swelled, hesitated, and broke in a roar of foam," as Goethe put it when comparing them to the turmoil of a man's breast in his *Torquato Tasso*.[21] The dashing seas broke on the rocks of Fort Saint Christopher with such fury that they spattered with splotches of white spume the dry, yellowing leaves of the fig trees—summer trees that can thrive only in the rays of a hot sun, whose leaves, despite their firm surface, cannot stand the wounding touch of cold.

"Are you a cistern, Don Federico, that you're trying to catch all the water falling from the sky?" José the shepherd asked Stein. "Let's go inside; roof tiles were made for nights like this. My poor sheep would give a good deal to have a roof over them."

They went in together and found the Alerza family gathered around the fire.

To the left of the fireplace Dolores, seated in a low chair, was holding the infant. With his back to his mother, he was leaning against the arms which encircled and supported him like a balcony railing. His little legs and bare arms were moving incessantly as he laughed and screamed with joy at his brother Anise, sitting quietly on the edge of an empty flower pot in front of the fire, holding himself stiff and motionless, lest his posterior lose its balance and he fall into the pot, an accident his mother had predicted.

To the right of the fireplace Aunt María was spinning. Her

---

[21] A drama portraying the conflict of poetic genius with the prosaic world (1790), in the style of classic Renaissance poetry.

two little granddaughters were sitting on dried stumps of century plant, which make excellent seats, being light, firm, and secure. Big *Palomo* and sober *Morrongo* were asleep almost in the fire, in mutual tolerance born of necessity, yet keeping a respectful distance from each other.

In the middle of the room was a small low table where a brass lamp with four wicks was burning. Next to the table Brother Gabriel was at work on his reed baskets; Momo was mending *Golondrina's* harness while Manuel ˙shredded tobacco. A copper pot full of sweet potatoes from Malaga, white wine, honey, cinnamon, and cloves was boiling over the fire and the small fry were waiting impatiently for the aromatic dish to finish cooking.

"Come in, come in," cried Aunt María seeing her guest and the shepherd enter. "What were you doing outdoors in a storm like this that seems to want to swallow up the world? Don Federico, here, here; next to this inviting fire. Let me tell you the sick girl ate a supper fit for a princess and she's sleeping like a queen now. Her recovery goes like clockwork, doesn't it, Don Federico?"

"Her improvement surpasses my expectations."

"My stews," opined Aunt María proudly.

"And the donkey's milk," added Brother Gabriel in a low voice.

"No doubt about it," replied Stein, "and she should go on taking it."

"I'm not against it," said Aunt María, "for 'donkey's milk is like a caul; it may do no good, but it does no harm at all.'"

"Ah, how good it is to be here," said Stein, caressing the children. "If only one could live for the day, with no thought of the morrow . . ."

"Yes, yes, Don Federico," cried Manuel gaily. "A good fire is half of life; bread and wine the other half."

"And why should you need to think about tomorrow?" answered Aunt María. "Doesn't tomorrow usually spoil today for us? What we have to look out for is today, so tomorrow won't be spoiled for us."

"Man is a wanderer," said Stein, "and he must seek the way."

"True," said Aunt Maria, "man is a wanderer; but if he comes to a place where he's well off, he should say like Elias or Saint Peter, I'm not sure which: 'This is a goodly place; let us pitch our tents.'"

"If you're going to spoil our evening for us," said Dolores, "by talking about travelling, we'll think we've offended you, and that you don't like it here."

"Who's talking about travelling in the middle of December?" asked Manuel. "My dear man, don't you see how the sea is worked up? Listen to the merry tune the wind is singing. You start off in this weather, as you started for the war in Navarre, and you'll end by ruing the day, as you did then."

"Besides," added Aunt María, "your patient is not entirely well yet."

"Mother," said Dolores, who was surrounded by the little ones, "if you don't call off these children, the sweet potatoes won't be cooked until Judgment Day."

The grandmother set her distaff in a corner and called her grandchildren.

"We're not coming unless you'll tell us a story," they said with one voice.

"All right, I'll tell you one," said the good old woman.

The children gathered around her; Anise again took his seat on the flower-pot, and she began to speak as follows:

HALF-COCKEREL
A Fable

Once upon a time there was a fine-looking hen living a good life on a farm, surrounded by her numerous family, among which a deformed and crippled cockerel stood out from the rest. Well, he was the very one the mother loved best, as mothers always do. This particular monstrosity had come from a teeny-weeny little egg, with the consequence that he was only a half-cockerel. He looked almost as though Solomon's sword had carried out on him the judgment that wise king had pronounced on a certain occasion. He had only one eye, one wing, and one foot, but for all that he was even vainer than his father, the bravest, the most gallant, and the boldest cock to be found in any barnyard for twenty leagues roundabout. The poor cockerel considered himself the flower of his species. If the other cockerels made fun of him, he believed they envied him; and if the pullets mocked him, he said they were piqued because he paid so little attention to them.

One day he said to his mother:

"See here, Mother; I'm bored with the country. I've made up my mind to go to the Court; I want to see the king and queen."

"Why, child," she exclaimed, "who has put such nonsense into your head? Your father has never left his own land and he's always been a credit to his kind. Where would you find another barnyard like the one you have now? Where would you find a better dunghill? Better and more plentiful food? A more weather-tight henhouse near the horse-path, a family who would love you more?"

"*Nego* (I deny it)," said Half-Cockerel in Latin, for he had set himself up as well-read and a writer. "My brothers and sisters and my cousins are an ignorant and churlish lot."

"But, son," replied the mother, "haven't you ever looked at yourself in the mirror? Can't you see that you lack one leg and one eye?"

"Now that you've brought the matter up," replied Half-Cockerel, "I must tell you that you ought to drop dead of shame to see me in such a state. It's your fault and no one else's. From what sort of egg was I born into this world? I'll bet it was an old rooster's egg." [22]

"No, my child," said the mother, "only basilisks come from such eggs. You came from the last egg I laid; and you came out weak and imperfect because that was the last one of the lot. It was not my fault."

"It might be," said Half-Cockerel, his comb as red as a pomegranate, "it might be that I shall meet a clever surgeon who will put on me the members I lack. So, there's no help for it; I'm leaving."

When the poor mother saw that there was no chance of dissuading him from his intention, she said:

"Listen, at least, son, to the wise counsel of a good mother. Try not to go near churches where there's an image of Saint Peter; he's not very fond of cocks, and still less fond of their crowing. Also shun certain men, called cooks, who live out in the world. They're our mortal enemies; and they'll wring our necks before you can say scat. And now, my son, may God and the blessed Saint Raphael, the travellers' advocate, be with you. Go and ask your father for his blessing."

---

[22] It is a common popular superstition that old roosters will lay an egg from which a basilisk will emerge after seven years. They add that it can kill with a glance the first person it sees, but that it will die if that person sees it first. AUTHOR'S NOTE.

Half-Cockerel went to his father, bowed his head to kiss his foot, and asked his blessing. The venerable cock gave it with more dignity than tenderness, for in view of the son's bad disposition, he did not love him. The mother felt so upset that she had to dry her tears on a withered leaf.

Half-Cockerel started on his way, flapped his wing and crowcd three times by way of farewell. When he came to the banks of a stream that was nearly dry (for it was summer) he found that the thin thread of water was dammed up by some branches. Seeing the traveller, the stream said to him:

"You see how weak I am, my friend; I can hardly move; I haven't enough strength to push aside those miserable little twigs that are obstructing my path. Neither can I circle around them, for it would tire me too much. You can easily get me out of this fix by pulling them aside with your beak. In return, you can not only slake your thirst in my current, but you can count on me to help you after the water from heaven gives me back my strength."

The cockerel answered:

"I can but I don't care to. Do I look like a servant to poor and miserable brooks?"

"You'll remember me when you least expect to!" murmured the brook in a weak voice.

"Well, you certainly talk big!" said Half-Cockerel maliciously. "One would think you had drawn a three-number combination in the lottery, or else you're surely counting on the waters of the Flood."

A little farther along he met the wind which lay full length and almost lifeless on the ground.

"Dear Half-Cockerel," it said to him, "we all have need of one another in this world. Come closer and look at me. Do you see what the summer heat has done to me—to me, so strong and so powerful; to me who can stir up the seas, and level the fields; to me who can never find a foeman worthy of my thrust? These dog days kill me; I fell asleep drunk on the fragrance of the flowers I was playing with, and here I lie prostrate. If you'd raise me up two fingers from the ground with your beak and fan me with your wing, that would be enough to start me off in flight, so I can go home to my cavern where my mother and my sisters, the storms, are busy mending some old clouds I tore apart. They'd give me a bite to eat and I'd get my strength back."

"Too many times you've made sport of me, sir," answered the ill-natured cockerel, "pushing me from behind, and spreading my tail out like a fan so everyone seeing me could scoff at me. No, my friend; Saint Martin's day[23] must come to every pig, and as far as I can see, you're for it."

So saying, he crowed three times in a loud voice, and, preening himself, went on his way.

In the middle of a mown field, set afire by some laborers, a thin column of smoke was rising. Half-Cockerel went to it and saw a tiny spark dying out rapidly among the ashes.

"Dear Half-Cockerel," said the spark when it saw him, "you've arrived just in time to save my life. I'm at my last gasp for lack of food. I don't know where my cousin the wind has gone. He's always the one to rescue me at a time like this. Bring me some straws to start me off again."

"What's that to me?" answered the little rooster. "Go out if you want to, for I've cursed little need of you."

"Who knows but that you will need me some day," replied the spark. "No one can say 'I'll never drink this water.' "

"So!" cried the perverse creature, "you're still alive, are you? Well, take that!"

---

[23] November 11, the traditional hog-butchering day.

So saying, he smothered it with ashes; after which he began to crow as usual, as though he had done some great deed.

Finally Half-Cockerel reached the capital; he passed in front of a church which he had been told was Saint Peter's, stood in front of the door and burst into shrill crowing, simply to annoy the saint and for the pleasure of disobeying his mother.

When he drew near the palace and wanted to go in to see the king and queen, the guardsmen shouted at him, "Back!" Then he turned and went through a rear door into a very large room where he saw many people coming and going. He asked who they were and learned that they were His Majesty's cooks. Instead of fleeing, as his mother had warned him, he went ahead, strutting, crest and tail high; but one of the scullions seized him and wrung his neck in the twinkling of an eye.

"All right," he said, "some water to pluck this sinner."

"Water, my darling, sweet crystal," said the cockerel, "please don't scald me! Have pity! Have mercy on me . . ."

"Did you have pity on me when I asked you for help, you misbegotten knave?" replied the water, boiling with anger. And it poured over him from head to foot, while the scullions left him without a feather to his name."

Paca, kneeling at her grandmother's side, turned very pink and very sad.

"Then," went on Aunt María, "the cook grabbed Half-Cockerel and put him on the spit."

"Fire, brilliant fire," cried the wretch, "you, who are so powerful and so resplendent, pity my sad plight, hold back your heat, damp down your flames, don't burn me!"

"Rascal," replied the fire, "how can you have the face to appeal to me, after you put me out under the pretext that you'd never need my help? Come closer and you'll get what's good for you."

And indeed, the fire, not content to turn him a golden brown, burned him black as coal."

On hearing this, Paca's eyes filled with tears.

"When the cook saw him in such a state," continued the grandmother, "he took him by the leg and threw him out the window. Then the wind fell upon him.

"Wind," cried Half-Cockerel, "my dear, my revered wind; thou who dost reign over everything and dost obey no one, powerful among the potent, have pity on me! Leave me here in peace on this dunghill!"

"Leave you!" howled the wind, beating up into a whirlwind and turning him over and over in the air like a top. "Never, as long as I live."

The tears which had risen in Paca's eyes were now running down her cheeks.

"The wind," continued the grandmother, "deposited Half-Cockerel on the tip of a bell-tower. Then Saint Peter reached out his hand and fixed him there firmly. He's been there ever since, black, skinny, and plucked, whipped and shoved by the wind from which he always turns tail. He's not called Half-Cockerel now; he's a weathervane. But you must know that up there he's paying for his faults and his sins, his disobedience, his pride, and his wickedness."

"Grandmother," said Pepa, "look how Paca is crying over Half-Cockerel. What you've been telling us is only a story, isn't it?"

"Of course," said Momo, "not a word of it is true; but supposing it were, isn't it silly to cry over a rascal that got his just deserts?"

"When I was in Cádiz thirty years ago," replied Aunt María, "I saw something that made quite an impression on me. I'm going to tell you about it, Momo, and please God it won't be erased from your memory, as it has never been from mine. It was a gold sign above the door of the jail and it read: 'Hate the sin and pity the sinner.' Don Federico, that must be a verse from the Gospel, mustn't it?"

"If the words aren't the same the spirit is," replied Stein.

"Paca always has tears in her eyes," said Momo.

"Is it so bad to cry?" the child asked her grandmother.

"No, child, on the contrary; the crown of the Queen of the Angels is made from tears of compassion and repentance."

"Momo," said the shepherd, "if you say another word to upset my little goddaughter, I'll wring your neck as the cook wrung Half-Cockerel's."

"See how lucky you are to have a godfather?" said Momo to Paca.

"It's not so bad to have a goddaughter either," replied Paca proudly.

"Really?" asked the shepherd. "Why do you say that?"

Paca went to her godfather, who set her on his knees with many demonstrations of affection, and she launched into the following story, turning her little head to look at him.

"Once upon a time there was a poor man, so poor he couldn't afford to buy clothes for the eighth child the stork was going to bring, nor to feed the other seven. One day he went out of his house, because it broke his heart to hear them crying and begging for bread. He started to walk, not knowing where, and after walking, walking all day long, he was overtaken by night . . . I bet you can't guess where, Godfather? . . . Well, he found himself at the entrance to a cave of robbers. The captain came to the door. He was very cross. 'Who are you? What do you want?' he asked in a voice like thunder. 'Sir,' said the poor man, throwing himself on his knees, 'I'm a poor wretch who can do no harm to anyone. I left home so I wouldn't have to listen to my poor children asking for the bread I can't give them.' The captain took pity on the poor fellow, and after giving him something to eat and a purse full of money and a horse, he said: 'Go; and when the stork brings the other baby, tell me, and I'll be his godfather.' "

"Now comes the best part of it," said the shepherd.

"Wait, wait," went on the little girl, "and you'll see what happened. Well, sir, the man went back home so happy his heart would hardly fit in his chest. 'What a feast my children are going to have!' he was saying. When he arrived, the stork had already brought a little boy, who was in bed with his mother. Then he went to the cave and told the robber what had happened, and the captain promised him he would be at the church that night and would keep his word. And so he did. He held the baby at the baptismal font, and gave him a sack full of gold.

"But before long the baby died and went to Heaven. Saint Peter told him he could pass through; but the baby answered: 'I won't come in unless my godfather can come in with me.'

" 'And who is your godfather?' asked the saint.

" 'A robber captain,' replied the baby.

" 'Well, son,' said Saint Peter, 'you can come in, but not your godfather.'

"The little boy sat down at the gate with his hand to his cheek, very sad. The Virgin happened to come along, and said to him:

" 'Why don't you go in, my son?'

"The little boy said he didn't want to go in unless his

godfather could, and that Saint Peter had said he was asking the impossible. But the little boy went down on his knees, crossed his little hands, and wept so hard that the Virgin, the mother of mercy, took pity on his sorrow. The Virgin went away and came back with a little gold cup in her hands; she gave it to the little boy and said:

" 'Go and find your godfather and tell him to fill this cup with tears of contrition, and then he'll be able to come into heaven with you. Take these silver wings and fly.'

"The robber was asleep on a cliff with his gun in one hand and a dagger in the other. When he waked, he saw a beautiful naked little boy in front of him, sitting on a lavender bush, with silver wings that shone in the sun and a gold cup in his hand.

"The thief rubbed his eyes, thinking he was dreaming, but the little boy said to him: 'No, you're not dreaming. I'm your godson.' And he told all that had happened. Then the robber's heart opened like a pomegranate and his eyes poured tears like a fountain. So sharp was his grief and so keen his repentance that they stabbed his chest like daggers, and he died. Then the little boy took the cupful of tears and flew to heaven with his godfather's soul, where they entered, and where please God we all may enter."

"And now, Godfather," added the little girl, turning her head and looking the shepherd in the face, "you see what a good thing it is to have godchildren."

The little girl had barely finished pointing out the moral of her story when a great commotion arose; the dog got to his feet and pricked up his ears, ready to fight; the cat, his fur standing on end, his eyes wide with alarm, took precipitate flight; but merry laughter soon followed the scare. What had happened was that Anise had fallen asleep during his sister's narration, with the result that he had lost his balance, thus justifying his mother's warning, and fallen inside the pot where his tiny body was lost to sight except for his feet and legs, rising from the pot like some new kind of plant. His mother impatiently seized the collar of his jacket with one hand and plucked him from the depths. She held him, struggling, in the air, so that he looked like one of those cardboard dolls which hang from a thread and wildly move their arms and legs as they are manipulated.

While his mother scolded him and everyone laughed, Anise, who was high-spirited, as all small, chubby children are said to be (which does not mean that tall ones are not, too), burst into loud, angry weeping.

"Don't cry, Anise." said Paca, "Don't cry. I'll give you some chestnuts I've got in my pocket."

"Honestly?" asked Anise.

Paca took out the chestnuts and gave them to him; his tears ceased instantly and two rows of little white teeth shone in the child's face, gleaming by the light of the fire.

"Brother Gabriel," said Aunt María, speaking to the monk, "didn't you tell me that your eyes were bothering you? Why are you working at night?"

"They were bothering me," replied Brother Gabriel, "but Don Federico gave me some medicine that has cured me."

"Don Federico may very well know many cures for the eyes," said the shepherd, "but he wouldn't know the very best remedy."

"If you know it, I'd be glad to have you tell me about it," said Stein.

"I can't tell you," replied the shepherd, "for though I know there is such a thing, I don't know what it looks like."

"Who does know, then?" asked Stein.

"The swallows," [24] replied the shepherd.

"The swallows?"

"Why, yes, sir," the shepherd went on. "It's an herb called royal whistle, but no one sees it or recognizes it except the swallows; if their nestlings' eyes are plucked out, they go and wash them with this royal whistle and they get their sight back. This herb also has the virtue of breaking iron with a mere touch; and so when the tools of reapers or pruners break in their hands for no apparent reason, it's because they touched this royal whistle. But no matter how many people have looked for it, no one has found it; and it's God's mercy that they haven't, for if it were found by chance, there'd be little trade carried on in the world, because neither bolts nor bars, nor chains, nor crossbars would be of much use."

"The things that José will swallow! He has a gullet like a shark!" said Manuel, laughing. "Don Federico, do you know anybody who claims, and believes as an article of faith, that snakes never die?"

"Why, anyone can see that snakes never die," the shepherd replied. "When they see death approaching, they shed

---

[24] The matters of which the people speak and in which they believe, though adorned by their rich and poetic imagination, always have some source. In the second part of the work entitled *Unknown Simples in Medicine*, written by Brother Estéban de Villa, and printed in Burgos, in 1654, we find this paragraph which corresponds with what the shepherd said:

"The ibis (believed to be the stork) taught the use of enemas, which it gives itself by filling its mouth with water, the length of its bill serving for this purpose. The dog, the use of vomiting, by eating dog-grass, which acts as an emetic. The hippopotamus of bleeding; when it feels overcharged with blood, it opens a vein with a sharp-pointed reed which acts as a lancet; and he uses mud as a bandage, for by rolling in it he closes the incision. The swallow knows 'the celandine eyewash' with which it gives sight to its nestlings; it gave the name to the plant called 'hirundinaria,' so-called for its discoverer, *the swallow*, etc." AUTHOR'S NOTE.

their skins and run for their lives. As they grow old they turn into serpents; then little by little they begin growing scales and wings until they turn into dragons and fly off into the desert. But you, Manuel, you don't want to believe anything! Would you also deny that the lizard is the enemy of women and the friend of men? If you don't want to believe it, ask Miguel about it."

"What does he know about it?"

"Come, come! He knows about it because it happened to him."

"And what was it?" asked Stein.

"One day he was asleep in the fields," replied José, "and a big snake was coming toward him; but before it had quite got to him, a lizard inside the hedge came out to defend Miguel, and the snake and the lizard got into a fight, for the lizard was this big . . . very big. But as Miguel didn't wake up even for that, the lizard stuck the point of its tail into his nose. Miguel woke up then and began to run as though he had sparks in his feet. The lizard is a good and well-intentioned creature; it never takes shelter at sunset without climbing down the walls and coming to kiss the earth."

While this conversation had begun to turn on the subject of swallows, Paca had said to Anise, who looked like the Grand Turk in miniature as he sat among his sisters on the floor:

"Anise, do you know what the swallows say?"

"Not I. They've never talked to me."

"Well, listen. Here's what they say." The little girl began to recite very quickly, mimicking the trill of the swallow:

"Eat and drink; borrow, borrow;
If they seek you on the morrow
Just because you cannot pay,
Run, dear Pepa, run away!"

"Is that why they fly away?" asked Anise.

"That's why," stated his sister.

"I like them best! . . ." said Pepa.

"Why?" asked Anise.

"Because you know," replied the little girl, "that on Mount
Calvary

'Christ's five thorns were brushed away
By swallows, with their tails;
And little linnets with their beaks
Pulled out the three sharp nails.'

"What about the sparrows, what did they do?" asked
Anise.

"Sparrows," replied his sister, "have never known how to
do anything but eat and fight."

Meanwhile, Dolores, carrying her sleeping baby on one
arm, had set the table with her free hand and taken up the
sweet potatoes which she distributed around equally. The little
children ate from her plate; and Stein observed that Dolores
did not even taste the food she had prepared with such loving
care.

"Dolores, you're not eating," he said.

"Well, you know the old saying," she replied, laughing:
" 'He who has children beside him will not die of overeating.'
What they eat makes me fat, Don Federico."

Momo, who sat to one side of the group, drew back his
plate so that his brothers and sisters might not be tempted to
ask him for what was on it.

His father, who noticed this, said:

"Don't be greedy; that's a miser's vice; nor niggardly, the
vice of the base-born. You must know about the miser who fell
into a river. A peasant, who saw that the current was carrying

him away, stretched out his arm and shouted to him: 'Give me your hand!' Would he give it? He'd give nothing! . . . Before he'd give *anything,* he let the current sweep him on down. It was his good luck that the stream brought him near a fisherman, who said to him: 'Take this hand, man!' And as long as it was a matter of *taking,* our man was very quick, and was saved."

"You shouldn't tell your son that kind of story, Manuel," said Aunt María. "Instead, you should give him the example of that miserable rich man who refused to help a poor man, faint with hunger, by so much as a crust of bread or a sip of water. 'God grant,' said the poor man, 'that everything you touch may turn into that gold and that silver you're so fond of!' And so it happened! Every blessed thing in the miser's house was turned to metal as hard as his heart. Tormented by hunger and thirst, he went out into the countryside, and seeing a fountain of pure water, he flung himself at it, but as soon as his lips touched it, the wafer solidified and turned to silver. He went to pick an orange from a tree, and it turned to gold when he touched it; and so he died, raving and cursing himself for what his covetousness had done to him."

Manuel, the doubting Thomas of the circle, shook his head.

"You see, Aunt María," said José. "Manuel won't believe it! He doesn't believe either that on Assumption Day, at the moment of the elevation in high mass, all the leaves of all the trees join together in pairs to form a cross; the high ones bend down and the low ones stand on tiptoe, and every single one takes part. He doesn't believe, either, that on the tenth of August, the day of Saint Lawrence's martyrdom, when he was burned to death on a grate, coal can be found anywhere the earth is dug."

"When that day comes," said Manuel, "I'm going to dig a hole right in front of you, José, and we'll see if I can convince you that no such thing happens."

"And what would be so wonderful about not finding coal?" said his mother. "Do you think, by any chance, that you'll find it if you look for it without faith, Manuel? You imagine that whatever is not an article of faith needn't be believed, and that anyone who is credulous plays the fool. Not so, my son, he plays the wise man."

"But, Mother," said Manuel, "there's a happy medium between running and standing still."

"But why do you quibble so much over faith?" said the good old woman. "After all, isn't it the first of the virtues? What would you think, my dear son, if I were to say to you: 'I bore you, I raised you, I started you in life; now I've done my duty,' as if the love of a mother is to be regarded merely as an obligation?"

"I'd think you weren't a good mother, señora."

"Well, son, apply that to this other case; he who believes only as an obligation, and believes only what he can't help believing, is a poor Christian, though not a renegade. Just as I'd be a poor mother if I loved you only as a duty."

"Brother Gabriel," said Dolores, "how is it that you don't want to try my sweet potatoes?"

"It's a fast day for us," replied Brother Gabriel.

"What! There are no more convents, nor rules, nor fasts," said Manuel heartily, to encourage the poor old man to eat his share of the general treat. "Besides, you've already passed seventy; you won't be damned for that."

"You must forgive me," replied Brother Gabriel, "but I never fail to fast as I used to, as long as the prior has not given me a dispensation."

"Good for you, Brother Gabriel," said Aunt María. "Manuel, don't play the tempting demon with your rebellious spirit and your incitements to greediness."

Thereupon the good old lady got up and put the plate Dolores had served for the monk into a cupboard, saying:

"I'll keep it here for you until tomorrow, Brother Gabriel."

When the supper was over, they said grace. The men, who always wore their hats in the house, took them off.

"Blessed be the Lord
Who gave us this food
Which we do not deserve. Amen.
As he has given us his gifts,
May he give us His glory. Amen.
May God give likewise unto the poor
Who have it not. Amen."

Anise jumped to his feet at the last word as impulsively, straight, and sudden, as a fish jumping in the water.

CHAPTER X

Marysal was now on the road to recovery, as if Nature had wished to reward Stein for giving her the right treatment, and Aunt María for her charitable care.

The girl was decently dressed, and her hair, properly combed and done up in a chignon, did credit to Dolores, who had seen to her clothes.

One day as Stein was reading in his room beside the small window opening on the main patio where the children were playing with Marysal, he heard the girl begin to imitate the song of various birds with such rare perfection that he stopped reading to admire her extraordinary accomplishment. Soon afterward, the children started one of those games, so common in Spain, which are played to the accompaniment of singing. Marysal was taking the part of the mother; Pepa, that of a gentleman who had come to ask the hand of her daughter. The mother refuses; the gentleman attempts to possess his sweetheart by force; and the entire dialogue consists of couplets sung to a most pleasing melody.

The book fell from Stein's hands, for as a good German he was very fond of music. He had never heard such a beautiful voice. It was of the purest timbre, strong and clear as crystal, soft and flexible as silk. Stein hardly dared to breathe, fearing to lose the slightest modulation.

"You're all ears," said Aunt María, who had entered the room without a glance from him. "Didn't I tell you she's a canary without a cage? Now you can see for yourself!"

Whereupon she went out into the patio and told Marysal to sing a song.

With her characteristic rudeness, the girl refused.

Just then Momo came in, looking like a chimney sweep, preceded by *Golondrina* with a load of charcoal.

His hands and face were smudged, and black as ink.

"Melchior the King," cried Marysal on seeing him.

"Melchior the King! King Melchior!" echoed the children.

"If I had nothing more to do," replied Momo, furiously, "than to sing and jump around like you, you big lazy thing, I wouldn't be black from head to foot. Luckily, Don Federico has forbidden you to sing, so you can't torture my ears."

Marysal's reply was to burst immediately into full song.

The Andalusian people have an infinite number of songs. They are: *boleras*, now sad, now gay; the *olé*, the *fandango*, and the *caña*, all as beautiful as they are difficult to sing, plus many others with their own titles, among which the ballad form predominates. The melodies of the ballads are monotonous, and we venture to say that if they were written down and played, they might not satisfy either the dilettantes or the devotees of symphony music. But their pleasing quality, not to say their charm, lies in the modulations of the singer's voice; in the way some grace notes are introduced, so to speak, and gently trilled, falling, rising, stressing the sound or letting it die. Thus the ballad, made up of few tones, is extremely difficult to sing well and authentically. It is so much a specialty of these people that we have heard only them—and few of them —sing it to perfection; it seems that those who do, sing through intuition. At twilight in the country a good voice may be heard singing a ballad in the distance with plaintive improvisation, and it produces an extraordinary effect which we can compare only to the bugle calls of the postboys in Germany, vibrating so sweetly and sadly, repeated by the echoes through those magnificent woods and over those delightful lakes. Moorish tales or pious legends, or the sad stories of wrongdoers, are usually the subject-matter of the ballads.

This famous old ballad, handed down to us from father to son, like a tradition of melody, has rested more firmly on its few notes entrusted to the ear, than the grandeurs of Spain won by her arms and sustained by the mines of Peru.

The people also have very lovely and expressive songs whose melody was composed especially for the words, as those mentioned above are not. Innumerable verses are adapted around these melodies, and everyone has his own rich repertoire stored away in his memory.

María was singing one of those songs, which we shall transcribe here in all its simplicity and popular power:

"Once there was a cavalier
On the Island of León,
Enamored was he of a lady;
In his love he was not alone.
Tura lura lura, tura lura lay.

Enamored of him, she said:
'Will you stay a night or two?
My husband is far away
In those distant hills. Please do!'
Tura lura lura, etc.

He was making love to her
When the husband came home to his love:
'Now open the door, my darling,
Now open the door, my dove.'

Slowly she came down the staircase,
Her face was white with fear.

'Oh, have you been sick of a fever?
Or is there another man here?'

'No, I'm not sick of a fever,
Nor is there a stranger here;
But I have lost track of the key
To your dressing room, my dear.'

'If your key was fashioned of steel
I have mine that is fashioned of gold;
Now tell me, whose charger is that one
I heard neighing out there in the cold?'

" 'Tis thine, 'tis thine, dear master,
For my father sent it here
To fetch you to the wedding
Of my elder sister so dear."

"Now long may your father live
Though a stable of horses had I.
But tell me, whose rifle is hanging
From that nail in the wall so high?"

" 'Tis thine, 'tis thine, dear master,
For my father sent it here
For you to bring to the wedding
Of my elder sister so dear."

"Now long may your father live,
Though many rifles had I.
But tell me, who's the bold rascal
Asleep in my bedroom—and why?"

" 'Tis but my youngest sister,
For my father sent her here

To travel with me to the wedding
Of our elder sister so dear."

He dragged her away by the hand
To her father's home; with this plea:
'Father, take back thy daughter,
For she has played false with me.'

'You take her away, my poor son,
For the Church has bestowed her on thee.'
So he dragged her away by the hand
And out to the fields went he.

Then he took out his trusty dagger

And thrice he stabbed her through.
The lady was dead by one o'clock,
And her lover was dead by two.
Tura lura lura, tura lura loo." [25]

---

[25] The great writer, the great anthologist, the learned bibliophile, Don
Juan Nicholas Böhl de Faber, to whom Spanish literature owes *The
Spanish Theater Before Lope de Vega,* and *Collection of Castilian
Verse,* quotes the following old ballad by an unknown author in the
first volume of the latter, page 255. It has seemed to us worthy of
reproducing here as a curiosity, for it treats of the same theme as the
song. We are not competent to judge whether the popular song rose
from the people to the cultivated poet who rewrote it, or whether it
came down from the educated poet to the people, who simplified and
treated it in their own fashion, or whether indeed it may be that it
was sung by both simultaneously, though the language of the song
appears to be that of more modern folk:

'How white you are, my lady;
The sunlight is not so white.
I fain would take off my armor
And sleep without fear this night.

For seven long years—full seven—
My sword in my hand has been,

And darker than darkest coal-pitch
The hot sun has burned my skin.'

'Sleep now, my lord; sleep well,
Without fear and with arms laid aside,
For the count is away: he is hunting
In the hills of León far and wide.

May rabies destroy all his hound dogs,
May eagles his falcons all slay;
May the Moors drag the count off with them
To their castle so far away.'

Deep were the two of them sleeping
When the husband arrived, full of ire:
'What are you doing, fair lady,
Oh, daughter of treacherous sire?'

'I'm combing my long black tresses,
And with grief do I comb my hair,
For you went off to the mountains
And left me alone in despair.'

'All that you're saying, my lady,
Is nothing but treacherous talk.
Now whose is that warlike charger
That whinnied down there on the walk?'

'Master, 'tis one of my father's,
Sent to use at your beck and call.'
'Whose weapons are these, my lady,
That stand here in the hall?'

'O master, they are my brother's,
The gift he sent you today.'
'Whose, then, is that long lance yonder?
I see it as plain as day.'

'Take it my lord, O take it,
And run me through and through,
For full I merit, good master,
The death I'll receive from you.'

We could give still another version of this same theme, found in another Andalusian village; but, considering that popular poetry may not have for everyone the same charm it has for us, we shall forbear. AUTHOR'S NOTE.

Scarcely had Marysal's song ended when Stein, who had an excellent ear, took his flute and repeated it note for note. Then it was her turn to stand spellbound and absorbed, turning her head from side to side as though seeking the spot whence came that accurate and faithful echo.

"Why, it's Don Federico, blowing on a reed with holes in it," clamored the little girls.

María quickly entered the room where Stein was, and sat down to listen with the greatest attention, leaning forward with a smile on her lips and her soul in her eyes.

From that moment forward, Marysal's brusque rudeness toward Stein was converted into a measure of confidence and meekness which surprised the entire family. Aunt María, overjoyed, advised Stein to take advantage of the ascendancy he had gained over the girl to induce her to let herself be taught to employ her time in learning God's law, in working to make of herself a good Christian and a reasonable woman, born to be a housewife and the mother of a family. The old lady added that the best course to attain the desired end of taming Marysal's proud nature and her wild habits would be to ask Señorita Rosita to admit her to her school, for the girl should be tutored by a reasonable, God-fearing woman, skillful in needlework.

Stein approved of the proposal and prevailed upon Marysal to lend herself to carrying it out, promising in exchange to see her every day and entertain her with the flute.

The child's natural love for music awakened in her an extraordinary desire to cultivate it, and Stein's skill was what gave her the first impulse in that direction.

When it came to Momo's notice that Marysal was going to place herself under the tutelage of Mystical Rose to learn to sew, sweep, and cook, and especially, as he put it, to learn sense, and that the doctor was the one who had set her upon this course, he said he was immediately reminded of the story Don Federico had told him about certain men in his own land who were able to start all the rats to running away from the village when they played the pipe.

After her mother's death, Señorita Rosa had established a school for young girls, of the type known in the villages as a dame school, and called, more stylishly, an academy in the cities. The little girls in the villages attend such schools from morning to noon, and are taught only Christian doctrine and sewing. In the cities they learn to read, write, embroider, and draw. Obviously such establishments cannot be wellsprings of science, nor seed beds for artists, nor yet models of education for the emancipated woman. But on the other hand, they do turn out industrious women and excellent mothers, which is somewhat more worthwhile.

Once the sick girl was fully recovered, Stein begged her father to turn over his intractable daughter to a good woman who could take the place of the mother she had lost, and indoctrinate her in the duties appropriate to her sex.

When Señorita Rosa was asked to admit the fisherman's wild daughter to her house, her first response was a definitive no; people of her temperament are likely to react thus in such cases. But when she was given to understand the good effects such a labor of love might yield, she finally consented, as all religious people must in similiar circumstances, for to them duty is no mere convention but a straight line drawn with a firm hand.

What the unhappy woman suffered while Marysal was in her charge would hardly bear thinking about. The girl's rebellion and scoffing did not cease, and neither did the teacher's futile sermons and fruitless exhortations.

Two events wore out Señorita Rosa's patience, all the more

so because hers was not an innate virtue but one that had been laboriously acquired.

Marysal had worked up a kind of conspiracy in the ranks captained by Señorita Rosa. This conspiracy finally broke into rebellion one day, timidly and waveringly in the beginning, but daringly and high-handedly in the end. It came about as follows:

"I don't like roses by the pound!" said Marysal abruptly.

"Silence!" ordered the teacher, whose stern discipline would permit no one to speak during class hours.

Silence reigned.

Five minutes later another voice, very sharp and more than a little insolent was heard to say:

"I don't like pink roses."

"No one has asked you to," said Señorita Rosa, believing that this untimely declaration had been provoked by Marysal's.

Five minutes later another of the conspirators said, as she picked up her fallen thimble:

"I don't like white roses."

"What is the meaning of this?" exclaimed Mystical Rose then, her little dark eye shining like a ship's lantern. "Are you making fun of me?"

"I don't like rosebushes," said one of the smaller girls, instantly ducking under the table.

"Nor passion roses."

"Nor roses of Jericho."

"Nor yellow roses."

The strong clear voice of Marysal overrode all the others as she shouted:

"I can't stand dried-up roses."

"I can't stand dried-up roses," all the girls cried in chorus.

Mystical Rose, at first astonished at such insolence, got up, ran to the kitchen, and came back armed with a broom.

At sight of it, all the girls fled like a flock of birds. Mystical Rose stood alone, let the broom drop, and crossed her arms.

"Patience, Lord," she exclaimed, making a great effort to calm herself. "I've borne my nickname with resignation, as Thou didst carry Thy cross; but I yet lacked this crown of thorns. Thy holy will be done."

Perhaps she might have brought herself to forgive Marysal on this occasion if another had not arisen very soon after it. This finally forced her to make up her mind to dismiss her once and for all. It so happened that the barber's son, Ramón Pérez, a fine guitarist, used to come every night to play and sing amorous couplets beneath the sternly closed windows of the saintly lady.

"Don Modesto," she said to her boarder one day, "when you hear that locust Ramón flaying our ears with his song, please go out and tell him to take himself and his music elsewhere."

"But, Rosita," replied Don Modesto, "do you want me to offend that boy whose father (may God reward him) has been shaving me for nothing ever since I came to Villamar? And besides, you see . . . I like to hear him, for it can't be denied that he sings and plays the guitar very well indeed."

"Much good may it do you," said Señorita Rosa. "You must have noise-proof ears. I haven't. That business of coming to sing at the window of a decent woman does him no credit and is senseless besides."

Don Modesto's face mutely expressed a three-part reply. First, astonishment, which might be expressed as: "What! Ramón paying court to my landlady!" Second, doubt, as though he were saying: "Can that be possible?" Third, conviction, which might be summed up as: "The story's true then! Ramón is a daring young fellow."

"But, on second thought," went on Señorita Rosa, "don't bother, for you might catch a cold going from the warmth of your bed into the open air. It's better for you to stay still, and I'll be the one to tell that young upstart that if he wants to amuse people he'd better buy a monkey."

On the stroke of midnight, the strumming of a guitar was heard, and immediately following it, a voice singing:

My dark lady of the night
Is far lovelier than the white
Of the candid lily bright

"What nonsense!" cried Mystical Rose, getting up from her bed. "What a long account is owed to God for so much useless chatter!"

The voice went on singing:

"When you go forth to mass
  The church shines bright, my lass;
  And when you tread dry grass
  It springs up green where e'er you pass."

"God help us!" exclaimed Mystical Rose as she put on her third petticoat. "He drags the mass into his profane verses, and everyone who can hear him, knowing how close I am to the affairs of God, will say he's singing that to make a fool of me. Does that fuzz-face think he can make me a laughing-stock? This is far more than enough!"

Rosa went into the sitting room and what should she see there but Marysal peering out the window, listening to the singer with her whole attention! Rosa crossed herself, saying:

"And you not thirteen years old yet! Little girls aren't little girls any more!"

She gripped Marysal by the arm, pulled her away from the window, and took her place there, just as Ramón, striking the guitar loudly, began to bawl this verse:

"Come now to your window,
  Open wide those lovely eyes;
  Light us both with their luster,
  In the darkness hear my sighs."

And his strumming went on more violently and incoherently than before.

"I'll light you up with a brand from hell," screamed Mystical Rose shrilly and angrily. "Libertine, blasphemer, bawling and insufferable songster."

Ramón Pérez, coming to himself after the first shock, broke into a run swifter than a deer's, and never looked back.

This was the coup de grâce for Marysal. She was expelled forthwith, despite Don Modesto's timid plea on her behalf.

"Don Modesto," replied Rosita, "as the saying goes, 'burdens are burdens!' and as long as this barefaced creature was my burden, I had to account for her actions before God and man. All well and good; each has to answer for enough on his own behalf, without taking on anyone else's faults. Besides, as you see, this is a child that can't be kept to the right path; much as you try to lead her to the right, she'll always draw to the left."

CHAPTER XI

Stein remained in that peaceful backwater for three years. Adopting the temperament of the country where he was dwelling, he lived for the day, or, as the French say, *au jour le jour;* or, as his good landlady, Aunt María used to advise him in other terms, tomorrow must not spoil today, and one should take care not to let today spoil tomorrow.

During those three years the young doctor had kept up a correspondence with his family. His parents had died while he was with the army in Navarre; his sister Charlotte had married a well-to-do farmer who had made good farm helpers of his wife's two small brothers, poorly educated, but skillful and dedicated to their work. Stein thus found himself completely free, and master of his fate.

He had devoted himself to the education of the girl who owed her life to him, and though he was cultivating ungrateful and barren soil he had succeeded, by dint of patience, in causing the bud of education to sprout. But the harvest he reaped from the extraordinary musical gifts with which Nature had endowed the fisherman's daughter exceeded his hopes. Her voice was incomparable, and for Stein, a good musician, it was not difficult to guide her effectively, as the branches of the grapevine, at once flexible and vigorous, yielding and strong, can be trained.

But the teacher, who had a soft and tender heart and a propensity in his temperament for trust which bordered on blindness, fell in love with his pupil, thus adding his love to the adoration the fisherman felt for his daughter, and the admiration the girl had aroused in Aunt María; both of them exerted a certain sympathetic and communicative force which was bound to influence an open, well-disposed, and gentle spirit like Stein's. He convinced himself, like Pedro Santaló, that the girl was an angel, and like Aunt María, that she was a marvel. Stein was one of those men who can go to a masquerade ball and not remind himself that behind the absurd faces, the painted, cardboard features, are other faces and other features given each masked one by Nature.

So that if Santaló was blinded by his highly emotional love and Aunt María by her own consummate goodness, Stein was eventually blinded by both of them.

Yet in the end it was Marysal's pure, sweet, flexible, and expressive voice that most attracted him.

He used to say to himself when he was alone: "A girl who can interpret the most sublime feeling so eloquently must have an exalted soul."

But as the grain of wheat will sprout in rich soil and send out roots before the spears rise into the daylight, so this tranquil and sincere love sent out roots in Stein's heart. His love was sensed, rather than clearly defined.

For her part, Marysal had grown fond of Stein, too, not from gratitude for his efforts, nor because she could appreciate his superior natural gifts, nor yet because she was able to grasp the greatness of his spirit and intelligence, nor even in response to the attraction exerted by love on the person who inspires it, but only because she felt gratitude, admiration, attraction to, and inspiration from the musician—the teacher who had initiated her into her art. Moreover, the isolation of her life kept her away from anyone else who might have been able to dispute her preference for him: Don Modesto was not of an age to compete in the arena of love; Momo, who was not only unusually ugly, still retained his animosity toward Marysal. He had never ceased to call her the Sea Gull, while she looked upon him with the utmost scorn. True, lads were not lacking in the village, beginning with the barber's son who continued to sigh for her. But none of them was at all equipped to compete with Stein.

Three summers and three winters had passed in this tranquil state of affairs, like three calm nights and days, when what we are about to relate took place.

In tranquil Villamar (who would have thought it?) an intrigue was shaping up; its promoter and guiding spirit (who would have believed it?) was Aunt María; the partner (who would not be astonished?) was Don Modesto.

Even though it be an indiscretion, or, more accurately, an indignity, to eavesdrop, let us listen to them in the garden hidden behind an orange tree whose trunk remained sound while its leaves had fallen and its blossoms faded, as resignation remains in the heart after gaiety has fled and hope has died; let us listen, we repeat, to the colloquy wherein the two conspirators take counsel, while Brother Gabriel, a thousand miles away though right beside them, is tying up the heads of lettuce with string so they may grow white and tender.

"I'm not imagining it, Don Modesto," said the instigator, "it's a fact; you'd have to lack eyes in your head to miss seeing it. Don Federico is in love with Marysal, and the doctor is no mere bag of straw to her."

"Who wants to think about love affairs, Aunt María?" answered Don Modesto, in whose calm and serene existence the eternal, classical and invariable axiom of an inseparable alliance between Mars and Cupid had never been realized. "Who thinks about love?" repeated Don Modesto in the same tone as he would have said: "Who's thinking of a game of billiards, or of flying a kite?"

"Young people, of course, Don Modesto, young people; and if they didn't the world would come to an end. But the truth is that these two need a prick of the spur, for in my opinion that pair up yonder there are as slow as molasses. It's two years now since our man fell in love with his nightingale, as he calls her. That's as plain as daylight, and I'd be willing to bet that he's never so much as said, 'What fine eyes you have.' You, a man of authority, a gentleman for whom Don Federico has so high a regard, ought to drop him a hint on the subject, a word of good advice, for their own good and for the good of us all."

"Forgive me, Aunt María," replied Don Modesto, "but Ramón Pérez comes between me and a thing like that. He's a friend whom I don't want to hurt. He shaves me just for my honest face, and I'd be doing him a bad turn to get involved and to sponsor someone else. Seeing that Marysal doesn't love him, he's very much hurt, and he's grown so thin and pale it breaks your heart. The other day he said that if he couldn't marry Marysal, he'd smash his guitar and join the rebels since he couldn't become a monk now. You can see, Aunt María, that anything I might do would compromise me in the matter."

"Señor," said Aunt María, "how can you possibly take seriously what people in love will say? If Ramón Pérez, poor young fellow, is incapable of killing a sparrow, how do you think he could kill Christians? Just think that if Don Federico marries he'll stay here always; and wouldn't that be a good thing for everyone? I tell you it wrings my heart to hear him talk of leaving. Luckily, we've been able to get it out of his head so far. And what would become of the girl? You must know that Don Federico earns very good fees. When he attended the son of the mayor, Don Perfecto, and made him well, the mayor gave him a hundred *reales* like a hundred stars. What a fine couple they'd make, Commander!"

"I don't say they wouldn't, Aunt María," replied Don Modesto, "but don't assign me a role in the affair, and let me keep my strict neutrality. I'm not two-faced; I have only the one that Ramón shaves, and no other."

At that moment, Marysal came into the orchard. She was indeed no longer the little girl whom we met all dishevelled and ragged. Neatly dressed and with her hair beautifully combed, she would come to the convent every morning, drawn there, if not by affection and gratitude to those who lived there, at least by the desire to listen and learn music from Stein, plus the wish to leave the cottage and thus escape the boredom of being alone there with her father, who did not amuse her.

"Where's Don Federico?" she asked as she came in.

"He hasn't come back from his sick calls," replied Aunt María. "He was going to vaccinate more than a dozen children today. What a thing, Don Modesto! As he told it, he took the pus from the cow's teat, for cows have an antitoxin against smallpox! It must be true, because Don Federico says so."

"It's quite true," said Don Modesto, "and it was invented by a Swiss. When I was in Gaeta I saw the Pope's Swiss Guard; but none of them mentioned being the inventor."

"If I were His Holiness," went on Aunt María, "I'd reward the inventor with a plenary indulgence. Sit down, little grain of salt, I've been hungering to see you."

"No," replied Marysal, "I'm going."

"Where can you go to be loved better than you are here?"

"What do I care whether or not I'm loved?" replied Marysal. "What's there for me to do here if Don Federico's not here?"

"So that's it! You come here only to see Don Federico, do you, little ingrate?"

"Why else should I come?" replied Marysal. "To look for Momo with his eyes, his face, and his soul all twisted?"

"So you love Don Federico very much, then?" asked the good old lady again.

"I like him," replied Marysal. "If it weren't for him, I wouldn't set foot here, so I wouldn't have to meet that demon, Momo, who has a sting like a wasp in his tongue."

"And what about Ramón Pérez?" asked Aunt María teasingly, as if to convince Don Modesto that his protégé should put his hopes among the archives.

Marysal burst out laughing.

"If that Pérez the Mouse" she said, using Momo's nickname for the little barber, "were to fall into a whirlpool, I wouldn't be the little ant to sing and weep for him,[26] and particularly I wouldn't listen to him singing, because his singing attacks my nervous system, as Don Federico says, and he assures me that I have a nervous system tighter than the strings on a guitar. Let me show you how that Pérez the Mouse sings, Aunt María."

Marysal picked up an agave leaf off the ground with a quick movement. It was one of those Brother Gabriel used to place like a screen in front of the newly set tomato plants to keep the north wind off them. Fitting this to her arm, like a guitar, she began to mimic Ramón Pérez in a grotesque manner, and with her singular talent for mockery, she sang thus in his style of trilling and warbling:

'What ails you, man of God?
    You are so thin, and you si-i-gh.'

---

[26] El Ratón Pérez, Pérez the Mouse, was the subject of a folk-tale; hence Momo's nickname which is also a play on the sound of "Ramón."

Alas, I have lifted my eyes,
To a castle there on hi-i-gh!'

"Yes," said Don Modesto, recalling the serenade outside Rosita's window, "poor Ramon has always lifted his too high."

Subsequent events had never served to dissuade Don Modesto from his belief that Rosita was the subject of the aforementioned serenades; for, once an idea had entered Don Modesto's head, it lay there as if in a piggy bank. The pigeon-holes of his mind were so narrow and so well kept that an idea, having found its proper slot, stayed in place, embossed and encrusted *per in saecula saeculorum.*[27]

"I'm going," said Marysal, tossing away the agave leaf so that it struck Brother Gabriel with a sharp crack. He was stooping over with his back to them, tying his umpteenth string.

"Goodness," exclaimed Brother Gabriel, startled; but immediately he went back to tying his strings, without another word.

"What a good shot!" said Marysal, laughing. "Don Modesto, you can make me a gunner when you get the cannon for your fort."

"Those things aren't funny, Marysal; they're mean tricks, and you know I don't like them," said the good old lady crossly. "You may say what you like to me, but leave Brother Gabriel alone; that's all he asks of life."

"Come, don't be angry, Aunt María," answered the Sea Gull. "Console yourself that nothing about Brother Gabriel is made of glass except his spectacles. Commander, tell Señorita Mystical Rose she must move her school to your fort as

---

[27] Forever and ever, amen.

soon as you get some twenty-four pounders so the girls can be well guarded against the snares of the devil, planted by him in out-of-tune guitars. I'm going, since Don Federico hasn't come; I'll bet he's vaccinating the whole village, including Señorita Mystical Rose, the schoolmaster, and the mayor."

But the good old lady, accustomed to Marysal's bad manners, which consequently did not bother her, called the girl to her and told her to sit down beside her.

Don Modesto, inferring that the good woman was about to roll out the heavy artillery, said good-bye, made a half turn to the right and sounded the retreat, still clinging to his promised neutrality, but not before Aunt María had given him a couple of heads of lettuce and a bunch of radishes.

"My child," said the good old woman when they were alone, "why shouldn't you marry Don Federico, so you can be the Señora Doctor, and the happiest of women, with that man who is a Saint Luis Gonzaga,[28] who knows so much, who plays the flute so well and earns such good fees? You could be dressed like a lady, given food and drink like an heiress, and above all, my child, you could take care of your poor father, who is growing old. It's a worry now to see him going out to sea in rain, shine, or wind, just so you won't lack anything. Don Federico would stay with us, then, consoling and healing the sick, like the angel he is."

Marysal listened to the old lady with close attention, although she pretended she was watching something. When the old woman had finished speaking, the girl was quiet for a time, and then said indifferently:

"I don't want to be married."

---

[28] An Italian Jesuit of the Gonzaga family of Mantua who was canonized for the miracles he performed during his short life.

"Listen to her!" cried Aunt María. "Perhaps you'd like to be a nun, eh?"

Nor that either!" said the Sea Gull.

"Well, then," asked Aunt María, astonished, "Dont you want to be either fish or fowl? I've never heard the like! A woman, my child, must belong either to God or to a man; otherwise she fails in her vocation, both above, and below."

"Well, what do you want, señora? I have no vocation, either as a married woman or as a nun."

"Well, child," replied Aunt María, "it must be your vocation then to be a mule. Mariquita, I myself don't like anything that is out of the ordinary; and its especially bad for a woman not to do what the others do. Indeed, if I were a man I'd run away from a woman like that the same as I'd run from a wild bull. After all, your life is your own; you'll have to settle things for yourself. But," she added with her usual kindliness, "you're very young yet and you'll still have more turns to make than a key."

Marysal got up and left.

"Yes!" she was thinking as she tied her kerchief around her head. "he loves me; I know that already. But . . . it's as Brother Gabriel loves Aunt María, that is, it's the way old people love. I'll bet he wouldn't let himself get wet under my window for fear of catching cold. Now if he were to marry me, he'd give me a good life, it's true! He'd let me do whatever I please, he'd play his flute for me whenever I asked him to, and he'd buy me anything I'd want or anything I'd fancy. If I were his wife, I'd have a big, silk shawl, like Uncle Juan López's daughter, and a blond lace mantilla from Almagro, like the mayor's wife. Everyone would be green with envy. But Don Federico, who melts like bacon in a frying pan when he hears me sing, would as soon think of marrying me as Don

Modesto would think of marrying his beloved Rosa . . . the witch!"

During all this fine soliloquy there was not one thought nor one recollection of her father, whose well-being and relief had been the foremost reason adduced by Aunt María.

CHAPTER XII

Aunt María, convinced that she could expect neither support nor aid from the "gentleman of influence" with whom she had wished to associate herself in her matrimonial enterprise, made up her mind to carry it out all by herself, like Samson before the Philistines, confident of being able to overcome Maria's objections as well as whatever objections Don Federico might raise. Nothing discouraged her, neither Marysal's coldness nor Stein's inaction; for love is as persistent as a sister of charity and as intrepid as a hero; and love was the great moving force behind everything that excellent woman did. So it was that, without so much as a by-your-leave she said one day to Stein:

"Do you realize, Don Federico, that Marysal was here a few days ago and told us very plainly, with the wit that God gave her, that she comes here only to see you? What do you think of such frankness?"

"I think it would be sheer ingratitude, if it's true, and my nightingale isn't capable of that; it must have been one of her jokes."

"The thing is, Don Federico, that you can't put an old head on young shoulders, and the race goes to the swift. Does it seem to you so bad to be loved, my dear sir?"

"No, certainly not; we agree on that adage you often quote: 'Love never says enough.' But . . . Aunt María, I've always been better at giving love than at taking it."

"Don't tell me that!" exclaimed the good woman vigorously.

"No, truly, dear Aunt María," replied Stein, taking the

old woman's hand and pressing it between his. "Our feelings for each other are mutual, but I'm far behind in being able to show mine; I wish I were able to give you back some of my affection and my gratitude!"

"That's easy enough then, Don Federico, and I'm going to ask you to prove it."

"At once, my dear Aunt María; and what is the proof you want? Tell me quickly."

"That you stay with us, and that in order to do that you marry, Don Federico; in that way you'd relieve us of the constant dread we live in that you'll want to go back to your own country; for, as the saying goes: 'Where is your country?' 'Where my wife is.' "

Stein smiled.

"I marry?" he said. "But whom, my good Aunt María?"

"Whom? Who would it be? Your nightingale; that way you'd feel eternal spring in your heart. She's so beautiful, so fascinating, so well moulded to your ways that she could neither live without you nor you without her! And of course you love each other now like two turtle-doves. That's plain as daylight!"

"I'm old for her Aunt María," replied Stein, sighing and blushing as he realized that the good woman was correct about his feelings. "I'm old," he said again, "for a girl of sixteen, and my heart was hurt once; to spare myself I'd like to lead a quiet and tranquil life, and not expose my heart to new wound's."

"Old!" cried Aunt María. "What nonsense! Why, you're hardly thirty years old! Come, that's a ridiculous reason, Don Federico."

"What more could I ask," replied Stein, "than to enjoy with an innocent young girl the sweet and blessed domestic happiness which is the true, the only perfect, solid happiness a man can enjoy, and which is blessed by God, for it is what He has marked out for us. But, Aunt María, she can't be in love with me!"

"That's more like it! My word, the girl who falls in love with you, Don Federico, will have a very discriminating taste. Lord! Don't deny it; it would be foolish. The woman you love will surely be the happiest in the whole world."

"Do you think so, my dear Aunt María?"

"As I live and breathe, Don Federico. Anyone who wouldn't ought to be roasted alive."

On the following morning when Marysal came into the courtyard, she met Momo face to face. He was sitting on a millstone, breakfasting on bread and sardines.

"Here already, Sea Gull?" was Momo's suave welcome. "Some day we're going to find you in our boiled dinner at this rate. Don't you have anything to do at home?"

"I dropped it all," answered the girl, "to come and see your face which has bewitched me, and those ears that are the envy of *Golondrina*. Say, do you know why you have such big ears? When Father Adam found himself in Paradise with all the animals, he gave each one its name; your kind he named donkeys. A few days later he got the animals together and asked each one his name. All of them answered except your species which didn't even know its own name. Father Adam got so annoyed with him that he took the forgetful one by the ears and shouted at him as he pulled them out very long: 'Your name is doooonkey!'"

It was Marysal's luck that at the first bellow Momo uttered with all the strength of his ample lungs, he choked on a mouthful of bread and sardines, which brought on such a fit of coughing that she could escape him as swiftly as a real sea gull eludes the vulture.

"Good morning, my nightingale,'" said Stein, who had come into the courtyard at the sound of her voice.

"A nightingale, say you," muttered Momo between bouts of coughing. "Nightingale! She's the most tiresome locust hatched in any summer!"

"Come, Marysal," continued Stein. "Come and do your writing and read the verses I translated yesterday. Wouldn't you like to?"

"I don't remember them," she answered. "Were they the ones about a country where the orange blossom grows? They don't fit here, for these dried up because Brother Gabriel's tears weren't enough to water them. Lay aside verses, Don Federico, and play me Weber's *Nocturne,* with the words that go: 'Listen, listen my beloved, the song of the nightingale is heard; on every branch a flower blooms; before the bird is still, and the flowers fade, listen, listen, my beloved.'"

"Such big words that Sea Gull has learned!" muttered Momo. "They suit her like candy in a garlic grinder."

"After you've done your reading, I'll play the serenade by Karl von Weber," said Stein, who was able to persuade Marysal to learn what he wanted to teach her only by that kind of bribe.

She reluctantly took the paper that Stein handed her and began to read easily, though unwillingly, the following poem:

IN THE RETREAT
(Translation from the German poet, Salis)

'In the soft shade of the retreat I found peace, that peace which both softens and strengthens us, and which looks with *calm eyes at the blows of fate as the saint looks at the sepulchre.*

Sweet forgetfulness of the march of time, soft withdrawal from mankind, where you come to love them more than when you are among them. Gently you draw from the wound the dart that injustice has shot into the soul.

He who tolerates and appreciates, he who asks much of himself and little of others, will find the softest leaves of the olive tree budding for him, and with them he will crown his brow.

As for me, crown my household gods with lotus, and the cares of the future will not fall across my threshold, for the prudent man confines his happiness within a small circle.'

"Marysal," Stein said when the girl had finished the reading, "you, who do not know the world, can't judge how much profound truth lies in those verses, and how much philosophy. Do you remember that I explained to you what philosophy is?"

"Yes, sir," she answered. "The science of being happy. But for that, sir, there are no worthwhile rules nor any science; each person understands in his own way how to be happy. Don Modesto when they mount cannon in his fort, which is as dilapidated as he is; Brother Gabriel when they restore his convent, his prior, and his bells; Aunt María as long as you stay here; my father when he gets a good catch of congers; and Momo when he's making all the mischief he can."

Stein burst out laughing, and placing his hand affectionately on her shoulder, he said:

"And what about you? Where does yours lie?"

Marysal hesitated a moment over her reply, raised her big eyes to Stein, lowered them again, looked askance at Momo, smiled inwardly to see that his ears were redder than tomatoes, and finally answered:

"What about you, Don Federico; where would your happiness lie? In going back home?"

"No," Stein replied.

"Well, where then?" she persisted.

"I'll tell you, my nightingale," Stein answered, "but first you must tell me, what would yours consist of?"

"In listening to you play forever," she answered sincerely.

At that moment Aunt María came out of the kitchen with the good intention of putting a match to the kindling; like many another she smothered the very thing she wanted through an excess of zeal.

"Don't you see, Don Federico," she said, "what a beautiful girl Marysal is and how she's filled out?"

Hearing these words from his grandmother, Momo muttered as he bit the head off a sardine:

"She's just like her father's fishing pole! Arms and legs that make her as graceful as a grasshopper, tall enough and dry enough to make a cross-bar for my door. Aaaaah!"

"Go away, you lout, you fatty; you look like a cabbage without a stalk," replied the Sea Gull in a low voice.

"Yes, yes," Stein answered Aunt María. "She's lovely, her eyes are the sort the Arabs have so often mentioned."

"They look like two chestnut burrs, and they prickle with every glance," grumbled Momo.

"And this pretty mouth that sings like an angel?" went on Aunt María, taking her protégée's face in her hands.

"Look!" said Momo, "a mouth like a basket that spits out toads and snakes."

"And what about your pig's snout?" said Marysal with a fury she could no longer contain. "Your awful snout that reaches from ear to ear, or would if your face wasn't so wide it gets tired half-way there."

For reply, Momo sang on three different notes: "Sea Gull! Sea Gull! Sea Gull!"

"Flat Nose! Flat Nose! Flat Nose! Snub nose, nose like a duck's tail," sang Maria in her magnificent voice.

"How can you possibly pay attention to what Momo says just to annoy you, Marysal?" said Stein. "His jokes are foolish and rude, but without malice."

"That's a thing he has too much of and that you lack, Don Federico," replied the girl. "And I may as well tell you that I don't intend to put up with that dolt who's harder than a rock, more prickly than a briar patch, and rougher than rawhide. So I'm leaving."

So saying, the Sea Gull departed and Stein followed her.

"You're a shameless rascal," said Aunt María to her grandson. "There's more gall in your heart than warm blood in your veins. Those who wear skirts must be respected, you wretch! There's no one in the whole village as wayward and unloving as you are!"

"You're so set on reforming that beachcomber," replied Momo. "She made my ears like this, but she's aces high with the rest of you? Only the devil can tell what kind of a spell that jellyfish[29] has cast to make such fools of you and Don Federico. Fancy a sea gull knowing how to read and write! Has anyone ever seen the like? That's why that big lazy thing who cares for nothing all day long but making her voice quaver like water bubbling over the fire, won't so much as cook a meal for her father; he has to cook for himself; nor does she take care of her clothes; you have to take care of them. But her

[29] Agua-mala is the common name of a marine polyp which surrounds itself with a glutinous matter that floats in the sea. Contact with it will cause a sharp sting, similar to a nettle sting. AUTHOR'S NOTE.

father, and you, and Don Federico don't know where to put her, and you'd like His Holiness to canonize her. She'll pay you back! She'll pay you back! Just wait! You're raising a crow. . . ."

Stein had overtaken Marysal and was saying to her:

"Mariquita, what's the use of all I've tried to do to enlighten your mind if you haven't even achieved the little self-control needed to rise above foolish talk of no value nor importance?"

"Listen, Don Federico," replied the girl. "I understand that self-control will help me by making others think more of me, not less."

"My word, Marysal, how can you possibly twist the reins so? What self-control teaches is precisely not to deck yourself with laurels, and not to rebel against injustice. But," he added, smiling, "the things you say come from your almost infantile years, and from your effervescent Southern blood. By the time you have gray hairs like me you'll have learned how little such things matter. Have you noticed my gray hairs, Marysal?"

"Yes," she replied.

"Well, I'm quite young; but suffering ages the head very rapidly. My heart has stayed young, Mariquita, and I'd offer you the flowers of springtime if I weren't afraid that the sad signs of winter which whiten my brow would frighten you."

"It's true," she answered, unable to control her natural impulse, "that a gray-haired suitor looks ridiculous."

"I thought so," Stein said sadly. "My heart is faithful, and Aunt María was mistaken when she assured me happiness was possible and raised hopes in my heart, as a flower is born in the air, without roots, alone in the breath of the breeze."

Marysal now saw that by her rudeness she had rejected a

spirit too delicate to insist, a man so modest as to believe that a single objection was enough to cancel his other advantages. Abruptly she said:

"If a suitor with gray hair looks ridiculous, gray hairs on a husband don't look so bad."

Stein was greatly surprised by that brusque sally, the more so at the decisiveness and lack of emotion with which it was voiced. Then he smiled and said:

"Would you marry me, then, you lovely child of Nature?"

"Why not?" replied the Sea Gull.

"Mariquita," said Stein with feeling, "she who accepts a man for a husband and unites herself with him for her entire life, or to put it better, makes their two lives one, as two wicks of a candle will burn with a common light, does him greater service than the woman who takes him as a lover."

"What's the sense of flirting in the window?" said Marysal with a mixture of innocence and indifference, "And what good are guitar players, if they play and sing badly enough to scare away the cats?"

They had come to the beach and Stein begged her to sit down beside him on some stones. They were silent for a long time. Stein was deeply moved; Marysal, bored, had picked up a stick and was drawing figures with it in the sand.

"How Nature speaks to the heart of man!" said Stein at last. "What a bond unites all that God has created! A pure life is like a calm day; a life of unleashed passions like a stormy one. Look at those clouds moving slow and dark to come between the sun and the earth; they're like duty, which comes between the heart and an illicit love, chilling the heart with its cold but pure, clear rays. Lucky the earth not shadowed by their rolling! But our happiness will be as changeless as the skies of May; for you will always love me, won't you, Mari-quita?"

Marysal, whose rough, tempestuous spirit never felt the poetry or the ascetic sentiments of Stein, had no desire to reply. But since she could not avoid some sort of answer, she wrote in the sand with the stick she was using to distract her idle mind, "Always!"

Stein, mistaking her indifference for modesty, went on with feeling:

"Look at the sea. Can you hear its waves murmuring with a voice full of enchantment and terror? They seem to be imparting grave secrets in an unknown tongue. The waves, Mariquita, are those seductive and terrible sirens that the fertile imagination of the Greeks created out of fantasy, beautiful creatures without hearts, as seductive as they were terrible, who drew men to their own destruction with their sweet voices. But you, Mariquita, you don't attract me with your sweet voice only to repay me with ingratitude; no, you'll be the siren in attractiveness but not in perfidy. Isn't that so, Mariquita, that you'll never be unfaithful?"

"Never!" she wrote in the sand; and the waves took pleasure in erasing the words as though mimicking the power of the years, which are the waves of time and which gradually erase from the heart what one feels certain is engraved on it forever, as the waves erase the sand.

"Why don't you answer me with your sweet voice?" said Stein to her.

"What do you wish, Don Federico?" she answered. "My throat knots up at the thought of telling a man I love him. I'm dry and undemonstrative, as Aunt María says, but she doesn't love me the less for that; everyone is as God made him. I'm like my father, not a talker."

"Well, if you're like your father, I want nothing more, for good Uncle Pedro—I'll call him my father, Mariquita— has a heart too loving for any human breast. Hearts like his belong in the diaphanous breasts of the angels, and in those of chosen men."

"My father a chosen man!" said Marysal to herself, hardly able to restrain a mocking smile. "Well, let it go! It's better if he thinks so."

"Listen, Mariquita," said Stein, approaching her, "let's offer up our pure and blessed love to God; let us promise Him to make it pleasing by our faithfulness in complying with all the duties imposed when it is consecrated at His altar; and let me embrace you as my wife and companion."

"No, not that!" said Marysal taking a quick step backward and frowning, "no one can touch me."

"Very well, my pretty shy one," Stein answered softly, "I respect your delicacy, and I bow to your wishes. As one of your ancient and divine poets says, the greatest happiness lies in loving obedience, doesn't it?"

CHAPTER XIII

When the fisherman saw the man who had saved his daughter so deeply interested in her, his gratitude changed into an idealistic friendship comparable only with the admiration aroused in him by Stein's great natural endowments.

The rude seaman and the polished scholar had been congenial since they met; for people with similar good inclinations are attracted when they come together, and conquering distance, immediately hail each other as brothers.

Consequently when Stein offered himself as a son-in-law, the good father was speechless with joy, but deeply moved in his heart, and the only thing he asked of Stein, taking his hand, was to let them go on living in the cottage; Stein consented gladly. Then the fisherman seemed to regain the strength and suppleness of youth in order to set about improving, tidying, and beautifying their dwelling. He cleared out the little attic, to which he retired, leaving the second-floor rooms for his children. He whitewashed and painted the walls, leveled the floor and later covered it with a handsome palm-leaf matting which he wove, and finally turned over to Aunt María the task of choosing appropriate, simple furniture.

The news of Stein's wedding aroused equally great rejoicing among all the people who knew and loved him. Aunt María could not sleep for three nights out of sheer delight. She prophesied that none of the inhabitants of that part of the country would die of anything but old age as long as Don Federico was going to be living there.

Brother Gabriel was manifestly so pleased with the decision and especially with seeing Aunt María so happy, that, overflowing with her sentiments, he ventured to make a joke, the first and last in his life. He remarked in a low voice that the priest was going to forget the *De Profundis*.[30]

This mild jest pleased Aunt María so much that for a fortnight she could talk with no living soul without immediately quoting it, to the honor and glory of her protégé; but the astonishing success of his joke caused the monk so much embarrassment that he took a vow never to fall into the temptation of making another as long as he lived.

Don Modesto was of the opinion that the Sea Gull had drawn first prize in the lottery, and the villagers second prize; for if he had met a surgeon as clever as Stein at the siege of Gaeta, he would not be crippled in one arm.

The opinion of Dolores was that, if the fisherman had twice saved his daughter's life, God's will had twice given the girl happiness, in alloting to her such a fáther and such a husband.

Manuel noted that there was a cake kept in heaven for men who never repented of being husbands; and that thus far no one had tasted it. His wife replied that that was because Saint Peter had promised Saint Genevieve that husbands wouldn't go to heaven.

As for Momo, he maintained that if the Sea Gull had found a husband, all the ills of the world need not lose hope of finding their mates, too.

Mystical Rose took it in her own fashion. Marysal had added to her catalogue of grievances with another of recent date. The month of May had arrived, and some pious ladies were meeting to sing couplets in honor of the Virgin, to the accompaniment of a broken-down clavichord played by the

---

[30] Psalm 130, which begins: "Out of the depths have I cried unto Thee, O Lord."

old, blind organist. Rosita presided over this musical and religious gathering. A few pure and pleasant voices joined in the chorus with hers which was, inevitably, shrill and rasping. Rosa, not unaware of Marysal's great talent, buried the hatchet in deference to the month of Mary, and decided to make use of Don Modesto as mediator to ask the fisherman's daughter to take part in that Virginal choir.

Don Modesto grasped his walking stick and started on his way.

Marysal could hardly be called pious, and was not at all fond of practicing her art under that particular keyboard master. She answered the veteran with a flat and final no.

This monosyllable was more terrifying than a cannonade to Don Modesto; he did not know what to do.

Don Modesto was one of those kind-hearted men with a sincere desire for the good of his friends, but he lacked both the necessary courage to achieve his end, and sufficient imagination to find the means.

"Uncle Pedro," he said to the fisherman after that peremptory rejection, "I'm shaking in my boots. What shall I tell Rosita? What will the priest say? What will people say? Couldn't you find some way to persuade your daughter?"

"She doesn't want to! What can I do?" replied the fisherman.

Accordingly, poor Don Modesto had to resign himself to being the bearer of bad tidings, bound not only to offend but to scandalize his mystical landlady.

"I'd a thousand times rather face all the batteries of Gaeta than face Rosita with this no on my lips," he was saying as he went back to Villamar. "Lord, how she's going to take on!"

He was right; in vain did he adorn his message with a mollifying exordium; in vain did he annotate it with explanatory footnotes; in vain embellish it with flowery paraphrase; Rosita was nonetheless deeply offended, and exclaimed in a sententious tone:

"He who has received gifts from Heaven and fails to employ them in its service, deserves to lose them."

Consequently, when she learned of the proposed marriage, she said, heaving a sigh and raising her eyes to the skies:

"Poor Don Federico! So good, so devout, so blessed! May God grant them happiness, as only He can, for nothing is beyond His omnipotence."

With characteristic malice, Momo took pleasure in conveying the news of the wedding to Ramón Pérez.

"Listen, Pérez Mouse," said he, "now you can eat onions till they come out of your ears, for the devil has tempted Don Federico, and he's going to marry the Sea Gull."

"Honestly?" exclaimed the barber in consternation.

"Does that surprise you? I was even more surprised. Some people have their taste in their mouths! Just think of pledging yourself to that heartless girl who looks like a snake on two feet, shooting sparks from her eyes and poison from her mouth! But with Don Federico, it's a case of that old saying: 'he who marries late, marries badly.' "

"It doesn't surprise me that Don Federico loves her," answered Ramón Pérez. "But what does surprise me is that Marysal should love that ungainly fellow, that tow-head with a face like an orange and eyes like a dead fish. That ungrateful girl ought to bear in mind that 'whoever goes far away to marry, goes either deceived, or to deceive.' "

"I'll take my oath it won't be the first, for he is one of the good ones; that goes without saying. But that black-hearted girl has fooled him with her singing that goes on from sunrise to sunset. And that's all she does. I already told him: 'Don

Federico, the old saying is 'take a house with a hearth, and a woman who knows how to spin,' but he paid me no heed. As for you, Pérez Mouse, your nose is more out of joint than a swordfish."

"It's always been plain to see," replied the barber, turning the peg of his guitar so tight that the treble string broke, "that someone would come from the outside to throw us out of the house. But let me tell you, Momo, it doesn't matter a straw to me. It takes all kinds to make a world. The king is dead; long live the king."

And setting himself to strumming his guitar furiously, he sang in an arrogant voice:

"They say you do not love me;
  I don't care a bit!
  A mulberry stain can be covered
  By a fresh one over it!

Your ungrateful love
  Isn't worth a sou;
  I'll find a new love for myself
  And get revenge on you."

CHAPTER XIV

The wedding of Stein and the Sea Gull took place in the church in Villamar. The fisherman was wearing a white, stiffly starched shirt in place of his red flannel one, and a new jacket of blue homespun, in which he felt so embarrassingly dressed up he could scarcely move.

Don Modesto, one of the witnesses, appeared in the full pomp of his old uniform, worn out with much brushing. Its owner having grown thin, it was too big for him. The nankeen trousers which Mystical Rose had washed for the thousandth time and rinsed in straw-water, which unfortunately wasn't the Fountain of Youth, had shrunk so much that they came half-way up his leg. His epaulets had turned copper-colored. His tricorn, with its stiff shape unaltered by the passage of forty years, occupied its lofty perch with dignity. But at the same time the Cross of Honor, bravely won on the field of battle, shone on the honorable chest of the poor disabled man, like a pure diamond in a damaged setting.

As usual, the women were dressed in black for the ceremony, but they changed their dresses for the festivities. Marysal was in white. Aunt María and Dolores wore dresses which Stein had given them for the occasion. They were of cotton tissue, smuggled in from Gibraltar. The design was in the current mode called "Rainbow" because it was a meeting ground of the most clashing colors, least apt to harmonize with one another. It almost seemed as though the manufacturer had intended to make fun of his Andalusian customers. In short, all of them, except Momo, were gotten up in their best, but he did not care to be bothered about an occasion like that one. This gave the Sea Gull some reason to say to him:

"You did right, you clown. It's like that thing that goes: 'Though you dress a monkey in silk, he'll still belong with his ilk.' I need you at my wedding as dogs are needed at mass."

"I suppose you imagine that when you get to be a doctor's wife, you won't be a Sea Gull any more," replied Momo, "and that because you're all fixed up, you're pretty. Yes, you're pretty all right in that white dress. If you put on a red cap, you'd look like a match."

Then he started to sing in an off-key voice:

"You're white as a crow,
  Pretty as the dead,
  You're pink as white wax
  And fat as a thread."

Marysal riposted immediately:

"Your mouth's like a basket—
  For setting clothes to bleach;
  You teeth are like pendants—
  They have three dangles each."

Then she turned her back on him.

Momo, never the man to be left behind in bandying invective and insult, replied angrily:

"Go on, go on, let them give you their blessing; it'll be the first time you've been blest in your whole life, and I'll bet it will be the last."

The wedding took place in the village, in Aunt María's house, for the fisherman's cottage was too small to hold such a crowd. Stein, who had put aside some savings from his professional practice (although for the most part, his treatments were free) wanted to make a great celebration of the wedding, and to provide entertainment for everyone; consequently, there were three guitars and a great abundance of wine, of *mistela*,[31] biscuits, and cakes. The guests danced, sang, drank, shouted and made the usual rustic jokes and witticisms.

Aunt María came and went, serving the drinks and playing the role of godmother at the wedding. All the while she never stopped saying:

"I'm as happy as if I were the bride."

To which Brother Gabriel unfailingly added:

"I'm as happy as if I were the bridegroom."

"Mother," said Manuel as she went past him, "the color of that dress is very gay for a widow."

"Be still, long tongue," his mother replied. "Everything ought to be gay on a day like this; besides, you don't look a gift horse in the mouth. Here, Brother Gabriel, take this glass of *mistela* and this cake. Drink a toast to the newlyweds before you go back to the convent."

"I'll drink to the health of the newlyweds before I go back to the convent," said Brother Gabriel.

After draining the glass, he slipped away, and no one except Aunt María noticed either his presence or his absence.

The gathering was growing more animated.

"A toast!" shouted the sacristan, who was very short, bent, and lame.

Everyone was quiet for the announcement.

"I drink," he said, "to the health of the newlyweds, to the health of everyone in this honorable company, and to the repose of the souls of the blessed."

---

[31] A kind of punch made of wine, water, sugar, and cinnamon.

"Bravo! Let's drink! Hurrah for the province of La Mancha, which yields wine instead of water!"

"It's your turn, Ramón Pérez; give us a song and don't save your voice for a better occasion."

"For the bride: best wishes
  I certainly bring;
  For the groom: except envy
  I have not a thing."

"Good! Well said!" they all shouted. "Now for the fandango! Everybody dance!"

At the opening strains of that eminently national dance, a man and a woman spring simultaneously to their feet, taking a position facing each other. They executed their graceful movements almost without moving from the spot, with elegant twists of the body, marking time with the gay clicking of the castanets. After a time the two dancers yielded their place to another couple who came forward as the first couple withdrew. This was repeated again and again, according to the custom of the country.

Meanwhile, the guitarist was singing:

"The girl went to church
  And there 'Yes' she said;
  The girl went in single
  And came out wed."

"A toast!" shouted a man who was considered a wit. "I drink to the health of the quack who was sent to this country so we could all live longer than Methusaleh; with the condition that when the time comes he won't try to prolong the life of my wife and my purgatory."

This speech brought an explosion of *vivas* and clapping.

"And what have you to say to all this, Manuel?" they shouted.

"What I have to say," replied Manuel, "is that I have nothing to say."

"You can't get away with that. If you're going to keep mum, go to the church. Give us a toast and look alive."

Manuel took a glass of *mistela* and said:

"I drink to the newlyweds, to our friends, to our commander and to the resurrection of Saint Christopher."

"Long live the Commander! Long live the Commander!" shouted the crowd. "And you, Manuel, give us a verse. You know how to do it."

Manuel sang the following:

"Man, be careful when you wed
 A girl who's young and gay;
 Fear will never leave you, man,
 Until you're old and gray."

After he had sung several other verses, he said he'd played the comedian long enough.

"Manuel, sing some of those nonsense rhymes that have no meaning; you know how to say things with a good swing, and all the more so when you're tipsy. Give us a stanza in honor of the newlyweds, and take that glass of wine to loosen your tongue."

Manuel took the glass of wine and recited:

"Come to me, my solace,
 Cheer me when I pine;
 Grown among green leaves,
 And trampled into wine.

Come, warm my warbling throat,
And make my tones so fine
That I may toast the newlyweds,
And drain this glass of mine."

"Now it's your turn, Ramón, my lad. Has liquor dulled your throat? You're colder than a tomato salad."

Ramón picked up his guitar and sang:

"When to mass she goes, so sweet,
I approach her, and we nod.
All my happiness I meet
And kiss the ground where she has trod."

When he followed this verse with another that was somewhat risqué, Aunt María went to Stein and said:

"Don Federico, the wine is beginning to take hold; it's twelve midnight; the children are at home alone with Momo and Brother Gabriel; Manuel has bent his elbow more than usual; and I think it would not be a bad idea to sound the retreat. The donkeys are saddled. Do you want to take French leave?"

A moment later, the three women were riding their burros toward the convent. The men accompanied them on foot, while Ramón, in a sudden burst of jealousy and scorn, bawled rather than sang the following couplets, playing his guitar with unusual spirit:

"You handed me the mitten,
I'll wear it with my gloves;
I'd rather wear the mitten
Than be counted with your loves."

"What a beautiful night!" Stein was saying to his wife as he raised his eyes to the heavens. "Look at that starry sky, look at that moon, at the full, as I am at the full of my good fortune . . . It lacks nothing and needs nothing, like my heart!"

"And I was having such a good time!" Marysal answered impatiently. "I don't see why we had to leave the party so early."

"Aunt María," said Pedro Santaló to the good old woman, "now we can die in peace."

"That's true," she replied. "But we can also live in contentment, and that's better."

"Why can't you ever know when you've had enough once you have a glass in your hand?" Dolores was saying to her husband. "When you decide to spread your sails, there's no hawser that can hold you."

"Hell!" said Manuel. "What do you care if I've drunk too much? If you say another word I'll put about and go back to the party."

The songs of the drinkers could still be heard:

"Viva La Mancha that yields wine instead of water!"

Dolores held her tongue, fearing Manuel would carry out his threat.

"José," said Manuel to his brother-in-law who was among the group, "is the moon full?"

"Of course it is," replied the shepherd. "Can't you see what's in its eye? Don't you know what that is?"

"It must be a tear," said Manuel, laughing.

"It's just a man."

"A man!" cried Dolores, fully convinced of what her brother told her. "Who is the man?"

"I don't know," replied the shepherd. "But I know his name."

"What's his name?" asked Dolores.

"His name is Venus," José answered.

Manuel burst out laughing. He had drunk more than usual, and, as they say, he was a happy drunk.

"Don Federico," said Manuel, "do you want me, as an elder in the fraternity, to give you some advice?"

"Be quiet, Manuel, for heaven's sake," said Dolores.

"Why don't you leave me alone? If you don't, I'll go back. Listen, Don Federico. First of all, it's the same thing with women as with dogs: food in one hand and a stick in the other."

"Manuel!" said Dolores again.

"Will you leave me alone or shall I go back?" Manuel replied.

Dolores said nothing.

"Don Federico," Manuel went on, "marriage and dominance need neither force nor noise."

"Please be quiet, Manuel," interjected his mother.

"Well, this is a fine how-do-you-do," grumbled Manuel. "We might as well be going to a funeral."

"Can't you see, Manuel," observed the shepherd, "that Don Federico doesn't like those jokes of yours?"

"Don Federico," said Manuel, saying good-bye to the newlyweds, who were going to the cottage, "when you begin to repent of what you've just done, we'll get together and sing a duet with the same words."

And he went on to the convent, his good, clear voice singing in the silence:

"If my horse and my old woman
    Should both collapse and die,
    The devil with my woman's death!
    But the horse would make me cry."

"Go to bed, Manuel, and be quick about it," said his mother when they reached home.

"My wife will see to that," he replied. "Isn't that so, sweetheart?"

"All I wish is that you were asleep now," answered Dolores.

"Liar! How would you like to keep your sermon in your mouth? Then I won't have to gag you between sleeping and waking, so as to get any sleep tonight! It would be easy to do!"

"Don't you know how to shut her mouth?" asked his brother-in-law, laughing.

"Listen, José," replied Manuel, "have you ever found anything in the brambles or the caves of the countryside that can shut a woman's mouth? See here, if you've found it, you won't lack for a customer who'll pay a gold peso for it; I've never found it in the whole wide world nor heard tell of it in God's time."

Then he began to sing:

"It's easier to quench
 The sun's flaming fire
 Than to stay the hot tongue
 Of a woman's ire.

Flattery's no good,
And it's no use getting rough;
Being kind won't do it,
Nor will being tough."

CHAPTER XV

Three years had gone by. Stein, one of the few men who ask very little of life, believed he was happy. He loved his wife dearly; daily he grew more attached to his father-in-law and to the good family that had taken him in when he was at the point of death, and whose affection for him had never faltered. His uneventful rustic life was in harmony with his modest tastes and the gentle and peaceable temper of his spirit. Moreover, monotony does not lack attractions. A life that is always the same is like a man in a peaceful, dreamless sleep, like melodies composed around a few notes that form a soft lullaby. Perhaps there is nothing that leaves behind such pleasant memories as monotony, that endless chain of days, none of which differs from the one following it or preceding it.

Imagine the surprise of the people of the cottage, then, to see Momo coming on the run one morning, shouting agitatedly to Stein to go without a moment's delay to the convent!

"Has someone in the family been taken sick?" asked Stein, frightened.

"No," replied Momo, "it's a nobleman called His Excellency, who was hunting wild boar and stag in the district with his friends; when he jumped a ravine, his horse slipped and they both fell in. The horse was killed and the nobleman broke every bone in his body. They brought him there on a stretcher, and the whole place is a Tower of Babel. It seems like Judgment Day. They're running around like a flock of sheep when the wolf comes. The only one who's kept his head is the one who had the bad fall. He's quite a fellow, by all the signs. Everybody there is standing around quiet, not know-

143

ing what to do. My grandmother told them that one of the best doctors lives here, but they don't believe it. But as it would take two days to get one here from Cádiz, and more than that to bring one from Seville, his lordship said he wanted the one my grandmother recommended, and that's why I had to come, because it looks like there's nobody in all the world nor Kingdom Come to do things but me. Now I give you my word that if I were you, I'd hang back after they turned me down."

"Even if I were capable," replied Stein, "of refusing to do my Christian and professional duty, I'd have to have a heart of bronze to see a fellow man suffer and not do everything I can to relieve him. Besides, those gentlemen couldn't have confidence in me without knowing me, and that's no fault of theirs, nor would it be even if they knew me."

With these words, they arrived at the convent.

Aunt María, impatiently awaiting Stein, took him to the stranger. They had put him in the prior's cell where they had hastily made up a bed as well as they could. Aunt María and Stein passed through the milling servants and hunters who surrounded the injured man. He was a tall young man. His black, curly hair fell around his handsome, pale, but self-controlled face. Stein had hardly looked at him before he gave a cry, and rushed toward him; but fearful of touching him, he stopped abruptly, and clasping his trembling hands, exclaimed:

"Good God! It's the Duke!"

"Do you know me?" asked the Duke, raising his head and fixing his large black eyes on Stein, unable to place the man who had spoken to him.

"He doesn't remember me!" murmured Stein, while two big tears ran down his cheeks. "That's not strange; generous spirits forget the good they do, while the grateful keep forever in memory what they have received."

"A bad start!" said one of those present. "A surgeon who cries. A fine thing!"

"What a terrible mischance!" added another.

"Doctor," said the Duke to Stein, "I place myself in your hands. I trust in God, in you, and in my lucky star. Let's get to work."

Hearing these words, Stein raised his head; his face was perfectly serene, and with a modest, but firm and authoritative air, he sent the bystanders out of the room. Immediately thereafter he examined the patient with a hand skilled and dextrous in this type of practice; all with so much sureness and expertness that everyone was silent and nothing could be heard in the room but the sound of the patient's rapid breathing.

"The Duke," said the surgeon upon concluding his examination, "has a dislocated ankle and a broken leg, doubtless because it took all the weight of the horse. I think, however, that I can vouch for his complete recovery."

"Shall I be lame?" asked the Duke.

"I think I can assure you that you won't."

"If you can accomplish that," said the Duke, "I'll say you're the greatest surgeon in the world."

With no change in demeanor, Stein sent for Manuel, whose strength and gentleness were already known to him, and on whom he could rely with complete confidence. With Manuel's help, he went to work on the treatment which was undeniably painful; but Stein seemed to ignore the suffering of the patient, who was on the verge of fainting. At the end of a half-hour the Duke was resting, still in pain, but self-possessed. Instead of the former lack of confidence and suspicion on the part of the Duke's friends, Stein now received their fulsome congratulations and expressions of appreciation and admiration. Once more his shy and modest self, he acknowledged them all courteously. But Aunt María was in seventh heaven.

"What did I tell you?" she said over and over again to each of those present. "Didn't I tell you?"

Reassured, the Duke's friends went on their way at his urging. The patient had asked them to leave him alone under the care of his able doctor, his old friend, as he called him, and he even sent away most of his servants.

Thus he and the doctor were able to renew their acquaintance at their leisure. The Duke was one of those high-minded, unmaterialistic men, not bound by habit, who pay little attention to their physical well-being; one of those privileged people who can rise above circumstances, not in sudden, random spurts, but constantly, through strength of character and by virtue of a strong, stout heart, expressed in a "What does it matter"; one of those hearts that used to beat beneath XVth Century armor, and whose like can be found only in Spain today.

Stein told the Duke all about his campaigns, his misfortunes, his arrival at the convent, his love, and his marriage. The Duke listened with keen interest, and the narrative awakened in him a desire to meet Marysal and the fisherman, and to see Stein's house which he valued more highly than a grand palace. Accordingly, on his first venture out, he turned toward the seashore, accompanied by his doctor. Summer was coming in and the cool breeze, the pure breath of the immense sea, brought pleasure to them on their outing. Fort Saint Christopher was decked with its green crown, in honor of the important guest, before whose eyes it was displaying itself for the first time. The tiny flowers which covered the roof of the cabin, like the gardens of Semiramis,[32] bowed to one another as they were stirred by the gentle breeze, like shy girls whispering of their love in each other's ears. The sea sent its swells slowly and gently toward the Duke's feet as though welcoming him. The song of the lark could be heard, but the bird was so high aloft that it was invisible. The Duke, somewhat tired, sat down on a big stone. He was a poet and he enjoyed that beautiful scene in silence.

Suddenly he heard a voice singing a simple, plaintive melody. The Duke looked at Stein in surprise; Stein smiled. The voice went on singing.

"Stein," said the Duke, "are there sirens on these waves or angels in the air?"

By way of reply to the question, Stein took out his flute and echoed the melody.

Then the Duke saw a dark young girl come half-running, half-leaping toward them. She stopped short at seeing him.

"This is my wife," said Stein. "My María."

"She has the most marvelous voice in the world," said the Duke enthusiastically. "Señora, I've been in every theater in Europe, but I've never heard a voice more worthy of my admiration."

If Marysal's changelessly dark, smooth skin had been capable of changing color, a blush of pride and satisfaction would have reddened her cheeks to hear such high praise from such an eminent personage.

"Between the two of you, you have all you need to open a path for you in the world. Do you want to stay buried in

---

[32] An Assyrian princess c. 800 B.C., credited with creating the hanging gardens of Babylon.

obscurity and oblivion? It can't be that you don't want to share your advantages; I repeat it can't be that, it mustn't be."

"We're so happy here, Duke," replied Stein, "that any change in my situation would seem to me ungrateful to fortune."

"Stein," exclaimed the Duke, "where's that calm, firm boldness I admired in you when we were sailing together on board the *Royal Sovereign?* What has become of your love for science, of your desire to dedicate yourself to suffering humanity? Has happiness enervated you? Can it be true that happiness makes men selfish?"

Stein lowered his head.

"Señora," went on the Duke, "at your age and with your gifts, how can you decide to stay attached to your rock forever, like those ruins?"

Marysal, her heart beating faster with intense joy and beckoning hope, nevertheless answered with apparent coldness:

"What do I care?"

"What about your father?" asked her husband in a reproachful tone.

"He's fishing," she answered, feigning not to understand the real meaning of the question.

At once the Duke launched into a long explanation of all the advantages to be derived from that talent which would make her fame and fortune.

Marysal listened avidly, while the Duke admired the play of expression on that face, now cold, now enthusiastic, now frozen, now vivid.

When the Duke was saying good-bye, she spoke in Stein's ear and said with the greatest urgency:

"Let's go! Let's go! Think of it! When Fortune is calling me and offering me a crown, shall I turn a deaf ear? No! No!"

Downcast, Stein followed the Duke.

When they entered the convent, Aunt María asked the Duke, who treated his nurse with great kindness, what he had thought of her dear Marysal.

"Isn't Marysal a pretty little girl?" she asked.

"Certainly," said the Duke. "She has the kind of eyes that could stare back at an eagle, as one poet expressed it."

"And her grace?" went on the good old woman. "Her voice?"

"As for her voice," said the Duke, "it's too good to be wasted in this wilderness. You have enough with your nightingales and your linnets. Husband and wife must come with me."

If a bolt of lightning had struck at Aunt María's feet she could not have been more terrified than she was by those words.

"Do they want to?" she exclaimed with dread.

"They've got to want to," answered the Duke, going into his room.

Aunt María stood perplexed and confounded for a few moments. Then she flew to look for Brother Gabriel.

"They're going!" she said, streaming tears.

"Thank God!" replied the monk. "They've already ruined the marble paving stones in the prior's cell. What will his reverence say when he comes home?"

"You misunderstood me," said Aunt María, interrupting him. "The ones that are going are Don Federico and his wife."

"They're going?" asked Brother Gabriel. "They can't be!"

"Is this possible?" asked Aunt María of Stein who had come to look for her.

"She wants to!" he answered dolefully.

"That's what her father always says," said Aunt María, "and he'd have let her die with that answer of his if it hadn't been for us. Ah, Don Federico, you're so well off here! Are you going to be like the good Spaniard who wanted to be better?"

"I couldn't hope nor believe I'd be better off in any other place in the world, my good Aunt María," said Stein.

"Some day," she said, "you'll be sorry. And poor Pedro! Dear Lord! Why did the outside world have to come here to upset us!"

At that moment Don Modesto arrived. For some time his visits had been growing infrequent, not that the Duke would have failed to receive him cordially, nor because he himself might fail to exercise the same irresistible attraction for the veteran as for everyone who came in contact with him. But as Don Modesto lived by rule, he had imposed on himself a regulation that he was not to appear before the Duke, a general and an ex-Minister of War, except with rigid ceremony. Mystical Rose had told him, however, that his uniform was not fit for active duty, and it was for this reason that he spaced his visits widely. When Aunt María observed that the Duke intended to start on his way in two days, Don Modesto immediately withdrew. He had formed a plan and needed time to carry it out.

When Marysal told her father she had made the decision to follow the Duke's advice, the poor old father's sorrow would have wrung a heart of stone. But his was a mute sadness. He listened to his daughter's grandiose plans, neither censuring nor applauding them, as well as to her promises to return to the cottage, neither exacting nor rejecting those either. He looked upon his daughter as a bird does upon its fledgling when it tries to fly from the nest, never to return. The good father often shed inward tears, if that can be said.

Soon the horses, the servants, and the pack animals came,

as the Duke had ordered for his departure. Shouts, oaths, and the bustle of travel echoed through every corner of the convent. Brother Gabriel had to go to work on his baskets beneath the ivy in whose shade the chain pumps had once worked.

Morrongo climbed to the highest roof and sunned himself, casting a look of disdain at the tumult in the courtyard. *Palomo* barked, growled, and protested so loudly against the foreign invasion that Manuel ordered Momo to shut him up.

"There's no doubt," said Momo, "that my grandmother, the most headstrong nurse under the sun, has a lodestone to draw sick people to this house. This one makes three; probably she'll go to work healing St. Lazarus in heaven."

The day of departure came. The Duke was all ready in his room. Stein and Marysal had arrived, followed by the poor fisherman, who never raised his eyes from the ground and whose body was bent over with a sorrow that had aged him more than all his years and the storms at sea. As soon as he had come, he sat down on the steps by the marble cross.

Don Modesto also came, but with consternation painted on his face. His eyebrows were arched to a prodigious height. The little topknot of hair was hanging limply to one side. He was heaving deep sighs.

"What's the matter, Commander?" asked Aunt María.

"Aunt María," he replied, "today is the fifteenth of June, my saint's day, a day that's sadly memorable among the feast days in my life. Oh, Saint Modesto! How could you possibly treat me like this on the very day the Church prays to you?"

"But what is it that's wrong?" Aunt María asked him again with some uneasiness.

"Look," said the veteran, raising his arm and revealing a hole where a big strip of cloth had been ripped off. Through it the white lining showed, like teeth bared in a derisive smile. Don Modesto identified himself with his uniform; in losing it he would have lost the last symbol of his calling.

"What a pity!" said Aunt María sadly.

"It will give Rosita a sick headache," went on Don Modesto.

"His Excellency requests the Commander to be kind enough to go to his room," said a servant at that moment.

Don Modesto drew himself up; he took out a carefully folded and sealed paper, pressed the arm beneath which the hole had appeared as close as he could to his body, and presenting himself to the personage, he greeted him respectfully, holding himself at stiff attention.

"I wish Your Excellency a most pleasant trip," he said, "and hope you will find my lady the Duchess and all your family in the best of health. I have taken the liberty of begging Your Excellency to place in the hands of the Minister of War this statement relating to the fort which I have the honor to command. Your Excellency has been able to judge for himself how urgently the castle of Saint Christopher needs repairs, particularly in view of the talk of war with the Emperor of Morocco."

"My dear Don Modesto," replied the Duke, "I cannot venture to be responsible for the outcome of that petition; I'd advise you instead to erect crosses on the battlements of the fort as upon a sepulcher. But, on the other hand, I promise to see to it that some of your back pay may be made available."

This welcome promise did little to wipe away the sad impression made on the Commander by the kind of death sentence pronounced on the fort by the Duke.

"Meanwhile," continued the Duke, "I beg you to accept a remembrance from a friend . . ."

And so saying, he pointed to a nearby chair.

What was the surprise of that excellent man to see lying there a complete, new, shining uniform, with epaulets fit to adorn the shoulders of the greatest captain of the century! Don Modesto was naturally confused, astonished, dazzled to see so much splendor and magnificence.

"I hope, Commander," said the Duke, "that you may live as long as this uniform lasts, and that it will last as long as its predecessor."

"Ah, Your Excellency," replied Modesto, somewhat recovering the use of his voice, "this is too handsome for me."

"Not at all, not at all," replied the Duke. "There are a great many wearing fancier uniforms than this without deserving them as much. I know, too," he went on, "that you have a friend, an excellent landlady, and that you won't mind bringing her a remembrance. Please give her this small, friendly token."

It was a rosary of gold filigree and coral.

Without allowing Don Modesto time to emerge from his bewilderment, the Duke went at once to the family, whom he had asked to gather together so that he might thank them and leave them all mementos of him. The Duke never did a good deed indifferently, nor with scornful and perhaps offensive liberality, as rich people often do, but more in the manner of those who are not rich; that is, by making a study of the needs and tastes of each individual. Thus all the residents of the convent received what they needed or wanted most. Manuel, a cape and a good watch; Momo, a full suit of clothes, a yellow silk sash and a shotgun; the women and children, materials for dresses, and toys; Anise, a kite so huge that his tiny person disappeared beneath it when he held it up, like a mouse behind the shield of Achilles. The Duke gave Aunt

María a lifelong annuity for her tireless nursing of her illustrious guest, and for her skillful composition of nourishing
stews.

As for poor Brother Gabriel, he got nothing. He made
such a small ripple in the world, and had hidden so often from
the Duke's sight that the Duke had scarcely seen him.

Aunt María, unobserved, cut some lengths from one of
the pieces of linen the Duke had given her, and with two
cotton handkerchiefs, she went to look for her protégé.

"Here you are, Brother Gabriel," she said, "a little gift
from the Duke. I'm going to see to making you a shirt."

The poor fellow was even more overcome than the Commander, for Brother Gabriel was more than modest; he was
humble.

Everything being in readiness for the trip, the Duke went
out into the courtyard.

"Good-bye, Momo, the honor of Villamar," said Marysal,
"if I miss you, I won't remember."

"Good-bye, Sea Gull," he answered, "if everyone were as
sorry to see you go as my mother's son, they'd have to set the
bells to ringing."

Pedro stayed where he was, on the marble steps. Aunt
María was at his side, crying bitterly.

"Anyone would think I was going to China," said Marysal, "and that we wouldn't see one another again as long as we
live. Come, this looks like a gypsy funeral! You're determined
to dampen my pleasure in going to the city!"

"Mother," said Manuel, moved at seeing his mother's tears,
"if you're crying so hard now, what would you do if I were to
die?"

"I wouldn't cry, dear son," said his mother, smiling

through her tears. "I wouldn't have time to cry for your death, for I'd be coming right behind you."

The riding horses were ready. Stein threw himself into Aunt María's arms.

"Don't forget us, Don Federico," said the good old woman, sobbing. "Come back!"

"If I don't come back," he replied, "it will be because I'm dead."

The Duke had arranged for Marysal to mount at once the mule chosen for her, so as to remove her as quickly as possible from such a painful parting. The animal broke into a trot, the others followed it, and the whole party had soon disappeared around the corner of the convent.

The poor father stretched out his arms to his daughter.

"I'll never see her again!" he cried, choking, and lowered his face to the steps of the cross.

The travellers went forward at a faster trot. When Stein reached the Calvary, he eased the grief oppressing him by a fervent prayer to the Lord of Succour, whose benign influence spread through the district like the light around the star that sends it forth.

Mystical Rose was at her window when the travellers crossed the village square.

"May God forgive me!" she exclaimed when she saw Marysal riding beside the Duke. "She never even spoke to me, nor so much as looked at me! The demon of pride has already breathed into her heart!" Putting her head out the window, she added, "I'll bet she won't speak to the priest there on the portico of the church, either. Yes, she is speaking, but because the Duke set her the example. Hello, he's stopping to speak and he's handing him a purse. It must be for the poor! . . . He's a good and very liberal man. He's done a lot of good. May God repay him!"

Mystical Rose did not yet know of the double surprise which awaited her.

As Stein rode by, he saluted her sadly with a wave of the hand.

"Go with God!" said Rosa, waving a handkerchief. "The best of men! Yesterday when he said good-bye to me, he cried like a boy. What a pity he isn't going to stay in the village! And he would stay if it weren't for that crazy Sea Gull, as Momo so rightly calls her."

The party had come to a hill and had begun to descend it. The houses of Villamar quickly disappeared from Stein's view. He could hardly tear himself away from the place where he had lived so quietly and so happily.

Meanwhile, the Duke had taken on the unneeded task of consoling Marysal by painting flattering plans for her future.

Stein had eyes only for the scene he was quitting!

In their turn the Cross of Calvary and the chapel of the Lord of Succour vanished from sight. Later the huge mass of the convent seemed to sink gradually into the earth. Finally nothing could be seen of that tranquil corner of the world but the ruins of the fort, its dark mass outlined against the deep blue of the sky, and the tower which, as a poet had put it, was pointing with mute eloquence to heaven, like a finger.

CHAPTER XVI

In Spain, whose national character is inimical to affectation, what is called "high society" is neither needed nor recognized. Good taste is natural here; for in Spain everything that is natural is elegant in itself.

AUTHOR'S NOTE.

The month of July had been extremely hot in Seville. Groups of friends met in those delightful patios where beautiful marble fountains, their jets playing, were hidden behind a great mass of flowerpots. From the ceilings of the hallways, big lanterns of crystal globes hung, shedding floods of light around them. Flowers perfumed the air, and rich furniture contributed to a setting of grace and splendor, further adorned by the pretty Sevillian women, whose gay and lively conversation competed with the soft whisper of the fountains.

One night toward the end of the month there was a huge gathering in the house of the young, pretty, and elegant Countess of Algar. It was considered great good fortune to be received into that house, though certainly nothing could be easier, for the lady was so amiable and sociable that she received everyone with the same cordiality. The ease with which all those presented to her were admitted was not to the taste of her uncle, General Santa María, a soldier of Napoleon's time, and like most soldiers of those days, somewhat brusque, a little exclusive, a trifle despotic and haughty; in short, a classical son of Mars, fully convinced that all relations among men consisted in commanding or obeying, and that the principal purpose and use of society is to classify every one of its members.

Otherwise, he was as Spanish as Pelayo[33] and as gallant as The Cid.[34]

The general and his sister, the Marchioness of Guadalcanal, who was the mother of the Countess, were playing *tresillo*[35] with several other persons. Some were talking politics, strolling through the corridors; the young of both sexes, sitting near the flowers, were chatting and laughing as though the earth produced nothing but blossoms and the air echoed nothing but happy laughter.

The Countess, half reclining on a sofa, was complaining of a bad headache, but this did not prevent her from being gay and smiling. She was small, slender, and white as alabaster. Her thick, blond hair was curled in ringlets in the English style. Her large, dark eyes, her nose, her teeth, her mouth, the oval of her face, were models of perfection, her grace incomparable. She was loved to excess by her mother, adored by her husband, who, disliking society, still gave her unlimited freedom, for she was virtuous and he trusted her. In truth, the Countess was a spoiled child. But, thanks to her fine character, she did not abuse her privileges as such. Without any great intellectual endowments, she possessed the talent of the heart: she was sensitive and delicately perceptive. Her whole ambition boiled down to amusing herself and to be pleasing without excess, like the bird that flies without knowing how, and sings effortlessly. That night she had come home from an outing tired and somewhat indisposed; she had taken off her dress and put on a simple white organdy blouse. Her white,

[33] and [34] *Pelayo,* first King of Spain, and also an epic poem by José de Espronceda (1808-1842), very popular at the time this novel was written. El Cid, the national hero of Spain, was the protagonist of the 12th Century epic poem of the same title.

[35] A three-handed card game also called *ombre*.

round arms showed through the lace of its loose sleeves; she had forgotten to take off a bracelet and her rings. A young colonel, recently arrived from Madrid after distinguished service in the war in Navarre, was sitting next to her. The Countess had all her attention fixed on him.

From time to time General Santa María glanced at them, biting his lips with vexation.

"New fruit!" he was saying. "She wouldn't be a daughter of Eve if she didn't like something new. A coxcomb! Twenty-four years old and a colonel already! When was there ever such prodigality with rank? Five or six years ago he was still in school, and now he commands a regiment! We'll doubtless be told that he got his rank through brilliant action. Well, what I say is that courage doesn't confer experience, and no one is fit to command without experience. A colonel in the army at twenty-four! I had to wait until I was forty, after having served in Rosellon,[36] in America, and in Portugal, and I didn't win my general's rank until I came back from the North with the Romana Division, and after fighting in the War of Independence. Gentlemen, the truth is that we've all gone mad in Spain, some from what they're doing, and others from what they've left undone."

At that moment an outcry was heard. The Countess herself recovered from her languor and got up in one bound.

"At last, the lost is found!" she exclaimed. "A thousand times welcome, luckless hunter and hapless horseman. But what is this? You look as if you'd never taken a fall. Is it true what they're saying, about a marvelous German doctor, who came out of the ruins of a fort and a convent, like one of those legendary creatures? Tell us, Duke, all about those extraordinary goings-on!"

---

[36] A district in France.

The Duke, after being congratulated by all those present on his return and his recovery, took a seat facing the Countess and embarked on the story which the reader already knows. Finally, after talking a great deal about Stein and Marysal, he ended by saying that he had arranged for them to come to live in Seville so that Stein could practice his science and she could reveal the unusual gifts with which Nature had favored her.

"You did wrong," ruled the general in a firm tone.

The Countess quickly turned to her uncle.

"And why is it wrong, señor?" she asked.

"Because those people were living contentedly without ambition, and from now on that won't be true, for as the title of a Spanish play puts it, 'No one should leave the certain for the doubtful.' It is a wise saying."

"So you believe," replied the Countess, "that that woman, privileged to have such a voice, will miss the rock she was stuck fast to like an oyster, with no advantages, no glory for herself, for society, nor for art?"

"Come, niece, do you really expect us to believe that human society will be advanced very much by a woman climbing on the stage and setting herself to singing *di tanti palpiti?*"

"Indeed!" said the Countess, "it's well known that you're not a music lover."

"Thank God for that," answered the general. "How could you expect me to lose my head, as so many do, with all this musical madness, that flood of notes that has spilled out over Spain like a deluge, or an avalanche, as they express it so poorly today? Would you want me to swell the overweening pride of those kings and queens of warbling with my idiotic enthusiasm? Do you think my money should go to add to their colossal incomes, while so many battle-scarred officers are starving to death, while so many women of solid merit and Christian virtue spend their lives weeping, with only a crust of bread to put in their mouths? That cries to heaven, and it's true irony, as they say today, too, that this is a period when those hypocritical bawlers never let the word 'humanity' fall from their lips! Well, I'd be likely to toss garlands of flowers to a prima donna whose shabby talents can be reduced to *do, re, mi, fa, sol!*"

"My uncle," said the Countess, "is the living personification of the status quo. Anything new displeases him. I'm going to grow old as quickly as possible just to please him."

"You'll do no such thing, niece," replied the general, "and neither will you ask me to become rejuvenated to flatter the younger generation."

"What is my brother arguing about?" asked the Marchioness, who, absorbed in the game, had not paid attention to the conversation.

"My uncle," said a young officer who had entered quietly and sat down beside the Duke, "is preaching a crusade against music. He has declared war on the *andantes;* he has doomed the *moderatos,* and will give no quarter to the *allegros.*"

"Dear Rafael!" cried the Duke, embracing the officer, a relative whom he liked very much.

Rafael was small, but slender, well-formed and graceful; his face was one of those called too pretty for a man.

"I'd have let my two legs be cut off to spare you the bad time you've just had!" replied the officer, pressing the Duke's hand in his. "But we're talking about opera and I don't want to sing in the style of melodrama."

"Good idea," said the Duke. "I'd rather hear you tell me what's happened here during my absence? What's the gossip?"

"They say that my cousin, the Countess of Algar," said Rafael, "is the pearl of the Sevillian women."

162   FERNÁN CABALLERO

"I asked you what's new," said the Duke, "not what everyone knows."

"Duke," went on Rafael, "Solomon said, and many wise men (I among them) repeat, that there's nothing new under the sun."

"I wish that were true," said the general, sighing. "But my nephew Rafael Arias is a living contradiction of his own adage. He's always bringing new faces to our friendly gatherings, and that's unbearable."

"My uncle is now slashing at the foreigners with his sword," said Rafael. "Foreigners are General Santa María's bugaboo. Duke, if you hadn't appointed me your adjutant when you were Minister of War, I wouldn't have established relations with foreign diplomats in Madrid and I wouldn't be constantly vexed with letters of recommendation. Do you suppose, Uncle, that it's very amusing for me to have to act as guide to every visiting fireman as I've had to do ever since I came to Seville?"

"Who obliges us to open our doors wide to anyone who comes and to place ourselves at his disposal?" answered the general. "That isn't done in Paris, much less in London."

"Each nation has its national character," said the Countess. "And every society its own customs. Foreigners are more reserved than we are, even among themselves. We must be fair."

"Have any come recently?" asked the Duke. "I ask because I'm expecting Lord G., one of the most distinguished men I know. Is he already in Seville?"

"He hasn't arrived yet," replied Rafael. "But first of all we now have here Major Fly, whom we call The Fly. He's serving in the queen's guard, and is a nephew of the Duke of W., one of the leading peers of England."

"Yes, the nephew of the Duke of W.," said the general putting on a drawl, "just as I'm the Grand Turk."

"He's young," Rafael went on, "elegant, and a good-looking chap, but a Colossus in height; so that you have to stand some distance away to get the right view of him. Close up, he seems so huge, so robust, so angular, so rough that he loses a hundred per cent. When he's not at table, he's always at my side, indoors or out; when my servants tell him I'm out, he says he'll wait for me, and as he comes in the door, I go out the window. He has a habit of brandishing his stick, and though his thrusts are innocent and wound nothing but the air, his arm is so strong and so long and my room is so small that he's poking holes in the walls and has broken several window panes. He sits down on the chairs, he rocks, he throws himself about and leans back, with the result that he's broken four of them. My landlady was furious when she saw that. Sometimes he picks up a book and that's the best thing he can do, for then he falls asleep. But his point of pride is his amorous conquests; they're his hobby, his fixed idea, and his great hope, though still unrealized. With regard to the fair sex, he has the same illusions as the Galician who went to Mexico thinking the streets were paved with gold. I've tried to disillusion him, but I was a voice crying in the wilderness. When I try to talk to him about it, he smiles with an air of incredulity, twirling his enormous mustache. He's engaged to a millionairess and the strange thing is that this thirty-year-old Ajax, who devours four pounds of beefsteaks and drinks three bottles of sherry in one sitting, has convinced his fiancée that he's travelling for his health. The other intruder, as my uncle calls him, is a Frenchman; the Baron de Maude."

"Baron!" said the general slyly, "yes, a Baron, as I'm the Grand Turk."

"But, goodness, Uncle," said the Countess, "why shouldn't he be a baron?"

"The reason, niece," said the general, "is that real barons, not Napoleon's barons, nor Constitutional barons, but barons of the Old Régime don't travel or write for money, nor are they so ill-bred, so curious, and so full of tiresome questions."

"But, heavens, Uncle, he could be a baron and still ask questions. One doesn't lose one's patent of nobility by asking questions. When he goes back to his own country, he's going to marry the daughter of a French nobleman."

"He'll marry her," answered the general, "as I'd marry the Grand Turk."

"My uncle," said Arias, "is like Saint Thomas: seeing is believing. But, coming back to our baron, it must be admitted that he's a man with a very good appearance, though, like me, he finished growing before it was time. He has an amiable disposition; but he sets himself up as learned and literary, and he talks equally of politics and art, of history and music, of statistics, philosophy, property, and styles. He's now writing a serious book, as he calls it, which is to serve him as a ladder to climb to the Chamber of Deputies. It's entitled: A Scientific, Philosophic, Physiologic, Artistic, and Geological Tour of Spain (Iberia), with Critical Observations on its Government, Cuisine, Literature, Roads and Canals, Agriculture, its Boleros, and its Tax System. He's affectedly careless in his dress, and is serious, circumspect, and economical to an extreme. He's getting to be one of those insipid fruits from the greenhouse of public men which breeds forced plants, with no spring, no life-giving breezes, and no open air; fruits without taste or scent. Those men fling themselves into the future, with all steam up, searching for what they call a position, and sacrificing everything else to that; sad, tormented lives, for whom life has no dawning!"

"Rafael, that's philosophizing," said the Duke, smiling. "Do you know if Socrates were living today, you'd be one of his disciples rather than my adjutant?"

"I wouldn't exchange being an adjutant for being a disciple, General," replied Arias. "But the truth is that if there weren't so many stupid students there wouldn't be so many perverse teachers."

"Well said, nephew," cried the old general. "So many new teachers, and each one teaches some one subject and preaches the latest and most addled doctrine! Progress! Magnificent and never-sufficiently-praised progress!"

"General," replied the Duke, "for this globe of ours to keep in balance, there must be gas and there must be ballast; each ought to regard the other as necessary and reciprocal, instead of each wanting to annihilate the other with such fury."

"What you are stating," replied the general, "is the odious doctrine of the happy medium, which is precisely what has ruined us with its shameful opinion and its corruscating terminology, as the common people say. They speak with more sense than the illustrious followers of conservatism, great hypocrites with a fair exterior and a rotten interior, adorers of the Supreme Being who don't believe in Jesus Christ."

"My uncle," said Rafael, "hates the moderates so much that he loses all moderation when he combats them."

"Be still, Rafael," said the Countess, "you argue and make fun of every opinion yet you have none yourself as long as you won't take the trouble to defend it."

"I'm a Liberal, cousin," cried Rafael. "My empty purse will testify to that."

"Why should you be a Liberal!" said the general in a strident voice.

"And why shouldn't I be one, señor! The Duke is one, too."

"Why should you be a Liberal!" repeated the veteran in a loud, emphatic voice, like the roll of a drum.

"Come," murmured Rafael. "Seemingly my uncle won't permit anything but the arts by that name to be liberal. Sir," he added, addressing his uncle, whom he took delight in angering, "why shouldn't the Duke be a Liberal? Whom is he bothering if he takes a notion to be a Liberal? Is he any uglier for being a Liberal? Why can't we be all Liberals, sir; why not?"

"Because," answered the general, "a soldier is not and should not be anything other than the support of the throne, the maintainer of order, the defender of his country. Is that what you are, nephew?"

"But, Uncle. . . ."

"Rafael," interrupted the Countess, "don't get yourself in over your head, and go on with your story."

"I obey. Ah, cousin, there would never be an insubordinate man in an army under your command. We have another foreigner in Seville, a certain Sir John Burnwood. He's a young fellow of fifty, strikingly handsome, with a great mane of tawny hair like an authentic lion of the Atlas Mountains, a monocle, a fixed smile, handshakes to right and left, a great chatterbox, a busybody, uproarious when he's trying to appear lively, like the German who jumped out of the window for the same reason; very fond of betting; a celebrated sportsman; the owner of huge coal mines which bring him in an income of twenty thousand pounds."

"Presumably," said the general, "that would be twenty thousand pounds of coal."

"Uncle is like the stockbrokers who raise and lower incomes at will," said Rafael. "Sir John made a bet that he would climb the Giralda[37] on horseback, and that's the great purpose which brings him to Seville. It's true that one of our ancient kings did it; but when the poor horse had climbed up he couldn't go down, and there he stayed like Mohammed's coffin, suspended between heaven and earth; they had to kill him in his high place. Sir John is in despair because they won't allow him to enjoy that monarchical pastime. Now, following the example of Lord Elgin[38] and Baron Taylor, he wants to buy the Alcázar[39] and take it to his manorial estate, stone by stone, not omitting those stones that are forever stained with the blood of Don Fadrique, whose murder was ordered by his brother, King Don Pedro, five hundred years ago, so they say."

"There is nothing the *milords* are not capable of," said the general, "nor is there any idea, no matter how wild, that wouldn't occur to them."

"That isn't all," Rafael went on. "The other day he asked me if I could get the cathedral chapter to sell me the gold keys that the Moorish king presented to Saint Ferdinand in a silver font when he conquered Seville, and the agate goblet from which the great king used to drink."

The general struck the table such a blow that one of the candelabra fell.

"General," said the Duke, "can't you see that Rafael is painting his pictures in garish colors, and that everything he's saying is sheer extravagance?"

---

[37] A statue on the cathedral tower of Seville that revolves like a weather-vane. It represents Faith.

[38] A Scottish art collector of the nineteenth century who nearly stripped Athens of its ancient sculptures, now known as the Elgin Marbles.

[39] A beautiful Moorish palace, built in the twelfth century, and later used as a palace for the Spanish kings.

"There's no extravagance that would seem unlikely to the English," replied the general.

"But the best is yet to come," went on Rafael, fixing his eyes on a pretty girl at the side of the Marchioness, watching her play. "Sir John is desperately in love with my cousin Rita, and has asked for her hand. Rita, who absolutely does not know how to pronounce the monosyllable 'yes,' gave him a bare, hard 'no' like a shot from a canon."

"Is it possible, Rita," said the Duke, "that you've refused twenty thousand pounds in income?"

"It wasn't the income I refused," replied the girl emphatically, without taking her eyes from the game, "what I refused was the man who has it."

"She did well," added the Marchioness. "A Protestant! God spare us!"

"And what have you to say, Countess?" asked the Duke.

"I say the same as my mother," she answered. "It's no joking matter when the head of the family belongs to another faith than hers; I think like my uncle, that everyone should marry in his country, and I say the same as Rita: that I'd never marry a man only because he has twenty thousand pounds in income."

"Besides," said Rita, "he's in love with the dancer, Lucía del Salto; so that even if the gentleman were to my taste, I'd have given him the same reply. I'm not fond of competition, especially with people from the stage."

Rita was a niece of the Marchioness and the general. She had been an orphan since early childhood, reared by one of her brothers who loved her tenderly, and by her nurse, who adored and spoiled her, but, despite all that, she had grown into a good and pious girl. The solitude and independence in which she had spent the first years of her life had impressed on her character the dual seal of shyness and determination. She was one of those contradictory people, at once haughty and kind, capricious and simple, mocking and reserved. Her piquant character was enhanced by the most seductive and beautiful physical endowments. She was of average height; her figure, never subjected to the imprisonment of a corset, had all the suppleness, all the flexibility that French novelists falsely attribute to their heroines tightly encased in whalebone. Spanish women owe their famous attractiveness to graceful contours and movements, combined with a frank and natural manner, so charming when accompanied by grace and kindliness. Rita had the clear and uniform finish of a marble statue; her beautiful hair was black, her notably large eyes were dark gray, fringed with long black lashes and crowned with eyebrows that seemed to have been drawn by Murillo's hand. Her fresh mouth, usually serious, opened a little from time to time to emit a quick, gay laugh which displayed her very white teeth, but with her habitual reserve, she suppressed it immediately, for nothing was more offensive to her than to call attention to herself, and when this happened, she felt cross.

She had made a vow to the Virgin of Sorrows to wear a habit. Accordingly, she was always dressed very simply in black with a patent-leather belt and a small gold heart pierced by a sword.

Rita was the only woman her cousin Rafael Arias had ever seriously loved, not with a lachrymose and elegiac passion, which would be out of character for him, the most unsentimental of dry, east-coast Mediterranean Spaniards, but with a keen, sincere, and constant affection. Rafael, a fine young man, loyal, sensible, and noble in spirit and birth, heir to a good patrimony, was the husband Rita's family wanted for her. But she had already given her heart, unknown to her brother, despite his vigilance.

The object of her choice was a youth of illustrious family; an arrogant boy, but a gambler; and this was enough to cause Rita's brother to oppose his suit to the extent of sternly forbidding her to see him or speak with him. With her firmness of character and her Spanish perseverance, Rita was serenely waiting, uncomplaining, with no sighs nor tears, for the day when she would reach twenty-one, the age at which she could marry over her brother's opposition, without causing a scandal. Meanwhile, her lover, dressed like a gallant and superbly mounted, courted her from the street, and they wrote to each other daily.

That night Rita had entered the group as usual, without creating a stir, and had sat in her accustomed seat, near her aunt, to watch her play. The aunt had not noticed her niece's nearness until the Duke asked her about the match she had refused, and she had been obliged to answer.

"Gracious, Rita," said the Marchioness, "you scared me! How did you get here without our being aware of it?"

"Would you like me to come in like a regiment with drum and trumpet?" Rita replied.

"But at least," said the Marchioness, "you might speak to a person."

"That would distract the players," said Rita. "Look at your own cards. Diamonds have been played, but you were about to renege, just to give me a scolding."

During this exchange, Rafael had sat down behind his cousin, and was saying in her ear:

"Rita, when can I ask for the dispensation?"

"When I tell you to," she replied.

"And what can I do to hasten that blessed day?"

"Commend yourself to my saint; she's the advocate of the impossible."

"Cruel girl, some day you'll be sorry you refused my white hand. You'll be losing the best and most grateful of husbands."

"And you the most ungrateful of wives."

"Listen, Rita," went on Arias, "has our uncle, there in front of us, some custody over your head that keeps you from turning your face to whoever speaks to you?"

"I've got a stiff neck."

"This stiff neck is named Luis de Haro. Are you still infatuated with that card sharp?"

"More than ever."

"And what does your brother have to say to that?"

"Ask him, if you're interested."

"So you'll let me perish?"

"Without batting an eyelash."

"I'll make a vow in the parish church to the devil under Saint Michael's feet that I'll gild his horns if I can once meet up with your Luis de Haro."

"Wish him ill; the evil wishes of the envious will do him good."

"It seems to me I'm boring you," said Rafael, seeing his cousin yawn after a few moments of silence.

"Hadn't you noticed it before?" Rita answered.

"So you want me to go away. I catch on! Luis the Card-sharp is jealous!"

"Jealous of you?" his cousin replied, bursting into sudden laughter. "He's as jealous of you as of the fat Englishman."

"Thank you for the comparison, dear little cousin; and good-bye forever!"

"Vanity!" answered Rita without turning her head.

Rafael got up, stung by her words.

"What's the matter, Rafael?" asked a young girl in a languid voice as he passed by her.

This new speaker had just come from Madrid, where an important lawsuit had demanded her father's presence. She had returned from her trip completely modernized; so rabidly infected by what she chose to call foreign high society that she made herself utterly ridiculous. Her incessant occupation was reading—French novels almost exclusively. She practiced a kind of cult of fashion; she adored music and despised everything Spanish.

Hearing her question, Rafael tried to compose himself and answered:

"Eloise, I am one day older than yesterday, and have one day less of life."

"I know what ails you, Arias; and I know you're suffering."

"Eloise, you're going to make me nervous, like Don Basilio," and he sang, *'What a scowling face!'*

"It's useless for you to hide it; there are tears beneath your laughter, Arias."

"But tell me, for heaven's sake, Eloise, what's wrong with me? It's an act of mercy to enlighten someone who doesn't know."

"You know very well what's wrong with you, Arias."

"What?"

"A deception," murmured Eloise.

"A what?" asked Rafael, who had not understood her.

"A deception," repeated Eloise.

"Ah, I see. I understood you to say desertion, and my honor as a soldier was outraged. As for deceptions, they happen to me a hundred times a day, as they do to every mother's son, my friend; and it's no small feat to awaken pity instead of pleasure in you, which is what I should prefer to do."

"But of all deceptions, there's one that darkens your life which may ironically bring you happiness by making you regard the grave as a rest and death as a smiling friend."

"Ah, Eloise," Rafael replied, "I'd have given a finger from my hand for such thoughts during the battle of Mendigorria, not to mention when they took me to the hospital with a bullet in my side. Devil a smile I got from death or the grave!"

"How prosaic you are!" exclaimed Eloise indignantly.

"Is that scorn, Eloise?"

"No, it's a compliment."

"The honest truth is," said Rafael, "that you're very lovely with that hair style, and that dress is in excellent taste."

"Do you like it?" cried the stylish girl, suddenly abandoning her sentimental tone. "It's the latest rage, from Chez Ledru-Rollin."

"It's no wonder," said Rafael, "that that Englishman there in front of you, a head taller than the flower-pots, is crazy about Spain and Spanish women."

"What poor taste!" said Eloise, gesticulating.

"He says there's nothing in the world prettier than a Spanish girl wearing her mantilla," went on Rafael. "That's the costume he likes best on her."

"How unfair!" said the girl. "Does he think a hat is too elegant for us?"

"He says you use your fans with incomparable grace," persisted Rafael.

"What slander!" said Eloise. "We stylish women don't use them any more."

"He says those little feet, so cunning, so small, so pretty, cry out for silk stockings and shoes instead of those horrid boots, buskins, or whatever you call them."

"He's insulting us," cried Eloise. "He wants us to go back half a century, as the illustrated press in Madrid so nicely puts it."

"He says Spanish girls' black eyes are the most beautiful in the world."

"How vulgar! Eyes like those belong to villagers, to cooks, and cigarette girls."

"He says the Spanish girls' manner of walking—so light, so graceful, so alluring—is the most enchanting that can be imagined."

"But doesn't that gentleman realize he's looking upon us with scorn," said Eloise, "and that we're doing everything possible to mend our ways and walk properly?"

"The best thing for you to do is to convert him," said Rafael. "I'm going to present him to you."

Arias hastened away, thinking: "Eloise has a soft heart and she fanices herself a romantic. She's made to order for the major; she's hunting for just such a big bird."

Meanwhile, the Countess asked the Duke if the Villamar nightingale was pretty.

"She's neither pretty nor ugly," he answered. "She's dark and her features wouldn't pass for regular. She has fine eyes; in short, one of those combinations you see wherever you go in our country."

"As long as her voice is so unusual," said the Countess, "we must make her an eminent prima donna for the honor of Seville. Mayn't we hear her?"

"Whenever you wish," replied the Duke. "One of these

nights I'll bring her here with her husband, who is a fine musician and her teacher."

With this, the time had come for him to leave.

When the Duke went to the Countess to say good-bye, she shook a finger at him in a warning gesture.

"What does that mean?" asked the Duke.

"Nothing, nothing," she said. "It just means 'take care!'"

"Take care? Why?"

"Are you pretending not to understand me? There's none so deaf as he who will not hear."

"You're keeping me in suspense, Countess."

"So much the better."

"For heaven's sake, won't you please explain?"

"Now that you force me to, I will. When I said take care, I meant take care that you're not hanging a millstone around your neck."

"Ah, Countess," replied the Duke heatedly. "For heaven's sake, I hope no unjust and false suspicion will come to shadow that woman's reputation even before anyone knows her. This woman, Countess, is an angel."

"Oh, of course," said the Countess. "One doesn't fall in love with devils."

"And yet you have a thousand admirers," replied the Duke, smiling.

"Well, I'm not a devil," said the Countess, "but I am a diviner."

"When the shot misses the target, it's a poor shot."

"I'm summoning you to appear for trial right here in six months, invulnerable Achilles," replied the Countess.

"For goodness' sake, be still, Countess!" exclaimed the Duke. "What is a light jest in your lovely mouth would be venom in the mouths of the vipers who crawl through society."

"Don't worry, I'll not be the one to cast the first stone. I'm as tolerant as a saint, or a great sinner, though I'm neither."

The Duke left, not at all pleased with the conversation. At the door General Santa María stopped him.

"Have you ever seen anything like it, Duke?" he said.

"Like what?" asked the Duke, irritated.

"What a thing to ask!"

"Well, I am asking, and I'd like a reply."

"A twenty-four-year-old colonel."

"He is indeed somewhat young," replied the Duke, smiling.

"It's a blow to the Army."

"No doubt about it."

"It gives the lie to common sense."

"Of course!"

"Poor Spain!" exclaimed the general, offering his hand to the Duke and raising his eyes to heaven.

CHAPTER XVII

The Duke had arranged for Stein and his wife to live in a boarding-house run by a poor but honest and decent family. In a chest, to which Stein had been given the key when he took possession of his quarters, he had found a sum of money sufficient to surpass his most extravagant dreams. With the money was a note which said: "A fitting tribute to the surgeon's skill. The care and the night watches of a friend cannot be repaid except with sincere gratitude and friendship."

Stein was overcome.

"Ah, Marysal," he cried, showing the paper to his wife, "this man is great in everything: his rank, his heart, and his virtues. He imitates God by raising little, humble people to his own level. He calls me friend when I'm just a poor surgeon; and he speaks of gratitude when he heaps favors on me!"

"What's all that gold to him?" replied Marysal. "A man who has millions, according to what the landlady says, and whose estates are as big as whole provinces! Besides, if it weren't for you, he'd be lame for the rest of his life."

Just then the Duke came in, and, cutting short Stein's expressions of appreciation, he said to Marysal:

"I've come to ask a favor of you. You won't refuse, will you?"

"What could we refuse you?" Stein hastened to reply.

"Very well, María," the Duke went on. "I've promised a very close friend that you'd go to sing at her house."

Marysal did not answer.

"Of course she'll go," said Stein. "Heaven didn't give her

such a precious gift as her voice without imposing the obligation to share this grace with others."

"All right, then, it's agreed," the Duke went on. "And
since Stein plays the piano as well as the flute, you'll have one
at your disposal this afternoon, together with a selection of the
best pieces from modern opera. You'll be able then to choose
those you like best and practice them; for she must shine and
cover herself with glory. Her fame as a singer depends on
that."

At these last words, Marysal's eyes lit up.

"Will you sing, María?" asked the Duke.

"Why not?" she replied coldly.

"I know," said the Duke, "that you've already seen many
of the good things Seville has to offer. Stein already knows
Cean,[40] Ponz and Zúñiga[41] by heart. But what you haven't seen
is a bullfight. I'm leaving you some tickets for this afternoon's
performance. You'll be near me, for I'd like to see what you
think of this spectacle."

Shortly afterward, the Duke left.

That afternoon when Stein and Marysal arrived at the
bullring, it was already full of people. A lively and continuous
babble of voices served as a prelude to the performance, like
waves rising and roaring before a storm. That immense crowd,
made up of almost the entire population of the city and its
surrounding countryside; that agitation like the pounding of a
heart in the throes of violent passion; that ardent, intoxicating
atmosphere reminiscent of a bacchanal; that fusion of innumerable emotions into one; that fever of expectancy; that exaltation, frenetic but held within the bounds of order; those

---

[40] Bermúdez Cean, founder of the Academy of Fine Arts in Seville.
[41] Antonio Ponz, a famous theologian, antiquarian, painter, and writer
of eighteenth-century Valencia. Diego Ortiz de Zúñiga, eighteenth-
century Sevillian who wrote the Annals of the city.

strident, but not unmannerly shouts; that impatience on which
fear acts like a tonic; that eagerness which sends shivers of
pleasure, all form a kind of emotional electric charge to which
one must yield or flee.

Stein, bewildered and tense, would gladly have preferred
to flee. But his shyness detained him. Seeing that everyone
around him was happy, gay, and animated, he did not venture
to make himself conspicuous.

The bullring was full; twelve thousand people formed a
huge concentric circle around it. The rich spectators sat in the
shade; the common people, in the sun, displayed the many-
colored Andalusian costume.

In the big theaters where La Grisi, Lableche, Rachel, and
Macready are stars, the auditorium is not full except when it
is time for the performance of the favorite artist; but the barbarous performance carried out in this immense circus has
never been thus humbled.

The arena was cleared, and for a time it lay clean and
empty. Then came the picadors mounted on their unlucky
horses. With their drooping heads and their sad eyes, they
looked (as indeed they were) like victims going to the sacrifice.[42]

Only to watch those poor animals, whose fate he could
foresee, converted the kind of uneasiness Stein was experi-
encing into painful pity. He had not thus far had occasion
while in the war-torn provinces of the Peninsula to attend

---

[42] We offer our sincere good wishes to the periodicals which have taken
the initiative in the Spanish press in opposing the unheard-of cruelty
with which the poor animals are treated here. These pioneers have
begged that the agony of the wretched horses be ended humanely. As
freedom of the press is never of any use to the "good" causes it could
serve, this just and charitable admonition has not been heeded. AU-
THOR'S NOTE.

these grandiose national and popular festivals where the remnants of the light, brilliant tactics of the Moors are combined with the fierce courage of the Gothic race. But he had heard of them, and he knew that the success of a bullfight is gauged today by the number of horses killed. Hence his pity was directed mainly toward those wretched animals which, after serving their masters well, contributing to their prosperity and perhaps saving their lives, were repaid, when old age and overwork had exhausted their strength, with a terrible death that, through a refinement of cruelty, they are forced to seek for themselves; a death against which instinct warns them, and which some resist, while others, more resigned and beaten down, go to meet docilely in order to cut short their agony. The torments of these hapless creatures would wring a heart of stone; but the fans had no eyes, no attention, no feeling, except for the bull. They are under a veritable spell; and this communicates itself even to foreigners most set against Spain, and especially, against this savage sport. Moreover, it must be confessed, and we confess it with sadness, that in Spain compassion for animals, especially among men, is generally a theoretical rather than a practical sentiment. In the lowest classes it does not exist. Ah, Mr. Martin! [43] How much more meritorious you are in recognizing what humanity is than are many philanthropists of our time, who do so much harm to man without advancing the general welfare one iota!

Bullfights delight foreigners with depraved tastes, or those whose zest for life has become cloyed and who long, as for

---

[43] Mr. Martin from Galway, a member of the British Parliament, was the man who introduced a celebrated bill to prevent and punish cruelty to animals. He founded, moreover, a society for the same purpose; a society that, after the famous founder's death, has striven with tireless zeal along the line of the principles of conduct he had set forth. AUTHOR'S NOTE.

cool water, for some emotion to shake and revivify them; or they delight the mass of Spaniards, energetic and unsentimental men who, moreover, have been accustomed since childhood to this kind of spectacle. On the other hand, many attend through force of habit; others, especially the women, to see and be seen; still others are not amused; they suffer, but they stay, thanks to that carnal aspect of our human nature with which we are liberally endowed.

The three picadors saluted the president of the bullfight, preceded by the *banderilleros*[44] and the splendidly dressed *chulos*[45] in gay and brilliant colors. At the head of them all strode the star matadors and their substitutes whose costumes were still more luxurious than the others'.

"Pepe Vera! Here's Pepe!" the crowd shouted. "The pupil of Montes! What a fine boy! How gallant! How well he sets his feet down! How elegant from top to toe! What firm, calm eyes!"

"Do you know the great lesson Montes teaches his pupils?" asked a young man sitting next to Stein. "He pushes them in front of the bull with their arms crossed and says to them: 'Don't be afraid of the bull.'"

Pepe Vera went up to the barrier. His suit was a clear, bright cerise, with epaulets and heavy trimmings of silver. From the small pockets of his waistcoat the points of two batiste handkerchiefs stuck out. A jacket of rich silver lamé, and a small, graceful velvet hat with pompons completed his elegant, rich, and colorful bullfighter's costume.

After saluting the authorities with great suppleness and grace, he went to take his place, like the other fighters.

---

[44] The men who place the darts (*banderillas*) in the shoulders and neck of the bull.
[45] Assistants to the chief actors in the bull fight, who supply weapons, hold capes and divert the bull in moments of danger.

The three picadors took theirs at equal distances apart, near the barrier. The matadors and *chulos* were scattered over the arena. Then a deep silence fell as if that mass of people, so clamorous a few moments ago, had suddenly lost the power to breathe.

The mayor gave the signal; the trumpets sounded, and as the trump of the Last Judgment will, they brought about a general rising. And then, as if by magic, the wide doors of the bull pen swung open in front of the authorities' box. A reddish-colored bull plunged into the arena and was greeted by a universal explosion of shouts, whistles, insults, and eulogies. When the bull heard this tremendous outcry, he stopped short, raised his head, and seemed to ask with his burning eyes if all those provocations were addressed to him—to him, the great athlete who until then had been generous and had spared man, such a tiny and puny enemy; he reconnoitered the terrain, turning his menacing head quickly from side to side. He still hesitated; the shrill, penetrating whistles grew louder; then he launched himself straight at a picador with a speed that appeared incompatible with his weight and his bulk.

But he drew back when he felt the pain caused by the sharp point of the lance in his neck. He was a stupid animal, one of those called "bullocks" in bullfighting terminology, which was why he drew no blood in his first rush, but attacked the second picador instead.

This one was not so alert as his predecessor, and his thrust was neither so straight nor so firm, so that he wounded the animal without stopping him. The horns buried themselves in the body of the horse which fell. A cry of horror arose in the circus; immediately all the *chulos* surrounded that dreadful group; but the fierce animal had his prey down and was not to be distracted from his vengeance. At that moment the shouts of the crowd became a deep, wordless cry that would have terrified the entire city had it not been in the bullring.

The critical moment was prolonged in all its horror. The bull was concentrating upon the horse; the horse was crushing the picador with his weight and his convulsive movements, and the picador was squeezed beneath both huge masses. Then a young man sheathed in silver which shone like a star came up as lightly as a bright-plumaged bird, calmly as a child going out to pick flowers. He approached the bull from behind, and this youth, delicate in structure and fine in appearance, took the brute by the neck with his two hands and drew it toward him, as though it were a lap-dog. The bull, surprised, turned around furiously and plunged toward his adversary, who, facing him while walking backward, evaded the first rush with a half-turn to the right. The bull wheeled around and again attacked, and the youth again eluded him with a twist to the left, continuing in the same manner until he was close to the barrier. There he vanished before the animal's astonished eyes and the anxious gaze of the public, which, drunk with enthusiasm, thundered its applause; for it is always a moving sight to see men play thus with death, with no bravado nor affectation, and with an expressionless face.

"See how well he's learned his lessons from Montes! Look how Pepe Vera knows how to play the bull!" cried the young man sitting next to Stein, in a voice grown hoarse from shouting.

The Duke then turned his attention to Marysal. For the first time since their arrival in the capital of Andalusia, he saw emotion on that cold and disdainful face. Until that moment he had never seen her animated. Her harsh make-up, too vulgar to yield to the exquisite sense of wonder, and too indifferent and cold to register surprise, had not deigned to admire nor to show an interest in anything. To make any impression, to get any reaction from that hard metal, fire and a hammer were needed.

Stein was pale and upset.

"Duke," he said with an air of gentle reproach, "can this possibly amuse you?"

"No," answered the Duke with a kind smile, "it doesn't amuse me; it interests me."

Meanwhile, they had raised the horse. The poor animal could not keep on its feet. From its ripped belly its intestines hung to the ground. The picador was also on his feet, shaking in the *chulos'* arms, furious against the bull, and wanting with all his heart to remount and continue the attack with blind courage, despite being stunned from his fall. It was impossible to dissuade him, and he did indeed mount the poor victim again, sinking his spurs in the ripped flanks.

"Duke," said Stein, "perhaps I'm going to appear peculiar to you, but the truth is that it's impossible for me to remain at this spectacle. María, shall we go?"

"No," replied Marysal, whose whole soul seemed concentrated in her eyes. "Am I squeamish? Are you afraid I may faint?"

"Well, then," said Stein, "I'll come back for you when the bullfight is over."

And he left.

The bull had already killed a considerable number of horses. The unfortunate one we have just mentioned was letting himself be pulled by the bridle, with his entrails hanging, to a door through which he went out. Others, unable to get up, were lying full length, convulsed with agony; at times they would lift their heads on which the picture of terror was painted. When they showed such signs of life, the bull returned to the charge, goring his still-quivering victims again with his cruel horns. Then he ran around the arena, his forehead and horns covered with blood, his attitude provocative and challenging, now raising his head proudly to the stands, where the shouting had never stopped for a second and now toward the bright-colored *chulos* who were passing in front of him like meteors, placing the *banderillas*. Sometimes, little birds would emerge from a net hidden among the rosettes on the *banderillas,* and would fly around. Who could have been the first to think of effecting this striking contrast? He must certainly not have had the intention of symbolizing defenseless innocence, rising effortlessly above the horrors and the fierce passions of the earth. Rather, he must have been one of those people with poetic ideas which arise spontaneously even in the hardest and cruelest hearts of the Spanish people, as a mignonette plant will flower spontaneously in Andalusia among the stones and mortar of a balcony.

At a signal from the president, the trumpets sounded again and there came a moment of rest in that bloody struggle when all was quiet once more.

Then Pepe Vera with a sword and a red cape in his left hand walked toward the official box. He stood before it and bowed, indicating that he was asking permission to kill the bull.

Pepe Vera had noticed the presence of the Duke, whose fondness for bullfighting was well known. He had also observed the woman beside him; for this woman with whom the Duke would often chat never took her eyes off the matador.

He went to the Duke, and taking off his hat, he said:

"I dedicate this bull to Your Excellency, and to the lovely girl at his side."

And, saying this, he flung his hat on the ground with a

gesture of inimitable carelessness, and went where his duty called him.

The *chulos* were watching him closely, ready to carry out his orders. The matador chose the place that suited him, then, pointing it out to his troupe:

"Here!" he shouted to them.

The *chulos* ran toward the bull to incite him, and the bull, pursuing them, came face to face with Pepe Vera, waiting for him in a firm stance. That was the moment of truth. A profound silence succeeded the raucous tumult and the vehement cheering that had been lavished on him as the champion matador.

The bull, seeing that tiny enemy which had mocked his fury, stopped as if to reflect. Doubtless he feared that the man might escape him again. Anyone entering the bullring just then might have believed he was attending not a public spectacle but rather a solemn religious ceremony. So great was the silence.

The two adversaries studied each other.

Pepe Vera shook the cape he was carrying in his left hand. The bull rushed him. With a single light movement, he made a pass with the red cape, followed by a series of graceful passes, and when the brute once more attacked, he aimed the sword between the shoulders, so that the animal, continuing his charge, helped with all his strength to drive the steel full-length into his own body to the hilt. He fell flat on the ground, lifeless.

It is quite impossible to describe the outburst of shouts and applause which echoed throughout the bullring. Only those who are accustomed to attending such events can envisage them. At the same time the military band struck up.

Pepe Vera calmly crossed the arena in the midst of those frenetic testimonials of passionate admiration, of that unanimous ovation, saluting to right and left with his sword, in grateful acknowledgement, without any feeling of surprise nor pride at a triumph that more than one Roman emperor might have envied. He went to bow before the city officials, and then to the Duke and the girl.

The Duke slipped her a purse of gold coins, and she threw it into the arena, wrapped in her scarf.

When Pepe Vera made the natural demonstrations of thanks, his black eyes met Marysal's. If a classical writer were to record that meeting of the eyes, he might say that Cupid had wounded both their hearts with as much skill as Pepe Vera had wounded the bull. We who lack the temerity to ally ourselves with that severe and inflexible school, shall merely say that those two natures were born to understand and harmonize with each other, and that indeed they did so.

Pepe Vera had been truly admirable. Everything he had done in a situation where he stood between life and death had been carried out with a dexterity, a suppleness, a calm, and a grace that never faltered for a second. To achieve this a strong character and supreme courage are essential, combined with a degree of exaltation that can only be aroused by twenty-four thousand eyes watching and twenty-four thousand hands applauding.

CHAPTER XVIII

During the scenes we have been attempting to describe
in the preceding chapter, Stein was strolling around Seville,
following the line of its ancient walls, built by Julius Caesar,
as this inscription over the Jérez gate testifies:

> HERCULES BUILT ME
> JULIUS CAESAR ENCIRCLED ME
> WITH WALLS AND HIGH TOWERS,
> AND THE BLESSED KING WON ME
> WITH GARCI-PÉREZ DE VARGAS.[46]

Turning to the right, Stein passed in front of the convent
of Pópulo, today a jail; there he saw close at hand the beautiful gate of Triana, and farther along the Royal gate, through
which Saint Ferdinand made his entrance, and some centuries
later, Philip II.

Facing him was the convent of Saint Laureano, where Ferdinand Columbus, son of the immortal Christopher, founded
a school and established his observatory. Later on, Stein passed
the gate of Saint John, and Baqueta Gate, with which so
many memories are linked. A certain distance away, on the
banks of the river, the sumptuous monastery of Saint Gerónimo could be seen. The statue of the saint, considered one of
the most perfect ever to have issued from an artist's hands, now
adorns the hall of the museum. This thought came to Stein:
"Would the ancient artists have turned out masterpieces, if,

---

[46] The king was Ferdinand the Saint, who recaptured Seville from the
Moors in 1248. Garci-Pérez de Vargas was one of his most distinguished
and valiant knights.

instead of dedicating them to the veneration of devout souls, as objects of worship and prayer, they had known that their final resting place was to be a museum where they would be exposed to the cold analysis of art lovers and admirers of form?"

Farther on he looked at Saint Lazarus, a hospital for lepers, and at the immense proud hospital of the Five Wounds of the Lord, commonly called the Hospital of the Blood, one of the magnificent public works on which the Enríquez de Rivera family had spent millions. Their trustees have retained the charity and public zeal of the founders, both greater than their great work, for posterity.

Stein studied the gate of La Macarena, which takes its name from a daughter of Hercules to whom, some say, Julius Caesar dedicated it, while others claim it was the name of a Moorish princess who once had a palace there. Pedro the Cruel[47] often came through the gate as a conqueror; as did Don Fadrique, his brother, whom Don Pedro had murdered to satisfy a grudge. A little farther along, Stein passed the Cordovan gate; above it could still be seen the narrow cage, now turned into a chapel, in which Saint Hermenegildo was imprisoned and martyred at the command of his father, Leovigildo, the king of the Goths, about 586. In front of the gate is the Capuchin monastery, on the spot, they say, once occupied by the first church in Spain, founded by Saint James the Apostle, although Zaragoza disputes this glory with Seville. Farther on was the convent of the Trinity, on the site once occupied by the Roman jail, and the dungeon where the holy virgins, Justa and Rufina, patron saints of the city, were once imprisoned. An altar has been built in the dungeon around a

---

[47] King of Castile (1333-1369), ruler at sixteen, constantly at war with Aragon, and perpetrator of a series of murders. Fadrique was his bastard brother, whom he had put to a violent death before his eyes in the Alcázar.

marble pillar to which the two saints were bound, and on which they traced with their weak fingers a cross that can still be seen.

Beyond the Sun and the Osario gates, he found the gate of Camona, one of the most beautiful in the district, where the main highway starts and runs parallel with the aqueduct that provides Seville with her water. This road crosses the entire Peninsula in length, bounding like a goat through the rugged terrain of Despeñaperros. An anecdote is connected with this gate, portraying to the life the character of the Sevillian noblemen of the time. It was in 1540. The Sevillians were leaving the city through the gate to rescue Gibraltar. Don Rodrigo de Saavedra was carrying the city's standard; but the arch in those days was so low that the standard could not pass through unless it was lowered. Don Rodrigo went up over the gate, hauled by ropes, preferring this inconvenience to seeing his noble design humbled.

On the left are the large, colorful suburbs of Saint Roque and Saint Bernardo, together with the King's Garden, so called because it once belonged to a Moorish king named Ben-Joar. Stein came to the Carne gate, near the fine cavalry barracks, leaving the elegant San Fernando gate to his right. This was built in 1760 at the same time as the adjoining magnificent tobacco factory, which cost thirty-six million *reales*; and leaving on his left the cemetery which death works as constantly to fill as the Danaïdes[48] their cask, he came to the beautiful public walks, like flower gardens, which adorn the city along the banks of the Guadalquivir.

---

[48] The fifty daughters of King Danaus of Argos, betrothed to the fifty sons of Egypt, who were ordered by their father to slay each her own husband on her wedding night. In punishment the maidens were condemned forever to dip water in a sieve to fill a cask.

The only sound breaking the silence of the beautiful Promenade of Las Delicias was the birds' salute to the sun at its setting. The stillness of the river was such that it would have seemed frozen if it had not been made to ripple from time to time by the caress of a bird's wing or the leap of some playful little fish. On the opposite bank rose the Convent of Los Remedios, with its crown of cypresses, their tall heads proudly erect, unaware that the building was cracking in deep fissures, as an abandoned plant will dry up when there is no hand to water it. The shadows of twilight were beginning to cover the city, while the beautiful and colossal gilded bronze statue of Faith, reigning atop the Giralda, shone in the last rays of the sun, radiant and ardent as the glory of the great men who placed it there to crown the immense basilica. The canons paid for it out of their own purse in 1401, thereby pledging themselves and their successors, whoever they might be, to live a communal life so as to apply all their income to the construction of the church. Every single man of them kept his promise, perhaps without a parallel in the history of the arts. A splendid example of abnegation, of religious zeal, and of artistic intelligence, and a worthy complement to the memorable contract decreeing the erection of that temple, which we cannot forbear to quote: "Let us make," it said, "such a church, and so great, that there may not be its equal in the world, and let them take us for madmen in the future."

The round Gold Tower was to Stein's right. Some say it was so named because it once was the depository for the gold arriving from America.

This derivation is unlikely, however, for it had borne the name before the discovery of the New World. More likely it comes from the yellow tiles that once faced it, some of which are still there. This very ancient tower, built long before the

Christian era, is like the club of Hercules tossed in among children's toys, so conjoined is it with reminders of the days of the heroes, standing there among the varicolored ship's pennants, the wisps of smoke from the steam vessels, the walks built yesterday and the flowers born today, with its foundations that can count the centuries as if they were decades.

Among those reminders is one of very slight, though historical importance. It has often caused us to smile (a rare enough occurrence in view of the state of the world) at its portrayal of the nature of the man, King Don Pedro, whose memory ranks second only to that of the sainted King Don Ferdinand in Seville.

Near the Gold Tower there is a wharf which the canons ordered built while the church was under construction to accommodate the discharge of the materials for the church. All those who landed there were charged a wharfage fee. Don Pedro, pressed for money, made use of those funds as a forced loan. It seems that this monarch, then very young, had such a poor memory for debts that the chapter considered turning to the courts to recover the promised payment. But where could they find a clerk bold enough to present himself to Pedro with a writ in his hand? A secretarial Cid or Pelayo was needed, and there are few of those in the world. The ecclesiastical court sought ways and means; and the following expedient came to hand: one day when the king was taking a horseback ride near the aforementioned wharf, he saw approaching a small vessel which stopped at a respectful distance from him. There was a kind of crow or big black bird of ill omen on that boat. The king was astonished to see such a sight on the river, for people dressed in black are generally no more devoted to Neptune than to Mars. But his astonishment was greatly increased when he heard a harsh voice saying: "To you, Don Pedro, we issue this court order." It could say no more, for the king, with sparks shooting from his eyes, drew his sword, set spurs to his mount, and plunged into the water with no thought of what he was doing. Imagine the terror of the black bird! He dropped the papers, seized an oar, and sheared off to safety. It may be assumed that the people, as admiring of daring courage as scornful of judicial maneuvers, applauded the king with enthusiasm. We, who admire anything great, even though it be a royal rage, have told this anecdote because birds truly black, that is, those whose plumage and tongues had both been dipped into an inkwell, took their revenge later to slander the unfortunate man, availing themselves of their customary weapons of cunning and calumny.

Poor Don Pedro! Perhaps he was evil because he was unhappy. His cruelty was the outgrowth of desperation; but he had an able mind, an energetic character, and a heart capable of love.

Stein, his head resting on his hands, was feasting his eyes on the magnificent spectacle spread before him, and breathing that pure, balsam-scented air with delight. From time to time a prolonged roar took him out of his gentle ecstasy and touched his heart with sadness. It was the shouting in the bullring.

"Dear God!" he said to himself, recalling the war, "they call that glory and this," alluding to the bullfight, "they call pleasure!"

CHAPTER XIX

Marysal was spending all her time concentrating on the perfection of her art which promised a brilliant future, a glorious career, and a status that would flatter her vanity and satisfy her fondness for luxury. Stein never tired of wondering at her constancy in study and her admirable progress.

Nevertheless, the moment of her introduction to high society had to be postponed owing to the illness of the son of the Countess.

At his first symptoms she had forgotten everything around her: her salons, her wardrobe, her amusements, Marysal and her friends, and in particular, the elegant young colonel of whom we have spoken.

Nothing in the world mattered to this mother but her son, at whose bedside she had spent two weeks weeping and praying, without food or sleep.

The child was having trouble cutting his teeth, which could not pierce the swollen and painful gums. His life was in danger. The Duke advised the stricken mother to consult Stein; and when she had done so, the clever German saved the boy by lancing the gums. Thenceforth, Stein became a friend of the family. The Countess embraced him, and the Count paid him a fee fit for a prince. The Marchioness used to say he was a saint; the General admitted there might be good doctors outside Spain. Rita, for all her asperity, deigned to consult him about her migraine headaches, and Rafael swore he was going to break his ribs one fine day for the pleasure of being treated by Frederick the Great.

One morning the Countess was sitting, pale and ill-looking, at the bedside of her sleeping son. Her mother was in a low chair, keeping her fan in constant motion against the heat. Rita had settled down in front of a large frame and was embroidering a magnificent altar piece she had undertaken to make in company with the Countess.

Rafael came in.

"Good morning, Aunt; good morning, Cousins. How is the Algar heir?"

"As well as can be expected," replied the Marchioness.

"Then, my dear Grace," went on her cousin, "it seems to me the time has come for you to come out of your prison. Your absence is a notable eclipse of the sun which is throwing the city into consternation. Your usual visitors are heaving such deep sighs they're going to strip the trees in Las Delicias of their leaves. Baron de Maude is adding to his string of questions some more about your invisibility. He was scandalized at your excess of mother love. He says that in France ladies are permitted to write some pretty verses on this subject; but they wouldn't tolerate a young mother's endangering her health, letting the bloom fade from her cheeks, depriving herself of rest and food, and forgetting her own well-being at her child's side."

"Nonsense!" cried the Marchioness. "Are you trying to tell me there's a country in the world where a mother would leave her child for one single second when he's ill?"

"Well, the Major is worse yet," Rafael went on. "When he heard about what you're doing, he somehow opened his astonished-looking eyes still wider, and he says he wouldn't have believed the Spanish people were so barbarous as not to have a nursery in their houses."

"And what is that?" asked the Marchioness.

"As he explains it," Rafael replied, "it's a Siberia for English children. Sir John bets you've grown so slight and thin you'd pass for a daughter of Zephyr with better reason than the Andalusian mares that enjoy that reputation. He says they'd fall far behind his English mare, Atlanta,[49] in a horse race unless someone should scatter a measure of oats on the track to distract her. Cousin, the only one who has consoled himself during your absence has been Polo, who has brought out a volume of poetry, and we almost had a quarrel over it."

"Tell us about it, Rafael," said Rita. "I'd like to have been present at your dispute; it would have amused me a great deal."

"As you know," said Rafael, "all our modern *enlightened* people are aspiring by any and all means to the title of *notabilities*."

"Nephew," exclaimed the Marchioness, "for goodness' sake stop using those foreignized words. They make me sick."

"Forgive me, Aunt," Rafael replied, "but they're essential to my story; in fact they're its very essence. As these gentlemen, especially those of them who have drunk from French springs, have noticed that in France, the particle *de* signifies nobility, they want to adopt it, too. But as in Spain it means absolutely nothing, anyone can flatter his ears with the sonorousness of that innocent monosyllable, a caliph among names, as it were, each one the son of his father and mother. This may dazzle foreigners who do not know that in Spain the *de*, plus a long string of surnames, is practically arbitrary and may be used *ad libitum*."

"Of course," said the Marchioness. "It would be a strange thing if anyone must be of noble blood to have two letters in front of his name. Married women add their maiden name to

---

[49] Daughter of the king of Arcadia, whose hand was won by Hippomenes, who raced against her and won by dropping three golden apples which she stopped to pick up.

their husbands' with the usual *de*; and so, your mother signs herself Rafaela Santa María de Arias. Many noble names don't have it. In Seville, the Marquis of C . . . is J.P. The Count of A, F.E. The Marquis of M . . . A.S. My brother calls himself León Santa María, and the Duke of Rivas puts Angel Saavedra on the front cover of his books."

"Returning to our Polo," went on Rafael, "not satisfied with having a name so suitable to the title page of a collection of poetry, he's had the idea of placing his mother's and his grandmother's there, too, according to whether the syllables are more or less harmonious, and has had the satisfaction of ordering them in Gothic script on the title page of his work: By A. Polo de Mármol; and he was very happy to see his prosaic name stretched out, ennobled, sonorous, distinguished and proud there on calfskin, like an ancient paladin emerging from the tomb with his armor all rusty, and thinking himself a different man from what he once was; admired and respected by himself like that Portuguese officer who, seeing himself in a mirror armed from head to heel, began to tremble in fear of himself. Polo's enthusiasm rose to such heights that he ordered his calling cards engraved with the newly discovered formula, adding an imaginary coat of arms where a castle appears . . ."

"Playing cards!" said the Marchioness testily.

"A lion," continued Rafael, "an eagle, a leopard, a fox, a bear, a dragon; in short, the whole Noah's ark of heraldry, and topping it all, an imperial crown. Unfortunately, the engraver being neither an Estévez nor a Carmona, was unable to find room for the strings on a lyre which formed a part of the Polo arms; but that's a small contretemps that no one minded. I congratulated him on his new name, assuring him that the name 'de Mármol' fitted beautifully after the 'A. Polo,' for an

'Apollo of Marble' is worth more than an Apollo of plaster
of Paris. He took it as a slur on him, and got so furious that
he threatened to write a satire on the vanity of nobles. I asked
him if the satire on the male nobles would be extended to the
females, also. Then he was reminded of you, my dear cousin.
He heaved a sigh and let the mighty pen fall from his hand;
he combed his hair, slicked it down and covered the serpentine locks of his Nemesis with pomade, and so I got out of it
very well, thanks to my cousin's beautiful eyes. But," added
Rafael, seeing Stein enter, "here comes the most precious of
precious stones,[50] a melodious stone like Memnon.[51] Don Federico, since you are an observing physiologist, admire how all
the situations of life in Spain are unchangeable: evenness of
temper, benevolence, and even gayety. We have none of the
melancholy of the Germans, the spleen of the English, or the
ennui of our French neighbors. Do you know why? Because
we don't ask too much of life, because we do not sigh for a
fleeting happiness."

"Thats' because we usually have the tastes appropriate to
our respective ages," said the Marchioness.

"It's because our beautiful sky sheds well-being on our
spirit," observed the Countess.

"It's because everyone does as he pleases," said Rita.

"I think," said Stein, "it's because of all those things, and
of the national character, besides. The poor Spaniard who con-
tents himself with a crust of bread, an orange, and a ray of
sunlight, is in harmony with the patrician who is almost always

---

[50] A play on words. Stein means stone in German.
[51] Memnon, the beautiful son of Aurora, was an Ethiopian king killed
in the Trojan war. A statue was erected to him with a stone in its lap
which sends forth a sound like a harp string when the dawn light
(Aurora) strikes it.

happy with his lot, and he becomes a noble Procrustes,[52] his own arbiter of ethics, fitting his aspirations and his well-being to his situation."

"You're saying, Don Federico," said the Marchioness, "that in Spain everyone is satisfied with the fate that's dealt him. Ah, Doctor! How sorry I am to say that we're no longer what we were in that respect. My brother says that in current jargon a word has been invented by the spirit of evil and pride, a kind of lever that the foundations of society cannot resist, which has caused the human species more misery than all the despotism in the world."

"What is the word?" asked Rafael, "Tell me so I can shut my ears to it."

"That word is *noble ambition*," said the Marchioness, sighing.

"Señora," said Rafael, "ambition has become the general mania of the nobility."

"Aunt," cried Rita, "if we're going to get into politics and you're going to repeat Uncle's strictures, I warn you that Don Federico is going to lapse into German melancholy, Rafael into English spleen, and I into French *ennui*."

"How impudent you are!" said her aunt.

"To avert such a misfortune," ventured Rafael, "I make a motion that among us all we compose a novel."

"I second the motion," cried the Countess.

"What nonsense!" said her mother. "Do you want to turn out one of those beauties my daughter reads me, one of those serials the French write?"

---

[52] A Greek giant, called the Stretcher, with an iron bedstead to which he tied travellers who fell into his hands. If they were shorter than the bed, he stretched them to fit it; if longer, he lopped off the necessary amount from their legs.

"Why not?" asked Rafael.

"Because no one will read it," answered the Marchioness, "unless it's proclaimed to be French."

"What does that matter to us?" Rafael went on. "We'll write as birds sing—for the pleasure of singing, and not for the pleasure of our listeners."

"At least do me the favor not to drag in by the tail any seductions or adulteries," went on the Marchioness. "It's a fine thing to make women interesting only for their faults! Nothing is less interesting in the eyes of sensible people than a feather-brained girl who lets herself be seduced, or a light woman who betrays her husband. Don't profane the sacred texts of Scripture, either, as is the scandalous custom of new-fangled novelists. Is there anything more scandalous than to see on a slick paper-back book with a suggestive drawing on the cover the very words of our Lord, such as: 'Much may be forgiven her, for she has loved much.' Or, 'Let him who is without sin cast the first stone.' And this to justify vice! It's a profanation! Don't those simple-minded writers know that those sacred words of mercy devolved upon the anguish of repentance and are the merits of contrition?"

"Wonderful!" said Rafael. "What a burst of eloquence! Auntie is inspired, enlightened; I'll vote for her for Congress!"

"Don't introduce suicide either—that terrible thing that was never known here until lately, and that has succeeded in weakening religion and even banishing it. Nothing like that befits us."

"You're right," said the Countess. "We must not paint the Spanish people as foreigners; we'll paint ourselves as we are."

"But if we accept the restrictions the Marchioness demands," said Stein, "what kind of romantic outcome can a novel have? Mustn't it be built on an unrequited passion, as usual?"

"Time," answered the Marchioness; "time writes the outcome to everything, whatever the novelists who dream when they should be observing may have to say. Besides, isn't there any other topic but unrequited passion?"

"Aunt," said Rafael, "what you're saying is as prosaic as a stew."

"Will you kill yourself if I marry Luis?" said Rita.

"I! I, an innocent and interesting individual, become my own hangman? I, my own Herod? God spare me, lovely ingrate," replied Rafael. "I shall live to see and enjoy your repentance, and to replace your Luis Trumps, if he takes it into his head to play *monte* with his companion Lucifer in his kingdom."

"Don't have any ostentation in your novel," pursued the Marchioness. "No foreign words and phrases that we don't need. If you don't know our language, here's the dictionary."

"Well said," replied Rafael. "We shan't give house room to the *sveltes,* the *notabilities,* nor the *dandies;* perverse intruders, poisonous parasites, dangerous emissaries of Revolution."

"What you are saying is truer than you think," answered the Marchioness.

"But, Mother," said the Countess, "with all the restrictions you're setting up, we're bound to end up with something insipid."

"I'm counting on your good taste," replied the Marchioness, "and on what Rafael is capable of inventing and contriving so that it won't be insipid. Another warning: if you mention God's name, call Him by His own name and not by one of those names that are fashionable today: Supreme Being,

Supreme Intelligence, Moderator of the Universe, and others of that ilk."

"What, dear Aunt!" cried Rafael. "Are you denying God His powers and prerogatives?"

"Certainly not," replied the Marchioness. "But the name God embraces everything. To seek other more high-sounding names is to gild the lily. It seems to me that everything that's done here from the top down is the same sort of thing, taking away the title of the king to call him president, first consul, or protector. I'm sure that before his rebellion had been fully consummated, Lucifer called God the Supreme Being."

"But, Aunt, you can't deny," observed Rafael, "that it's more respectful and even more submissive."

"Go along with you!" said the Marchioness impatiently. "You're always contradicting me, not from conviction, but to annoy me. Give to God the name that He gave to Himself, for no one is going to give Him a better one."

"You're right, Mother," said the Countess. "Let's leave out the weaknesses, the tears, and the crimes, and the high-sounding phrases. Let's make something good, elegant, and gay."

"But, Grace," said Rafael, "it must be admitted that there's nothing so insipid as pure virtue in a novel. For example: let's suppose I'm going to write a biography of my aunt. I shall say she was an excellent young girl; she married a man who suited her, as her parents wished her to; and that she was a model wife and mother, with no other weakness than to be somewhat attached to the past and a little too fond of cards. This is all very fine for an epitaph, but you must agree it's pretty flat for a novel."

"And wherever did you get the idea that I aspire to be the model for the heroine of a novel?" asked the Marchioness. "How absurd!"

"Let's write a Gothic novel, then," said Stein.

"By no means," said Rafael. "That's all right for you Germans, not for us. A Gothic Spanish novel would be an unbearable affectation."

"Very well," continued Stein, "a heroic or a sad novel, then."

"God save and defend us!" cried Rafael. "That's all right for Polo."

"A sentimental novel."

"Just to hear of it makes my hair stand on end," said Rafael. "There's no type less suited to the Spanish temperament than the weepy type. Sentimentality is as inimical to our character as sentimental jargon to the Castillian language."

"What are we going to write, then?" asked the Countess.

"To my feeble mind there are two types that suit us: the historical novel, which we shall leave to learned writers, and the novel of customs, which is precisely suited to mediocre writers like us."

"Let it be a novel of customs, then," said the Countess.

"That's the best kind of novel," went on Rafael, "useful and agreeable. Each nation should write its own. Written with accuracy and the true spirit of observation, they would add much to the study of humanity, history, moral practice, acquaintance with places and times. If I were the Queen, I'd order a novel of customs written in every province, leaving out nothing in the way of reference and analysis."

"In fact it would be a sort of geography," said Stein, laughing. "What about the writers?"

"There'd be no lack of them if they were sought," replied Rafael, "as men are never lacking for any enterprise if they're sought with enough diligence. The proof is that here am I,

and right now you're going to hear a novel composed by me
that will belong to both types."

"You'll see," said the Marchioness, "that it will come out
looking something like Berthold,[53] Don Federico."

"As my cousin wants something good and simple; my
aunt, something moral, minus passion, weaknesses, crimes, and
Scriptural texts; and my cousin Rita, something festive, I'm
going to choose as my subject the honorable and moral life of
my uncle, General Santa María."

"The one thing lacking was for you to make fun of my
brother," said the Marchioness. "It seems to me he doesn't deserve that. Indeed!"

"No," replied Rafael, "I certainly respect and appreciate
my uncle above anyone in this world, and I know that his
military virtues, which are sometimes excessive, have earned
him the name of the Don Quijote of the Army; but this doesn't
keep him from having his own story, for if Mme. de Staël said
that the life of a woman is always a novel, it might be said
with equal truth, I think, that the life of a man is always a history. Listen, then, incomparable doctor, to the history of my
uncle in compendium. Santiago León Santa María was born
predestined to the noble career of arms, for he first saw the
light of day, or, more accurately, the shades of night, at the
very moment when the tattoo for night quarters was being
sounded, so that he made his entry in the world to the beat
of the drum."

"That is true," said the Marchioness, smiling.

"I never lie . . . while I'm telling the truth," gravely
continued Rafael. "As a token of that predestination, he was
born with a sword on his chest, the color of blood, drawn by

---

[53] An early German prose writer, whose sermons were published in 1824.

Nature's hand with the greatest appropriateness; so that all the women of the district gathered to salute the General *in partibus* of Her Catholic Majesty's armies."

"No such thing," said the Marchioness. "He has a birthmark on his chest, it's true, but it's in the shape of a radish, a mark our mother had."

"You see, Doctor," said Rafael, "how my aunt depreciates and depoetizes the history of her dear brother? A radish on the chest of a brave man, instead of a military symbol! Come, Aunt, could anything be more ridiculous?"

"What's ridiculous about being born with a birthmark on the chest?" demanded the Marchioness.

"Go on, Rafael," said Rita. "I never knew any of these details. Go on, without so many interruptions."

"There's no rush, Rita," said Rafael. "What's our hurry? One of the advantages we have over other nations is that we don't live at headlong speed, like unwelcome runners.

"So hardly had León Santa María reached the age of twelve when he entered a regiment as a cadet, and from then on he went ahead straight as a ramrod, serious as a sermon, and sober as a funeral. While he was drilling troops and fighting like a brave lad in Rosellon, time was passing, and my uncle had reached the age when the heart sings and sighs."

"Rafael, Rafael," said his aunt, "be careful what you're saying."

"Don't be afraid, Aunt. I shall speak only of platonic love."

"Meaning," said the Marchioness, "this is only the vanguard; but you know that the main body of troops comes behind it; so let's turn the page on this chapter."

"Señora Marchioness," said Rafael, "don't worry. My history shall be such that, after hearing it, anyone would be able to picture my uncle with the sword in one hand and the palm in the other.

"His first love was a beautiful girl from Osuna, where his regiment was quartered. The order to march came unexpectedly. My uncle swore he would return and she began to sing: 'Marlborough went off to the war,' and she would be singing it yet if a husky farmer had not offered his mutton-fist and his fortune. At first, however, she was inconsolable. She wept like the clouds of autumn, and day and night she kept exclaiming: 'Santa María! Santa María!' until a servant girl who slept near her was answering devoutly, 'Pray for us,' thinking that her mistress was saying the Litany.

"My uncle," continued Rafael, "was ordered to America; he came back to take part in the War of Independence, and he had no time to think of love. The result was that, being unable to be on terms of intimacy with any beauties other than those he could order to march to the drumbeat, he acquired such a sour temper that he became known as General Sour Grapes."

"How dare you?" cried his aunt.

"I'm not daring anything, Aunt," replied Rafael. "I'm only repeating what other people have said. Softly, softly he reached the age of sixty, which brought with it the usual accompaniment of rheumatism and colds, which gave signs of becoming chronic. My aunt and all his friends advised him to retire and marry so as to lead a tranquil life. Think, Doctor, of the remedy; to marry in order to live in peace! You can see that my aunt leans to homeopathy." [54]

"You mean that new system which prescribes stimulants to moderate a fever?" asked the Marchioness. "Don't you believe it,

---

[54] The branch of medicine which holds that disease is cured by remedies producing effects similar to the symptoms of the malady.

Doctor, and don't give that kind of remedy to the little boy."

"Well, as I was saying," continued Rafael, "there was a middle-aged spinster here who hadn't wanted to marry her father's choice, while her father hadn't wanted to let her marry her own choice; this lady had many whims, in view of which she named her daughter Doña Pancracia Cabeza de Vaca.[55] Very well, this noble part of the animal . . ."

The Marchioness interrupted him.

"You may laugh all you like, as you laugh at everything; this is a privilege that Nature has given you, as the sun was given to shine. But, Don Federico, you must know that this name, so ridiculous in my nephew's eyes, is one of the oldest and most illustrious in Spain. It owes its origin to the battle at Navas de Tolosa . . ."

"Which," added Rafael, "took place in the year 1212, and was won by King Alfonso IX, called the Noble, father of Queen Blanche of France, the mother of Saint Louis; and with that deed he freed Castille from the Saracen yoke."

"Just so," said the Marchioness. "I've already heard all that from my sister-in-law. The Defender of the Faith, as she tells it, had retired to a height where he dug himself in with his treasure in a kind of corner built of iron chains. A river separated this height from the Christian army. The king was in despair because he couldn't cross it. Then an old shepherd came to him in his gown and cape and showed him a place where the river could be forded with ease. 'Follow the bank,' he said, 'downstream, and where you see the head of a cow that was eaten by the wolves, there will be the ford.' Owing to this information, that memorable battle was won. The grateful king knighted the man who had performed such a signal service, and gave him and his posterity the name of Cabeza de Vaca. My

---

[55] Meaning, literally, "cow's head."

sister-in-law says that the statue of the patriotic shepherd and
the chains from the Caliph's encampment are kept in the cathedral in Toledo."

"Six hundred years of nobility are a bagatelle compared
with ours," said Rafael, "for you must know, Doctor, that the
name of Santa María eclipses all the Cabezas de Vaca, even if
their family tree had been rooted from the horns of the cow
that Noah took on his ark. For your information, we are related
to the Blessed Virgin, no less, and to prove it, one of my grand-
mothers used to say the rosary with her servants, according to
good Spanish custom . . ."

A custom that's being lost," interrupted the Marchioness,
sighing.

Rafael went on: "She used to say, 'God save thee, Mary, my
cousin, and my Lady,' and the servants responded: 'Holy Mary,
Her Excellency's cousin and Lady.' "

"Don't say such things in front of strangers, Rafael," said
the Countess, "because, either they're so set against us they
won't believe them, or else, believing them, they'll be malicious
enough to repeat them. What you've just told is something
that everyone knows; a joke invented to make fun of our family's exaggerated pretensions to antiquity."

"Apropos of what strangers say, do you know, Cousin, that
Lord Londonderry has written *Voyage to Spain,* in which he
says there's only one pretty woman in Seville and that's the
Marchioness of A . . . , supposedly disguising her name in the
strangest fashion?"

"He's right," said the Countess. "Adela is very beautiful."

"She's very beautiful," agreed Rafael, "but to say she's the
only one seems to me the biggest piece of nonsense. The Mayor
is furious, and he's going to sue for libel, with the full support

of la Giralda, who rates herself the best-looking girl in all Seville."

"That's being more royal than the king," said Rita with a gesture of disdain, "and you may assure the Mayor in the name of all the Sevillian women, that we couldn't care less whether he finds us ugly or beautiful. But do go on with your story, Rafael; you left us at the preliminaries to our uncle's marriage."

"Before Rafael picks up the hour-glass," interrupted the Marchioness, "I shall tell you, Don Federico, that our family's patents of nobility were already recognized in the year 737, because one of our ancestors killed the bear that had taken the life of the Gothic king, Don Favila, and we therefore have a bear on our coat of arms."

Rafael broke into such hearty laughter that he broke the thread of his aunt's narrative.

"Come," he said, "here's the second part of the Cousin and My Lady story. The Marchioness has a collection of genealogical data, one as true as another. She knows the family tree of the Dukes of Alba by heart, and that's worth a fortune!"

"I shall be infinitely grateful if you'll be good enough to tell me, Señora Marchioness," said Stein.

"Gladly," said the Marchioness, "and I hope you'll credit my words more than that boy does who's so proud of knowing more than those who were born before him. You know that nothing so ennobles a man as courageous deeds."

"By that reckoning," said Rita, "José María could be noble and more besides; a grandee of Spain of the first class."

"How my nephews and nieces like to contradict! cried the Marchioness impatiently. "Very well, then, señorita. José María could be noble if he weren't a thief."

"Now that we're talking about José María," said Rafael,

"I'm going to tell Don Federico about a valorous deed by that personage. I have it on good authority."

"We don't want to hear about the deeds of the heroes of the blunderbuss," said the Marchioness. "Rafael, you talk without periods or commas."

"Listen to my story about José María," Rafael went on. "A robber hero, gentlemanly, elegant, gallant, and distinguished, he's a fruit that grows only in our soil. You foreigners may have many Dukes of Alba, but you surely don't have a José María."

"What are you saying?" said the Marchioness. "The foreigners may have many Dukes of Alba. Oh, yes, indeed! That would be easy! Listen, Don Federico, when Saint Ferdinand the king was before the walls of Seville, he suggested to the Moorish king that as the siege had become so prolonged . . ."

"Whose name was Axafat, upon my word of honor," interjected Rafael.

"His name doesn't matter," said the Marchioness. "He proposed, then, as I was saying, that the fate of the besieged city be decided by single combat between the two monarchs, face to face. The Moor was ashamed to refuse the challenge. King Ferdinand concealed his design from everyone, and when the hour agreed upon arrived, he went out alone by night from his tent, walking toward the chosen spot. A soldier of his guard who saw him go had some suspicion of his intent and, fearing that the king might fall victim to some trick, he armed himself and followed at a distance. The monarch had reached the place that is still called the King's Fountain, then a very wild place, where he stopped and waited for the Moor to appear. But the longer he waited, the less the other thought of rushing to the engagement. So the night went by, and at break of dawn the king was about to withdraw, convinced that his opponent would not be coming, when he heard a noise in the bushes and ordered whoever was there to come forward.

"It was the soldier, and he obeyed.

"'What are you doing here?' asked the king.

"'Sire,' replied the soldier, 'I saw Your Majesty go out of the camp alone and I guessed your intention; I was afraid of a trap and I came to defend your person.'

"'Alone?' asked the king.

"'Sire,' replied the soldier, 'are Your Majesty and I not enough for two hundred Moors?'

"'You went out of my camp a soldier,' said the king, 'and you will go back the Duke of Alba.'"

"So you see, Don Federico," said Rafael, "how that legend from the people arranges midnight challenges and creates dukes at will."

"Be still, Rafael, for goodness' sake," said the Countess, "and leave us our beliefs, for I like that origin of the title."

"Yes," replied Rafael, "but the Duke of Alba wouldn't thank your mother for her *enlightenment*. Let's see now what there is on the subject."

So saying, Rafael ran from the room and soon came back with a large vellum-bound book that he had taken from the library of the Countess.

"Here is the *Creation, Privileges and Antiquity of Castilian Titles*," he said, "by Don José Berni y Catalá, solicitor of the Royal Council. Page 140: 'Count of Alba, now Duke. The first was Don Francisco Alvarez de Toledo, created Count of Alba by Juan II, 1439. Don Enrique IV made him Duke in 1469.

"'This illustrious and lofty family is of royal blood, and has borne the highest offices of Spain in war and politics. The

Duke was in command of the entire army during the conquest of Flanders and of Portugal, where he performed marvels.

" 'This very illustrious family is of such brilliance and so many merits that it would require volumes to enumerate them.' So you see, Aunt, that the story you told us, although very widely circulated, is apochryphal."

"I don't know what that Greek or French word means," said the Marchioness. "But to get back to the Santa Marías; this name was given to . . ."

"Aunt, Aunt," cried Rita, "please excuse us from listening to our genealogical history. Haven't we had enough with the Cabezas de Vaca and the Albas? When you're planning to marry again, then you can spread these genealogical goodies before the lucky man's eyes."

"The surname of the Dukes of Alba," said Stein, "is Alvarez, and so is my landlord's; he's a good, honorable man, a retired shopkeeper. It surprises me very much to find that the most illustrious names in this country are common to both the highest and the lowest classes. Is it true what they say in my country that all Spaniards believe they are of noble blood?"

"That's a confusion of ideas," answered Rafael, "like all the others that foreigners have with respect to things Spanish; hence there's no foreigner who doesn't believe firmly that every rustic at the plow carries the distinctive sword of knighthood hanging at his side. Undoubtedly there are many common surnames used in Spain as if by common consent; but this arises in great part from the fact that in times past the gentlemen who kept slaves gave them their names on freeing them.

"These names, taken by the freed Moors, must have multiplied, especially those of the rich, in proportion to the number of slaves they had. Some of those new families distinguished themselves and were knighted, for many of them were descended from Moorish nobles. But the grandees of Spain with those same names take just as much offense at being confused with those families as with those of the laborers who also bear them. It must be noted, too, that many have taken their names from the localities from which they came; thus we have hundreds of Medinas, Castillas, Navarros, Toledos, Burgoses, Aragoneses, and so on. As for those aspirations to noble blood that are so widespread among the Spaniards, there is some foundation, because it's true that this people has pride as well as delicate and distinguished inclinations; but these national traits of character should not be confused with the ridiculous affectations of nobility that we've seen in modern times. The Spanish people do not care to deck themselves with worthless ribbands nor to emerge from the class in which Providence placed them; but they do grant equal importance to the purity of the blood and to their honor, especially in the northern provinces, where they can boast of having no admixture of Moorish blood. This purity of race is considered lost through illegitimate birth, through a more or less dubious alliance with mulatto or Jewish blood, and through the offices of hangman and night watchman, or through infamous punishments."

"Heaven help us!" said Rita. "How tiresome you are with your nobility! Please, Rafael, do us the favor of going on with the history of our uncle."

"Oh, fiddlesticks!" cried the Marchioness.

"Aunt," said Rafael, "a story is never all bad as long as the teller is asked to tell it. So, Don Federico, Santa María and Cabeza de Vaca were united like two turtle-doves. I've often heard tell that my aunt, this aunt present here, cried with joy and tenderness to see such a mutually harmonious union. My uncle's misgivings inspired by the name of his better half were calmed with one look at her."

"Rafael, Rafael!" warned the Marchioness.

"But to everyone's astonishment," continued Rafael, "and no one's more than my uncle's, the Cabeza de Vaca gave birth to a little Santa María after nine months. He was about the size of a fan, and would seem to have been fathered and mothered by an X and a Z. The Cabeza de Vaca was more puffed up than Jupiter when he produced Minerva. A great matrimonial debate grew out of the event. The lady wanted the sweet fruit of her love to be named Pancracio, a name that had been given the first-born son in the family ever since the battle of Navas de Tolosa. My uncle had set his heart on the future scion of the venerable Santa Marías bearing no other name than his father's, a sonorous, soldierly name. My aunt got them to agree by proposing that the baby be christened León Pancracio; with the result that his father has always called him León, and his mother always Pancracio."

The narrative was suddenly interrupted by the General, who came into the room pale as death, his lips compressed and his eyes flashing.

"Dear Lord!" said Rafael to Rita in a low voice, "I'd like to be seven feet under the earth right now, along with the Roman statues that the Moors used as the foundation of the Giralda."

"I'm furious!" said the General.

"What's the matter, uncle?" asked the Countess, as red as a tomato.

Rita bowed her head over her embroidery, biting her lips to keep from laughing.

The face of the Marchioness was longer than Don Quijote's.

"This goes beyond making fun of people," said the General, his voice trembling. "It's an insult!"

"Uncle," said the Countess, making her voice as soft as she could, "when there's no evil intent, when it's nothing but frivolity, a prank, the desire for a laugh . . ."

"Desire for a laugh!" interrupted the General. "Laugh at me! Laugh at my wife! Upon my word, this goes beyond being a joke. I'm going to complain to the police right now."

"The police!" cried the Marchioness. "Are you out of your mind, Brother?"

"If I ever get out of this," said Rafael to Rita, "I'll make a vow to Saint John the Silent to imitate him for a year and a day."

"My dear León," continued the Marchioness, "I beg you, for goodness' sake, not to pay so much attention to a childish jest. Calm yourself. I know that he loves and respects you. Do you want to start a scandal? Family complaints shouldn't be aired before the public. Come, León, Brother, let's keep this to ourselves."

"Who's talking about family complaints?" replied the General, turning to his sister. "What does the family have to do with the unheard-of insolence of that outrageous Englishman who's come here to insult the people of this country?"

Hearing these words, his sister and the nieces and nephew breathed easily, as if a weight had been lifted from their chests. Their fear that our story-teller had been overheard by the stiff-necked veteran was without foundation, and Rafael asked in a ringing voice:

"What has that huge amphibian done?"

"What has he done?" replied the General. "Well, I'll tell you what he's done. You know that, unfortunately for me, he lives across the street from my house. Very well. At one o'clock in the morning, when everyone is enjoying his best sleep, this 'mister' opens his window and starts—to play the trumpet!"

"I know he's crazy about that instrument," said Rafael.

"In addition to that," the General went on, "he plays it horribly, and the breath from his vast chest draws sounds from the instrument loud enough to wake the dead for twenty leagues around; so all the dogs in the neighborhood start to howl. This will give you some idea of the kind of nights we've been spending thanks to him."

All the efforts his listeners had made until then to suppress their mirth were now in vain. Their burst of laughter was so simultaneous and so unrestrained that the General suddenly stopped talking and glared at them indignantly.

"This is the limit, children! That you should think such barefaced insolence, such contempt for people, a laughing matter is too much. Laugh! Laugh! We shall see whether your friend, this fellow that you've taken up, will laugh, too!"

Whereupon he left the room as resolutely as he had entered it, on his way to the police.

Rita was laughing uncontrollably.

"Gracious, Rita," said the Marchioness, who was in no laughing mood, "it would be more fitting for you to be indignant at such a lack of sense instead of laughing at it."

"I know very well what I should do, Aunt," replied the girl, "but I'd have to laugh if it killed me. I promise you I'll take revenge for my uncle on that Major Fly when he comes to me babbling flattery. I won't stop at turning my back. I'll say: 'Save your breath to blow the trumpet.'"

"You'd do better to imitate the foreign young ladies who blush when they say good morning and turn pale when they say good night," said Rafael.

"That might be better," said Rita. "But I prefer to do worse."

"Now after all this," said Stein with his German perseverance, "you promised me, Señor de Arias, to tell me about José María's deed of valor."

"It will have to wait until another day," replied Rafael, and, taking out his watch, he added. "Here's my commanding officer. It's a quarter of three and I've been invited to dine at the Captain General's house. If I were you, Doctor, I'd go and minister to my aunt Cabeza de Vaca in the critical state to which the Major's trumpet has reduced her."

CHAPTER XX

The Countess's son had completely recovered, and the evening set to receive Marysal had arrived. Some guests had already gathered there when Rafael Arias made a precipitate entry.

"Cousin," he said, "I'm going to ask a favor of you; if you refuse me I'll throw myself headlong into bed right now, under the pretext of a terrible migraine headache."

"Heavens!" said the Countess, "What can I do to prevent such a misfortune?"

"I'll tell you," went on Rafael. "Yesterday I had a letter from one of my friends in the Embassy: Viscount de Saint-Léger."

"Take off the Saint and the Viscount and leave Léger plain and simple," said the General.

"Well," said Rafael, "my friend, who is neither viscount nor saint, according to my uncle, has referred an Italian prince to me."

"A prince! Quite likely!" said the General slyly. "Why can't things be called by their right names? He'll probably turn out to be a member of a secret society, a propagandist, a veritable pest. Where is this prince from?"

"I don't know," answered Rafael. "All I know is that the letter reads as follows: 'I should be most grateful if you would introduce him to the most beautiful and charming women, to the most exclusive gatherings, and the most noteworthy historical landmarks of beautiful Seville, that Garden of the Hesperides.'"

"He must mean the Garden of the Alcázar," noted the Marchioness.

"Very likely," said Rafael. "When I found myself burdened with that task, I didn't know where to turn, but I had the bright idea of coming to my cousin and begging leave of her to bring the prince to her salon; for in that way he'll be able to meet the most beautiful and charming ladies, the choicest society, and," he added in a low voice, pointing to the card table, "the most noteworthy antiquities of Seville."

"You can see that my mother is there," murmured the Countess, laughing in spite of herself. "You're impudent;" and she added aloud, "I'll be very pleased to receive him."

"Good, very good!" exclaimed the General, shuffling the cards violently. "Spoil them, open your doors wide to them, take them around by the hand! They'll amuse themselves at your expense, and afterward they'll make fun of you!"

"Believe me, Uncle," replied Rafael, "we get our own back. They certainly make it easy for us. Some come with the one aim—to look for adventure, fully persuaded that Spain is the classical land for such intrigues. Last year I had one who was filled to the eyebrows with this monomania. He was an Irishman, a relative of Lord W."

"Yes, as I'm a relative of the Grand Turk," said the General, using his favorite phrase.

"The spirit of the hero of La Mancha had taken possession of my Irishman, whom I shall call Emerald Erin since I've forgotten his right name. One afternoon as we were walking in the Duke's Plaza, the sky turned dark and a sudden storm blew up. I tried to find a shelter, but he kept on walking, because he wanted to experience a Spanish storm. When I rightly observed that he was going to be soaked to the skin, he replied

that everything he was wearing on the outside was water-proof
—his hat, his coat, his trousers, his gloves, his boots—everything. I left him to his fate."

"Is that possible, Rafael?" asked the Countess.

"More than that, it's probable," said the General. "No
Englishman ever goes to bed without having committed some
extravagance during the day."

"Go on, Rafael; go on, son," begged the Marchioness. "I
can already see that this daring fellow is going to learn by
experience that he shouldn't tempt God."

"Well, my Erin was taking the water like Noah's Ark,"
continued Rafael, "when lightning struck the tree he was sitting
under."

"Come, come!" they all shouted, "That's a story. One of
Rafael's stories."

"As I live and breathe, it's the truth," he exclaimed warmly.
"You can ask a hundred people who saw the thing happen if
you want to. I assure you that a whole, real acacia tree fell on
my poor Erin. Luckily he was caught in such a way that the
trunk missed him, but he was a prisoner among the branches
like a bird in a cage. In vain he shouted, in vain he promised
and offered bank notes to anyone who would come and rescue
him. He had to wait in his arboreal prison throughout almost
the entire shower. Finally the storm passed over and people
returned to the street. They went to his aid then; but the thing
wasn't so easy. They had to bring saws and axes and cut off
the thickest branches. As the walls of his jail fell, the sad figure
of the son of Ireland was uncovered little by little. All his
water-proofs had gone to pieces. His arms and his hair and
the brim of his hat were hanging down sadly, perpendicular to
the ground. He looked like a ship in the doldrums. Imagine the
jests, the jokes heaped on that poor Erin by our Sevillians who

are so lively and fond of joking. The poor man not only had
to endure the scare and the shower, but Homeric laughter also,
the like of which he'd never dreamed of at home. I'm ashamed
to confess that after I'd gone back with the intention of joining
him, I lost my courage and ran away."

"And didn't that happening bring any consequences?"
asked the Marchioness. "Didn't it give him something to think
about?"

"The accident had no consequences, of either a physical
or moral nature. The English people have nine lives like a cat.
The only thing that happened was that his faith in water-proof
clothes was shattered. But that was not the most tragic of my
hero's adventures. He brought to Spain with him a great fancy
for thieves; he wanted to meet them at any cost. The pleasure
of being robbed was his idea, his whim, the object of his trip;
he'd have given ten thousand sacks of potatoes to see José María
close at hand in his beautiful Andalusian suit with its set of
buttons made of pieces of eight. He had brought expressly for
him a dagger with a gold hilt and a pair of Manton pistols."

"Arming our enemies!" exclaimed the General. "That's
their great desire. It's always the same."

"He wanted to go to Madrid," Rafael continued, "and
knowing that the stagecoach had the bad taste to carry an
armed guard, he decided to go in the mail coach. All my attempts to dissuade him were in vain. He did leave, and beyond
Cordoba his burning desire was granted. He met some thieves,
but not well-bred thieves, nor fashionable thieves like José
María, who looks like a red-hot coal mounted on his spirited
red sorrel. These thieves were more or less the ordinary kind;
on foot, common, and vulgar. You know what being vulgar
means in England. There's no pest, no leper that awakens in
an Englishman as much loathing as something vulgar. Vulgar!

At the mere word, Albion covers herself with a thick fog; the dandies feel the blackest spleen; the ladies have the vapors; the young girls feel queasy, and the leaders of fashion have an attack of nerves. It isn't to be wondered at, then, that Erin felt degraded by letting himself be robbed by vulgar thieves, and he therefore defended himself like a lion. He wasn't defending his fortune, however, for he had entrusted it to me until his return, and the most valuable things to him that he had with him were a willow branch that hung over Napoleon's tomb, a satin dancing shoe, about the size of a walnut, and a collection of caricatures of Lord W., his uncle."

"That portrays the man," said the General.

"But I'm doing nothing but chattering," said Rafael. "Good-bye, Cousin, I'm stopping, and I'm going."

"What? You're going, leaving poor Erin in the hands of thieves?" said the Countess. "You'll have to finish your story."

"All right," said Rafael. "I'll tell you in a couple of words that the thieves were annoyed. They beat him and left him unconscious, tied to a tree where a poor widow found him, had him carried to her hut, and took care of him like a mother while he lay ill as a consequence of that episode. I didn't hear from him for some time; and as the common saying goes, 'hope was green and was eaten by a donkey.' I was thinking that some misfortune had befallen my Emerald Erin when he wrote me telling me what had happened. He asked me to give ten thousand *reales* to the woman who had rescued and cared for him without the faintest idea who he was, for when they found him he was dressed as when his mother bore him. As you see, the reward was decent; no one can deny that the English are generous. But here comes Polo looking like an undertaker's mute. The Prince is waiting for me. I'm going to run, even if I fall down."

Whereupon he disappeared.

"Heavens!" said the Marchioness. "Rafael makes my head swim; he seems to be made of lizards' tails. He moves around so much, gesticulates so much, chatters so fast and incessantly that I miss half the things he says."

"You don't miss much," said the General.

"Well," said the Countess, "if I didn't already love Rafael so much for his worth, I'd love him because he amuses me."

"Here, dear Grace," said Eloise, entering and embracing the Countess, "here's Dumas's *Voyage Through the South of France*."

The Countess took the volumes. Polo and Eloise gave a dissertation on the writer's work; a dissertation we'll spare the reader, who will thank us for it.

"Poor Dumas!" said the Countess to the Colonel.

"Poor!" cried the Colonel. "Do you call a man poor who's rich and important, whom everyone fetes, flatters, and applauds? Or is it because he's sometimes criticized?"

"Because he's criticized?" answered the Countess. "No, certainly not; I sometimes take the liberty of doing that myself. Anyone who goes before the public confers the right to do that. I don't say *poor* when I hear him criticized; I say it when I hear some of the praise given him."

"Why, Countess? Eulogies are always flattering."

"I can't explain it very well," said the Countess, "except by a comparison, for I'm not as eloquent as Eloise. A while ago one of our relatives came from Jérez to see us—a very devout woman whose husband is fond of the arts. The first thing I tried to show her, of course, was our beautiful cathedral. On our way to it another person from Jérez attached himself to us and we couldn't get rid of him. He was very ordinary, but a very rich man, and we had to agree to let him join our party.

When we entered that peerless building, my cousin raised her head, clasped her hands, crossed the nave quickly, and knelt down, streaming tears, at the foot of the main altar. Her husband stood as if stunned, unable to take a step forward. But the rich man exclaimed: 'A good property! What a fine store it would make!' Do you understand what I'm getting at?"

"Of course," replied the Colonel, laughing. "You mean a stupid eulogy is worse than a criticism; Iriarte's fable has already said it:

'If the wise man disapproves, that's bad.
If the fool applauds, that's worse.'

But your little story has a good dash of salt and pepper."

"I should be sorry for that," said the Countess. "I was reminded of it when I heard apologies for Dumas's work made by these admirers of his."

"Countess," said the colonel, "if, sometime, Dumas should come to Spain, I promise to bring him to you so he can thank you for the way you evaluate his work."

"You mustn't do any such thing."

"Why not? Wouldn't you like to meet him?"

"Knowing authors of great merit has its drawbacks, generally speaking."

"Why, Countess?"

"Because it usually happens that personal acquaintance makes you think less of the author. A friend of mine, a person of great talent, used to say that great men are the opposite of statues, for the statues appear larger and the men smaller the closer one comes to them."

"As for me," she went on, "if I should choose to become an author some day (which might happen, for as the saying goes we all have a touch of the poet and the madman), I should at least hold the advantage of being heard but not seen, thanks to my small size, the scant brilliance of my pen, and distance."

"Do you believe, then, that the author is bound to be one of the heroes of his fiction?"

"No, but I should be afraid I'd find him giving the lie to the ideas and sentiments he expresses. Then the charm would be gone, and if I recovered what he had snatched from me while reading him, I shouldn't be able to rid myself of the notion that the man had been writing with his head and not his heart."

"How the French can write!" Eloise was saying meanwhile, reverting to the literary controversy mentioned above.

"Name one thing those sons of liberty can't do well!" replied Polo.

"But, señorita," said the General, "why don't you read Spanish books?"

"Because everything Spanish carries the stamp of gross stupidity," replied Eloise. "We're dreadfully backward in all our concepts and in all branches."

"What can you expect a cultivated writer to write about in this detestable country," added Polo, somewhat nettled, "since we're ahead in nothing, and can only imitate? How are we going to portray our country and our customs, if we can find nothing elegant, good, or characteristic in it?"

"Unless," said Eloise with a mincing smile, "we praise our orange blossoms with the Germans, our bolero with the French, and our sherry wine with the English."

"Ah, Eloise," cried Polo with enthusiasm, "that *spirituelle* jest! If it isn't French, it ought to be!"

As usual, Polo had stolen a well-known French word.

Luckily, the General had just been dealt a good card combination which kept him from hearing this precious dialogue.

At that moment, Rafael came in with the Prince and presented him to the Countess, who received him with her usual amiability but, according to the Spanish custom, without rising. The Prince was tall and thin; he looked about forty-five years old, and though a prince, was not distinguished in appearance or manner. With his arrival, the party was complete and all were waiting impatiently for the promised singer, not without grave doubts as to her merit.

Major Fly waddled to his chair, near the young girls, ogling them with glances as killing as thrusts with his sword. Sir John had his monocle trained on Rita, who took no notice of him. The baron, seated near an aged judge, was asking him whether the Moors whitewashed their houses.

"I lack the data to answer that," replied the magistrate. "It's a point that has escaped the attention of Zuñiga, Ponz, Don Antonio Morales and Rodrigo Caro." [56]

"How ignorant!" the baron was thinking.

"What a stupid question!" the judge was thinking.

"You have a very pretty cousin," the Prince said to Rafael.

"Yes," he replied, "she's a rosewater Ondine[57] to whom an angel gave a soul, if love did not."

"And that general playing cards, who looks so distinguished?"

"He's the retired Nestor[58] of the army. You wouldn't find a better preserved ruin in Pompeii."

---

[56] All historians of Seville.

[57] The reference is to a fantastic novelette by the German author, La Motte Fouquet, entitled *Ondine*. AUTHOR'S NOTE. Ondine was a water sprite.

[58] A king of Pylos, noted for his wisdom, justice, and knowledge of war.

"And the lady he's playing with?"

"His sister, the Marchioness of Guadalcanal; she's a kind of Escorial, that is, a solid made up of monarchical and monastic sentiments with a heart that is a pantheon of throneless kings."

Just then a loud noise was heard; it was the major, who had knocked over a flower-pot as he was rising to go and join Rafael.

"The major announces himself," said Rafael. "Doubtless he's coming over to sigh like an organ over the short shrift the ladies are giving him."

"They must be discriminating in their tastes," observed the Prince, "for the major has a fine figure."

"I don't deny that," said Rafael, "he's a very beautiful Samson, but in the first place, he already has his Delilah who will soon be legally his (thanks to the millions her father made from tea and opium in India). She's waiting for him amid the fogs of their island, while he's vacationing under the beautiful Andalusian sky. The foreigners who come to Spain, moreover, are bent upon counting among the pleasures they expect to enjoy a good climate, bullfights, oranges, the bolero, amorous conquests. And they're often disappointed. How many complaints I've listened to from those who came like Caesars and left like Dariuses."

Meanwhile, the Baron had approached the table and was watching the play.

"The señora," he said, speaking to the Marchioness, "is the mother . . ."

"Of my daughter, yes, señor," answered the Marchioness.

Rita gave one of her sudden peals of laughter.

"Baron," said the Countess whose sofa was near the card table, "are you fond of music?"

"Yes, señora, I admire and venerate it, that is, profound, wise, serious music, philosophical music, as Haydn, Mozart, and Beethoven understood it."

"What is he saying?" the General asked Rafael who had drawn near to speak to Rita. "Serious and wise music indeed! The philosophy of the tra, la, la! How can he say such ridiculous things in front of sensible people?"

"What can you expect, Uncle," answered Arias, "the sylphs from the garden of Lutetia[59] have been turned into teutonic gnomes in the Black Forest."

"That doesn't make them any more lovable," added the Marchioness.

Rafael, fleeing from the Major, threaded his way through the groups formed by the guests. He came to a cluster of young girls, some of whom were related to him. He was a great favorite of theirs, but seeing that he was neglecting them to take care of his guests, they had turned against him and wanted to avenge themselves. He had hardly approached them when they all suddenly fell silent and serious.

"Have I been changed into Medusa's head without knowing it?" said Arias.

"Oh, so it's you?" said one of the conspirators.

"I think so, Clarita," replied Rafael.

"It's just that I haven't seen you for such a long time I didn't recognize you. It seems to me you're getting oldish. How can you tear yourself away from your foreigners?"

"Mine!" replied Arias. "I renounce ownership. As for my having aged, I was already a hundred years old when I was born, Clarita, so you figure it out."

---

[59] Paris. This refers to the switch in the conversation from French literature to German music.

"It must be the hard work and the fatigue of taking care of your charges that has brought on this aging."

"Some people say," added another girl, "that the foreigners are taking up a subscription to raise a statue to you."

"And that the Queen is going to make you the Marquis of Itálica," [60] said another.

"And that you're wearing out the paving stones of the Alcázar with your boots."

"And that Murillo's *Saint Felix* knows you by sight and blesses you when he sees you come in with a new admirer."

"Señoritas," cried Rafael, "is this a declaration of war, a conspiracy? What's up?"

Then they all united in raking him with enfilading fire.

"Heavens, Arias, you reek of coal!" "Rafael, when you speak to me you leave an after-taste, you know." "Arias, you're getting unkempt." "Arias, you're blushing."

"Arias," said Polo, "you look like a bear in a swarm of bees."

"That comparison isn't very poetic coming from a disciple of the nine muses. Apollo will object to being your namesake. But you stay here, like the rose among the bees, lavishing your honey on them, while I go for my umbrella to protect me from the swarm."

At that moment the guests gathered near the door to the patio made way for Marysal, whom the Duke was leading by the hand. Stein was following them.

---

[60] Roman Italica, where many ancient ruins could be seen, was much visited by foreigners going to Seville. It was the villa of the Emperor Trajan. AUTHOR'S NOTE.

CHAPTER XXI

Marysal, whose landlady had helped her in her choice of clothes, was exceedingly badly dressed. A printed foulard gown, too short, its figures in glaring colors; an unbecoming hair-do, bedecked with stiff red bands; a mantilla of white and blue tulle trimmed with Catalonian lace—these were her adornments, which could not fail to add up to a bad effect.

The Countess went forward a few steps to meet her. As she passed Rafael, he said in her ear, alluding to the fable of the crow by La Fontaine:

"If the song is like the plumage, she'll be the phoenix of these woods."

"How grateful we are for your kindness in coming. We want so much to hear you!" said the Countess to Marysal. "The Duke has praised you so highly."

Without a word in reply, she let herself be led by the Countess to a large chair placed between the piano and the sofa.

Rita had left her usual post to be near her, and standing next to Eloise she said when she saw Marysal, "Heavens! She's darker than a black pudding from Extremadura."

"She looks as if she's been dressed by her worst enemy," Eloise added. "Like a Judas on Holy Saturday. What do you think, Rafael?"

"That wrinkle in her forehead," said Arias, "makes her look for all the world like a unicorn."

Meanwhile, Marysal was not showing the least sign of timidity nor humility in the presence of such a numerous and brilliant company; not for an instant did she lose her unalterable calm and aplomb. Ten minutes' observation enabled her to see and sum up everything with appraising and penetrating glances and the quick comprehension and precise judgment of Spanish women.

"Here I am," she was saying to herself while taking stock. "The Countess is good and wants me to shine. The smart young girls are making fun of me and my get-up, which must look awful. As for the foreigners who are eyeing me through their monocles with disdain, I'm a Miss Simplicity to them; to the old people I'm a mere cipher. The rest are neutral, ready to praise or censure me, out of consideration for the Duke, my patron, according to his opinion pro or con."

All this while, the good and amiable Countess was making every possible effort to start a conversation with Marysal; but her laconic replies frustrated good intentions.

"Do you like Seville?" she asked kindly.

"Well enough," said Marysal.

"And what do you think of the cathedral?"

"Too big."

"And our beautiful walks?"

"Too small."

"Then what have you liked best?"

"The bullfight."

Here the conversation came to a halt.

After ten minutes of silence, the Countess said: "May I ask your husband to take his place at the piano?"

"Whenever you wish," replied the girl.

Stein sat down at the piano. Marysal stood at his side, after the Duke had led her there by the hand.

"Are you shaking, Mariquita?" asked Stein.

"Why should I be?" she answered.

Everyone was silent.

Various expressions could be read on the faces of the people present. For the most part, curiosity and wonder; on the part of the Countess, a kindly interest; at the card tables, or, as Rafael put it, the Upper Chamber, the most complete indifference.

The Prince was smiling with scorn.

The Major opened his eyes wide as though to hear through them.

The Baron closed his.

The Colonel was yawning.

Sir John made use of the interval to take out his monocle and polish it with his handkerchief.

Rafael fled to the garden to light a cigarette.

Stein played the *ritornello* from *Casta Diva* without flourishes or affectations. But as soon as Marysal's voice rose, pure, serene, smooth, and strong, it seemed as though a magic wand had touched all the listeners. An expression of surprise and admiration was painted on every face.

The Prince gave an involuntary exclamation.

When she had finished, a storm of applause burst unanimously all over the room. The Countess set the example, clapping her delicate hands.

"Lord help us!" cried the General, covering his ears. "We might as well be in the bullring."

"Let them, León," said the Marchioness. "Let them enjoy themselves. It would be worse if they were whispering about their neighbors."

Stein bowed to all sides. Marysal went back to her seat, as cold, as impassive as she had got up from it.

Later she sang some extremely complicated variations where the melody was obscured by an intricate and difficult network of flourishes, trills, and rapid runs. She executed them with admirable ease, effortlessly, without strain, and aroused ever greater admiration.

"Countess," said the Duke, "the Prince would like to hear some Spanish songs which he's heard highly praised. María excels in this genre. Would you like to lend us a guitar?"

"Gladly," replied the Countess.

Her desire was immediately satisfied.

Rafael had seated himself next to Rita, after installing the Major at Eloise's side. She was attempting to prove to the Englishman that Spanish women were rising to the level of foreign women in affectation and artifice; for it is well known that those who imitate servilely always copy the defects.

"What eyes you have!" Rafael was saying to his cousin. "How beautifully they're trimmed with those thick, long lashes! They have the color and drawing-power of magnets, Rita."

"It's you who are the magnet to the foreigners," replied Rita. "Why did you put the Major near Eloise? Listen to the nonsense she's telling him. I warn you, Cousin, that you're acquiring the look and the dress of a guide-book."

"Leave off, leave off, I say," cried Rafael, striking the chair-arm with his fist. "We're not talking about that, Rita; we're talking about my love for you that will last forever. A man really loves only one woman in his lifetime. The others are paper loves."

"I know that," said Rita. "Luis has told me often enough. But listen to me. You're turning into a very tiresome repeater watch."

"What is the meaning of this?" Eloise exclaimed, seeing a guitar brought in.

"It means that we are about to have some Spanish songs,"

said Rita, "and I'm very glad indeed. These are truly amusing and lively."

"Spanish songs!" cried Eloise, indignantly. "What a horror! That's all right for the common people, not for smart society. What are you thinking of, Grace? You see why people from other countries rightly say we're backward because we won't model our manners and tastes on theirs; because we stubbornly insist on dining at three, and we won't persuade ourselves that everything Spanish is foolish from birth."

"But," said the Major in his bad Spanish, "I think you do very well in being what you are."

"If that's a compliment," replied Eloise emphatically, "it's so exaggerated that it seems like a sneer."

"That Italian gentleman is the one who asked for Spanish songs," said Rita. "He's a fan and he understands them, which proves they're worth listening to."

"Eloise," said Rafael, "the barcarolles, the songs of the Tyrol, the *ranz des vaches,* are the folk songs of other countries. Why shouldn't our boleros and our other folk songs be privileged to enter the society of refined people, like those?"

"Because they're more vulgar," replied Eloise.

Rafael shrugged; Rita gave one of her laughs; the Major missed the point.

Eloise rose, pretending to have a headache, and left, accompanied by her mother, to whom she was saying:

"At least let them know there are señoritas in Spain refined and delicate enough to shun such buffoonery."

"How unlucky the Abelard of that Eloise!" said Rafael, seeing her leave.

In addition to her beautiful voice and her excellent technique, Marysal, as a daughter of the people, knew the Andalusian songs innately, with all their wit that a foreigner can enjoy and understand only after long residence in Spain, and only insofar as he identifies himself, so to speak, with the national temperament.

In this music, as in the dances, there is an abundance of improvisation, such a strong magnetism, such a series of surprises: laments, crackling joy, languors, demonstrations of rejection and attraction, a certain something, implicit but not explicit; and all this so fixed, so ruled by the hypnotic beat, if it may be so expressed, of the voice in the song and of the body in the dance; while excitement and languor follow one another so rapidly that they intoxicate and captivate the hearer and hold him in suspense.

And so it was when Marysal took up the guitar and began to sing:

> "If I'm lost, then let them seek me
> Beside the Southern sea,
> In the land of sun-bronzed maidens,
> Where wine and wit flow free."

Admiration was turned to enthusiasm. The young people beat time with their hands, repeating "Good, good," as though to encourage the singer. The cards fell from the hands of the stodgy card players; the Major, wishing to follow the general example, began to clap, too, without rhyme or reason. Sir John swore it was better than "God Save the Queen." But the greatest triumph of the national music was that it smoothed out the General's frown.

"Do you remember, Brother," asked the Marchioness, smiling, "when we used to sing the *zorongo* and the *tripili?*"

"What are the *zorongo* and the *tripoli?*" asked the Baron of Rafael.

"They're the forerunners of the *sereni,* the *cachucha,* and

the forbears of the *jaca de terciopelo,* of the *vito,* and other
modern songs."

Those peculiarities of the national songs and dances, of
which we have spoken, might appear to be in bad taste, and
doubtless would be in other countries. To yield unreservedly
to the impressions our songs and dances carry with them, our
kind of character is needed; rudeness and vulgarity must be
unknown, as in this country:—they are two things that do not
exist. A Spaniard may be insolent but he is seldom rude, for
that is unnatural to him. He always lives to the full, following
his own inspiration which is usually correct and refined. This
is what gives the Spaniard that natural elegance, that easy
frankness that makes knowing him so pleasant, even though
his education may have been neglected.

Marysal left the house as pale and impassive as she had
entered it.

When the Countess was among her family, she said to
Rafael with an air of triumph:

"And what does my dear cousin have to say now?"

"I say," replied Rafael, "that the song is better than the
plumage."

"What eyes!" cried the Countess.

"They look like two black diamonds in a case of Russian
leather," said Rafael.

"She's self-possessed but not haughty," said the Countess.

"And as shy as a girl from Madrid's lower classes!" Rafael
went on.

"But what a voice!" added the Countess. "What a divine
voice!"

"They'll have to engrave on her tomb the epitaph the
Portuguese composed for their renowned singer, Madureira:

Here lies Senhor Madureira,
Who had this world's finest voice;
He died because God willed it so:
'Twas only by God's own choice.

He needed that voice in His choir,
So God said: 'Sing here on high.'
He listened—then told all His angels, 'Be off;'
And He called Madureira to die.

"Rafael," said the Countess, "can anyone escape your razor tongue, you everlasting mocker? I'm going to order your portrait painted as a mocking bird, like the one of Paul de Kock's as a rooster."

"I'd rather be a male harpy," said Rafael as he was leaving; "that would give me the advantage of being able to propagate my kind."

CHAPTER XXII

Summer had gone and September had come. The days still held the heat of summer, but the nights were now long and cool. It was about nine o'clock, and there was no one in the Countess's salon as yet except her closest and most intimate friends, when Eloise came in.

"Sit down on the sofa beside me," said the hostess.

"Thank you, Grace, but your sofas here are stuffed with horsehair or tow; they're the hardest and most uncomfortable you could find anywhere."

"They're cooler that way, my child," said Rita, at whose side Eloise had seated herself in a studied pose.

"Do you know the latest?" said the poet Polo, playing with a yellow glove and stretching out a leg to show a fine patent-leather shoe. "They're saying that Arias is being appointed major of the garrison; but I think it's just idle talk."

"That sort of thing is for hamlets, villages, and small towns like this," replied Eloise mincingly. "Rafael deserves something better. He's a very spiritual man, a very fashionable youth, and a brave soldier."

"What's that you say, señorita?" asked the General, who was listening, absorbed, to the conversation of the two modish young people.

"I'm saying, señor, that your nephew is a brave officer."

"And what do you mean by that?"

"What his service record says, señor, and what all who know him will echo: that he has distinguished himself in the war as a man of honor."

"Well, if that's what you meant, why didn't you say so?

Why didn't you use the famous expression of Don Juan Nicasio Gallego, as well as of the Duke de Rivas, Quintana, Bretón, Martínez de la Rosa, Hartzenbusch, and many others who committed the blunder of being eminent men and first class poets without ceasing to be Spaniards in form and essence? Did you mean to say courageous, by any chance?"

"Well, of course, General. Didn't I say that?"

"No, señorita," said the General impatiently. "What you said was that he was 'brave,' a term I've heard applied only to untamed bulls, and to half-wild ones to describe their brutal ferocity. Upon my word, you don't need to use such a term for the lack of others suitable to the case, for, in addition to courageous, you could have chosen such words as gallant, valorous, intrepid, and so on, and so on."

"Heavens, señor; those are old-fashioned words, quite vulgar and stupid. We must admit new ones for the sake of style and good manners, in spite of the dictionary and its heavy-footed compilers and specialists."

"Lord, give me patience!" cried the General, throwing down his cards.

"What has stirred up our uncle this way?" asked Rafael of Rita as he entered.

"The news that's going around."

"What news?"

"That you've been named major of the garrison; he took it as irony."

"He's right. I don't aspire to a title higher than that of minor of the garrison. But I'm bringing a piece of news that might more properly be called major."

"A piece of news? News belongs to everyone. So pass it on quickly."

"Well, I must tell you," said Rafael, raising his voice, "that the Grisi[61] of Villamar is ready to mount the stage to display her voice."

"Oh, what happiness to think there'll be some notable event to take this monotonous town out of the rut where it's been vegetating since Saint Ferdinand founded it!" exclaimed Eloise.

"He conquered it," said her sympathetic friend, Polo, under his breath.

But Eloise went on, paying him no heed:

"What opera will she make her debut in?"

"What? Has she decided to make her debut?"

"Yes, and Stein is going to a play for her." [62]

"What nonsense!" said the good lady.

"Mother," said the Countess, "don't you see that Rafael is playing the fool in his own laudable and inveterate fashion?"

"Ever since they presented the *Pata de Cabra*,[63] no theatrical title can surprise me," said the Marchioness, "and ever since Lucresia, Angela, Anthony, and Charles the Bewitched, I wouldn't consider any theme incredible."

"As the theater is the school of customs," said the General ironically, "they fix it at the level of the manners they want to introduce."

"How right the French are when they say Africa begins beyond the Pyrenees," Eloise was saying to Polo in a low voice, meanwhile.

"They don't say it since they occupy a part of the coast," he replied. "It would be too flattering to us."

---

[61] Giuditta Grisi, an Italian mezzo-soprano, or Giulia Grisi, who first sang in Paris in 1832 and later in London.

[62] The next two sentences, which are plays on words, cannot be translated. AUTHOR'S NOTE.

[63] Goat's foot.

Eloise stifled a laugh in her tiny lace-trimmed handkerchief.

"Those two are conspiring," said Rita to Rafael. "Polo has an infernal machine between his glasses and his eyes, and Eloise is hiding in the handkerchief that she's holding to her mouth a mutiny against our churlish Spanish backwardness, pickled in musk."

"Bah! They're not conspirators," replied Rafael.

"What are they, then, an infernal machine of contradiction?"

"They are . . . , I'll tell you so you can judge them in all their loftiness."

"Tell me, Slow-poke."

"They are misunderstood revivalists," he said solemnly.

A few nights after this scene, the wide terraces of the Countess's house were deserted. No one was there but the characters from the Old Testament, as Arias called the card players.

"How late they are!" said the Marchioness. "Eleven-thirty and still they're not here."

"Time doesn't drag for music-lovers," said her brother, "as long as they're at the opera swooning with delight, like dolts."

"Who would have thought," said the Marchioness, "that woman would have the training and courage necessary to go on the stage so soon?"

"As for her training," said the General, "once you know how to sing, not so much is needed as you might think. As for her courage, I wouldn't ask for more than one regiment of grenadiers like her to assault Numancia or Zaragoza."

"Let me tell you what's happened," said one of the group. "When this Italian company came here, three months ago, our future prima donna took one of the boxes nearest the stage for the series. She never missed a single performance, and even managed to be present during the rehearsals. The Duke succeeded in getting the star to give her some lessons, and later persuaded the impresario to let her join the company. But the role the impresario agreed to for her was that of a supporting voice—a proposal she promptly rejected. By one of those chance happenings which always favor the daring, the prima donna came down with a serious illness, and the Duke's protégée offered to replace her. We shall see how the engagement will turn out."

At that moment the Countess entered the room with her coterie. She was animated and sparkling.

"What an evening we've had, Mother!" she cried. "What a triumph! What a wonderful, magnificent thing!"

"Please tell me, Niece, how it matters, and how the fact that any guttersnipe with a good throat can sing well on the stage can arouse as much enthusiasm and exaltation in you as an heroic deed or a noble act?"

"Think of it, Uncle!" said the Countess. "What a feather in our cap, what glory for Seville, to be the cradle of an artist who's going to fill the world with her fame!"

"Like the Marquis de la Romana?" replied the General. "Like Wellington, or Napoleon? Is that it, señora?"

"Well, what do you wish, señor?" replied the Countess. "Can't anything be famous but a war trumpet? How divinely that peerless woman sang! What good taste she showed in her presence on the stage! She's a prodigy. And then, how the enthusiasm and excitement spread from person to person! I was very happy, too, to see the Duke so pleased and Stein so moved . . ."

"The Duke," said the General, "must be pleased about something else, too."

"General," said the guest who had spoken earlier, "those are just human weaknesses. The Duke is young . . ."

"Oh!" the Countess exclaimed. "There's nothing baser than to suspect or cause others to suspect evil where there is none. The world taints everything with its foul breath. You all know, don't you, that the Duke, not satisfied to practice the arts, is a patron of artists, learned men, and anyone else who can advance the mind? Besides, isn't she the wife of a man to whom the Duke owes a great deal?"

"That's all very well and good, Niece," replied the General, "but it doesn't quite cover what looks suspicious. It's not enough in this world to be exempt from censure; it's essential to appear so, too. By the very fact that you're young and pretty, you'd be wise not to openly defend certain causes."

"I have no ambition to be considered perfect," said the Countess, "nor to set up a court of justice in my house. What I do want to be taken for is a loyal and staunch friend, and I respect and defend those who consider me such."

At that moment Rafael Arias entered.

"Come, Rafael," said the Countess, "what have you to say now? Are you going to make fun of that charming woman?"

"To please you, Cousin, I'm going to imitate the public and burst with enthusiasm, like the frog when he was trying to swell up to the size of the ox. I've just witnessed the royal ovation made to that eighth wonder."

"Tell us about it," said the Countess. "Tell us about it."

"When the curtain came down, there was a moment when I thought we were going to witness a second run of the Tower of Babel. The *Diva Donna* had ten curtain calls, and she'd have

had twenty if it weren't for the insolent stage assistants who
were tired of so much work and were beginning to curse and
turn out the lights. The Duke's friends pressed him to take
them to congratulate the heroine. We all threw ourselves prostrate at her feet."

"You, too, Rafael?" said the General. "I thought that under that madcap surface you were too sensible."

"If I hadn't gone where the others went I wouldn't have
had the satisfaction of telling you now how this Queen of the
Orient, this Empress of Sharps and Flats, received us. In the
first place, all her replies were made along a kind of chromatic
scale, as is her habit, consisting of the following semi-tones:
first, self-possession, or better, indifference; then coolness, followed by coldness, and finally, disdain. I was the first to pay
her homage. I showed her my hands, flayed by clapping, and
assured her that the sacrifice of my skin was but a feeble tribute
to her supernatural skill, comparable only with that of Madureira. Her reply was a grave nod of the head, worthy of the
goddess Juno. The Baron begged her by all the saints in
Heaven to go to Paris, the only theater capable of applauding
her properly, in view of which French *bravos* would resound
in every corner of the universe, under the tricolor. She answered him with the greatest coolness: 'You can see that I
don't need to go to Paris to be applauded, and as for applause,
I prefer my country's to the French.' "

"Did she say that?" demanded the General. "Who'd have
thought that woman could say such a rational thing?"

"Major Fly," continued Rafael, "told her with his unfail-
ing clumsiness that of all the singers he had heard, only Grisi
could sing better than she. She answered him coldly: 'Well,
any time that Grisi sings better than I, you do wrong to listen
to me instead of to her.' Sir John arrived immediately after,

shaking hands and stepping on everybody. He told her her voice was a marvel, and that if she'd like to sell it, he was ready to pay her fifty thousand pounds. She answered with scorn that it was not for sale. But now, Cousin, what have you to say, after all this, about the mysterious way this affair was handled?"

"What mystery are you talking about?" asked the Baron, who had approached during the conversation.

"About that brilliant stage debut," replied Arias, "which burst as suddenly as a bomb. Now I'm beginning to add up certain things . . . The Duke's interviews with the impresario, that budding Norma's constancy in attending the rehearsals . . . Now my *qui vives* are gradually waking up."

"*Qui vives* waking up?" said the Baron. "What an extraordinary expression!"

"It's a very common metaphor," replied Rafael.

"I never heard it," said the Baron, "and I don't understand it. Would you be good enough to explain it to me, Señor Arias?"

Rafael gave his cousin a sly glance, lifted his eyes to heaven as if he were about to make a sacrifice, and said:

"When an accident happens without warning, it's because the attention has let it happen without giving the *qui vive*. That is, without determining whence it came or where it was going. If another accident, similar to the first one, happens, we're forced to remember the first, and we say our attention which was lazy or sleeping the first time is waking up; that is, our *qui vives* are gradually coming to. We have several loose phrases of this kind in Spain which explain as much as many words could. One word may suffice to cover a great deal of meaning. Of course both invention and comprehension are needed for this. There's an expression among the country people that illustrates this. They say of an intelligent, alert man: 'He's one of those who are *already right here.*' This expression originated because when an overseer in the country has to give an order or make a request of one of his workers who is far away, he calls and the man answers, indicating he has undertaken what he's been ordered to. He's *already right here.* But the phrase that struck your attention (since not everyone is the sort that people label *already right here*) is said to have originated as follows: A Spaniard who was in Saint Petersburg was astonished to hear a rather pleasant sound in the air as he was out walking one beautiful spring morning with a Russian friend. This sound sometimes came from nearby, sometimes from far away; now from the right, now from the left. It was merely a repetition in various tones of the words *qui vive.* The Spaniard thought it was birds, but he raised his head and saw nothing. Was it a song? Was it an echo? No, because it did not come from any particular direction, but could be heard from all directions. Then he thought his friend was a ventriloquist, and he stared at him. The Russian started to laugh. 'I see,' he said, 'that you don't know where those voices are coming from. Every year they can be heard at this season. They are the *qui vives* spoken by the sentries in the garrison during the winter. They freeze in the cold and melt in the first warm days, echoing through the spring air which brings them back to life.' "

"Not badly told," said the Baron absently.

"You flatter me," replied Rafael, dropping an ironic curtsy.

"Ah, here's the Señorita Ritita," said the Baron, seeing her come in after taking off her mantilla. "It seems to me, señorita, that I had the honor of seeing you in Catalanes Street this morning."

"I didn't see you," answered Rita.

"That's too bad," Rafael said to Rita. "That wouldn't have

happened to Major Fly nor to La Giralda, whom he wants as lady colonel of his regiment of Life Guards."

"I saw you," the Baron continued, "near a big cross attached to the wall. I asked . . ."

"I'll take care of this," said Rafael Arias in a low voice.

"And they told me that it's called the Negro's Cross. Can you tell me, señorita, why it's been given such an odd name."

"I don't know," replied Rita. "Perhaps because a Negro was crucified on it."

"Doubtless that's it," the Baron said. "It must have been at the time of the Inquisition," and he muttered, "What a country! What a religion! But," he added with that intolerable sarcasm, that insolence that unbelievers adopt toward those who believe and who cling to their faith, "could you tell me why a crocodile is hanging from the roof in that aisle of the cathedral near the patio of the orange trees, as you go in by the gate to the right of the Giralda? Was the cathedral also used as a museum of natural history?"

"That big lizard?" said Rita. "It's there because it was trapped above the arch of the church roof."

"Ah!" cried the Baron, laughing. "In this cathedral everything is gigantic. Even the lizards!"

"That is a story the common people have spread," said the Countess, while Rita went to take her accustomed place without listening to the Baron. "That crocodile was presented to King Alfonso the Wise by the famous ambassador sent by the Sultan of Egypt. An elephant's tusk, a bridle, and a rod are also hanging from the same arch. These things and the lizard represent the four cardinal virtues. The lizard is the symbol of prudence; the rod, of justice; the elephant's tusk, of strength; and the bridle, of temperance. Those symbols have been hanging at the entrance of that great and noble edifice for six hundred years, like an inscription that the people can understand if they don't know how to read."

The Baron was sorry he could not accept Rita's version. The true explanation had cruelly robbed him of a precious satirical article—critical, humorous, and mocking. Who knows but that the crocodile might have played the role of the Holy Ghost in an amusing story by that Frenchman, who had the national advantage of being born malicious? Meanwhile, the Marchioness was saying to Rita:

"Why did you tell him that nonsense about the crucified Negro? Wouldn't it have been better to tell him the truth?"

"But, Aunt," replied the girl, "I don't know why that cross is called the Negro's; besides, it would have bored me to tell it."

"Then," her aunt continued, "you should have told him that you didn't know, and not have led him into such crass error. I'm sure he'll include that bit of foolishness when he writes his *Voyage to Spain.*"

"What does it matter?" Rita said.

"It matters, Niece," replied the Marchioness, "because I don't like them to speak ill of my country."

"Yes," said the General sourly, "he's going to stop the river at its source. (He'll do it as sure as you're born.) But why do you wonder if foreigners speak ill of our country when we ourselves are the first to blacken her? Not to mention the old saying that 'he who considers himself evil is evil.' "

"So that you won't make such a mistake in the future," said the Marchioness, "I must tell you that the name of that cross comes from a devout and pious Negro of the Seventh Century. Seeing that the mystery of the immaculate conception of the Virgin was being attacked, he sold himself on the spot where that cross stands so that he could use the money for a solemn mass of atonement to the Virgin for the wrongs done her. This commemoration of pious and fervent self-sacrifice is a somewhat different story from the one you've made the Baron believe."

"You might also scold that crazy Rafael, Sister," the General said, "for having told Monsieur le Baron a similar story in answer to his question concerning the Thieves' Cross near the Carthusian monastery. Rafael said it's called that because the thieves go there to pray God to favor their undertakings."

"And did the Baron believe it?" asked the Marchioness.

"As firmly as I believe he is not a baron," the General replied.

"It's mischievous," the Marchioness went on, irritably, "for us to give them grounds ourselves for believing and repeating such absurdities. The cross was raised on that spot owing to a miracle that Our Lord performed there; for in those times there were miracles because there was faith. Some thieves had entered the Carthusian monastery and stolen the treasure from the church. They fled in fear, running all night, and on the following morning, they found themselves only a short distance from the monastery. Then, clearly seeing the Lord's hand, they were converted, and they erected the cross to commemorate this miracle, and the people have kept their name. I'm going to have a few words to say to that scatterbrain. . . . Rafael! Rafael!"

Meanwhile, Grace, seated on the sofa, was saying:

"I'm in heaven! It's going to be wonderful for us!"

"It won't last long, Countess," the Colonel said. "The story is going around that the Duke wants to take the new Malibrán[64] to Madrid."

"What *nom de guerre* has she taken for all this?" the

---

[64] María Felicita Malibrán, a Spanish soprano who made her Paris debut in 1824.

Countess asked. "I presume it won't be Marysal, though it's pretty and rather affectionate, it's not serious enough for a first-class artist."

"Perhaps she'll want to go under the nickname of Sea Gull," said Rafael. "One of the Duke's servants told mine that was what she was called in her village."

"She could use her husband's name," said the Colonel.

"How awful!" cried the Countess. "She needs a sonorous name."

"Very well; let her take her father's: Santaló."

"No, sir," said the Countess. "She must have one that ends in i to lend her prestige. The more i's, the better."

"In that case," said Rafael, "let her choose Mississippi."

"Let's consult Polo;" said the Countess, "and by the way, where has our poet slipped off to?"

"I'll bet anything that right now he's busy confiding to paper the harmonious inspirations that the divinity of the day has brought to bud in his soul," said Rafael. "Tomorrow without fail we'll read in *The Sevillian* one of those compositions that, according to Uncle, will certainly cast him into the Lethe, since it wouldn't be easy to raise him to Parnassus."

Just then the Marchioness called Rafael.

"I'm sure," he said to his cousin, "that Aunt is doing me the honor to call me so she can have the satisfaction of giving me a scolding. I can see a sermon sprouting between her tight lips, a Philippic on her clouded brow, and a bulky reprimand riding on her threatening nose. But forewarned is forearmed."

With these words, Rafael got up, went to the Baron, to whom the magistrate was just then offering his snuff box, took the Baron's arm, and went to the gaming table with him. The Marchioness held her fire until a better occasion.

Rita put her handkerchief to her mouth to stifle her

laughter. The General tapped the floor with the heel of his boot, an infallible sign of irritation with him.

"Is the General uncomfortable?" asked the Baron.

"He suffers from a nervous tic," replied Rafael under his breath.

"What a pity!" cried the Baron. "This is a tic douloureux. What caused it? Perhaps a tendon injured in the war?"

"No," Rafael replied. "It was caused by a powerful moral reaction."

"It must have been a terrible one," observed the Baron. "And what caused that?"

"A saying of your King Louis XIV."

"What saying?" insisted the Baron with astonishment.

"The celebrated saying THERE ARE NO MORE PYRENEES," Rafael replied.

With all the talk concerning the new singer at the social gatherings, a significant event that occurred that night was overlooked.

Pepe Vera had been following Marysal's footsteps ceaselessly, and as he was a public favorite, it had been easy for him to enter the temple of the Muses despite their sworn enmity to bullfights.

She was making her entrance to the sound of applause when she unexpectedly met Pepe Vera with some other youths in the wings.

"Blessed be," said the famous bullfighter, spreading his cape on the floor as a carpet for her, "blessed be that crystal throat, the envy of all the nightingales of May!"

"And those eyes," another added, "which have wounded more Christians than all the daggers of Albacete."[65]

---

[65] The capital of the inner part of the ancient kingdom of Murcia, once the Sheffield of Spain, especially famous for its daggers.

Marysal passed by, as scornful and impassive as ever.

"She won't even look at us," said Pepe Vera.

"Listen dear, a king will look at a cat. Never mind, gentlemen, she's a fine-looking girl, even if . . ."

"Even if what?" said one of his companions.

"Even if she is cross-eyed," Pepe Vera replied.

When Marysal heard that, she could not suppress an involuntary start, and she turned her big, astonished eyes on the group. The young men burst out laughing, and Pepe Vera blew her a kiss.

She realized at once that he had spoken only to make her turn her head. She could not help smiling, and she dropped her handkerchief as she went ahead. Pepe was on it like a shot and approached her as if to return it.

"Come to your window tonight," he said rapidly in a low voice.

At the stroke of midnight, Marysal got up from her bed and went on cautious feet to make sure her husband was lying fast asleep. Indeed Stein was dreaming with a smile on his lips, intoxicated with the acclaim she had received that evening. Meanwhile a black silhouette loomed at one of the window grilles on the ground floor of the house where she and Stein were living on one of the narrow little streets so common in Seville. She could not make out the features of her visitor, for an official hand had already extinguished the street lights.

CHAPTER XXIII

Already the Sevillian theater had grown too cramped for Marysal's ambitious eyes, and for the thirst for applause that was eating at her heart. Moreover, the Duke was obliged to return to the capital and wanted to introduce the prodigy whose fame had preceded her. In addition, Pepe Vera was scheduled to fight in the Madrid bullring and he asked her to make the trip, which she did.

The triumph that crowned her in her new setting surpassed her achievement in Seville. It seemed as though the days of Orpheus and Amphion[66] and the lyric marvels of mythological times had been reborn. Stein was stunned. The Duke was intoxicated. Pepe Vera said to the singer one day:

"Caramba! They clap more for you than if you'd killed a seven-year-old bull!"

Marysal was surrounded by a numerous court. All the distinguished foreigners then in the capital were part of it; among them some notable for their own merit, others for their rank. What was motivating them? Some went to be smart, as the modern phrase puts it. (What is smartness? It is the servile imitation of what others do.) Some were motivated by the kind of curiosity that impels the child to try to find the hidden springs in his toy.

It was through no effort of Marysal's that she felt completely at home in the midst of that large circle. Her cold and haughty temperament had not changed in the least; but there was more elegance in her bearing and more taste in her

---

[66] Son of Jupiter and Antiope, queen of Thebes. When Amphion became king he fortified the city with a wall. As he played his lyre, the stones moved of their own accord and set themselves in the wall.

dress—outward and mechanical acquisitions that in the eyes of some people may disguise the lack of intelligence, of tact, and good manners. On the stage at night, when the reflections from the footlights lightened her pallor and increased the luminosity of her big black eyes, she looked truly beautiful.

The Duke was fascinated by that woman in whose triumphs he had played a part, for she had realized his prophecies; and such was the enthusiasm her singing aroused in him that he saw no harm in asking her to give lessons to his daughter, even though he had not forgotten the forecast made by his sweet Sevillian friend, and shuddered when he thought of what the Countess had said to him. He had every intention then of respecting the innocent woman whom he himself had introduced to the brilliant and treacherous stage she was treading.

Let us now say a few words about the Duchess.

She was a virtuous and beautiful lady. Although in her early thirties, her fresh complexion and the innocence of her face made her look younger. She belonged to a family as illustrious as her husband's, to which she was related. Leonor and Carlos had loved each other almost since early childhood, with that truly Spanish affection, deep and constant, which neither wanes nor grows cold. They had been married very young. Leonor gave her husband a daughter at eighteen. He was twenty-two at the time.

Like some of the great families, the one from which the Duchess came was highly devout, and Leonor had been reared in that tradition. Her reserve and her austerity kept her apart from the noise and amusements of the world, and in addition they had no appeal for her. She was not a reader; she never picked up a novel. She was entirely unaware of the dramatic effects of grand passions. She had never learned from books or the theater what a great role had been assigned to adultery. Consequently it was an abomination in her eyes, on a par with murder. She would never have believed, had she been told so, that a banner proclaiming the emancipation of women was being raised in the world. Furthermore, even if she had believed it, she would not have understood it, like many others who led less retired and less austere lives than the Duchess.

Had she been told that there were those who justified divorce, that there were even detractors of the holy state of matrimony, she would have believed she was dreaming or that the end of the world had arrived. An affectionate and submissive daughter, a generous and steadfast friend, a loving and unselfish mother, a wife exclusively consecrated to her husband, the Duchess of Almansa was the kind of woman whom God loves, whom poetry portrays in song, whom society venerates and admires, and whom some people today would like to depose in order to enthrone those Amazons who have lost the fine, soft, feminine instinct.

Consequently it was long possible for the Duke to yield to the attraction Marysal held for him without causing the smallest cloud to darken the serene and heavenly pure peace of his wife. The Duke, however, so affectionate until then, was neglecting her increasingly. The Duchess wept but said nothing.

Later she heard the singer who had taken all Madrid by storm was her husband's protégée, and that he was spending all his time at the woman's house. The Duchess wept, but was not convinced.

The Duke had brought Stein to his house to give lessons to his son, and later, as we have said, he wanted Marysal to teach his daughter, a charming child of eleven.

Leonor vigorously opposed this, claiming that she could

not permit a woman of the theater to have the least contact with her innocent little girl. The Duke, accustomed to seeing his wife yield without a struggle, considered her opposition the scruple of a devout woman, lacking in worldliness. He persisted in his notion. The Duchess yielded at the order of her father confessor; but now she wept bitterly on two accounts.

She received Marysal, then, with excessive circumspection, with a cold, though urbane reserve.

In keeping with her quiet tastes, Leonor lived a very withdrawn life. She received few visitors, mainly relatives; the others were priests and a few intimates. Accordingly she was present at her daughter's lessons with open persistence, and was so careful never to take her maternal eye off the child that she could not fail to offend Marysal. The people who came to see the Duchess did no more than speak frigidly to the teacher. Thus the woman to whom the public of Madrid knelt found the position she occupied in that noble and austere household an extremely humiliating one. Marysal was fully aware of it, and her pride was outraged; but as the exquisite courtesy of the Duchess never flagged, as there was never a scornful smile or haughty look on the modest and beautiful face, she could not complain. Furthermore, how could the Duke permit anyone to complain of his wife, he being so dignified and fastidious? Marysal had enough insight to realize that she must remain silent in order not to lose the Duke's friendship (which flattered her), nor his protection (which she needed), nor his gifts (which were very welcome). Hence she was obliged to hold herself in check until some situation could put an end to such a strained position.

One day when she entered the house of the Duchess, dressed in silks, dazzling all eyes with her jewels, and wearing a magnificent lace mantilla, she met the father of the Duchess, the Marquis of Elda, and the Bishop of . . .

The Marquis was a grave old gentleman, deeply attached to the old ways. He was Spanish to the fingertips, Catholic, and an ultra-royalist. Since the death of the king, whom he had served in the War of Independence, he had been living in retirement from the Court.

A measure of coolness had developed between the Marquis and his son-in-law, whom the old man accused of lowering himself to the notions of the time. This coolness came to a head when the severely virtuous old man heard open rumors of the patronage extended by the Duke to a singer in the theater.

As Marysal entered the parlor the Duchess rose, intending to thank her and dismiss her for that day out of respect for the guests present. But the Bishop, knowing nothing of what was going on, manifested a desire to hear the little girl sing, for she was his god-daughter. The Duchess sat down again, nodded to Marysal with her usual urbanity, and sent for her daughter, who appeared promptly.

The little girl had barely finished the last notes of Desdemona's plea when three soft knocks were heard at the door.

"Come in, come in," said the Duchess, indicating by her manner of calling that she knew who was there. And displaying a vivacity new to Marysal, she rose and went to meet the visitor with extraordinary courtesy.

But Marysal was even more surprised to see this newcomer. She was an ugly woman of some fifty years, common in appearance. Her dress was coarse, worn, and strange.

The Duchess received her with great demonstrations of consideration and a cordiality all the more noticeable by contrast with the glacial reserve she had shown toward the teacher. She took the woman's hand and presented her to the Bishop.

Marysal was at a loss. She had never seen such a dress nor a person less in harmony with the position she seemed to occupy among these distinguished and high-born people.

After a quarter of an hour of animated conversation, the woman rose. It was raining. The Marquis insistently offered her his coach; but the Duchess said:

"Father, I've ordered mine."

As she spoke, she was accompanying the departing caller, who refused to make use of the carriage.

"Come, daughter," said the Duchess, "come to say good-bye to your good friend, with your teacher's permission."

Marysal did not know what to think of what she was seeing and hearing. The child embraced the woman whom the Duchess called her good friend.

"Who is that woman?" she asked as the little girl went back to her place.

"She's a Sister of Charity," the child replied.

Marysal was humiliated. Her stiff-necked pride, which challenged any superiority—the dignity of the nobility, the rivalry of fellow-artists, the power of the authorities, and even the prerogatives of genius—bent like a reed before the greatness and the supreme merit of virtue.

Soon afterward she rose to leave. It was still raining.

"You have a carriage at your disposal," the Duchess said to her as she took her leave.

Marysal noticed when she went down into the patio that the Duchess's horses were being unhitched. A lackey dismounted from a hired carriage with a respectful air. Marysal entered it, her heart swelling with impotent rage.

On the following day she told the Duke resolutely that she would not continue giving lessons to his daughter. She took good care not to reveal to him the true reasons, and she was astute enough to lend her withdrawal all the aspect of an act of prudence. The Duke was so hallucinated by his enthusiasm for Marysal and by her wiles, which she knew very well how to use, that he supposed his wife had been the cause of that decision and was even colder toward her.

CHAPTER XXIV

The arrival in Madrid of the famous singer, Tenorini, crowned Marysal's glory with the admiration that that great figure heaped on her, and the ardor he displayed at having a voice worthy to join his as an accompaniment to his singing. Tonino Tenorini, called The Great, had come from goodness knows where; some people said he had been born into the world not in a swan's egg like Castor and Pollux, but in a nightingale's. His splendid and noisy career began in Naples where he had completely eclipsed Vesuvius. Later he went to Milan, thence successively to Saint Petersburg and Constantinople. At that time he was coming from New York, by way of Havana, with the intention of going on to Paris, where the people had rioted to vent their anger at being denied the chance to stamp their decisive vote on such a titanic reputation. From Paris Tenorini would deign to go to London, where music-lovers were in a bad humor out of sheer envy, and where the *season*[67] was in danger of collapse should the great notable fail to take pity on the ills born of his absence.

A peculiar thing which surprised all the Polos and the Eloises: this sublime artist did not fly in on the wings of genius! The churlish dolphins of the Atlantic had not borne him on their music-loving shoulders as those of the Mediterranean had carried Arion[68] in happier times. Tenorini had come on the stagecoach. . . . How awful!

---

[67] The period when Parliament is sitting, when the smart people gather in London. AUTHOR'S NOTE.

[68] A musician whom sailors had robbed and thrown overboard, but whom a dolphin, charmed by his song, had rescued.

And what is worse, he was carrying an overnight bag!

There were plans to celebrate his arrival by a general ringing of bells, by illuminating the houses, and by raising an arch of triumph with all the instruments of the orchestra around it. The Mayor would not agree to that, and this reactionary spoil-sport barely escaped a noisy demonstration in front of his house.

Meanwhile, as Marysal was sharing the extravagant ovation offered to the great singer by a public that humbly venerated him on bended knee, a scene of quite a different character was taking place in the poor cottage she had left a little more than a year earlier.

Pedro Santaló was lying prostrate in his bed. He had hardly lifted his head since his separation from his daughter. His eyes were closed, and he opened them only to stare at the little room once occupied by Marysal, separated from his by the narrow passageway which led to the attic. Everything there was kept just as she had left it; her guitar was hanging on the wall by a knotted cord that once was pink but now was faded like a vanishing memory and hung like a forgotten promise. On the bed lay a scarf of Indian silk, and small shoes still peeped from under a chair. Aunt María was sitting at the head of the bed.

"Come, come, Pedro," the good old woman was saying. "Forget you're a Catalan and don't be so stubborn; let yourself be led for once in your life and come with us to the convent, for obviously there's no lack of room there. I'll be able to help you better, and you won't be here alone and isolated in a lonely bay, like an asparagus plant."

The fisherman made no reply.

"Pedro," Aunt María continued, "Don Modesto has already written two letters and mailed them, which they say is the quickest and surest way for them to get there."

"She won't come," muttered the sick man.

"But her husband will come, and that's what matters now," Aunt María replied.

"I want her, her!" cried the poor father.

An hour after this conversation, Aunt María was on her way back to the convent, having failed to persuade the intractable and stubborn Catalan to let himself be moved. The good old woman was mounted on the redoubtable *Golondrina,* peaceful dean of the local donkey society. In view of the lapse of time since she was given the name of *Golondrina* (Swallow) we have not been able to discover why she deserved it—certainly not for flying, nor yet for running; nor had she ever manifested the slightest inclination to migrate to African regions in the autumn.

Momo, now a grown man, was driving the donkey. He had not lost an iota of his native ugliness.

"Listen, Grandmother," he said, "are these daily little outings to visit this sea wolf going to last much longer?"

"Of course," his grandmother replied. "Since he doesn't want to come to the convent. I'm afraid he'll die if he doesn't see his daughter."

"That's an illness I'd never die of," said Momo, bursting into a guffaw.

"Listen, son," Aunt María went on, "I don't take much stock in the mail, no matter how safe they say it is. Don Modesto doesn't trust it either; so there's no sure way to let Don Federico and Marysal know how sick poor Pedro is than for you yourself to go to Madrid and tell them; for after all we can't stand around here with our arms folded watching a father die, calling for his daughter, without doing whatever we can to bring her to him."

"I! I go to Madrid to look for the Sea Gull?" cried Momo, his hair standing on end. "Are you in your right mind, señora?"

"So very much in my right mind that if you don't want to go, I'll go. I went to Cádiz and I didn't get lost and nothing happened to me; it'll be the same in Madrid. It breaks my heart to hear that poor father calling for his daughter. But, Momo, you lack the bowels of compassion; it hurts me very much to have to say so. I don't know where you got your disposition, for neither your father's nor your mother's side of the family is like that. But there's a Judas in every family."

"Such a thing wouldn't have occurred even to the devil himself, who thinks of nothing but damning Christians," Momo was muttering. "And that isn't the worst of it, for if you take such a notion into your head, you're going to carry it out. I wouldn't bet one penny I won't be crippled in my legs and feet for a month!"

So thinking, he vented his rage by striking poor *Golondrina* a cruel blow on the flank.

"Barbarian!" his grandmother exclaimed. "Why are you hitting this poor creature?"

"Go on!" said Momo. "She was born to bear blows."

"Wherever did you get such traits? Where, son of Herod? Nobody knows how I pity poor animals that suffer without complaining, helpless to help themselves, with no consolation or compensation."

"Your pity, Grandmother, is like the spread of the sky, which covers everything."

"Yes, son, yes. God forbid that I should ever witness suffering without feeling pity, or become one of those heartless people who can listen to a groan as if it were just rain falling."

"You can say that about your neighbor and God bless you! But about animals—what the devil!"

"You think they don't suffer? And you think they're not God's creatures? Here we are burdened with the curse and punishment passed on to us from the first man; but what sin did the Adam and Eve of the burros commit to bring on to these poor animals such a miserable life? That beats me!"

"They must have eaten the apple peeling," said Momo with a laugh like a drum roll.

Just then they met Manuel and José, who were going home to the convent.

"How is Pedro, Mother?" asked Manuel.

"Sick, son, sick. It breaks my heart to see him so sick, so sad and alone. I told him to come to the convent; but no, it would be easier to move Fort Saint Christopher than that hard head. A twenty-four-pounder wouldn't budge him. Brother Gabriel will have to move over there with him, and Momo will have to go to Madrid to bring his daughter and Don Federico."

"Let him go;" said Manuel, "that way he'll see the world."

"I!" exclaimed Momo. "How am I to go, señor?"

"One foot after the other," his father replied. "Are you afraid of getting lost, or that a bogeyman will eat you up?"

"The point is I don't want to go," Momo answered exasperatedly.

"Well, I'll make you want to go with an olive switch; do you hear, you spoiled brat?"

Momo had no choice but to undertake the trip, cursing Pedro and all his kind. He joined a troupe of muleteers in the Aracena Mountains who had come to Villamar for fish. With them he went as far as Barracarrota, thence to Badajoz, through which the old road from Madrid to Andalusia runs. From there he went straight on to Madrid. Don Modesto had written in letters as big as walnuts Stein's address, which the latter had sent after he and Marysal had arrived in Madrid. With this slip of paper in his hand, Momo set out for the capital, muttering new strings of curses on the Sea Gull.

Meanwhile, Aunt María had left the fisherman's house one afternoon, more uneasy than ever.

"Dolores," she said to her daughter-in-law, "Pedro is going to leave us: he's plucking at the sheets on his bed, and this means he's packing his bag for the journey from which there's no return. *Palomo*, who was with me, started to howl. And still those people don't come! It makes my blood run cold. It seems to me that Momo ought to be back by now; he's been gone ten days."

"Mother," Dolores replied, "there's a lot of ground to cover from here to Madrid. Manuel says he can't be back for four or five days yet."

But what was their astonishment suddenly to behold Momo in person in front of them, looking upset and out of sorts.

"Momo!" they exclaimed in unison.

"The very same, in the flesh and in the spirit," he replied.

"And what about Marysal?" Aunt María asked anxiously.

"And Don Federico?" asked Dolores.

"You can wait for them till Judgment Day," Momo replied. "That's how much good my trip has done! Thanks to Grandmother, I got myself into a mare's nest that still . . ."

"But what's the matter? What happened to you?" the mother and grandmother asked.

"I'm going to tell you so you can wonder at God's judgments and bless Him that I'm here safe and sound, thanks to my good legs."

The mother and grandmother were bewildered at those words, which boded ill.

"Tell us, man, tell us. What happened?" they both exclaimed. "We're on tenterhooks."

"When I arrived in Madrid," Momo said, "and realized I was alone in that den of thieves, I was scared to death. Every street looked like a soldier, every square like a patrol. With that piece of paper the Commander gave me, a paper that could talk, I went to find a tavern. I met a tipsy fellow there, who was willing to do me a favor. He took me to the house the paper told about. The servants there told me their master and mistress weren't at home, and they were about to shut the door in my face, but those birds didn't know whom they were dealing with.

"'Hey,' I said to them, 'do you know who you're talking to? I'm nobody's servant and I haven't come to beg; though I could, because we took Don Federico into my house when he was dying and had no place even to die in.'"

"You said that, Momo!" his grandmother exclaimed. "The idea! You don't say things like that! What a disgrace! What must they have thought of us? Throwing a favor in their faces! Whoever heard of such a thing?"

"Well, wouldn't you have said it? Go on! I said more than that. For your information, I said my grandmother had been the one who brought their mistress to our house when she was sick from running around and screaming on the rocks like the Sea Gull she was. The stupid things looked at one another and laughed and made fun of me, and they told me I was mistaken, that she was the daughter of a general commanding the troops of Don Carlos. Daughter of a general! Do you understand? What the devil! What could be a more barefaced lie? Calling Pedro a general! Pedro, who was never even in the service!

" 'Hurry up!' I said. 'My business is urgent, and all I want is to get away fast and be rid of you, your masters, and all Madrid.'

" 'Nicolás,' said one of the maids then, as brazen as her mistress, 'take this chump to the theater; he'll see the señora there.'

"Notice that when she was talking about me the long-tongue called me a chump, and when she was talking about that lazy Sea Gull she called her señora. Would you believe it? Madrid manners! Curse them!

"Well, sir, the servant put on his hat and took me to a very big, very tall house like a church; only in place of candles it had lamps that lit everything up like so many suns. All around it were some seats, like, where more than ten thousand women were sitting, stiffer than spindles, and all dressed up like drugstore flasks. There were so many men down below it looked like an ant-hill. Christians! I don't know where so many people came from! 'Why,' I said to myself, 'the loaves of bread in the city of Madrid if laid end to end would be something!' But you'll open your mouths at this; all those people had gone there, why? To hear the Sea Gull sing!"

Momo came to a pause, holding out his open hands at about the level of his face.

Aunt María nodded as a sign of her satisfaction.

"I don't see any reason in all this why you came back so hurriedly and so upset," said Dolores.

"I'm coming to it, I'm coming. I'm not a shotgun," Momo replied. "I'm telling things as they happened. Just think of it, then, suddenly and without anyone telling them to, more than a thousand instruments—trumpets, pipes, and some violins as big as confessionals which they play down near the floor—all began to play at once. Holy Mary, I was stunned! I shrank up and gave thanks to God."

"But where did all that music come from?" asked his mother.

"How do I know? Maybe the blind men all over Spain were conscripted. But that isn't the best of it, mark you. A kind of thing like a garden there in front disappeared, I don't know how or where. It looked almost as if the devil had managed it."

"What are you talking about, Momo?" Dolores said.

"I'm not telling a single thing but the honest truth. Instead of the garden, there was something like a stage with carpets all around, like a palace. There was a woman with a long train, with more velvets embroidered in gold and more trinkets than a statue of the Virgin. 'This is Queen Isabel the Second,' I said to myself. But no, sir, it wasn't the queen. Do you know who it was? The Sea Gull, the wicked Sea Gull no less, the very one that used to run around barefoot and barelegged! The same thing must have happened to her as happened to the garden; the barefooted and barelegged Sea Gull must have been carried off by the devil, and a princess must have taken her place. I was paralyzed with amazement. All of a sudden an older man came in, all dressed up. How mad he was, mad enough to chew nails! His eyes were glaring. 'Gosh!' I said to myself, 'I wouldn't like to be in that Sea Gull's shoes.' Added to that, what brought me up short was that they were quarreling and singing at the same time! It must be the style there among important people. All the same, I couldn't make out what they were talking about; but what I did get clear was that he must have been Don Carlos's general, for she called him father, but he didn't want to recognize her as his daughter, no matter how hard she begged him on her knees.

" 'Good for you!' I shouted, 'Be hard on the imposter.' "

"Why did you interfere?" said his grandmother.

"Why! Because I know her, and I could testify to it. Doesn't silence give assent? But it seems you can't speak the truth there, for my neighbor, who was a police warden, said to me: 'Would you like to keep still, my friend!'

" 'No, I wouldn't!' I told him, 'and I'm going to shout right out loud that that man is not her father.'

" 'Are you crazy, or are you from the backwoods?' the cop said.

" 'Neither one, you miserable wretch,' I told him. 'I'm smarter than you are, and I'm from Villamar where her real father, Pedro Santaló, is.'

" 'You've got a head like a block of cork. Go away and get the bark off,' said the little man from Madrid.

"I flew into a rage and raised my fist to give him a punch, but Nicolás grabbed my arm and took me out to get a drink.

" 'I catch on now,' I told him, 'that general is the one that renegade Sea Gull wants to claim as her father. I've heard of a lot of wicked things: deaths, robberies, even piracies, but never in my life have I heard of denying your father.'

"Nicolás nearly split his sides laughing; it seems that kind of indignity doesn't shock them at all.

"When we went back in, the general must have ordered the Sea Gull to cut out the blandishments, because she came out all dressed in white material that looked like a winding sheet. She started to sing, and she took a guitar, a very big one she put on the ground and played with both hands. What won't that Sea Gull think of! And now comes the cream of the jest, for suddenly a Moor comes on."

"A Moor?"

"But what a Moor! Blacker and more bad-tempered than Mohammed. With a dagger in his hand as big as a machete. I was petrified!"

"God save us!" exclaimed his mother and grandmother.

"I asked Nicolás who that ogre was, and he told me his name was Thello. To make a long story short, the Moor told the Sea Gull he was going to kill her."

"Holy Mother of God!" cried Aunt María. "Was he the executioner?"

"I don't know if he was the executioner or if he was a hired killer," Momo replied. "What I do know is that he grabbed her by the hair and stabbed her several times; I saw it with these eyes that the worms will eat; and I can testify to it."

Momo put his fingers to his eyes with such expressiveness that they looked as if they would jump from their sockets.

The two good women screamed. Aunt María sobbed and wrung her hands in distress.

"But what were all the people there doing?" asked Dolores, weeping. "Wasn't there anybody to arrest that wicked man?"

"That's what I don't know," Momo replied, "for after I saw that, I took to my heels like a shot, in case they should call me as a witness, and I didn't slow down until I'd put several leagues between the city of Madrid and my father's son."

"This terrible thing must be kept from poor Pedro," said Aunt María between sobs. "Oh, what a pity! What a pity!"

"Who'd have the courage to tell him?" replied Dolores.

"Poor Marysal! She was like the Spaniard who didn't know when he was well off, and look what happened."

"Everyone gets his just deserts," said Momo. "That heartless deceiver was bound to come to no good end. She couldn't escape it. If I weren't so tired, I'd be on my way to tell Pérez the Mouse about it."

CHAPTER XXV

The word that the fisherman's daughter had been murdered spread quickly through the village.

Thus the selfish, dull-witted, and wayward Momo, abetted by his hostile spirit and selfish instincts, believed what he saw in the theater to be true. Not only had he made a useless trip, for he failed to carry out his commission, but he also communicated to all those good people the error into which his own stupidity had led him.

Don Modesto's face lengthened two inches.

The priest said a mass for Marysal's soul.

Ramón Pérez tied a black cord to his guitar.

Mystical Rose said to Don Modesto:

"I hope God has forgiven her. I was right when I said she'd come to a bad end. You'll recall that no matter how hard I tried to guide her right, she always swung left."

Aunt María, assuming in view of the tragedy that it would not be possible for Don Federico to come at that time, decided to entrust Pedro's treatment to a young doctor who had replaced Stein in Villamar.

"I have no faith in his ability," she would say to Don Modesto, who had recommended him. "He doesn't know enough to prescribe anything but boiling water, and there's nothing that weakens the stomach more. He orders boiled chicken for food. Now can you tell me how a pap like that can strengthen anybody? Everything is topsy-turvy, Commender, but let a little time pass, and they'll be undeceived and go back to what the experience of many centuries has found good, for after a thousand years water will go back to its source. What reckless hands have thrown down, time will raise up; but only after many souls have been cast to perdition and many bodies into the pit."

The doctor pronounced Pedro so seriously ill that he should prepare himself for death.

In Catholic terminology, to prepare one's self for death is to place one's self in a state of grace; that is, to settle all earthly accounts, doing good and undoing evil insofar as it lies in our power to do so, both in the eternal and the temporal order of things, and thus to seek through prayer and repentance the mercy of God on behalf of our souls.

If we explain something so well-known and so common, it is not only because it is possible that this story may come into the hands of some who do not belong to the body of our holy Catholic religion, but also because we have seen many who do not observe this religious practice in all its great and magnificent phases.

Aunt María began to cry bitterly at hearing the doctor's pronouncement. She summoned Manuel and charged him with the duty of informing the sick man with all due precaution, for she felt she had not the courage to do it.

Manuel entered the patient's room.

"Hello, Pedro," said he. "How are you?"

"I'm sinking," the sick man replied. "Is there something you'd like in the next world? Tell me quickly, for I'm weighing anchor, son."

"What! Pedro, you're not that bad off. You'll live longer than I. But . . . as the saying goes, there's no harm in doing what has to be done . . . It means . . ."

"Say no more, Manuel," Pedro answered with no change of expression. "Tell your mother I'm ready. I've seen the end coming for some time, and I'm thinking only of that," and he added in a tired voice, "and of her."

Manuel left, so moved that he was wiping his eyes though he had seen a great deal of blood and many deaths during his military service. How true it is that the most stoical nature will soften at the sight of death, when man is not forced to think of the soul as an atom launched into the bottomless abyss dug for so many thousands by the pride and ambition of those in authority who wrongfully try to impose their own will and opinions on the world!

On the following day the equinox brought one of its violent, noisy, and exciting storms. The wind blew in several keys, like a hydra with its seven heads all whistling at once.

It dashed against the cabin which rustled dolefully; it could be heard sounding mournfully among the echoing vaults of the upper ruins of the fort; it screamed among the tossing branches of the pine trees; it keened among the storm-tossed reeds of the garden; it blew itself out moaning in the open plains as shadows on a landscape gradually fade away.

The surface of the sea was whipping up with the violence of a Fury shaking her serpentine hair. The clouds, like Danaïdes, poured water incessantly, each her quota, which fell in torrents on the branches and broke them, and opened deep running ditches in the earth. Everything shuddered, trembled, or groaned. The sun had fled, and the sad color of the day was dark and uniform as a shroud.

Although the cabin was protected by the cliff, the storm had taken away part of its roof during the night. To prevent its total destruction, Manuel, with Momo's help, had weighted it with some timbers taken from the ruins.

"Now that you don't want to shelter your owner any

longer," said Manuel, "at least wait until he's dead before you bury him."

If any eye but God's had been able to scan that wilderness through the storm lashing it, it would have descried a group of men walking parallel with the shore, wrapped in their capes, fighting the fury of the storm in a withdrawn and silent manner, their bodies leaning forward and their heads lowered. A sober-faced old man was following them with measured step, his arms crossed on his breast in the manner of the Orientals, preceded by a boy who rang a little bell from time to time. Despite the raging of the hurricane, the old man's serene and sonorous voice could be heard at intervals, saying: *"Miserere mei Deus, secundum magnam misericordiam tuam."* And the men reply in chorus: *"Et secundum multitudinem miserationum tuarum, de iniquitatem meam."* [69]

The rain was soaking them, the wind was tearing at them, but they pursued their even, sober march impassively.

This group was composed of the priest and some devout Catholics of the brotherhood of the Most Blessed Sacrament, with Manuel as its chief officer, which was going to bring the last sacraments to the dying, the final consolation of Christianity.

Nothing could give greater reality and life to this moral truth than what we have just described: that in the midst of the tumult, and the tempests, and the evil passions, the voice of the holy faith makes itself heard at intervals, sober and powerful, soft yet firm, even to those who forget and renounce it.

---

[69] The priest says: "Have mercy on me, O God, according to Thy great mercy." The men answer: "And on my iniquity according to Thy boundless mercy."

The priest entered the sick man's room.

The children who had gathered there were reciting these lines which they had learned when they learned to talk:

"Jesus Christ is coming;
And I would die for God
As God did die for me.
The angels are singing,
The whole world adores
The merciful God
Who comes at this hour."

The poor dwelling had been cleaned and made ready with care and decency, thanks to the labors of Aunt María and Brother Gabriel. A crucifix, candles, and flowers had been set on a table, for lights and perfumes are the outward homage paid to God. The bed was clean and fresh.

At the end of the ceremony, none but the priest, good old María, and Brother Gabriel remained with the sick man. Pedro was lying quietly. After a time he opened his eyes and said:

"Hasn't she come?"

"Pedro," answered Aunt María, while two tears traced themselves down her wrinkled cheeks unseen by the sick man, "it's a long way from here to Madrid. She wrote that she was going to start out and we shall see her here soon."

Santaló sank back into his coma. An hour later he came out of it and fixing his eyes on Aunt María, he said to her:

"Maria, I've asked my divine Savior who has deigned to come to me, to forgive me, to make her happy, and to repay you for all you have done for us."

Later he lost consciousness, came to again, opened his eyes, now glassy in death, and said almost incoherently:

"She hasn't come!"

Immediately his head fell back on the pillow and he cried out in a loud, firm voice:

"Mercy, Lord!"

"Say the Creed," said the priest, taking the dying man's hands in his and putting his mouth to his ear to make him aware, through the growing dullness of his senses, of the words of faith, hope, and charity.

Aunt María and Brother Gabriel prostrated themselves.

Catholics retain all the solemn respect for death that God has given it through offering Himself as a sacrifice in expiation for man's sins.

Silence and a majestic tranquillity reigned in that humble corner where death had just come.

Outside, the storm continued to howl unabated.

Within, all was repose and peace, for God robs death of its horrors and its anxieties when the soul rises to heaven in a cry for mercy, surrounded by fervent hearts who echo it on earth: "Mercy, mercy."

CHAPTER XXVI

The world is a commingling of contrasts. This observation is neither new nor original; but each day shows us sunrise and sunset, filling us always with surprise and wonderment, despite its repetition.

So it was that while the poor fisherman was offering his humble and pious friends the grand and august spectacle of a good Christian death, his daughter was offering the frantically enthusiastic public the sight of a prima donna without a drop of Italian blood in her veins already eclipsing the great Tenorini in the exercise of his art. This was enough to revive the ancient and noble pride of the days of Charles III; to free us forever and ever amen from the rage and the itch to imitate. We were recovering our pure and unsullied nationality; in short, there was reason to say to the monument to the Second of May and the statues of Philip IV and Cervantes: "Bow down, illustrious shades, for here comes one who surpasses your greatness and your glory." There was no lack of enthusiasts who were thinking of petitioning the Queen to give Marysal a title, conferring on her a coat of arms whose motto might read: "To Andalusia, high and low, she gave new glory," in paraphrase of the motto of the Dukes of Veragua:[70] "To Castile and Leon Columbus gave a New World." In short, so great was the impression made by the singer on the public of Madrid that the offices issued no writs and the colleges did no studying; even the smokers forgot to go to the tobacco shops. The indignant tobacco factories trembled to

---

[70] The name given to the Columbus family when they were granted a dukedom.

their foundations, even though it is an established fact that
their basements are so deep they go down to America. All the
enthusiasm we have tried unsuccessfully to sketch was evident
at the door of the theater one night, symbolized by a group of
youths, and shared by two recent foreign arrivals. Those members of the intelligentsia not only extolled, examined, and
analyzed the quality of the voice, the flexibility of throat and
every other remarkable phase of Marysal's singing, but they
also passed judgment on her looks. Another young man stood
near that group, motionless and silent, wrapped to the eyes in
his cape; but when they began to talk about her physical endowments, he stamped his foot angrily.

"I'll bet a hundred guineas, Viscount Fadiese," our friend
Sir John Burnwood was saying (having failed to obtain leave
to carry off the Alcázar, he was thinking of asking for the
Escorial), "I'll bet that this woman would make more of a
stir in France than Mme. Lafarge, than Tom Thumb in England or Rossini in Italy."

"I don't doubt it, Sir John," the Viscount replied.

"What Arabian eyes," added the Don Celestino Harmo-
nía. "What a slim waist! As for her feet, they don't show, but
one can speculate. Magdalen might envy her hair!"

"I'm impatient to see and hear this wonder," cried
Viscount Fadiese excitedly. (As his name indicated he was
always a semi-tone higher than other Viscounts.) "Let's get
our glasses ready and go in."

Meanwhile the cloaked youth had vanished.

Marysal, dressed as Semiramis, was ready to go on stage.
Several people stood around her.

The man in the cloak, none other than Pepe Vera, suddenly entered and went up to her. He said in her ear too low
to be overheard:

"I don't want you to sing," and then went away with an air of indifference.

Marysal turned pale with astonishment and then instantly reddened with indignation.

"Come," she said to her maid, "Marina, adjust the folds of this dress properly. They're going to start," and she added loudly enough so that Pepe Vera could hear her as he went. "One doesn't play games with the public."

"Señora," said one of the stage-hands, "shall I order the curtain raised?"

"I'm ready," she answered.

But she had hardly spoken when she gave a sharp cry.

Pepe Vera had passed behind her, and seizing her arm with brutal strength, had repeated:

"I don't want you to sing."

Overcome with the pain, Marysal threw herself into a chair, weeping. Pepe Vera had vanished.

"What's the matter? What's happened?" asked the by-standers.

"I have a pain," she replied.

"What's the matter, señora?" asked the director, who had been told what had taken place.

"It's nothing," Marysal answered, getting up and drying her tears. "It's gone. I'm ready. Let's go."

At that moment, Pepe Vera, pale as a corpse, and with eyes burning like open flames, came and interposed himself between the director and Marysal.

"It's cruel to send a girl on stage when she can hardly stand up," he said coolly.

"What is it, señora," exclaimed the director. "Are you ill? A moment ago I saw you looking fine, gay and animated!"

She was going to reply, but she lowered her eyes and did

not open her lips. The terrible eyes of Pepe Vera fascinated her as a snake charms a bird.

"Why shouldn't the truth be told?" Pepe Vera went on inexorably. "Why shouldn't you admit that you're in no state to sing? Is that by any chance a sin? Are you a slave to be forced to do what you aren't able to do?"

Meanwhile, the public was growing impatient. The director was at a loss. The authorities had sent to learn the cause of the delay; and while the director was explaining what had happened, Pepe Vera led Marysal away under the pretext that she needed help, clutching her wrist with such strength that it seemed he would break her bones, and saying to her in a muffled but firm voice:

"Caramba! Isn't it enough for me to say I don't want you to?"

When they were alone in her dressing room, her anger burst forth.

"You're insolent; you're a wretch!" she cried in a voice half stifled with anger. "What right have you to treat me this way?"

"The right of loving you," Pepe Vera answered coolly.

"Damn your love!" said Marysal.

Pepe Vera burst out laughing.

"You say that as if you could live without it," he said, laughing again.

"Go away, go away," Marysal exclaimed, "and never show your face in front of me again."

"Until you call me."

"I call you! I'd sooner call the devil."

"You can do that, too; I won't be jealous."

"Go away, go away this instant; leave me alone!"

"Granted," said the bullfighter. "I'll go straight to Lucía del Salto."

Marysal was very jealous of this woman, a dancer whom Pepe Vera had courted before knowing her.

"Pepe! Pepe!" she shrieked. "You villain! You're adding insult to injury!"

"That's just what I want to do," said Pepe Vera. "You're getting too upstage for me. If you want us to be good friends, you'll have to do the things I want you to. If you want to command and not to obey, you have your dukes, your ambassadors, your insipid and sickly excellencies."

He finished speaking and started to walk toward the door.

"Pepe! Pepe!" cried Marysal, crushing her fine handkerchief in her twitching hands.

"Call the devil," Pepe Vera replied ironically.

"Pepe! Pepe! Mind what I'm saying. If you go to Lucía, I'll let the Duke make love to me."

"What'll you bet you don't dare to?" answered Pepe, coming back a few steps.

"I'll dare anything to have my revenge."

Pepe stood firmly in front of her, his arms folded and his eyes fixed on hers.

Marysal stared back into his eyes, as penetrating as darts.

The attraction between these two harsh and brutal lovers seemed more suited to wild animals than to human beings. Nevertheless, the love that "modern" literature generally attributes to distinguished gentlemen and elegant ladies is described in just those terms!

In that brief moment the two natures were sounding each other out, and both recognized that they were of the same temper and strength. They must either cut short their relations or call a truce. Each knew this instinctively, and each renounced the victory.

"Come, dear Mariquita," said Pepe Vera, who had been

the aggressor, "let's be friends, and throw our quarrels overboard. I won't go to Lucía's house; but, on the other hand, to make us sure of each other, I'm going to hide in your house tonight so I can be a witness to the Duke's visit and convince myself you're not deceiving me."

"You can't," Marysal answered coldly.

"All right," said Pepe. "You know where I'm going when I leave here."

"You're vile," she answered, her fists clenching with rage. "You put me between the devil and the deep blue sea."

An hour after this scene, Marysal was at home, reclining on a sofa; the Duke was sitting near her; Stein, standing, was holding his wife's hand, noting her pulse.

"It's nothing, Marysal," he said. "It's nothing, Duke; a nervous attack that has passed. The pulse is perfectly normal. Rest, Mariquita, rest. You're killing yourself with work. Your nerves have been extraordinarily excitable for some time. Your nervous system is reacting to the strength you spend on your roles. I'm not at all worried, so I'm going to attend a man who is critically ill. Take the sedative I'm going to prescribe; when you go to bed, take a dose, and in the morning, some milk." Then, speaking to the Duke, "Much as I dislike to leave, Duke, it's my duty to go."

Again recommending calm and rest for his wife, Stein left with a low bow to the Duke.

The Duke, who was seated facing Marysal, stared at her for a long while.

"Are you tired?" he asked with the gentleness that love alone can impart to the human voice.

"I'm resting," she replied.

"Would you like me to go?"

"If you wish . . ."

"On the contrary, I should dislike it very much."

"Well, then, stay."

"Marysal," said the Duke after a few moments of silence, as he drew a sheet of paper from his note-case. "When I can't talk to you I sing your praises. Here are some verses I composed last night; for I dream by night without sleeping. Sleep has fled my eyes since peace has fled my heart. Forgive me, Marysal, if these words welling up from my heart offend your innocent feelings, as pure as your voice. When you suffer, I suffer, too."

"You can see," she replied, yawning, "that it hasn't been anything to worry about."

"Would you like me to read you the verses?" asked the Duke.

"Very well," Marysal responded coldly.

The Duke read her a pretty composition.

"Very beautiful," she said, somewhat more animatedly. "Is this going to be published in *The Herald*?"

"Would you like that?" the Duke asked, sighing.

"I think it's good enough," she replied.

The Duke was silent, supporting his head on his hands.

When he raised it, he saw a live spark in Marysal's eyes, fixed on the glass door of her bedroom. It was instantly extinguished. He turned his head toward the door but could see nothing.

In his distraction, the Duke had rolled up the paper on which the verses were written and which Marysal had not asked for.

"Are you going to make the sonnet into a cigar?" she asked.

"At least it would be worth something if I did," replied the Duke.

"Give me it, I'll keep it," she replied.

Inside the roll of paper the Duke handed her a magnificent diamond ring.

"What!" said Marysal. "The ring, too?"

She put it on her finger, letting the paper fall to the floor.

"Ah!" the Duke thought then, "she has no heart for love, no soul for poetry! It hardly seems she has blood enough for life! And yet heaven lies in her smile, hell in her eyes; and all that heaven and earth contain is in the tones of her superb voice."

The Duke rose to his feet.

"Rest, Marysal," he said. "Rest serene in your fortunate peace of mind, unworried by the thought that others lie awake and suffer."

CHAPTER XXVII

The Duke had hardly closed the door when Pepe Vera came out of the bedroom doubled over with laughter.

"Will you please be still?" Marysal said, turning the ring to reflect the light from the solitaire the Duke had just given her.

"I'll die laughing," said the bullfighter. "I'm not jealous any more. No more jealous than a sultan in his harem. Poor woman! What would become of you with a husband who makes love to you with prescriptions and a suitor who courts you with couplets? What would become of you if you didn't have someone who knows how to seduce you with his own fascinations? Now that one of them has gone to dream awake, and the other to watch asleep, let's you and I go out to supper with the gay people who are waiting for us now."

"No, Pepe, I don't feel well. The upset I had, and the cold air when I left the theater, have given me a chill."

"You and your royal whims," said Pepe Vera. "Come with me. Supper will do you more good than that silly medicine, and a couple of glasses of good wine will help you more than that nasty milk. Let's go, let's go!"

"I'm not going. There's a north wind off the Guadarramas. It's one of those that can blow out a candle and kill a Christian."

"All right," said Pepe. "If that's what you want, and if you'd rather take care of your health, good night."

"What!" cried Marysal. "You'd go out to supper and leave me? Alone and sick as I am through your fault?"

"Well!" replied the bullfighter. "Do you want me to go on a diet, too? No, not that, my dark lady. They're waiting for me and I'm going. You've wasted a lot of my time."

Marysal rose with an angry movement, knocked over a chair, and went out of the room, slamming the door. She soon came back, dressed in black and wrapped in a shawl. They went out together.

Very late that night, when Stein came home, the servant handed him a note. He opened it in his room. It read as follows:

"Dear Doctor:

Don't think this is an anonymous letter; I want to make everything clear. I'll begin by telling you my name, which is Lucía del Salto. I think it's a fairly well-known name.

Husband of Marysal Santaló, you'd have to be as good and as stupid as you are not to have caught on that your wife is carrying on with Pepe Vera who was my sweetheart, as I can say because I'm not married and am deceiving no one. If you want to have your eyes opened, go to No. 13 Tal Street to-night, and act like Saint Thomas."

"How can anyone do such a shameful thing!" Stein exclaimed, dropping the note on the floor. "My poor Mariquita is envied by the women of the theater. Poor girl, she's not well and probably she's sleeping quietly. But we shall see if she's sound asleep. Last night her pulse was fast and her voice was tight. There's so much pneumonia in Madrid just now!"

Stein picked up a light, went out of his room, passed the parlor into which his wife's bedroom opened, entered it on tiptoe, approached the bed, half opened the curtains . . . No one was there!

To a man of integrity, as trusting as Stein, the conviction of base deceit was slow to come, and he struggled against it.

"No," he said after a moment's reflection. "It's not possible. Something must have happened, something unforseen."

"But," he went on after another pause, "I must not keep a thing like this in my heart. I must be able to answer back to slander with scorn, and be able to give the lie to it with positive proofs."

With the aid of the night watchman he easily found the place named in the letter.

There was no doorman at the house; the street door was open. Stein went in and climbed a flight of stairs; but at the first floor he did not know which way to turn.

The first flush of resolution had faded, and he began to feel ashamed of what he was doing.

"Spying is a filthy business," he was saying. "If Marysal knew what I'm doing she would resent it bitterly, and she'd have a right to. Lord, how the first cloud in the sky of love can arise from suspicion! Can the despicable note of an even more despicable woman reduce me to this?"

"I'll go on home. Tomorrow I'll ask Marysal what I'd like to know. That's the proper way, the natural way, the honorable way. I have to settle my mind and clear it of suspicions, as the sun can clear the air of dark shadows."

He heaved a deep sigh, for he felt smothered, and wiped his damp forehead with his handkerchief.

"Oh!" he exclaimed. "How suspicion can generate the idea of deceit in a mind where it never existed! Oh, base suspicion, born of evil instincts and worse insinuations. For a moment my spirit was so poisoned by it that I think I'll always feel like blushing before Marysal."

Just then a door to the landing where Stein was standing swung open, letting out the sound of clinking glasses, singing, and laughter. A servant emerged, carrying empty bottles and stepped back to let Stein pass. His appearance and dress inspired her respect.

"Go on in," she said, "you're late, for they've had supper."

Stein found himself in a small anteroom, whose door

opened on an adjoining parlor. Stein went in. At his first glance into the interior, he stopped short and stood as if turned to stone.

All the good and pure impulses of his heart had been blinding Stein regarding Marysal, just as lofty and spiritually ennobling sentiments had been blinding the Duke. To the husband's stupefaction, he saw her sitting on a stool at the table[71] with Pepe Vera at her feet on a low chair, a guitar in his hands, and singing:

> "An Andalusian woman
>   Holds sunshine in her eyes;
>   The dawn is in her smile,
>   And in her arms lies Paradise."

"Bravo, Pepe, bravo!" the company shouted. "Now it's Marysal's turn to sing. Let Marysal sing. We don't belong to high society, but we have ears the same as they. When it comes to ears, there's no rich and no poor. Go ahead, Mariquita, sing for your own kind who can understand you; the people with the ribbons and the decorations only know how to clap in French."

Marysal took the guitar which Pepe Vera offered her on his knees, and she sang:

> "I'd rather be poor and eat peppers
>   And have fun, high and wide,
>   I'd rather eat hot roast peppers
>   Than have a noble gentleman
>   Lying spineless at my side."

---

[71] Here originally I wrote "with her mantilla off" but I suppressed this phrase, which might have given translators unfamiliar with the fact that the mantilla is a headdress, an opportunity to make the indecent statement that Marysal's neck and shoulders were bare. AUTHOR'S NOTE.

A storm of applause greeted this verse, applause so loud and lively that the window panes shook.

Stein turned red as a pomegranate, less with indignation than with shame.

"That Pepe Vera was born lucky, all right," said one of his friends.

"He has more luck than he needs!"

"Right this minute, I wouldn't trade her for an empire," replied the bullfighter.

"What does her husband have to say about that?" asked a picador, the oldest man in the group.

"The husband?" repeated the bullfighter. "I know his worship only to be useful to him. Pepe Vera has dealings only with brave bulls."

Stein had vanished.

CHAPTER XXVIII

On the day following the events related in the preceding chapter, the Duke was sitting in his library in front of his portable writing desk. He was holding his pen motionless and upright like an artilleryman awaiting an order.

The door opened slowly to reveal the beautiful head of a six-year-old boy almost submerged in a profusion of black curls.

"Daddy," he said, "are you alone? May I come in?"

"Since when, Angel," replied the father, "have you needed permission to come into my room?"

"Since you don't love me as much as you used to," replied the boy, climbing on his father's knee. "And I'm very good; I study hard with Don Federico as you told me to, and to prove it, I'm going to say something in German."

"Really?" said the Duke, taking his son in his arms.

"Really and truly. Listen: *Gott segne meinen guten Vater.* That means: God bless my good father."

The Duke hugged the beautiful child, and the boy, putting his small hands on his father's shoulder and leaning back, added:

"*Und meine liebe Mutter.* And that means: and my dear mother. Now, give me a kiss," the boy went on, flinging himself on the Duke's neck.

"But," he interrupted himself, "I forgot. I have a message from Don Federico."

"From Don Federico?" asked the Duke, wondering.

"He says he wants to speak to you."

"Let him come, let him come. Go and tell him that, son. His time is valuable and we mustn't waste it."

The Duke concealed the sheet of paper on which he had written some lines as Stein entered.

"Duke," he said, "you're going to be very much surprised. I've come to pay my respects, to thank you for so many kindnesses, and to tell you that I'm going away immediately."

"Going away!" echoed the Duke with an expression of utter astonishment.

"Yes, señor, without delay."

"Without delay? What about Marysal?"

"She is not coming with me."

"Come, Don Federico, you're joking. That can't be!"

"What cannot be, Duke, is for me to stay here."

"What's your reason?"

"Don't ask me that, for I cannot tell you."

"I can't conceive of a single thing that would be enough to justify such madness," said the Duke.

"It would have to be quite imperative," Stein answered, "to force me to such an extreme step."

"But, Stein, my friend, what is your reason?"

"I'll have to keep it to myself, señor."

"You have to keep it to yourself?" the Duke repeated with increasing astonishment.

"I think so," said Stein. "And that deprives me of the only consolation left me, which would be to open my heart to the noble and generous man who held out his powerful hand and deigned to call me friend."

"Where are you going?"

"To America."

"That's impossible, Stein. I repeat, it's impossible!" exclaimed the Duke, rising with an agitation that was growing by the minute. "There can be nothing in the world to oblige you to abandon your wife, leave your friends, desert your work, and leave your patients without a word, like an irresponsible and giddy person. Haven't you any ambition? Or have you been offered greater advantages in America?"

Stein smiled bitterly.

"Advantages! Hasn't my good fortune surpassed all the hopes your erstwhile travelling companion could have dreamed of?"

"You baffle me," said the Duke. "Is this a whim? Is it a fit of madness?"

Stein was mute.

"In any case," the Duke added, "it's ungrateful."

At this cruel yet tender word, Stein covered his face with his hands and his long suppressed sorrow poured forth in deep sobs.

The Duke went to him, took his hand, and said:

"There's nothing indiscreet about sharing your troubles with a friend. There's no duty forbidding a man to take the advice of people who are interested in his welfare, especially in the crucial situations of life. Speak up, Stein. Open your heart. You're too upset to be able to act coolly. Your mind is too confused to give you good advice. Let's sit down on this sofa. Yield to my counsel in what seems to be a critical situation, as I'd yield to yours if I found myself in like case."

Stein was convinced. He sat down near the Duke, and both men were silent for a time. Stein seemed to be occupied with seeking a way to give the explanation demanded by the Duke's friendship. Finally he said, slowly lifting his head:

"Duke, what would you do if the Duchess preferred another man to you? . . . If she were unfaithful to you?"

The Duke sprang to his feet, his head high, and stared haughtily at the speaker.

"Doctor . . . that question . . ."

"Answer me, answer me," said Stein, clasping his hands in a gesture of deep anxiety.

"By the living God! said the Duke. "I'd kill them both."

Stein bowed his head.

"I won't kill them," he said, "but I'll let myself die."

The Duke began to glimpse the truth, and an uncontrollable shudder ran through him.

"Marysal!" he cried at last.

"Yes," replied Stein without lifting his head, as though his wife's infamy were a weight holding it down.

"And you surprised them!" said the Duke, hardly able to pronounce the words, his voice choked with indignation.

"In an absolute orgy," Stein replied, "both vulgar and licentious, where wine and tobacco were the perfumes and where the bullfighter, Pepe Vera, was boasting about being her lover. Oh, Mariquita!" he cried, covering his face with his hands.

The Duke, like all even-tempered men, had great control over himself. He took several turns around the room. Then halting in front of his poor friend, he said solemnly:

"Leave her, Stein."

Stein rose and took the Duke's hands in his own. He tried to speak but could not.

The Duke embraced him.

"Courage, Stein," he said, "and good-bye until we meet again."

"Good-bye, and forever!" muttered Stein, rushing from the room.

When the Duke was alone, he paced for floor. As the agitation aroused by the overwhelming shock of hearing Stein's revelation abated, a smile of contempt rose to his lips. The Duke was not one of those men of sluggish, corrupt, and vulgar inclinations on whom the follies of women act as a stimulant to their rude passions instead of arousing repugnance and revulsion. In his haughty, upright, high-minded, and aristocratic temperament, love and contempt could not exist side by side, nor could the most delicate emotions live together with the most debased.

Hence contempt smothered illusion in his heart as snow will put out the flame of the sacred fire on the altar where it is burning. The woman he had praised in his verses and whom he had seduced in his dreams no longer existed.

In response to the powerful influence of his reflections, the Duke left his study in haste and went to his wife's room. He entered through a private door. As he neared the room where the Duchess customarily spent the day, he heard voices and his name. He stopped short.

"So the Duke has made himself invisible," a bittersweet voice was saying. "I've been in Madrid for two weeks and my dear nephew hasn't once deigned to come and see me, but I saw him elsewhere."

"It may be that he doesn't know you're here, Aunt," the Duchess replied.

"Not know that the Marchioness of Gutibamba has arrived in Madrid! That's impossible, niece. He'd be the only person in the capital who didn't know it. Besides, it seems to me you've had plenty of time to tell him."

"That's true, Aunt; it's my fault that I forgot to."

"But it's no wonder," the bittersweet voice went on. "How could he enjoy my company or the society of people in his own class when he spends all his time with actresses?"

"That's not true," answered the Duchess dryly.

"You're either blind," said the Marchioness in exasperation, "or you acquiesce."

"I shall never acquiesce," said the Duchess, "in letting my husband be attacked by slander here in his own home, and to his wife."

"You'd do better to stop your husband from giving cause for all the talk in Madrid about his conduct," the voice continued, losing much sweetness and gaining much bitterness, "than to defend him, to drive all your friends away from here with such rude and repulsive remarks, which you've doubtless prepared at your father confessor's orders."

"You'd do better to consult your father confessor," replied the Duchess, "about the language to be used to a married woman, your own niece."

"Very well," said the Marchioness of Gutibamba. "Your austere, reserved, and self-centered character has driven your husband away, and you'll end by driving away all your friends, too."

The Marchioness departed, well pleased with her peroration.

Leonor remained seated on her sofa, her head bowed and her lovely face pale and wet with the tears she had long restrained.

Suddenly she turned with a cry. She was in her husband's arms. Then she burst into sobs; but her tears were no longer bitter. Leonor realized that this man, always frank and loyal, was giving back to her a sincere heart and a love that were indisputably hers.

"My Leonor! Would you, could you forgive me?" he said, falling on his knees before his wife.

She covered her husband's mouth with her pretty hands.

"Are you going to spoil the present with memories of the past?"

"I want you to know my faults," said the Duke, "faults that are being judged too severely by the world, as well as my repentance."

"Let's make a bargain," said the Duchess, interrupting him. "You'll never speak to me of your faults, and I'll never speak to you of my grief."

Angel came running into the room at that moment. The Duke and Duchess quickly moved apart, for in Spain where speech is over-free, there is extreme reserve in action.

"Is Mama crying? Is Mama crying?" asked the child, turning red and on the brink of tears. "Have you quarreled with her, Daddy?"

"No, son," replied the Duchess. "I'm crying because I'm happy."

"Why?" the child asked, a smile replacing his tears.

"Because tomorrow without fail we'll all go to our place in Andalusia," the Duke replied, taking the boy in his arms and drawing near his mother. "Your mother wants to see it, and we'll all be as happy there as the angels in heaven."

The boy gave a shout of joy, put one arm around his father's neck and the other around his mother's, bringing their two heads together and covering them alternately with kisses.

At that moment the Marquis of Elda came in.

"Grandfather," shouted his grandson, "we're all going away tomorrow."

"Really?" the Marquis asked his daughter.

"Yes, Father," replied the Duchess, "and I lack only one thing for my happiness, and that is that you'll come with us."

"Señor," said the Duke, "how can you deny your daughter anything? If she weren't an angel, she'd be a saint."

The Marquis looked at his daughter whose face was bright with an intense joy; then at the Duke, who was displaying the utmost satisfaction. A tender smile softened the natural austerity of his expression, and going to his son-in-law, he said:

"Give me your hand, and count me in."

CHAPTER XXIX

Marysal, ill since before she went to the supper, had grown worse, and the next morning she had a fever.

"Marina," she said to her maid after a brief, restless sleep, "call my husband. I feel sick."

"The master has not come home," Marina answered.

"He must be on a sick call," said Marysal. "So much the better! He'd prescribe a long string of remedies, and I loathe them."

"You're very hoarse," said Marina.

"Very," Marysal answered. "I must take care of myself. I'll stay in bed today and take something to make me sweat. If the Duke comes, tell him I'm asleep. I don't want to see anyone. My head is driving me crazy."

"What if someone comes in by the secret door?"

"If it's Pepe Vera, let him come in, for I have to talk to him. Close the shutters and go away."

The maid left and came back after a few steps, smiting her brow.

"Here's a letter the master left for Nicolás to give to you," she said.

"Go along with your letter," said Marysal. "I can't see in here, and anyhow I want to sleep. What would he have to say to me? He's probably telling we where 'his duty calls him.' What do I care about that? Leave the letter on the dresser and go away."

A few moments later, Marina came in again.

"Once more and I'll hit you!" her mistress screamed.

"It's because Pepe Vera wants to see you."

"Let him come in," she said, recovering herself quickly.

Pepe Vera entered, threw open the shutters to let the light in, flung himself into a chair, smoking, and stared at Marysal, whose burning cheeks and swollen eyes indicated a severe indisposition.

"You're in a fine state!" he said. "What will Pontius Pilate say?"

"He's not at home," Marysal answered with increasing hoarseness.

"So much the better. And I hope to God he keeps on going like the Wandering Jew, till Judgment Day. I've just come from looking at the bulls for this afternoon. They're awful brutes! One of them is black. His name is *Midnight,* and he's already killed a man in the ring."

"Do you want to make me feel worse than I do by frightening me?" said Marysal. "Close the shutters; I can't stand the glare."

"Such foolishness!" Pepe Vera replied. "Pure squeamishness! The Duke isn't here to worry whether the light will bother you. Neither need your quack of a husband be afraid a breath of air might get in and kill you. It smells in here of patchouli, of civet, of musk and all the other drugstore concoctions. Those filthy things are doing you harm. Let the air in and freshen the room, and that'll do you good. Tell me, darling, are you going to the bullfight this afternoon?"

"Do I look as though I can go?" she answered. "Close that window, Pepe. I can't stand that bright light and so much cold air."

"And I can't stand your whims," said Pepe. "You're not so sick as you make out. You talk as if you were about to breathe your last! Well, little bitty lady, I'll go and order your coffin and then I'll kill *Midnight* and dedicate him to Lucía del Salto. It won't make her vain, thank God."

"The devil take that woman!" cried Marysal, raising herself with a furious gesture. "Aren't they saying she's going off with an Englishman?"

"They're saying she's going to that country where no one ever sees the sun except through curtains and where the people sleep standing up!" said the bullfighter.

"Pepe, you wouldn't really do what you say. That would be a vile thing!"

"It would be vile," said Pepe Vera, planting himself before her with arms crossed, "if instead of being there to encourage me with your presence when I go out to risk my life, you should stay in your house to receive the Duke with complete freedom, under the pretext of having a cold."

"Always the same theme!" said Marysal. "Wasn't it enough for you to hide in my room spying to convince yourself with your own eyes that there's nothing between the Duke and me? You know that what he likes about me is my voice, not me personally. As for me, you know very well . . ."

"What I know very well," said Pepe Vera, "is that you're afraid of me! And you should be, believe me! But God knows what can happen if you're left alone, certain that I can't surprise you. I don't trust any woman! Not even my own mother!"

"I, afraid!" Marysal replied. "I!"

But Pepe Vera went on, refusing to let her speak.

"Do you think I'm so blind I can't see what's going on? I don't know whether you're making up with your husband because you've taken it into your thick head that that dull doctor of yours will be appointed surgeon to the Queen, as I've just heard on good authority!"

"That's a lie!" Marysal shrieked hoarsely.

"Mariquita! Pepe Vera is not the man to mistake a mule for a horse. Get it into your head that I know the tricks of brave bulls as well as the tricks of cunning bulls."

Marysal burst into tears.

"That's right," Pepe said. "Cry your eyes out! That's the sinner's refuge for women. You believe in the old saying: 'Woman weeps to conquer.' No, darling. There's another one that goes: 'Put no faith in a dog's limp and a woman's tears.' Save your tears for the theater; we're not acting out a comedy here. Mind what you're doing. If you're playing me false, you're endangering a man's life. So think before you act. My love isn't a thing of prescriptions and verses. I don't want to be repaid with sobs, but with deeds. And you'd better understand that if you don't go to the bullfight this afternoon, you're going to be sorry."

So saying, Pepe Vera left the room.

At that time he was being assailed by two emotions so powerful that an iron temperament was needed to conceal them under the calmest exterior, as he was doing, under the most impassive face and the most offhand indifference. He had studied the bulls that were to be fought that afternoon. Never had he seen more formidable, more ferocious brutes. The sight of one of them had made a sinister impression on him, one of ill omen, a thing that often befalls those in his profession, so that they deem themselves safe and sound if they are spared that particular bull, and will not worry about any of the others.

In addition, he was jealous. He, who had never known anything but conquest and applause, jealous! He had been told that he was being made fun of, and in a few hours he was going to have to stand between life and death, between love and treachery. So he believed.

When Pepe Vera left Marysal's bedroom, she clawed the embroidered borders of the sheets, scolded Marina sharply, and wept. Later she dressed, sent a message to another actress, and went with her to the bullfight.

Marysal took the seat Pepe Vera had reserved for her, shaking with fever and excitement.

The noise, the heat, and the confusion increased her malaise. Her cheeks, always pale, were scarlet; a feverish flame burned in her dark eyes. Anger, indignation, jealousy, injured pride, anxiety, terror, and physical illness sought in vain to draw a complaint, a sigh, from that tightly closed mouth, mute as the grave.

Pepe Vera saw her. A faint smile brightened his face. It made not the slightest impression on Marysal; it slid off her glacial front beneath which her wounded pride was vowing revenge.

Pepe Vera's costume was similar to the one he had worn in the bullfight we mentioned earlier, with the difference that the background was green and the ornamentation of gold.

One bull had already been fought and another matador had dispatched it. It had been good, but not so ferocious as the fans had believed.

The trumpet sounded, the gate opened to its dark full width, and a black bull entered the arena.

"That's *Midnight*," the crowd shouted.

Midnight was the bull of the afternoon, king of the function.

Midnight, however, did not go charging out, like the others, as though seeking his freedom, his pastures, his open spaces. He was seeking revenge, above everything; he wanted to prove he was no plaything for despicable enemies; he wanted to punish. Hearing the usual clamor wash over him, he stood still.

There can be no doubt that the bull is a stupid animal. But, whether rage may have the power to sharpen the dullest intelligence, or passion to transform brute instinct into cunning, the fact is that there are bulls able to divine and mock the most astute minds in the field of bullfighting.

The first to attract the attention of the terrifying animal were the picadors. He charged the first and threw him to the ground. He did the same with the second without slowing down or being halted, or even being lightly wounded by the lance. The third picador met the same fate.

Then the bull, horns and forehead blood-stained, planted himself in the center of the ring, tossing his head at the ranks of spectators whence came a terrific uproar, roused by admiration for such wild courage.

The *chulos* got the picadors behind the barriers. One of them had a broken leg and was taken to the infirmary. The other two went for fresh horses. The extra horse was mounted, and while the *chulos* attracted the animal's attention with their capes, the three picadors took their places with their lances at rest.

Two minutes after the bull had seen them, all three were lying on the sand. One was bleeding from the head and unconscious. The bull attacked the horse, and its torn body served the luckless men as a shield.

Then came a moment of dark terror.

The *chulos* tried in vain to distract the brute's attention by exposing themselves; but he seemed thirsty for blood and wanted to slake his thirst on his victim. At that terrible moment, one *chulo* ran toward the animal and threw his cape over its head to blind him. For an instant he was successful, but the bull shook his head, freed himself of the obstruction, saw the aggressor fleeing, flung himself after him, and after throwing the man to the ground, went straight on, blind with fury. When he wheeled around, with no intention of abandoning his prey, the agile bullfighter had got to his feet and hurdled the barrier, applauded by the crowd with glad acclaim. All this had taken place with the speed of lightning.

The heroic selflessness with which bullfighters aid and defend one another is the only truly fine and noble aspect of these cruel, inhuman, and immoral festivals which are an anachronism in a century that prides itself on its enlightenment. We know that Spanish and foreign fans like the Viscount of Fadiese, the latter always more enthusiastic than the former, would greet our opinion with cries of anathema. We therefore refrain from pressing it on others, and limit ourselves to maintaining our position. We may not argue it, nor support it, for, like M. Joubet, we hold that "the labor of argument greatly exceeds its usefulness."

The bull was still strutting alone, in full possession of the field. A sense of terror dominated the crowd. Many opinions were offered. Some wished the Judas oxen would come into the ring and lead the formidable brute out, as much to avoid new disasters as to preserve him as a stud for a valiant progeny. This is sometimes done, but as a rule the bulls thus exempted do not survive the inflammation of the blood resulting from combat. Others thought he should be hamstrung so as to be safely killed at once. Unfortunately the great majority held it would be a pity to let such a brave bull die without all the honors of the art.

The president was undecided which side to take. Directing

a bullfight is not so simple as it appears. Sometimes it is easier to preside over a legislative body. What often happens there finally took place on this occasion. The loudest shouters prevailed, and it was decided that the powerful and terrible brute should die according to the rules with all his means of defense intact.

Pepe Vera then came out armed for the struggle. After saluting the authorities, he went to stand in front of Marysal.

He was pale. Marysal was burning up, and her eyes were starting from her head. Her breathing was noisy and fast like the rattle of the dying. The rail which she was clutching with her fingernails was supporting her as she leaned against it, for she loved that young and handsome man she saw so self-controlled in the face of death. She delighted in a love that subjugated her, that caused her to tremble, that drew tears from her, for she knew that brutal and tyrannical love was also deep, passionate, and concentrated. It was the kind of love she needed, as certain men of a rough temperament need to get drunk on strong drink instead of sweet liqueurs and delicate wines.

The most profound silence reigned. It was as if a dread presentiment had taken possession of the whole audience, darkening the brilliance of the festival as a cloud obscures the sun.

Many people got up and left the bullring.

Meanwhile, the bull stood in the center of the ring, arrogantly challenging his adversaries, serene as a dignified man with arms crossed and head erect.

With his customary calm and indifference, Pepe Vera chose the spot which suited him, and signalling the *chulos* with a finger he called: "Here!"

The *chulos* came flying like rockets from a powder magazine. Instantly the animal went after them. The *chulos* vanished. The bull stood face to face with the matador.

This crucial situation did not last long. The bull charged immediately with such speed that Pepe Vera was unprepared and had to flee from the attack. But the brute did not rush ahead on the impetus of his furious charge. He suddenly wheeled, threw himself at the matador like lightning and caught him up on his horns.

Thousands of voices gave a cry that only Dante's imagination could have conceived: a deep, mournful, long-drawn wail!

The *chulos,* like a flock of birds whose nest is pillaged by a hunter, surrounded the brute which was tossing the unconscious matador on his horns like a trophy.

"The *medias lunas!* The *medias lunas!*" [72] shouted the crowd. The president echoed the call.

Those dreadful weapons were produced and the bull was quickly hamstrung. He bellowed with pain, shook his head furiously, flung Pepe Vera some distance away, and fell at the blow of a dagger stuck into his neck by the ignoble bull-killer.

The *chulos* lifted Pepe Vera.

"He's dead!" The cry was breathed in chorus by the gaudily-dressed group surrounding the luckless youth. It ran from mouth to mouth, rose to the last rows of seats, and spread over the plaza like a funeral banner.

✦   ✦   ✦

Two weeks had gone by since that tragic spectacle.

In a bedroom where some decent furniture still remained,

---

[72] A crescent-shaped weapon with a curved knife at the tip, used to hamstring unmanageable bulls.

though the most luxurious had disappeared, a pale, wasted, and weak girl was lying in an elegant bed, its embroidered sheets soiled and stained. She was alone.

The woman seemed to awaken from a long, deep sleep. Raising herself in the bed, she stared around the room with wondering eyes. She raised a hand to her head, as though trying to collect her faculties, and called in a weak, hoarse voice:

"Marina!"

Instead of Marina, another woman came in carrying a drink already prepared.

The sick woman stared at her.

"I know that face!" she said with some surprise.

"Perhaps so, sister," replied the newcomer in a sweet voice. "We go into the houses of the poor and the rich."

"But where is Marina? Where is she?" said the sick girl.

"She went off with the manservant, after they had stolen everything they could lay their hands on."

"And my husband?"

"He's gone away, no one knows where."

"Oh, God!" the sick girl exclaimed, putting her hands to her head.

"And the Duke?" she asked after a few moments' silence. "You must know him, for I believe it was in his house I saw you."

"In the Duchess of Almansa's house? Yes, it's true that the lady asked me to distribute some alms. She has gone to Andalusia with her husband and family."

"Then I'm alone and abandoned!" cried the sick woman, whose memory was returning, the most distant recollections first, as usually happens when a person awakens from a long delirium.

"What? Am I no one?" said the good Sister of Charity,

taking Marysal in her arms. "If I had learned of it earlier, you wouldn't be in such a state."

Suddenly a rasping cry rose from the sick girl's aching chest:

"Pepe! . . . The bull! . . . Pepe! . . . Dead!"

She fell back unconscious on the pillow.

CHAPTER XXX

Six months after the events related in the preceding chapter, the Countess de Algar was in her parlor with her mother. They were busy decorating a straw hat with ribbons, and trying it on her son.

General Santa María came in.

"Look, Uncle," she said, "how well the straw hat becomes this little angel."

"You're spoiling him to your heart's content," the General replied.

"It doesn't matter," the Marchioness intervened. "We all spoil our children, but that doesn't keep them from growing into useful men. Our mother spoiled you, but that didn't prevent you from being what you are."

"Mama, give me a biscuit," the child lisped.

"What do you mean by using *tú*[73] to your mother, you little polliwog?" said the General. "You don't speak that way; you say, 'Mother, will you please give me a biscuit?' "

At the sound of his uncle's stern voice, the little boy started to cry. The mother gave him a biscuit on the sly.

"He's so little," remarked the Marchioness. "He can't distinguish between *tú* and *usted* yet."

"If he doesn't know," cried the General, "he should be taught."

"But, Uncle," the Countess said, "I want my children to use *tú* with me."

---

[73] Tú, the familiar form in Spanish, is used by close contemporary friends, relatives, or to servants. Until somewhat recently it was not used by the children of good families to their parents. Instead the more formal *usted* was used.

"What, Niece!" the General exclaimed. "Do you want to follow that fashion that's come to us from France, like everything else that corrupts good manners?"

"Then using *tú* between parents and children will corrupt manners?"

"Yes, Niece. Like everything else that helps to undermine respect, whatever it may be. That's why I like the old custom of the Spanish grandees, which requires the very best manners of their children."

"*Tú*, which puts parents and children on an equal footing, ought not to be used between them. There's no doubt that it lessens respect," said the Marchioness. "They say it increases affection but I don't believe it. Would you have loved me more, my daughter, if you had used *tú* to me?"

"No, Mother," said the Countess, embracing her tenderly, "but neither would I have respected you less."

"You've always been a good and obedient daughter," said the General, "but exceptions prove nothing. But let's change the subject. I'm bringing you some news that can't fail to please you. The beautiful corvette, *Iberia*, sailing from Havana, has just reached Cádiz. So tomorrow we'll probably be able to embrace Rafael. How lucky that boy is! He'd barely written us saying he wanted to come back to the Peninsula when the desired occasion arose, and the Captain General sent him back with some important dispatches."

The Marchioness and the Countess were still expressing the joy this news brought them when the door opened and Rafael Arias flung himself into his relatives' arms, closely embracing them again and again.

"How glad I am to see you, my dear, good Rafael!" the Countess kept saying.

"Heavens!" added the Marchioness. "Thank Our Lady of

Carmen that you're back! What was the necessity, in any case, for you, with a good inheritance, to go across the sea as if it were a pond? I'll bet you were seasick."

"That was the least of it," Rafael replied. "It's a bad crossing. But I had another illness growing worse by the day. It was the hunger for my country and the people I'm fond of. I don't know whether it's because Spain is a good mother or because the Spaniards are good sons, but it's a certainty we don't live except in her bosom."

"It's both, my dear nephew, both," said the General with a smile of deep satisfaction.

"Cuba is a very rich country! Isn't that true, Rafael?" asked the Countess.

"Yes, Cousin," Rafael replied, "and she knows how to enjoy it, like the great lady she is. Her wealth isn't something that came to her yesterday, a thing that rushes in like a torrent, floods, and passes on with a great commotion. Opulence flows softly and soundlessly there, like a deep, full river that derives its water from steady springs. Wealth is there on all sides, with no need for ostentation; everyone can see and feel it."

"How did you like the women?" asked the Countess.

"Well enough," Rafael replied. "I like all women everywhere—the young ones because they're young; the old ones because they were young; the little girls because they will be."

"Never mind begging the question, Rafael. Be specific."

"Very well, Cousin; the girls in Havana are beautiful, feminine sirens, dressed in batiste and lace with satin shoes that are mere useless adornments for the tiny feet they're made for, as I never saw a Havana girl standing. Their speech is like the nightingale's song; they live on honey like the bees; and they smoke like chimneys. Their black eyes are poetic dramas and their hearts like mirrors without quicksilver. Mournful and hair-raising dramas are not for that great flower-garden where the women spend their lives lolling in their hammocks, rocking among flowers, and cooled by their slaves with feather fans."

"Do you know that the word is going the rounds that you're about to be married?" said the Countess.

"Well, Lady Gossip, my dear Grace, has appropriated to herself the place formerly held by the royal court jesters. Like them, she says whatever comes into her head, never bothering whether it's true. So then, Lady Gossip has lied, Cousin."

"Well, she's saying more than that," added the Countess, laughing. "She's been dowering your future wife with two million dollars."

Rafael burst out laughing.

"I catch on now," he said. "The Captain General did in fact have some notion of endorsing that letter of credit for me."

"And what was my cousin-to-be like?"

"Ugly as sin. Her left shoulder leaned decidedly toward her ear, and contrariwise, her right shoulder shunned its neighboring ear."

"So what was your answer?"

"That I didn't care for pills, even gold-plated."

"You did wrong," said the General.

"It was her body that was wrong, sir," replied Rafael.

"And besides, knowing that . . ." said the Countess.

She had not completed the sentence before she noted an expression of pain shadow her cousin's face, like a bitter memory.

"Is she happy?" he asked.

"As happy as it's possible to be in this world," the Countess replied. "She lives a very retired life, particularly since she began to feel symptoms of being in that state of good hope, as

Don Federico used to put it, a German expression more heart-felt though less euphemistic than the English one—an interesting state—which we have adopted . . ."

"With that ridiculous spirit of foreignism and imitation which lives and rules here," added the General, "and the awful taste they inspire. Why can't you say clearly and properly, 'she's with child,' or 'pregnant,' in place of such ridiculous and affected translated phrases? You're doing as the French did in the past century when they played at being pagan gods with powder and hoop-skirts."

"What about him?" asked Arias.

"Completely changed since he was married and reconciled with his brother-in-law, who guides him in everything. Now he's managing his own estates, with my husband's advice, and spends whole weeks in the country. In short, he's the spoiled child of the family who have taken him in like the prodigal son."

"That shows," observed the General, "that 'a known evil is better than an unknown good,' as the wise old saying goes."

"And Eloise?" Arias asked.

"That's a sad story," said the Countess. "She was secretly married to a French adventurer who claimed to be a cousin of Prince Rohan, Dumas's collaborator, sent here by Baron Taylor to buy artistic curios. Unfortunately his name was Abelard. She found in her lover's name portents that their union would be predestined. She saw in him a literary man, an artist, and a relative of a prince all in one, and she thought she had met the ideal of her most golden dreams. She regarded her parents as tyrants of melodrama with backward notions and sunk in obscurantism because they opposed the match . . ."

"And sunk in Hispanism," added the General in an ironic tone. "The illustrious young lady, nourished on novels and weepy verses, married that rascal, already married twice, as we later learned. After a few months, when he had spent all the money she brought him, he abandoned her in Valencia where she had to seek out her hapless father and give him back a dishonored daughter—neither maid, wife, nor widow. You see, my children, what a false and exaggerated love of foreign things leads to?"

"You could have spared her her misfortunes, Rafael," said the Countess.

"I!" exclaimed her cousin.

"Yes, you," Grace went on. "You know very well how much she thought of you and how she valued your opinion."

"Yes," said the General, "because you took your opinion from foreigners."

"To change the subject, what's happened to our object of admiration, the outstanding A. Polo of Marble of the Cemeteries?" asked Arias.

"He's taken it into his head to be a politician," Grace replied.

"I knew that," said Rafael, "and that he's written an ode attacking the throne under the pseudonym of *Tyrranus*."

"Poor Tyranny," said the General. "Everyone cuts a fallen tree up into wood; but now it's being kicked by an ass."

"I knew, too," Rafael went on, "that he wrote another poem attacking preoccupations, among them the fatal augury attributed to the number 13, the infallibility of the Pope, the overturning of a salt shaker, and conjugal faithfulness."

"Go along with you, Rafael," cried the Countess, laughing. "He never said any such things."

"If not in those exact words," said Rafael, "still that's the spirit of the masterpiece, more or less. The public will classify it—"

"Among the worms eating away this society," said the General. "After it's destroyed, we shall see what will replace it!"

"I know, too," Rafael continued, "that our A. Polo has composed a satire (he felt inclined to that form a long time ago) against hypocrisy, where he proclaims it's a hypocrite's trait to demand that the clergy be paid and the excloistered nuns and monks be supported."

"Well, Nephew," said the General, "with such beautiful compositions he has won such high marks that he's a collaborator on an opposition newspaper."

"I see;" said Rafael, "and I can guess what happened, for farces such as that are acted out every day. He carved a new pen from the jawbone of an ass, and armed with it he attacked the Philistines in power."

"You're right on the bull's-eye like a wizard," said the General. "I don't know how he worked it, but right now he is in fact a great personage, with money and style, and he's playing it for all it's worth."

"I'm sure he'll give himself still another name now: A. Polo of Marble of Carrara, and he'll seek and get some honorific post at Court, such as, head groom in Parnassus, without quitting his writing against the nobility and class distinctions. What about the Duke, is he still in Madrid?" asked Rafael.

"No, but you could see him as you're going through Córdova, where he and all his family are living."

"The Duke finally took my advice," said the General. "He's withdrawn from public life. All the people of importance ought to retire to their tents like Achilles."

"But, Uncle," said Rafael, "if that were the case everything would be ruined."

"They say," said the Countess, "that he's dedicated himself entirely to literature. He's writing something for the theater."

"I'll bet the title of the piece will be: What is bred in the bone will come out in the flesh," said Rafael to the Countess in a low tone.

He was alluding to the love affair between Marysal and Pepe Vera, that was known to everyone with the exception of the two men who were so fond of her that they could never suspect her of wrongdoing: the Duke, owing to his high-mindedness, and Stein, owing to his trustfulness.

"Be still, Rafael," his cousin replied. "We ought to behave toward our friends as Noah's good sons[74] behaved toward their father."

"What did you say?" asked the Marchioness.

"Nothing, Mother," the Countess replied. "He's talking about a play he hasn't read."

"And what about Marysal?" asked Rafael. "Has she ascended to the capital in a chariot of pure gold, drawn by her fans?"

"She lost her voice," the Countess replied, "as the consequence of pneumonia. Didn't you know that?"

"I was so far from knowing it," said Rafael, "that I'm bringing with me some wonderful offers of engagements in the Havana theater. But where has she gone?"

"Now that she can't sing," said the General, "she'll probably follow the advice the ant gave the grasshopper in the fable: she will learn to dance."

---

[74] In Gen. IX 18-27, Noah is depicted as a drunkard: "And Noah began to be a husbandman, and he planted a vineyard and he drank of the wine and was drunken; and was uncovered in his tent . . . And Shem and Japheth took a garment and laid it upon both their shoulders and went backward and covered the nakedness of their father, and their faces were backward and they saw not their father's nakedness."

"Or, most probably she's weeping over her sins and the loss of her voice," said the Countess.

"But where is she?" Rafael insisted.

"I don't know," replied the Countess, "and I'm sorry I don't, because I'd like to offer to help her and console her, if that's what she needs."

"Save that for someone who deserves it," said the General.

"Every unfortunate deserves it, Uncle," replied the Countess.

"Well spoken, my daughter," her mother added understandingly. " 'Do good and don't ask questions. Do evil, and watch out,' as the saying goes."

"I have to try to find out where she is," said Rafael, "because I brought with me a letter for her."

"A letter? From whom?"

"From her husband."

"Have you seen him?" asked the Countess with interest. "Weren't they saying he was in Germany?"

"That's not true. He sailed on the same ship we did, for Havana. How changed and downcast he was! I'm sure you'd hardly have recognized him; but even so, he was always gentle, always obliging, always good! A short time after our arrival he died of yellow fever."

"He died?" exclaimed the Marchioness and her daughter in unison.

"Poor, poor Stein!" said the Countess.

"May God keep him in His glory," added the mother.

"The death of that good man is on the conscience of that damned singer!" said the General.

"Though I haven't had the disease, I believe I'm immune," Rafael went on, "and I went to see him when I learned he was ill."

"My good Rafael!" said the Countess, taking her cousin's hand.

"The illness was so violent that I found him almost at the last gasp, but he was as calm and full of good will as ever. He thanked me for my visit and told me it made him happy to see a dear face before he died. He asked me for paper and pen, and almost as he was dying he wrote some lines and begged me to address them to his wife and to send them together with his will. Suddenly he began to vomit and died, with one hand held by the priest who had administered the last rites and the other in mine. I'm entrusting this to you, Cousin, so you can send a reliable man to Villamar where she's probably retired to her father's house. Here's the letter," he added, taking a carefully folded piece of paper from his wallet. "I've read it several times as though it were an excerpt from a piece of religious literature.

The Countess unfolded the letter and read:

"Mariquita, whom I've loved so much and still love: If my forgiveness can spare you any remorse, if my blessing can add to your happiness, you have them both on my death-bed. Fritz Stein."

CHAPTER XXXI

If the reader wishes, before we separate forever, to take another glance at that tiny corner of earth called Villamar, doubtless quite alien to the distinguished guest it will take to its bosom, we shall lead him there, and he will not have to think of the strain or the cost of the trip. Indeed, we have already arrived without the need for planning. Very well, reader, here is Merlin's cap; please put it on, for if we remain visible we shall disturb that sleepy, quiet village with our presence, as any object cast into the clear, still water of a pool will shatter its tranquillity and repose.

It is now four years later, on a summer's day of 1848. You will find the village sitting peacefully on the seashore, like a fisherman with his rod. Let us catch up on whatever serious public and private events have happened during the interval.

Let us start with the luckless sign which had cost the illustrious mayor, a blacksmith by trade, such a lot of trouble. He used to say that iron was no harder than his subordinates' heads. This was the sign which had occasioned the schoolmaster some ugly bruises from a fall and Mystical Rose three days of indigestion. But in compensation, it had struck Don Modesto Guerrero dumb with admiration.

The other residents, however, had taken the inscription as a public notice—one of those that begin: "Four ducats fine for depositing any kind of rubbish in this place."

The heavy Andalusian rains, seemingly better designed for lashing the earth than for watering it, had fallen on the sign's handsome lettering, both large and small, and had nearly obliterated it.

The mayor, fearing that this might result in an analogous effacement of the residents' local pride, planned to stimulate this noble sentiment by other and more potent means. Moreover, the name, Royal Street, offended his egalitarian ears. He wanted to *patrioticize* it, and accordingly he posted a notice proposing that its evil-sounding name be changed to Sons of Padilla Street.

This proposal brought Villamar its little hour of insurrection. What corner of the globe can escape its mutinies in this century?

The fact was that one of the residents of the same street, a certain Cristóbal Padilla, had died and his sons had inherited the house he had owned. But the López family found themselves in like case, as did the Pérezes and the Sánchezes, and they protested the groundless preference with energy. The mayor tried in vain to explain to them that the so-called Sons of Padilla had been an association of free men at one time. To this they replied that they were aware that the Padillas were free men—no one was contesting that—but so were the Lópezes, the Pérezes, and the Sánchezes, and had been since the world began, and that they had no intention of letting themselves be humiliated by ranking below the Padillas, and that if the mayor persisted in his design, they would complain to competent authorities, for there had always been courts of appeal to serve as bulwarks against arbitrariness and injustice, unless they had fallen into ruin in such new-fangled times.

The mayor, wearied with so much outcry, consigned them all to the devil.

Knowing of no saint to whom he could turn so as to give Villamar a modern aspect which would raise it to the current level, he considered naming the road which ran from the village to the hill crowned with the cemetery and the chapel of Our Lord of Succour Urdax Road, after a battle which preceded the Convention of Vergara.[75]

But this time he came out even worse. The women mutinied; it was a regular mutiny, commanded by Mystical Rose herself. Their cries and lamentations would have awakened the dead.

"What is the meaning of Urdax?" one screamed.

"What is Urdax to us?" shrieked another.

"Who wants to be buried in Urdax?" shrilled an old woman.

"Your Honor," said an old widow, "if you're so anxious to make improvements, lower the taxes. Make them what they were before, in the time of the King, and leave everything with the name it's always had."

"If you like the name Urdax so much," said a young woman, "take it for yourself."

"Señor," said Mystical Rose sternly, "this road is the Way of the Cross, and you profane it with that Moorish name."

The mayor covered his ears and fled on the run.

With all his lovely ideas frustrated, he vowed that the inhabitants of Villamar were a lot of animals, stolid brutes, partisans of the abominable ways of absolutism, motivated solely by base pecuniary interests; the enemies of all social progress and improvements; despicable routinists unworthy of the name villagers, much less free citizens.

After this chilling anathema, Villamar and its inhabitants went right on as before.

Shortly afterward, there appeared in a newspaper of some weight:

---

[75] Vergara, a town in the Basque Provinces, was the site of the convention which ended the Civil War in 1839.

"Our correspondent from Villamar (lower Andalusia) reports: The public peace in this village has been threatened. Some malcontents, doubtless excited by the base agents of the odious opposition, have attempted to resist the introduction of worthwhile improvements, of useful proposals by our worthy mayor, Don Perfecto Cívico, under the absurd pretext that they were unnecessary. But the admirable coolheadedness and heroic courage demonstrated by that excellent official intimidated the daring, and order prevailed, thus averting grave and deplorable violence. Long live the good patriots in peace! Their brothers in Villamar will be ready to thwart the intrigues of our enemies.

"Now that we are into July, the temperature is very high. We are unable to state definitely what the reading is, for civilization has not yet furnished Villamar with the benefits of a thermometer.

"The crops look promising, especially the squash, whose quantity and size fill its honorable harvesters with joy and satisfaction. Signed: The Model Patriot."

Needless to say, this model of patriotism was the mayor himself, author of the item.[76]

This good man had been a veterinary surgeon, and had attained a high level of modern ideas and advanced views through his travels. He talked a great deal and listened to himself, thus never lacking an audience. He was also the sole representative of his party in Villamar; like the doctor who had taken Stein's place, he was "the happy medium."

The faction of the priest, Mystical Rose and the good women like Aunt María, was all for the old ideas. Ramón

---

[76] We recommend to our readers *Lágrimas*, another novel by our author, wherein the story of the good mayor-patriot, Don Perfecto Cívico and his family is told. AUTHOR'S NOTE.

Pérez and the other constant singers had no political coloration. José and other poor people of his class missed the good old days and deplored the present bad ones without analyzing their origin. There remained, then, the town clerk, a heartless rogue, as such men often are in small villages, a staunch defender of the winning side, and, worse, a vigorous persecutor of the conquered, a malicious and hostile brute that could be tamed only with silver.

But let us get back to our subject.

The tower of Fort Saint Christopher had fallen, and with it the last hopes cherished by Don Modesto of seeing his fort the equal of Gibraltar, Brest, Cádiz, Dunkerque, Malta, and Sebastopol.

But nothing had aroused so much admiration in our friends, the inhabitants of Villamar, as the change that could be noted in the barbershop of Ramón Pérez.

After the death of his father, which followed Marysal's departure by a few months, Ramón Pérez had been unable to resist the pull of the capital and the longing to follow in the steps of the ingrate who had sacrificed him to a spineless foreigner. Accordingly, he set forth and returned after two weeks bringing with him:

First: an inexhaustible store of lies and boasts.

Second: an infinity of Italian songs, each worse than the other.

Third: an air of swagger, a pose of nonchalance, a free and easy manner that vexed the people of Villamar, whose luckless ears and hapless jaws long bore witness to those deplorable acquisitions.

Fourth: lamentable aspirations to emulate that lion among barbers, Fígaro, which he had seen produced in a theater in Seville. Consequently, in imitation of his model, he had tried to swerve the mayor from the path of progress, to substitute the ways of the Count of Almaviva;[77] but in the first place, the mayor was married, hence he would have had a hard time finding a Rosina in Villamar willing to undergo such inconveniences. In the second place, the mayor's wife was a Galician of admirable strength and robustness, and in his eyes, she was more to be feared than Doctor Bartolo's ward.

Ramón Pérez had brought something else home from his travels, something he revealed to no one and which he had acquired by the following means:

One night as he was patrolling the street where Marysal was living, sighing like a bellows, he attracted the attention of a young man waiting at a corner, wrapped to the eyes in his cape, who came up to him and said two words:

"Get out!"

Ramón wanted to reply, but he received such a vigorous kick that the bruise from it made his return trip extremely painful, for it had been placed at the spot that came in contact with his pack-saddle.

The barber had succeeded, by means to be explained later, in gathering together a substantial sum of money. Thereupon his memories of Seville and Fígaro had awakened with new ardor. He had beautified his shop with Asiatic luxury: magnificent chairs painted emerald green; curtain rings as big as soup plates, holding fine towels an inch thick; engravings showing a very large Telemachus, a hairy Mentor, and a very fleshless Calypso. Such were the ornaments that competed to lend splendor to the establishment.

Ramón Pérez affirmed, the more staunchly for his belief

---

[77] Fígaro, a barber, was a cunning scamp who managed again and again to thwart Rosina's guardian, Bartolo, and promote her love affair with the Count of Almaviva. Fígaro appears in Beaumarchais's *The Barber of Seville* and several other operas.

that it was so, that the figures were Saint John, Saint Peter, and Mary Magdalen. Some malcontents had observed with a shake of the head that everything had been renewed in Ramón Pérez's shop except the razors. He replied that they were old-fashioned men who had not lost the old custom of looking at things on the inside, even though it was the order of the day to give importance only to outward appearances.

But what stunned the Villamariners with admiration was a huge sign covering the greater part of the barber shop's façade. In the middle of it, painted with marvelous art, a foot was depicted, a sort of Chinese foot, yellowish in color and spouting a stream of blood worthy to rival the fountains of Aranjüez and Versailles. On each side of it were two enormous half-open razors, like pyramids, and in their middle two colossal molars. Roundabout ran a garland of roses like a circle of beets, and from the garland hung a monstrous pair of scissors. As a final high touch of ostentation and luxury the painter had used gilt, at Ramón Pérez's command, and had distributed it on the thorns of the roses, the blades of the razors, and the toe-nails of the foot. This sign proclaimed what was already known —that its owner practiced the quadruple functions of barber, blood-letter, dentist, and chiropodist.

But the sign was so huge and so heavy that finally the wall of Ramón's house, made of mortar and rubble, could not hold it up. Two brick buttresses had to be erected at each side of the door to support it. The construction formed a kind of frontispiece or portal to the entrance of the house, which Ramón Pérez declared with the most sober and imperturbable effrontery to be an exact copy of the Sevillian produce exchange, known to be one of the masterpieces of our great architect, Herrera.

Now that the reader has been apprised of past events, let us again pick up the thread of the present.

The silence in that corner of the world was so deep that the voice of a man accompanying himself on the guitar could be heard from afar, singing not songs of Ronda, nor love songs, nor Andalusian songs, nor smugglers' songs; ah, no, but a mournful aria called *Atala!* To make matters worse, he adorned it with such trills, with such meaningless flourishes, with such regrettable cadenzas, and the verses were so bad, that Chateaubriand [78] would have been justified in hailing into court the composer and the singer as disturbers of the public peace.

This infernal caterwauling was emanating from the shop we have just described, and its executioner was the owner of that establishment, the distinguished Ramón Pérez.

He was bawling the words, "Sad Chactas" with an expression, an enthusiasm which so moved him that his eyes filled with tears. Facing the singer, erect as ever, stood Don Modesto Guerrero, in a pose of sober and judicious listening, like the respectable Mentor on the wall, with the difference that he was better shaved and his topknot stood up smooth and straight.

Suddenly the door in the back of the shop was thrown open and a woman with a child in her arms came out followed by another child, crying and hanging to her skirts. This woman was pale and thin, haughty and ill-natured in manner. She was dressed in a long, square shawl of crepe, old and faded. Her long, loosely-braided, uncombed hair hung straight down. She was shod in a pair of satin slippers and wore long gold earrings.

---

[78] *Atala* was a song composed by César Franck from a novel entitled *Atala* by Chateaubriand, the forerunner of the Romantic movement.

"Be still, be still, Ramón," she said in a hoarse voice as she entered the store. "Don't torture my ears. I'd rather listen to the cawing of all the crows in the district or the yowling of all the village cats than to your way of ruining serious music. I've told you a thousand times to sing the songs of Andalusia. That can be borne, such as it is. Your voice is flexible and you don't lack the grace this type demands. But your wrong-headed mania for singing as if you were a trained singer can't be borne. I tell you so, and you know that I know what I'm talking about. Your foolish flourishes wear on my nerves so that if you insist upon torturing me this way, I'll leave this house forever. "Be still," she added, slapping the head of the crying child, "be still. You bawl just like your father."

"By all means go, right now," replied the barber, his vanity cut to the quick. "Go on, start running and don't come back till I call you. At that rate, you'll never stop running."

"You say you won't call me back," replied the woman. "Would that be too much of a favor to do one who has been called back over and over by the grandees, by the ambassadors, by the whole Court! Do you realize, you clown, you lout, you dullard, how much it cost just to hear me?"

"If those same people could see you now with that vinegar face and could hear that voice like a hen with the pip, I'll bet they'd pay double not to see you or hear you," said the barber.

"Who put me in this hamlet, among this herd of rustics?" cried the furious woman. "Who married me to this whisker-scraper, this fool, who dares to insult me after devouring the dowry the Duke sent me? Me, the famous María Santaló, who made such a stir in the world!"

"It would have been better for you if you'd made less of a stir," said Ramón, endowed with unheard-of courage, born of the enthusiasm the song from *Atala* had aroused in him, and of his indignation at having it criticized.

At these words, his wife rushed at her diminutive husband. Thoroughly frightened, he had time only to set the guitar on a chair and start to run.

At the door he collided with a man standing at the threshold, whom he almost knocked down.

As soon as Marysal had time to think, her anger gave way to an impulse to laugh, no less violent.

The one who had aroused her laughter was Momo, with a horribly swollen cheek. He was wearing a handkerchief tied around his distorted face and had come to have the barber pull a tooth.

"What a horrible sight!" cried Marysal amid peals of laughter. "They say the sergeant of Utrera burst of his own ugliness. How have you escaped such a fate? You'd frighten fear with your looks. What made your cheek pregnant? It's about to give birth to a melon, and then you'll be able to exhibit it for a price. How frightful you are! Are you here to have your photograph taken for *La Ilustración* which is always on the lookout for such curiosities?"

"I've come to have Ramón Pérez pull a bad tooth for me," said Momo, "not to be stuffed with your shameless talk. But you always were a Sea Gull, you are a Sea Gull, and you will always be a Sea Gull."

"If you came to have what's wrong with you taken out," replied Marysal, "they could begin with your heart and your insides."

"By all the cats! Look who's talking about heart and insides," replied Momo. "The one who let her father die among strangers, forgetting the saint he was named after, without even sending him a plugged nickel."

"Who's fault was that, you evil lout?" replied Marysal. "None of that would have happened if you hadn't been such a savage that you came back from Madrid with your mission unaccomplished, spreading all over town that I was dead. And when I came back to the village, thinking my father was alive, they took me for a spirit from the next world. Only your brains, as flat as your nose, would have believed that a show was the real thing."

"Show!" replied Momo. "You're forever saying that was make-believe. The truth is if that Thello had been man enough to give you a proper stab, and if your husband hadn't cured you, (the man everyone mourns, except you) you'd be food for the worms now, to the relief of everybody who knows you. But you don't fool me, you sly thing."

"Well, you listen, face-and-a-half," said Marysal, waving her hand in front of his nose, "you'd have to scratch your nose a hundred years to make it the proper size."

Momo stared at Marysal with scornful dignity, incompatible with his damaged face, and said in a deep voice with a tone of finality, as he wagged his index finger:

"Sea Gull you were, Sea Gull you are, Sea Gull you will always be!"

Arrogantly he turned his back on her.

Don Modesto, perturbed by the shouts of the quarreling couple, and then hearing laughter following the explosion of anger—thanks to the ridiculous figure of Momo, whom Cruikshank, the famous English caricaturist alone could have portrayed—seized the chance to slip away from the field of battle unnoticed. Our readers know that Don Modesto, essentially serious and peaceable, had a profound antipathy to any kind of dispute, altercation, quarrel, or scuffle. But he had hardly entered his own house, pleased with his opportune withdrawal, before new terrors assailed him as he noted that Rosita's one good eye was looking as severe, angry, and threatening as an armed soldier; and that her tightly pursed and ominous mouth was like that of a judge on the bench. Don Modesto sat down in a corner and bowed his head, as a bird knowing a storm is coming will perch on the branch of a tree and hide its head under its wing.

First of all, it is apparent that with the years Rosita's good qualities and her bad ones had both increased. Her neatness had developed into an agonizing perfectionism. Don Modesto had to change his shoes every time he went in to see her. If she had heard of the carpet-slippers worn in Brussels by the curious who visit the palace of the Prince of Orange, she would doubtless have adopted the same means of preserving the woven feather-grass mattings which protected the cracked bricks of her parlor floor. If Don Modesto dropped an olive on the table-cloth, Rosita shuddered; if it was a drop of red wine, she wept. Her abstinence and sobriety had achieved the limits of the possible, and it was rumored that she longed to emulate Manuela Torres, the famous woman from the village of Gansar who had recently died after living forty years without food or drink.

"Rosita," Don Modesto would say to her, "you used to eat what a bird can carry in its beak, but now you're proving that what they say about the camel is no fake."

"You can see," replied Rosita, "that I enjoy perfect health; which proves that we need very little to keep alive, and the rest is pure greediness."

Her austerity had become something more than severe; it was caustic.

"How very becoming," she said to Don Modesto as he was praying wholeheartedly to Our Lady of Peace, "to a man of your age and dignity, one of the outstanding authorities in the village, a man whose name was printed in *The Gazette,* to go visiting those people, those monsters of vanity (not to say something else) and to get yourself mixed up with that quarreling couple who have become the scandal of the neighborhood."

"But, Rosita," replied Don Modesto, "I wasn't mixed up in their wrangle. It was she who started it while I was there."

"If you hadn't gone to that whisker-shaver's house, that everlasting singer, if you hadn't been there with your mouth wide open, listening to his immodest songs, you wouldn't have placed yourself in the position to witness such scandal."

"But, Rosita, you don't stop to think that I have to be shaved from time to time, or else look like a regimental sapper; and that Ramón Pérez shaves me for nothing, as his father used to do. Good manners and gratitude demand that if he undertakes to sing in front of me, I have to be patient and agree to lend an ear. Besides, he didn't sing anything improper. It was one of those songs that refined people sing, telling about a girl named *Atala* . . ."

"What nonsense are you talking, Don Modesto?" said Rosita indignantly. "As if I didn't know what the *Christian Year* had to say about Attila who was a king of the barbarians that invaded Rome, and who was won over by the eloquence of Saint Leo the Great, later the Pope! If you want to claim that it was a lovesick girl, contrary to what commonsense and the *Christian Year* have to say, you and Ramón Pérez are welcome to it. This enlightened century twists every idea, like that cannibal of a mayor who wants to change the Way of the Cross to Urdax, thinking he's enlightened. Very well, go ahead and believe it was a girl who headed the ferocious barbarian armies if that's what you want. As for profane and sacrilegious songs, they sound absurd to me at my age and to my way of thinking. But men always have their ears cocked for anything that's amorous. You melt when you hear songs about people like that: I've seen you do it, yes! . . . And I've seen you at the five-day devotion to Saint John Nepomuceno (the model of confessors) asleep like a log when they sing the couplets at the end."

"I! Rosita! Good Lord! You're as mistaken as you can be. I had my eyes closed, and you took my meditation for irreverent slumber."

"Let's not argue, Don Modesto, for you'd be capable of a barefaced sin against the eighth Commandment. But, coming back to what we were saying, let me tell you it's a shame for you to be hand in glove with those people."

"Ah, Rosita! How can you talk that way about that good Ramón who shaves me for nothing, and that famous Marysal who used to be applauded by generals and ministers?"

"That has nothing to do with the fact that she was an actress," Mystical Rose replied, "one of those women who were formerly excommunicated and who still ought to be. I'd like to know why they aren't any more."

"Probably," said Don Modesto, "the theater was a very evil thing at that time, but now it's the school for customs instead, as it says in the newspaper serial."

"The school for customs . . . , the theater! No two ways about it, Don Modesto, you're being perverted. This is worse than sleeping through the five-day devotions. What! Take the newspapers as texts from the Gospel? I tell you, sir, the Pope did very wrong in lifting the ban from those provocative women."

"Jesus, Mary, and Joseph!" cried Don Modesto, shocked.

"Rosita, how dare you condemn what the Pope does, especially right now when the paper says hymns are being sung in praise of him?"

"All right, all right," Rosita answered. "I know that better than you do. I shall take good care not to condemn what the Pope does. I'll confine myself to wishing we would not have to sing the Miserere after the hymn. But to get back to that woman whom so many personages have applauded, do you think all that foolish applause absolves her from her evil conduct and her perverse nature?"

"Don't be so quick to judge, Rosita. She's not a bad girl at heart. She made a cockade for my hat."

"She did it to make fun of you. Instead of a cockade she gave you a pleated frill as big as a plate. So you say she isn't a bad girl at heart, do you? That one who let her father who loved her so much die alone, poor and forgotten, while she was warbling on the stage?"

"But, Rosita, if she didn't know how serious . . ."

"She knew he was sick, and that was enough. When a father suffers, the daughter ought not to be singing. A woman whose carryings-on forced her poor husband to leave her and go away to die of shame there in the West Indies!"

"He died during an epidemic," the veteran observed.

"She's good, all right!" the stern schoolmistress went on, growing more and more angry. "She was the only woman in the village not at Aunt María's bedside during her last illness. And after she'd loved her so much, and had done so much for her. She was the only one missing at her funeral; the only woman who didn't pray for her in the church, nor weep for her at the cemetery!"

"She had just given birth, and it wouldn't have been wise before the forty days were up."

"What do you know about births or forty days?" exclaimed Mystical Rose, exasperated at seeing how persistently Don Modesto kept defending his friends. "Have you perchance given birth that you know about such things? So she's a good-hearted girl is she, when she burst out laughing at the time when Brother Gabriel followed his benefactress to the grave, and when she said she'd always thought people died of love and grief only in the theater!"

"Poor Brother Gabriel!" said Don Modesto, moved by the memories his landlady had awakened. "Every Friday of his life, he came to the Christ of Succour to pray for a good death. After the death of his benefactress, he used to come every day, for he had no one left but the Good Lord to understand and console him. And it was I who found him one Friday morning on his knees in front of the grille at Christ's chapel, his head resting on the bars. I called him, but he didn't answer. I went up close . . . he was dead, dead as he had lived, alone and in silence. Poor Brother Gabriel!" the Commander added after a brief silence. "You died without seeing your convent rehabilitated. And I shall die, too, without seeing my fort rebuilt!"

WORLD CLASSICS IN TRANSLATION

New Modern translations of foreign language classics introduced by interpretations of authors, works, literary and historical backgrounds. Everyone who reads for pleasure and relaxation should augment his library of the world's best by these charming yet inexpensive books.

BARRON'S EDUCATIONAL SERIES
Woodbury, New York